Hotel Déjà Vu

Christine Betts

for my son, who inspires me.

…and for lovers of Paris, everywhere.

This book would never have been written without my friend Deb Flueckiger. Your kind words and constant encouragement have been more appreciated than you can ever know. Thank you to everyone who read Hotel Déjà vu in its earlier iterations. Reading this second edition may cause a very real sense of déjà vu. It is different from the first edition of course, but better, I hope. At its heart, though, it is the same book, a story of love, Paris, and strong women.

Antoinette

5th Arrondissement, Paris. April 1944

The hunched figure shuffled along the pitch-black laneway; ruined arm pressed against her side. She had lost one shoe and the bare foot throbbed. For a moment, she imagined the bloody trail she was leaving for the police dogs to follow but part of her no longer cared who might come for her. Would tonight be the night they finally put a bullet in her back? At least death would end the pain and her father would no longer need to worry about her. Still, she shuddered at the thought.

The heat was spreading through her body as she stood disoriented in the dark. One of her father's favourite sayings echoed in her mind; ne paniquez pas, organisez vous. She calmed her breathing…un, deux, trois, quartre…don't panic, organise...

She stood rigid, listening for any sound, eyes closed - they were useless in the inky blackness. Again, she thought of her father and the last time she had seen him. They had argued of course, they always did, but this time the words were not barked at each other, a smirk playing at their lips, their familiar jousting. War was no time for games. Instead, they whispered urgently behind the closed door of his clinic. He had begged her to stay home.

'You are most certainly being watched, Ana…' He was tired but there had been an edge of anger in his voice that she had never heard before.

'You are putting this whole house at risk…'

She had raged inside, but then calmed herself knowing that dramatics and hysteria would not convince him of anything but her immaturity. Still, she spoke with force, the anger pulling her lips taut across her teeth.

'Papa, I know what you do. I know you tend people in the old servant's entry. This is a big house with many rooms, and I know you hide people. Do not lecture me on keeping this house safe. Men and women are dying this very minute on battlefields and in work camps. We all must play our part. Even your daughter…'

They stood inches apart. Neither was prepared to lose this time; the stakes were too high.

'You must be mindful of the children, they know nothing of the war, I have made sure of this. I am careful, but you, you are so reckless. Do you not recall the fates of those arrested last month? They were shot and tortured, and some were sent east. The collaborationists have even sent women to the guillotine. Women!'

Her father's face twisted in anger. She had never seen him so angry. Certainly, the raids and arrests over the previous weeks had made Antoinette more careful but had left her as one of the few chemists in Paris to carry on the work.

'Of course, I knew those people… Some of them were my colleagues at the university.' Her heart lurched at the thought of her friends, the American.

She felt the fight go from her as the sadness crept in. What she had not told her father was that one of those men, the American shot in the street, had been her… what had he been? She wasn't sure but perhaps he was the man, she'd hoped, might be her husband…after the war…although they had never spoken of it.

His face had softened. 'You want to help but making explosives is no work for a woman. There are so many ways you could be helping the war effort.'

'Until the war is won, this is my work, Papa. Who else can do it? I am your daughter, yes, but I am a scientist first, then a woman.'

He had said much more, by turns, warning and begging her, but she stopped listening. Finally, he had issued an ultimatum: if she returned to the laboratory, she would not be welcome at his home. She knew it was breaking his heart to say such a thing, but she knew it was for the best. Then he had turned his back on his last living child, bracing his hands on the old carved desk that had been his fathers before him. With tears in her eyes, she had kissed her sister's children and left that day knowing she would not return, until the war was won.

Pain dragged Antoinette back into the present, standing adrift in the dark alley somewhere behind her father's house, her body shattered. She had broken her vow by returning but she knew he would not refuse to help her. Without warning, she was paralysed by a deep, convulsing surge of pain. It threatened to overwhelm her, but she stood rigid, knowing if she sat on the wet cobblestones she would not stand again. She could not see her damaged arm in the darkness but could smell the smoke on her clothes, in her nose, taste the acid on her tongue and smell her burning flesh. The pain in her arm seemed to burn hotter at the thought of it. She squeezed her eyes shut against the appalling images of the moment the chemicals had caught alight.

Desperate to get her bearings, her eyes found the rooflines of the surrounding stone buildings. She and her twin, Marcel, had climbed those roofs as children, it had been their playground, while their little sister Marie-Louise had preferred playing house. There it was the distinctive mansard roof of the old convent house, illuminated by light shining through the remaining stained-glass. The house now converted to apartments, was no longer home to the tiny private school run by the order of nuns who had taught the de la Roche children for three generations. That had been a source of pride for the Sisters, until Antoinette darkened their doorstep. The Sisters had smacked Antoinette's soft pink hands for every act of will.

Flexing her hands at the memory she could feel the skin tightening on her burnt arm. She grimaced in pain, the tight skin on her face objecting to the sudden movement. But she knew where she was. She was nearly home, although she could not remember travelling the mile or so from the makeshift laboratory.

Taking small gulps of air, she looked back through the darkness towards the quai and the river Seine beyond. The sky was now glowing faintly and the stars that had only appeared a few hours earlier as she and the others had sat on the terrace with wine and cigarettes, feigning frivolity under the watchful eye of the enemy, had gone. The dawn was hours away and yet the sky over Paris glowed a sickly pink.

Her head swam and her gravelly breath seemed deafening in the quiet alley. She felt her way along the wall, searching for the low brick terrace she knew was only feet from the hidden door. It might have been a well-known refuge for injured members of the Resistance, but a place of last resort for her. To let her father see her like this…

She eased herself down until she was sitting on the cold stones. Great care had been taken to disguise the door, including painting it black and draping dirty tarpaulins across it. It had to be only feet from her, but she couldn't make it out. Normally there would have been a call, to alert her father that his expertise was needed, and he would be waiting near the door. Was there anyone left to make the call? She closed her eyes and carefully touched her left hand to the burned parts. The heat still radiated from her right arm, her shoulder, her face. The skin was tightening. She didn't have much time. Despite the pain, Antoinette bent to remove her remaining shoe and threw it against the wall hoping the noise would alert her father. Or the police. She no longer cared who came first.

She hung her head. She was épuisé, exhausted, 'done for' as the American liked to say. God knew he had enough cause to say it in his line of work. He was quick with a joke, but he had been the saddest man she had ever known and that was saying something in those bleak times. She never knew what, or who, he had lost but she knew loss when she saw it. She conjured his face in her mind, his unruly hair and those eyes. Her burnt skin protested now as she tried to smile at the thought of his arms around her. She pressed her back against the wall and clenched her jaw, waves of agony arcing through her body like electricity.

She coughed and the pain almost made her faint. As the echo of her cough died away, she heard a sound, a knocking sound on timber. A flicker of light caught her attention. Her limbs had begun to stiffen but Antoinette stood and walked towards where the light had been. A door opened and her father ushered her into the dark room. He bolted the door and turned towards the dimly lit lamp with shaking hands.

'Lie down,' he said, pointing at the settee.

She shuffled over to the little bed. He was turning up his sleeves as he approached her with the now bright lamp. He stopped, horror on his face as he took in her ravaged appearance. He tried to clear his throat.

'I heard the explosion. I…I knew I would be needed, but I didn't know it would be my own daughter…' She tried to speak but no words would come. She had to tell him about the explosion, the fire.

He helped her onto the settee. Antoinette let out an animal-like sound as she collapsed onto the clean white sheet. She fought to stay conscious. Her lips were parched but when she ran her dry tongue across them, the bitterness made her grimace. She knew that taste; a tincture to dull the pain.

Delirium replaced her terror and she muttered soundlessly to her father as he worked above her, bathing her wounds, monitoring her vital signs as well as he could in the tiny room. She tried to ask him to take her up to his clinic, but as confused as she was, Antoinette knew the police would come to see Herr Doktor de la Roche in the morning, if not sooner. They were both safer in the hidden room.

Sighing heavily, her father held her wrist and took her pulse again. He stood, head bowed, beside the bed. He replaced her hand on the bed and sat heavily on the stone floor, one hand on his own heart, forcing himself to take deep breaths.

…ne paniquez pas, organisez vous…

She watched him with terrified eyes, unable to help. He nodded at her and smiled. The face was lined but the eyes were warm. She tried to smile back.

'I am okay, chérie. I am an old man, it's normal to feel tired at this time of the morning.' He smiled at her again and nodded at the little clock on the shelf in the corner of the room, the clock that had not kept time for years. She tried to speak but no sound came. He stood and checked her vitals again.

'I have given you a tincture. Sleep now, I will be right here,' he said, as her eyes closed.

Antoinette had no idea how much time had passed, but for a moment, the delirium had subsided. She noticed that her father had stopped moving around the small space and tried to clear her throat.

'Papa, thank you.' She was surprised words had come.

Her father sat on the floor, his back against the old wooden door.

'I'm so sorry,' she sobbed, a cough gurgled in her raw throat.

'Don't talk, my love,' he said. He shuffled over towards the settee and knelt beside her. 'You will be well by morning. We will have tea with the children.'

Antoinette wasn't sure when her father had decided to lie to her. If she made it through the night, they would be lucky to be free citizens by morning, let alone sitting around the big wooden table eating Clementine's fresh baked bread.

She attempted to sit up but quickly abandoned the idea. She was drifting in and out of consciousness but could feel her father gently bathing her burnt skin. The room was stifling but they could not risk opening either the inner or outer doors. The police would surely be looking for her by now.

Jean-Claude thanked God for the thick walls, the solid door, as Antoinette groaned in pain and mumbled incoherently. Taking a deep breath, he reached for her good arm, testing her pulse once again. Her dark eyes were swollen but he could see her watching him in the lamplight. They sat in stillness, father and daughter, hands locked, silent except for their shallow breathing. Jean-Claude smiled and wiped a tear from his own cheek.

'Is my face very bad?' she whispered.

'You are…beautiful,' he said, his heart breaking.

Jean-Claude smiled although it pained him to see Antoinette's damaged features. She had always resembled her mother, the dark hair and fierce nature.

'Papa, please…'

'Yes, chérie…the burn is bad.'

Antoinette sobbed and coughed. Tears ran down her temples. Jean-Claude wrung out a cloth and gently sponged the tears away.

'Tell me stories of Maman,' Antoinette whispered.

He took her unburnt hand in his and began to speak. Surprised by the strength of her grip despite the terrible burns, he told her his favourite tales of her mother. Stories of her talent for cooking, her love of painting, her famously short temper. He spoke of her love for her three children.

Antoinette's breath became even more shallow but her grip on his hand remained. He then spoke of his own parents, their families. Jean-Claude's father had been an officer but had then become a surgeon, his mother, a painter. Theirs had been an arranged marriage, but they were a good match and raised a large family. He spoke of their grand home in Paris where like her, he had been born and lived his entire life, and of the ancient chateau in the countryside where he had spent long summer days with his cousins, long before his own children did the same.

For Jean-Claude it had been a charmed life filled with love and reading, sunshine, close-knit family, and his fulfilling work. He told Antoinette of his younger siblings with affection and humour but stopped short of recounting how they had all died, one by one in their thirties and forties, leaving him alone to run the family estates.

There will only be happy stories told in this room tonight, Jean-Claude thought. He began to speak of his own children. The lovely Marie-Louise with the softest heart, and brave Marcel, who had gone away to be a hero and returned home in a box, both now waiting with their mother in the family crypt. He wouldn't speak of death but of how they had both lived their lives to the fullest. The family summers at the seaside were his favourite times, the snatched moments away from the hospital, a few stolen weeks of relaxation when he would do nothing but watch his children play.

'Do you remember 1933, La Rochelle?' he asked, her hand squeezing his in response.

Antoinette tried her throat, but she could not speak. She remembered the Summer well. Marie Louise and Antoinette had convinced their father to give them two puppies they called Mimi and Joe. Sitting on the beach, the dogs yapping at the gulls, the family ate mussels fresh from the boats, boiled right there on the beach.

In the dark room, Jean-Claude told story after story, his words recreating that magical summer. The rambling chateau was being re-shingled, and they had camped in the gardens in a mishmash of tents, to the horror of Cook and the rest of the Paris staff. The children had been delighted. He asked her if she recalled the summer storm that hit two days after the roof was completed and the children were forced to abandon their tents to retreat to the safety and warmth of their bedrooms. That summer had indeed been idyllic.

Lost in the memory, Antoinette sighed in the dark and Jean-Claude smiled for what seemed like the first time in a year. Considering they were from an old family, they had had an enchanted, riotous childhood, even if their mother's absence was felt keenly at times.

Would that you were here now with me, mon amour, Jean-Claude thought, picturing his wife's face. He looked down at the ruined face of his daughter. 'Chérie, I will bathe your face and arm again.'

She squeezed his hand again. Her strength was going.

Rising slowly, still smiling at the thought of his wife by his side, Jean-Claude felt he might faint. He had been feeling ill since the morning and now feared he would collapse there on the floor, leaving them both locked in the tiny room. He had the only key, looped around his neck as it always was, on scarlet cord. A panic began to rise in his belly. He needed to open the door, to be free of the claustrophobic space, but could not leave Antoinette alone. Slowing his breathing, he decided to quickly check on his grand-children and fetch more of the tincture for Antoinette's pain. He would leave the key on the desk in his clinic. If the worst happened, at least the police would find them both.

13

'I've done all I can, my precious daughter. Please sleep now,' he said, his throat raw from talking. He gently leaned across and lifted her left hand. The pulse was weak. Her eyes closed. She was almost gone. He could not believe he would outlive all his children. He sniffed the air. Is that smoke?

Jean-Claude covered the lantern and unbolted the laneway door. Carefully shifting the tarpaulin aside, he stuck his head far enough into the alley to see the sky. There were no stars. The air reeked of smoke and worse, the sky over Paris glowed bright orange. The fire from the explosion was spreading.

Paris was burning.

He quickly replaced the tarpaulin and bolted the door. He had to get to the children, perhaps get them out of Paris, or at least to the river. That would mean leaving Antoinette. He did not want to think about it, but he was running out of time. He unlocked the heavy inner door and stood in the narrow corridor, breathing a sigh of relief that he was no longer in the airless room. Antoinette opened her eyes.

'I'll see you in the morning, chérie,' he said, but he couldn't look at her. They both knew what the morning would bring.

The clock on the small mantle ticked loudly in the silent room. It refused to keep time no matter how often it was wound, but the base was stuck in layers of varnish, so it remained. Jean-Claude opened the glass case and touched the hour hand lightly. He wound it anti-clockwise three or four times and hung his head, as though this small action had taken the last of his energy. 'Would that we could truly turn back the time,' he said.

Antoinette watched her father place his hand over his heart. She was desperate to help him, but she could not move. His hand found the little clock again and he clicked the glass door shut. She wanted him to stay, talk to her of La Rochelle, of her brother, her sister... She closed her eyes and thought of those puppies, that summer on the beach.

Antoinette heard the key turn in the old door and even though her father had taken the lantern, she thought she could see her brother waiting in the corner of the room.

Jean-Claude shuffled along the pitch-black corridor, exhausted. He had to get the children to the river, they would be safe at the river. Eight paces and a left turn would bring him to the stairs, a right turn, then nine paces to his cabinet de consultation, the clinic rooms that had been his fathers before him. The next landing led to the room Marie-Louise's orphaned children shared with their nanny.

He pushed the door open a fraction. They slept like the innocents they were, Clementine between them, like a protective mother hen. Jean-Claude wondered how life could be so incredibly beautiful in moments but could then bring such darkness in others. He began to speak, to rouse his household. No words came. He grasped the thick wooden door frame. He was on his knees before he realized what was happening and held his left arm as though his grip alone would keep him alive.

My heart is…breaking, he thought.

The cold sandstone under his cheek was not unpleasant after the grueling hours trying to save his daughter and he relaxed at once, deciding he would not fight it, as though he had a choice. Jean-Claude de la Roche smiled. He would soon see his wife again.

Paradise

Antoinette was surprised to wake at all, let alone with no fever or pain. Bright light forced its way in under the door, forcing her to cover her eyes. She was disoriented. Instinctively she felt her forehead and cheeks. Taking her own pulse, she closed her eyes and counted the beats.

Perfect, she thought, although she felt sure it shouldn't have been.

She cleared her throat and rolled onto her side, watching dust motes float in a shaft of light. There were so many questions running through her mind. In typical fashion, she attended to them one by one until she came to the large question that had been floating around in the background.

There had been…an explosion…

This was more of a statement than a question and it seemed to hang in the air, swirling with the dust. Her stomach lurched. She pressed her back into the mattress and ran her hands over her face and arms, sweat beads forming across her forehead. Her skin was smooth, but her clothes seemed to be in tatters. She felt sick. Screwing her eyes tight against spinning room, she forced herself to think about the night before. Her face and right arm had been burned, there was no doubt in her mind. She would remember that pain for the rest of her life.

Her father had saved her. The events of the previous night flashed into her mind as though lit by lightning…or an explosion. She could remember it all; the slick cobblestones, the stench of the chemicals, the skin stretching across her ruined face.

She sat up, her head swimming from the sudden elevation, and checked her feet. Her shoes were gone but her skin was perfect, better even than she recalled. Her father's reputation as a physician was widely known, but this recovery was nothing short of miraculous. Her hands moved quickly checking every part of her body but found no trace of the traumatic night before. Had it all been a dream, a nightmare? This seemed reasonable. She fondled the blackened fabric of her dress and felt the torn sleeves. Something terrible had indeed happened.

Lying back on the settee she was confused. Antoinette was not accustomed to feeling confusion. She remembered everything; dinner with her colleagues, flouting the curfew as they always did, somehow hiding in plain sight. She had met the new chemist, a young man she had once seen at the university. After serving and surviving at the front he had found he had a talent for explosives and a deep hatred for the enemy.

After dinner, they made their way slowly along the river, arm in arm, to the laboratory, but to the Boche they were just a couple walking home. Where was he now? She sat up again and felt along the hem of her skirt for the carefully concealed papers that would be her lifeline if the worst should happen.

'Think,' she said, clenching her fists…

…ne paniquez pas, organisez vous…

She had been thrown down into the alley at the back of the old disused stables that had been their laboratory. It had been part of an old abattoir being used again during the occupation, the perfect disguise for the strong smells of their operation. Obviously, she had been lucky, she thought as she ran her hands across her smooth skin.

'Perhaps I am dreaming,' she whispered to the room.

Antoinette de la Roche was not what you would call a dreamer. When trying to make a point, she could be dramatic, granted, but she considered herself practical and intelligent. She would be the last person to be given over to hysterics.

'If that wasn't a dream then I have died and gone on to the afterlife,' she said a little louder as though tempting someone to argue with her. A little startled by the sound of her own voice, she looked around the tiny room, disappointment the only emotion she could muster. 'Why does hell look exactly like the old servants' entrance in father's basement?' she said, laughing at her own joke.

She decided she'd had just about enough of this nonsense, whatever it was. She swung her legs over the edge of the settee and took a tentative step, and then two more. She leaned against the old outer door looking down at her bare feet, frowning at the dust motes swirling furiously now. The light should not be coming through. The tarpaulins have been taken down. Her heart began to race. The police would be looking for her. She put both hands to the latch and prepared to shove it as hard as she could, but the latch moved easily. Her father must have oiled it. The old bolt had often threatened to trap those who used the tiny room. She swung the door open, blinding sunlight flooded the room. She jumped back as though the light would harm her.

'Perhaps I am in heaven, after all,' she said. No, perhaps I am going mad.

A small grin edged across her mouth as she imagined the nasty mathematics mistress from her school days, Sister Marie, who would have dropped dead all over again to see the likes of Antoinette de la Roche in heaven.

Antoinette made her way into the street. Sunday morning in Paris was always quiet but as the occupation wore on it had become a ghost town. This morning somehow felt like the Paris of her youth. Parisians were out in force, soaking up the sunshine. The drizzle and low cloud of the previous week had departed in spectacular fashion; she hadn't seen a day like this since before the war, but considering it was heaven that made sense. She allowed herself a little smile at the thought.

Stopping at the curve in the laneway she looked towards the quai. There were crowds of people, strolling around Paradise or Paris, or whatever this was. She felt faint at the thought, but strangely elated, feeling she could run onto the street and throw her arms around everyone. Remembering her tattered clothes, she quickly retreated. Stopping abruptly, she looked up and down the length of the lane. Someone had removed the piles of building materials and barrels that her father had been storing on the brick terrace to disguise the doorway to the room. The alley was clean and bright on that impossibly warm morning, clear of everything except the washing lines she could see crisscrossing between the buildings at the end of the street.

If this is not the afterlife, the police must have searched the alley already, she thought. Her mind began to revolt at the idea of an alleyway in Paris existing in either heaven or hell. Where was the hellfire and brimstone? If this was heaven, then the streets were cobblestones as they had always been, rather than pavement of gold that the priests promised.

Confused and sweating in the warm air, she leaned against the low terrace wall, recalling the events of the night before as they jumbled about in her head. She had to get out of sight and think. Unlike the previous night, the door was now easily visible. She gripped the wrought iron handle to pull it open and stopped. The door her father had painted black was no longer black. It was blue. A shiny glossy blue, chipped in places, showing a deep grey paint underneath. She leaned her head against the door. It was warm from the sun.

She put her hand to her head and felt again for fever. The door had been deep cobalt blue during her childhood, but now it should be black. She opened the door slowly, running her hand over the blue paint lining the inside too. Without warning, her knees buckled, the floor rising to meet her. She sat for what seemed like an hour but must only have been minutes, staring at the door, the only sound in the room was the ticking clock and her own breath.

Deeply inhaling, she pulled herself upright. She had to find her family. Whether this was Paris or heaven, she had family here and she had to find them before the police found her. She rapped loudly on the heavy door but knew it was pointless. The outside door had always been left unlocked, but the internal door was usually bolted from inside the house for security, especially during the occupation. She pulled the handle, but the door wouldn't budge. It was at least four inches thick and far removed from the living areas, deep in the bowels of the house.

Antoinette pushed the outside door open again, catching sight of a small mirror propped on the mantel behind the old silver clock. She had not noticed it before. She picked it up and examined her reflection in the mottled surface. The clock that never worked showed it was just after 11 but had read 10:30 when she woke. The slim second hand was smoothly working its way around the face. She was more confused than ever.

Ignoring her tattered clothing, she propped the mirror against the clock and after combing her hair with her fingers, pulled it back into a chignon. She had never been interested in appearances but was grateful that her sister had taught her how to make herself presentable. There was nothing she could do about the state of her clothing, so she pulled the discarded top sheet from the settee and wrapped it around her waist like a long skirt.

She could either walk around the block via the quai or through the busy Sunday market to get to the front door, the old carriage entrance that now served as the entry to the house. Deciding to brave the quai rather than the crowded marché, she hesitated in the alleyway, surveying the crowds of people strolling along under the plane trees. Completely forgetting her bed-sheet skirt, she stood staring at the crowded street. Had the war ended overnight? Had the explosion somehow caused the enemy to turn tail and go back east? Confusion gave way to joy as she smiled at the happy people. It was delightful to see Paris as it should be - teeming with tourists and locals enjoying the beautiful city. She tore herself away from the glorious vision and turned towards Rue du Bièvre, and home.

'Bonjour, mademoiselle Antoinette,' said a quiet voice.

Antoinette looked up to see Monsieur Levy, the famous luthier and violinist, locking his studio, violin case tucked under his arm. He smiled warmly and waited for her to reply but Antoinette stood gaping, completely frozen in her tracks. The kind old gentleman nodded, tipped his hat, and continued towards the curb to a waiting taxi. Open-mouthed, Antoinette stared at the back of the elderly violinist. He didn't look up at her from the cab window, but she continued to stare as it drove away.

This day, this Paris, most definitely had to be Paradis, heaven. She was certain now. Monsieur Levy had confirmed it.

At some time in January 1940, Mr. Levy had left his home and studio as though he had simply popped out for the afternoon. He took his violin and a small bag. He was never seen again. He had in fact, moved to Scotland. And he had reportedly died peacefully surrounded by his nephews and their families in 1943. Jean-Claude had received a telegram.

The kind, generous Mr. Levy would never go to Hell, so Antoinette knew now that she must be dead, and had, by some stroke of luck, made it to Paradis. Her father had a lot of influence, but clearly even she had under-estimated his reach. She smiled, laughed at her own joke, a bizarre feeling bubbling up inside her. The trauma of the last few weeks had finally caught up with her and she felt her sanity slipping away.

A face seemed to float into her field of vision, and she reached her hand out to touch it. A gloved hand reached up to take hers and a voice from the past spoke to her. Antoinette's world tilted and she found herself on the warm cobblestone sidewalk, a couple hovering over her.

'Go. Fetch her father,' the girl's voice called to the boy running down the street towards her house.

'Antoinette, what happened to you? I saw you behind the church but when I walked over to you, you had already gone.'

'Genevieve?' Antoinette whispered. 'You're here too? How can you be here?'

'Paul has gone to fetch your father.' Genevieve patted her hand and took in her disheveled appearance.

'My father isn't in heaven, Genevieve, he is still alive. Unless…no…' Antoinette said. More faces swam into view.

'Marcel!' Antoinette screamed. A moment later she was off the ground and in his arms. Her twin had been her best friend, her ally, and her protector, until he was taken from her by the war. He looked so young. She held him in a violent embrace as he struggled to pull away from her grip. A young girl walked towards her; concern knitted on her brow.

'Marie-Lou?' Antoinette grabbed her sister and drew her into the embrace with Marcel, who was still trying to get away. She smiled at the small crowd of people gathered around her. 'You are all so young? I saw Mr. Levy, he's here in heaven too. And maman? Where is she?'

Marie-Louise looked at Marcel as though he could somehow translate the nonsense that was coming out of his twin's mouth.

'Chérie, let's take you home, and clean you up,' Marie-Louise spoke in a sing-song voice, as though to a small child.

'Yes, please let us go home and see maman,' Antoinette said. She took her sister's hand.

Not wanting to upset her deranged sister, Marie-Louise did what she did best. She held her head high and helped. It was her mission on earth, she had decided from a young age. Antoinette had the brains, the dreams and the schemes, and Marie's self-appointed role was to help her keep her hair and clothes neat while achieving those dreams.

They reached the huge entry doors, Genevieve's fiancé Paul rapping on the ornate iron knocker. Jean-Claude pulled it open, his smooth face became troubled as he saw the crowd of people at his door.

'Papa, why are you here?' Antoinette cried out, tears springing to her eyes.

She pushed passed him into the foyer and called out to their mother. Jean-Claude and Marcel moved forward to take her by the arms and guided her to a sofa as Marie-Louise closed the door on the crowd of neighbours who had gathered to see exactly what was disturbing their Sunday walk.

'Ana? What's happened to you?' Jean-Claude took in her appearance and the bed-sheet skirt. 'What are you wearing?' He pulled the sheet from around her waist, his brow furrowing at the sight before him. Marcel bolted from the room at the sight of his twin's tattered skirt. Marie-Louise moved forward to replace the sheet over her sister's bare legs, searching her eyes for answers.

'Get me some hot water and towels. Bring them to the clinic,' Jean-Claude said to his youngest daughter.

Marie-Louise ran to the stairs and raising a warning finger to her lips, directed the gathered staff to follow her. They had been preparing all week to depart for their summer home but that would have to wait now. For a tiny young woman, fifteen-year-old Marie-Louise ran her father's household like a benevolent dictator, a role she relished as much as her sister would have detested it. The girls boiled water and placed it carefully in the dumbwaiter with piles of freshly washed linens.

Antoinette had no interest in fashion, but Marie-Louise ensured that her clothes were fine-looking and well kept. She took clean stockings and undergarments from the trunk at the end of her sister's bed and a new dress from the armoire. Marie-Louise was worried. The dress was a strange style and appeared to be burned in places. She knew what that much blood on a woman's skirt could mean and she didn't like to think of what might have happened to her head-strong sister.

Or what might happen next.

Had Ana been assaulted in some way? Marie-Louise had no idea how her sister had managed to disappear after walking home from Mass that morning, to be found collapsed in the street, her clothing ruined.

Marie-Louise took the fresh clothes to the clinic, waiting in the cool, dark foyer for Jean-Claude to admit her. Time seemed to drag by, but eventually Jean-Claude opened the door and allowed her to see her sister. Marie-Louise quietly nodded to her father. Antoinette was sitting on an old over-stuffed chair, wrapped in a fresh linen sheet.

'Are you well, sister?' She was careful to look at her sister's face and not at the pile of soiled clothing and linens.

'Yes, I am very well,' Antoinette said, seeming quite her normal self again, 'better than I've been for a while, chérie!' She allowed Marie-Louise to help her dress, then pulled her into a warm embrace. 'It's so wonderful to be here, and to see you again.' Antoinette gazed into her sister's eyes and kissed her cheeks.

Marie-Louise turned to see their father come back into the room, his worried face down-turned.

'There's nothing physically wrong with her,' he said quietly.

Relieved, Marie-Louise turned back to her sister and hugged her.

'But it's not her body I'm concerned about.'

'Oh Papa, don't be dramatic,' Antoinette said. 'I simply fell asleep by the river after walking too far with my friends. Obviously, I've had a terrible dream, and torn my dress while sleep walking.'

Antoinette had told her father a most bizarre tale. A terrifying tale of death and of…war. He had made sure his daughter was physically safe, left her to clean herself up, and gone into the adjoining office where he had vomited. He had told her, and himself, that it was a nightmare. A bad dream, he consoled her as they both cried. It had been her mother's absence that confirmed for Antoinette that she was neither in heaven, nor hell, nor was she dreaming. No, this wasn't 1944; it was 1933. She was sixteen years old and she had had a terrible nightmare. Jean-Claude wondered if his daughter had been drugged, or even taken something voluntarily. She had always been wild, but her mother's death three years earlier had seen her spiral into a kind of mania. She pushed at every barrier before her and saw every rule as though it was there to be broken.

Too much time reading medical books and hanging around those women at the university; filling her young head with silly dreams. His daughter was fascinated by women in medicine and science, and fiercely proud that French women led the world in medical research, but her out-spoken nature and intellect had made her a target at the lycee. And her obsession with old photographs of murders and autopsies had given her the nickname 'Angel of Death' even amongst her friends.

Marie-Louise watched her father's face. He smiled at Antoinette, but they had all seen that smile before. That was what the three children called their father's 'we will discuss this later' smile.

'Keep her calm, ma petite chérie,' her father said. 'I need to talk to the staff. Perhaps we won't go to La Rochelle today.'

Antoinette shook her head. 'Oh no, papa, we must go. I am fine. We had…we will have the best summer.' Jean-Claude looked at Marie-Louise who nodded her head although she wasn't sure why.

'Very well, we will go, but in a few hours after you have rested. I will be upstairs if you need me,' he said.

The moment they were alone, Antoinette took two large steps towards her sister, roughly taking hold of Marie's slight shoulders. 'Fetch paper. And something to write with. Now,' she said in a harsh whisper.

…ne paniquez pas, organisez vous…

Marie-Louise knew better than to question her sister. She slipped into her father's study and snatched a wad of paper that he used in consultations with patients and one of his prized mechanical pencils. She presented them to Antoinette, who then sat, scribbling on sheet after sheet of paper. She stopped occasionally to stare at the wall, mumble and count on her fingers.

'I'm already forgetting things, like a dream.'

'But it was a dream, darling,' Marie-Louise said.

Antoinette's head flicked around to face her sweet sister. 'It was real, and it was so awful. Oh God, the camps…' Antoinette's shoulders hunched, and her pencil flew across the page.

Marie-Louise scanned the words with her eyes, her hand went to her throat. 'Why are you writing such things? The Great War was years ago. We were tiny children. Germany is chastened. Oh, Ana…'

Pulling the paper away from her sister's gaze, Antoinette continued writing and whispering to herself. 'A new war is beginning, it will take time, but it's coming. The new Chancellor of Germany… Lucifer personified.'

Marie-Louise clamped her hand over her mouth, tears springing to her eyes. 'Stop it, you're scaring me. It's not true. Stop…lying…'

Antoinette looked up again, her eyes boring into her sister. 'Lying? You think I am lying to you? When have I ever lied to you? Papa yes, but you, never! Now, please, hush…I need to remember everything that happened, that will happen… so I can stop…it.' She returned her attention to the paper and continued writing.

Marie-Louise turned and faced the huge cabinet of leather-bound journals that ran along the clinic wall. 'Even if I just save you and Marcel…'

Marie-Louise heard the mumbled words. Had she heard right? From the corner of her eye, she saw Antoinette's shoulders stiffen but she continued scribbling on the page. Marie spun on her heel to face Antoinette. 'What do you mean, save us?' Marie's voice was shrill, but her face was blank.

'Chérie, be quiet. Do not make Papa come back in here.' Antoinette arched her eyebrow and locked eyes with her sister. 'He will sedate me if you tell him anything and I may lose this…' she tapped the paper with her finger. 'Do you trust me?'

Marie-Louise did not answer, she stared at her sister in a mixture of horror and fear.

'Mary-Lou, do you trust me?' Antoinette eased back the chair, silently, moving slowly. She reached across and took her sister's thin, pale wrist. The young girl recoiled a little, but she nodded her head, her eyes not leaving Antoinette's face.

'This…this…whatever it is…has happened and I have an opportunity to fix things, save the people I love and do what I can to help others.' Antoinette's fingers began to tighten around her sister's wrist.

'You're hurting me, Ana,' Marie-Louise whispered. Antoinette released her arm.

'I'm so sorry, my darling, but I must finish this. You can read over my shoulder, but you must be quiet, no matter what you see. Let me write and we will talk about it later.'

'Why do you think you need to write all this?'

Antoinette sat back again and sighed. 'Because I need to remember what happened, to try to change things. I can't trust my memories; they are already slipping through my fingers. If I fail, all is lost. Paris will burn and so will we.'

Marie-Louise sunk onto the stool beside her sister as she gathered the bundle of papers and placed it in a neat pile. She flipped through the pages, reading what she had written, her lips moving slightly as she read.

'Genevieve and Paul must be warned to leave Paris,' she whispered, returning to her writing.

Marie-Louise sat staring at the paper. She was shocked to see that her sister had written her name and that of their brother. There were two sets of dates after their names, the way one would write dates of birth…and death. She tried to keep quiet, but she felt like she would scream. 'What will happen to me? To Marcel? This is a prophecy.'

Antoinette ignored her for many long minutes. The clock ticked, competing with the scratching of the pencil on the paper. Finally, she spoke. 'I am no prophet.' She sounded bitter. Marie-Louise had heard anger in her sister's voice before, but never bitterness. Marie-Louise looked at the floor.

'Marie,' Antoinette said and waited for a response. 'Marie-Louise, look at me.'

Antoinette reached over and caressed her sister's cheek. 'Terrible times are ahead for this family and for France if I ignore this. I don't care if papa does not believe me, but I need your faith. I will make sure it doesn't happen…again. You have to trust me, d'accord?'

Marie-Louise had always trusted her sister, but Antoinette had an alarming knack for getting herself into trouble. The young woman crossed her arms and stood at her full height. Even so she was inches shorter than Antoinette.

'I will trust you if you stay out of trouble.'

'Oh, my darling, my troublemaking days are over. I need to be quiet now and be very clever. I will be invisible…so I can stop…' she shuddered. Marie-Louise reached out to touch her arm.

'I trust you and I will do what I can to help,' she whispered and realised she meant it.

Antoinette returned to her writing and the only sound was the scratching of the graphite on the paper and their breath. Marie-Louise could feel her heart pounding in her chest. Antoinette finally pushed the sheets of paper away and turned to her sister, handing her the pencil.

'Ana, does anything good happen…to me?'

Antoinette sighed and drew her sister into an embrace. 'So many good things happen. You get married and have beautiful children.'

'I…get married? When? To…whom…?' Marie-Louise's cheeks flushed. 'Children?'

'Yes, my darling. And Marcel is elected to municipal council.'

'Oh, that's marvellous. It is perhaps easier to believe that something good will happen. I am too young, I think.'

Antoinette nodded. 'Yes, there are so many wonderful things coming.'

Antoinette clung to her sister. The sister she had lost and now found again. Was it a miracle? However, it had happened, she had managed to return to 1933, she had been given another chance to do things properly, to make right all the wrongs, but she wondered why she hadn't come back in time to save their mother.

She found the first page and printed carefully on the top, "I think I came back to this day because we were happy. I fell asleep last night thinking of the wonderful memories of that…this Summer."

'Shall we gather the staff and go to La Rochelle?' she said to a mystified Marie-Louise.

Karen

May 1990. Somewhere over Amsterdam.

Karen's eyes were fixed on the screen suspended from the ceiling midway along the cabin. She could see the route the plane had taken across the top of Europe. The captain announced that they had begun their descent to Paris but according to the map, they were somewhere over Amsterdam. She felt her stomach churn. It's just excitement, she told herself. The flight attendants seemed to be walking about a lot, she noticed. Is there a problem? She closed her eyes and tried to calm her breathing. She wondered if she had time to visit the toilet again.

Another announcement. She was so tired she couldn't seem to understand what the captain was saying, but then realised he was speaking French. Rubbing her eyes like a small child, Karen elbowed her travelling companion, Agnès, who opened one eye and mouthed an expletive at her over-excited friend. Twenty-two years old, sexy and world weary the way only French girls can be, Agnès was reluctantly returning to her family home in Paris, after a two year stay in Australia. She had travelled the world with her diplomat parents, and nothing troubled her.

Karen was always in a fluff about something. She wished she could be more like her friend. The only things that excited Agnès were fresh cigarette packets, surfing, and platform sneakers. Karen turned to look at her boyfriend, Peter, in the seat next to the aisle, his knuckles white on the arm rests. Unlike their well-travelled friend, Karen and Peter were experiencing air travel for the first time.

Agnès reached across Karen and patted Peter on the arm. 'We still have maybe ten minutes before we land. Try not to burst an artery,' she said.

Peter chuckled and relaxed a little. Agnès could always be counted on for a joke. He took a deep breath and rubbed his stubbled jaw. He didn't mind the flying, but the landings and take-offs would take a little getting used to. By the time the plane touched down Karen had managed to drop her passport and landing card between the seats, enlisting the help of the honeymooners in the row behind her to retrieve the documents. Agnès rolled her eyes affectionately and tucked Karen's loose hair into a stylish but messy bun on top of her head, securing it with two hair pins she had pulled from her own hair. Karen grabbed her makeup mirror and admired the effect.

'I will never learn to be as stylish as you if I live to be one hundred!'

'No. You won't.' Agnès pouted but then broke into the broad grin she had named her Aussie Smile. She didn't want to go home to Paris, having fallen in love with Australia. She was planning to return as soon as she could to work on an enormous cattle farm in the 'outback'. Paris versus the Outback? Karen loved her friend but thought she had rocks in her head.

Karen and Peter were nervous about navigating Customs without Agnès' help. She said she would be waiting, cigarette in hand, in front of the Arrivals hall. They had known each other for nearly a year, and she had been a true surprise package in the friendship department. Fiercely loyal, funny as hell and always up for a good night out, or in, if there was food and beer and perhaps a television. She and Karen were obsessed with sushi, Baywatch, and surfing but all the same, Karen half expected to emerge from arrivals to find her new friend had disappeared back into her French life like a beautiful dream. Karen still couldn't believe that someone like Agnès would want to be friends with her.

Happily, Customs was almost empty and the officer on duty was sweet and keen to practice his English skills. Upon finding two Australians in front of him he mimed a kangaroo jumping and, in a mix of heavily accented English and French, drilled Pete for information on the Australian Rugby team. After a few minutes of animated discussion, the Customs Officer welcomed the young Australians to France and directed them to the exit.

'He probably thinks you play rugby, Pete,' Karen said, once they were out of earshot. 'I don't think they've ever seen a bloke your size who wasn't a rugby player. I'm glad you didn't tell them you were a chef, or we'd still be there discussing the correct method for stuffing poultry.'

'I am so glad you said method, because of course, there is only one way…' Peter took a breath as though about to launch into a detailed description of such a method. Karen jammed her hands over her ears. Peter laughed.

To their relief, as Peter and Karen emerged into the morning sunlight, their friend could be seen smoking at the curb, as promised. She was waiting with a young, dark haired man who had the biggest eyes Karen had ever seen. Peter handed Agnès a bag of duty-free cigarettes, which she happily added to her own allocation. She believed you could never have too many cigarettes.

Karen reached for her sketchpad and pencil and started drawing.

'Guys, this is Jan. Jan, Karen and Peter.'

'It's great to meet you!' Jan shook Peter's hand energetically and smiled at Karen. He tilted his head to see what she was drawing. Karen looked up and smiled and added a few more lines. She showed him the quick portrait. His face lit up.

'C'est moi! This is me…' he said, intrigued. 'You are an artist…'

He said the word with a reverence not often heard where she was from. Karen blushed. He held the portrait next to his face so they could see the likeness. Peter and Agnès smiled and nodded.

'Err, Peter, perhaps you will come and work for my father?' Jan said without taking his eyes away from the drawing.

'Whoa, okay, I have a job offer before I leave the airport,' Peter laughed.

'Let's talk and drive,' Agnès interrupted, slapping Jan on the backside, 'I need some decent bread, some gum, and a fuck. In that order!'

They all piled into Jan's minivan and roared off into the quiet Sunday morning. Karen wondered who this enigmatic young man was, and would he be the one to help Agnès with the last thing on her list. Her friend had never mentioned a boyfriend. She slipped the drawing over the seat into Agnès lap, who looked back and mimed applause. 'It's a gift, for picking us up,' Karen said.

'It's beautiful,' Agnès said. Jan tucked the sketch into the visor so he could see it as he drove.

'You will be a famous artist one day and this will be worth thousands of francs. No, millions,' Jan said, smiling at her in the rear vision mirror. She would have preferred he watch the road.

Karen was mesmerised by the farmland surrounding the airport, glowing with beautiful golden light as the sun rose over the landscape. She was not sure what she had been expecting, but it certainly hadn't been farmland dotted with fat cows. Industrial sheds began to appear beside the road, along with huge parking lots, truck stops and the occasional power station in the distance. Karen could see apartment buildings ahead, which she had guessed was their destination, but they pulled into a gas station.

'I'm getting gum. Proper French gum! You want anything?' Agnès asked the rest of them.

'You should look at the market with Jan,' she said to Peter nodding in the direction of the tents in the next allotment. Peter smiled and sniffed the air for a tempting scent. The girls laughed at him and Jan looked around, confused.

'He smells everything!' Agnès nodded and smiled at Jan.

Peter handed money to Jan to pay for the fuel, but he declined. 'I was coming to the market anyway. It was the perfect opportunity to meet you and see if you want a job before someone else gets to you.'

Again, the offer of a job caught Peter off-guard. He was flattered but confused. 'What business are you in? What does your father do?'

Jan looked at Agnès and asked her in French why she hadn't explained it to Peter.

'His father owns three famous restaurants. He is desperate for his own Australian,' she said, as though this explained everything. She turned walked toward the convenience store.

'His own Australian?' Peter asked.

'Ha, yes, my father wants an Australian, because his greatest rival has an Australian and they are the best chefs, after the French, of course.' Jan laughed. 'Georges, Agnès' father told us all about you and how much you love food. My father is so happy!'

'Okay,' Peter said, slowly.

'So, you will come and meet my father and you can decide. No pressure, man.' Jan moved the van into a parking space and grabbed Karen and Peter's backpacks, securing them in what looked like a specially designed space under the floor.

'You can't trust anyone,' Jan explained, touching the side of his nose. 'In Paris, don't trust anyone,' he said again.

'Can we trust you?' Karen said.

'Of course. Of course. Sorry, yes. I work for the President. I am very trustworthy, and I have known Agnès since she was a baby, and I was two years old.' Jan handed Peter the keys to the van, in a show of good faith. They both relaxed, but Peter pocketed the keys all the same.

The little group made their way into the market, the two Australians felt they had entered a magical world. The dusty gas station seemed a distant memory as stalls piled high with seasonal vegetables stretched out in all directions, the two boys were soon lost in Culinary Heaven. Deep in thought, she hadn't noticed Agnès standing beside her, unlit cigarette in one hand and a long half-eaten bread stick in the other. She offered the bread to Karen who took a huge chunk off the top and devoured it. They hadn't eaten much since Jakarta, where they boarded the flight hung-over, sunburnt. She could see Jan and Peter walking towards them, somehow already laden with boxes of produce, matching grins on their stubbled faces.

'Jan, eh?' Karen mumbled, her mouth filled with bread.

'We're just friends, but he's sweet and we love sex together,' Agnès explained in her typical nonchalant manner.

Karen laughed. 'You're so… French!' Seconds later, the girls were laughing and choking on their bread in the middle of the market, while Jan and Peter looked on, puzzled.

'Let's get coffee, you crazy women,' Jan said, shifting the weight of the cartons in his arms, filled with white asparagus, tomatoes and tiny strawberries.

They piled the cartons around them and stood at the makeshift bar drinking strong coffee. Karen was amazed to see people with glasses of beer in their hands at eight in the morning. Having grown up in Sydney's inner eastern suburbs she was no stranger to people drinking at daybreak, but these were farmers and vendors, not drunks or party animals. She immediately felt at home in a country that was civilised enough for drinking to be acceptable at all hours, although she could hear her mother's judgmental tone in her head. The predictable wave of guilt soon followed, and she turned her back on the men in denim overalls.

Karen wondered when her mother's voice in her head would start speaking French. She looked over at Pete who was busy preaching on the finer points of tomatoes and why hydroponics will never be the future of growing food.

Agnès rolled her eyes and squeezed Karen's hand. 'You're going to love it here,' she enthused. 'We will go to the Louvre this afternoon.'

'The Louvre? Where is it?' Karen said, looking around.

'It's not here, you egg head,' her friend laughed, head back, mouth open.

The farmer closest to them tutted and made a hissing sound. Agnès stopped laughing and quietly apologised to the older man. Karen was astonished to see the unexpected display of deference from her friend, but made a note that in France, loud laughing in public, even at a truck-stop produce market in the middle of nowhere, would not be tolerated.

'When we get home, we will take a shower, have a rest and after lunch, we will go to the Louvre.'

It never ceased to amaze Karen how well her French friend had adapted to Australian life; how well she seemed to naturally understand everything around her, blend in. Karen hoped she would adjust to Paris as well as that, but feared Australia was a much more open society. She was so worried she would make a mistake, be immediately marked as 'Un-French' and banished from polite company. Agnès seemed to be reading her mind and squeezed her hand, offering her a drag on her cigarette.

'You will have to learn to smoke to fit in here, you know,' she said, blowing smoke elegantly over her shoulder. 'Everyone smokes.'

Karen carefully took the cigarette the way she had seen others do it and put it to her lips. Her mother's voice boomed in her head again and she quickly handed the cigarette back to her bemused friend.

'I don't care, I could never smoke,' she protested, screwing up her nose. 'I just couldn't.'

The boys had reappeared in time for Peter to see her put the cigarette to her lips. 'This day just keeps getting weirder.' He rubbed his hands through his messy hair.

'Let's go home,' Agnès announced, stabbing her cigarette out on the ashtray in front of them. 'And I am quitting smoking.'

'Yeah, right,' Jan, Peter and Karen said in unison, picking up boxes and bags of produce.

'You watch me. Once I've gone through all the duty-free!'

Karen didn't doubt that Agnès could do anything once she'd made up her mind. She realised she loved her French friend more than she loved Pete. Only a true friend would give up the thing they loved most in the world for you. Without being asked. Karen still couldn't believe that someone like her had found someone like Agnès, waiting at a bus stop in Bondi.

Home in Paris

To Karen's surprise, the van turned away from the apartment buildings she could see in the distance, retracing the route they had taken from the airport. The bright sunshine flickered through the trees lining the roadway, lulling her to sleep, her head on Peter's shoulder. Waking when the van stopped in an underground carpark, she was disoriented and parched. Her friends were all laughing quietly, sharing a joke, possibly at her expense.

'I was snoring, wasn't I?'

'Er…no, but you did a little fart,' Agnès teased.

Mortified, Karen swore them all to secrecy. She was sure that French women never farted, and if they did it would smell like perfume. Her face burning red, she swatted Peter.

'What was that for?'

'You should have woken me.' Karen tried out her best Parisian pout.

'Don't worry about it. It was a cute little fart, and you needed the sleep.' Peter put his hand to her cheek and kissed her forehead.

'Where are we?' Karen was surprised to see they were in a subterranean carpark surrounded by expensive cars. A light flickered on as two men approached the van. They looked like Secret Service guys.

'Home, apparently,' Peter said, pointing at Agnès who was hugging one of the men and happily draping her backpack strap over the outstretch hand of the other, who pulled her into a bear hug as soon as she was released from the first man's embrace.

'This is Jerome and Filipe. They are my big brothers.'

Karen and Peter must have looked confused, but Jan shook his head at them in a way that communicated that they should wait for later for an explanation of who these two men were. Agnès had told them she was an only child. Jan climbed back into the now empty van, the produce had presumably been delivered while Karen was sleeping and farting, which left her wondering how long she had been asleep and how many people had witnessed her passing wind. As the van revved, a previously unseen door began to rise twenty metres away, the now bright sunshine streaming in. There was an armed guard manning a boom gate at the top of a short steep driveway.

'We're not in Kansas anymore, Toto,' she whispered to Peter as a door hissed open directly in front of them to reveal an elevator.

Agnès could see the exchange of glances between her Australian friends and smiled. 'I told you my mum is a diplomat, right?'

'Well, yes, but we didn't really expect…,' Peter waved his hand in the general vicinity of the lift, the carpark, and Jerome and Filipe. 'Secret Service guys.'

'We're not terribly secret but we can kill you if you do the wrong thing. It goes with the territory,' Jerome explained.

'Licensed to kill?' Peter joked.

'Aah, yes, actually,' Filipe replied, his face stern.

'We were both fresh out of University when we first began working for the family. So, we are her big brothers if anyone asks. We did the school run often, so we are more like nannies.' Jerome expertly dodged a swat from Agnès. The men broke into broad smiles and ushered the three travellers into the elevator.

After a short ride, the elevator door opened onto an elegant lobby, complete with a secretary and metal detector. A door to the left was open, revealing an office lined with books, and Agnès' father, Georges, sitting at the desk in the middle of the room.

'Come in, come in, my children are home.'

They all laughed and lined up for hugs and not double, but triple kisses. The secretary in the entry way had not looked up from her desk, apparently oblivious to the three smelly backpackers in her vicinity. Jerome and Filipe had also disappeared along with their backpacks and hand luggage. The tired trio talked and laughed with Georges until a badly stifled yawn from Peter told him that jet lag was setting in.

'You must take a swim, eat and sleep. Then we will go for dinner at Peter's new place of work. You will consider the offer, yes?'

'I will definitely consider the generous offer. My head is spinning that I have barely landed, and I have a job already. A very good job.'

Peter was still shaking his head in disbelief when the secretary appeared in the doorway and Georges gestured to them to follow her. It took a minute for Karen to realise that the woman wore an earpiece and was multi-tasking while she buzzed them through the door, handing them a security pass accompanied by various sheets of paper.

'Read this, and don't do anything on the list,' she warned in a broad Scottish accent, which caught Karen by surprise.

'Agnès, be a lamb and show your friends their room. I have a million things to do and no time to play nanny.'

Agnès performed a strange little curtsey that seemed to go unnoticed by the busy secretary and led them to one of the doors off the entry lobby. She opened it with a dramatic swipe of her key card, head back like a matador, eliciting stifled laughter from Peter and Karen. They filed through the door as a slow beep began to emanate from the swipe-pad. Agnès shut the door firmly behind them silencing the beep, leaving the three standing in a long corridor with doors coming off at intervals. Karen wasn't sure what she had been expecting but this certainly wasn't it. Her skin began to prickle. She'd never had claustrophobia but there was a first time for everything. Agnès was saying something but Karen couldn't hear her over the pulse pounding in her ears. She could feel Pete's arm against hers. It was reassuring. Agnès' lips were still moving, so she smiled and nodded to show she was listening.

'Are you alright?' Agnès asked, moving to put her arm around Karen. Her face must have betrayed her unease. Agnès drew her into a quick hug.

'It's ok, chérie. You are safer here than anywhere in Paris! Security is everything to you, I know. Bon, you must read the list and promise me you won't fuck it up and you can stay here for as long as you want! Just so you know, we only get one chance, and I must stick to the list too, now that I am an adult. Here…is your room.'

Agnès nodded her head towards the first door on the right-hand side of the corridor, gesturing to Peter to use his swipe card. He waved it dutifully in front of the access panel that whirred and clicked. He pushed the elegant white door open to reveal a stylish living space with numerous doors leading from it. Peter's jaw dropped comically.

'Holy shit, are you kidding me? This is our room?'

'Yes, this is home sweet home. Your bags are here as you see. Make a mess, do whatever you want. This is your space. You must keep it clean though. The staff won't clean our rooms.' She pulled back the heavy drapes.

'Do you want to take a swim or sleep? Or we can eat?'

Agnès showed the astonished couple their bathroom, the pretty view of a typical Parisian street from the window, the walk-in wardrobes, finishing with a demonstration of the sound system.

'It's all soundproofed,' she bellowed over the booming music, dancing around the room and shouting.

Peter and Karen joined in and danced madly in the huge space, all collapsing on the Persian rug, laughing and exhausted. Peter picked up the typed sheet of paper that had been handed to them by the efficient and slightly frightening secretary on the way in, which Agnès referred to as the 'shit list'.

'No drinking, no smoking, no drugs, no visitors, no fun, no smiling…. It's all very straightforward,' Agnès laughed, lying back on the rug. 'I'm going to swim, then eat, then sleep. In that order!' She laughed at herself for once again using her favourite turn of phrase.

'I will buzz you in five minutes. Get your swimmers on, kids.'

Agnès loved using her Aussie accent.

Karen and Pater obeyed her direction, as they always did, and found themselves half an hour later dripping wet beside a heated roof-top pool under a glass conservatory, munching on fresh fruit and the best ham and tomato sandwiches they had ever eaten. Nothing ever seemed to go wrong when Agnès was in command, Karen thought to herself as she smiled over at Pete, who was chewing ecstatically, eyes shut.

'Now we sleep, then you will go with Dad and get your job. We,' Agnès nodded at Karen, 'will go and look at art.'

They followed her back to their beautiful rooms, amazed by their dumb-luck and the generosity of Agnès' parents. As it turns out, Karen thought, Paris is always a good idea.

Is it better to have loved and lost?

Weeks passed in a blur after that first visit to the Louvre. With a little help from Agnès' father, Karen became a volunteer at the museum, assisting with the cleaning of the sculptures, a task she referred to as 'poo patrol' but only in her head. Karen tried to take her work seriously, even if that included scraping pigeon excrement off marble plinths while tourists snapped photos in the Tuileries Gardens. Peter, still amazed by his sheer luck, had started work for Olivier, Jan's father, loving the long hours, the camaraderie of the kitchen. Agnès was writing freelance articles for a German language art magazine based in Paris, and Peter was working all hours. This left Karen free to immerse herself in art. Her mornings may have been spent cleaning pigeon poo from sculptures, but her afternoons were free to wander the museums, gardens and galleries and she discovered the many art supply stores dotted around the city.

Her tea-chest of art supplies arrived from Australia and supplemented by regular purchases from Sennelier on the left bank, Karen happily set up a makeshift studio in the ensuite bathroom after clearing the idea with Agnès.

Peter had Mondays off and would meet Karen at the museum. One icy afternoon in November, he collected her on Agnès' scooter. Karen waved a letter at him, her coat flapping in the wind, scarf trailing on the pavement.

'They offered me a job. They want to pay me to learn how to restore artworks.'

'Wow, that's incredible. Congratulations, babe. Let's go and find somewhere warm to celebrate. Angelina or Ladurée?'

After their celebratory hot chocolate, the ride home froze them to the core. No matter the weather, the Paris streets whizzing by never failed to excite Karen. She almost pinched herself, not believing she could be so lucky. Here she was in Paris with an amazing man, a job at the most famous museum in the world, and a best friend. They pulled into the underground garage and parked the scooter. Popping their heads into Georges' office to tell him the good news there were excited to see Agnès talking to her father.

'No, this is a disaster, Karen. You are here in Paris to make art, not just look at it, or clean shit off it all day.' Karen was crestfallen and Peter put his arm protectively around her waist.

'I'll take the job for just one year, so I can say I worked at the Louvre when I'm a famous artist.'

'You won't get to be a famous artist if you are working in the museum.'

Was this jealousy, Karen wondered. She was never good at understanding people's emotions nor their motives. 'I promise I will keep painting,' she said.

Agnès took charge and the mood lifted again. 'Okay, now let's go for a drink to celebrate your new commitment to your art career!'

Their celebratory drink took them to the Ritz, the only place to party according to Agnès. Karen always felt like a duck out of water in the luxurious bar, but as always felt grateful for Agnès ability to make her feel comfortable.

'I'm going to paint your portrait,' Karen slurred to her friend in the taxi on the way home. 'To prove to you that I am going to keep painting.'

'I believe you, but you better paint my portrait every day for a year if you want to prove anything to me.'

'You're on!' Karen and Agnès shook hands while Peter shook his head.

A week later the collection of portraits was already becoming too much for the suite they shared in the embassy. Peter stood brushing his teeth as Karen put the final touches on her latest piece.

'I don't think Agnès seriously wants 365 portraits of herself.'

'366. I think next year is a leap year,' Karen said. She was in another world as she expertly moved the drawing charcoal across the canvas.

Peter spat the toothpaste into the sink. 'I think we should get our own place, babe. I need a kitchen and you need more space to paint.'

Finally, Karen stood back from the canvas and nodded, first at the canvas, then at Peter. Surveying their comfortable surroundings, they both knew he was right. The time had come to find their own apartment in Paris, as daunting and exciting as that was. Peter floated the idea of throwing a wild going away party to see if the secretary would join in or have Jerome and Filipe remove them and their grubby back packs. Karen laughed as she washed her charcoal-covered hands in the bathroom sink. It would need a good scrub before they move.

Peter picked up the phone next to the toilet to call Agnès. They had made a pact to only use the phone above the toilet to call each other's rooms, such was the novelty for the two Australians to have a phone in the 'dunny' as they called it. Peter growled into the handset, trying to sound sexy.

'Guess where I am, Agnès,'

'I'm guessing in the bathroom because you sound constipated.'

'Ha, ha, that's the best come-back yet. You're getting good at this game,' he teased. 'Can you come in? If you're free? I want to show you something.'

A few minutes later, Agnès stood dumbstruck in front of the portraits Karen had painted so far. Karen stood with her back to her friend, looking at the walled courtyard. As always, she was battling with the inner critics that told her admirers of her work were simply being kind, that the art was rubbish, and she was doomed to be a sculpture cleaner for the term of her natural life. As much as she loved making her art, listening to people admiring it was almost worse than criticism.

Agnès looked around the cramped ensuite-cum-studio and understood it was time for them to move into their own place, and in fact, she said she knew a place that would be perfect for them. The trio laughed.

'Of course, you do!' Peter said.

The apartment was a few blocks from the metro station that would take Peter back into the 1st arrondissement for work. The move was easy. They loaded up their backpacks with their clothes and Jan dropped by with his van and two kitchen hands from the restaurant. The unfurnished apartment lacked even the basics, a surprise to two Australians accustomed to flats having built in kitchens and even wardrobes in some cases. Kitchen basics appeared over the course of the weekend, with Peter's boss buying them a new futon. Their generous friends gave them various kitchen appliances that elicited excited sounds from Peter and made Karen's eyes glaze over.

'I'm so lucky to have you, babe,' she told him as he excitedly showed her the new blender from Jan, 'I'd live on Pot Noodles if I had to cook.'

Trawling the flea markets all over Paris and taking Jan's van to brocantes further afield, they managed to furnish the studio in their preferred vintage style. They loved the apartment, relishing the feeling of independence and although Peter missed his passionate food-oriented conversations with

Georges, Agnès' father, neither of them missed the constant mildly intimidating presence of the secretary, who regularly reminded them of their luck at having such generous hosts.

Sculpture restoration was fascinating up to a point, but as predicted, Karen's own art-making all but dried up in the busy weeks after they moved even though the new apartment offered enough space to set aside a whole, albeit tiny, room as a studio. At first the room with the natural light had been their bedroom while she made a studio of the miniscule room that adjoined the living room. Who knew what the tiny space had been used for by previous inhabitants; perhaps a study or playroom if they had had children?

In the middle of their first frigid winter in the apartment, Karen had woken from a dream in which the space was lined with books, a sturdy chair tucked in one corner, draped in old wool throws. Unable to shake the feeling that it should be exactly that way she spent the following evening rearranging the rooms. As the winter sun was trying half-heartedly to push its way through the clouds, Peter arrived home to find their bed evicted to the living room, the studio set up in their former bedroom, and his now-manic girlfriend on the Minitel planning an excursion to Ikea for shelving for the books stacked in piles around the room.

He kissed her forehead and after his shower, curled up on the unmade futon to sleep the day away before heading back to the relative safety of a Michelin starred restaurant kitchen.

Agnès was concerned about her friend. 'Darling, you promised me you would keep painting. You can paint anything, it doesn't have to be me, just keep painting. It helps you…'

'What do you mean by that?' Karen placed her cup on the table and glared at her friend.

Agnès had never seen Karen so agitated. 'You are stronger when you paint. I am only saying this because I love you.' Agnès' eyes flicked from Karen's face towards the Louvre museum opposite the café.

Karen sighed heavily. 'Fine, I'll quit my job,' she said, as though she was doing Agnès a monumental favour. She secretly hated the work and was more than happy to quit and concentrate on her artwork.

Peter wasn't sure it was a good idea for Karen to paint alone all day, but she had already given her notice at the museum. His constant fatigue from working long hours in a hot kitchen and his new-found inability to read her moods resulted in nasty arguments in the small apartment. Karen would never apologise for her nasty words flung about in anger.

They were better in the warmer months; arriving home with fresh bread, the smell of coffee wafting from the tiny kitchen, he would shower, eat and flop naked onto the bed. Sometimes she would join him, and they would make love. But if it was cold, as it often was, flopping naked on the bed would be suicidal in their chilly flat so he would bundle himself in a layers and sleep like the dead, leaving her hunched muttering over her drawing table, unlit cigarette stuck to her lower lip. He had all but given up trying to make sense of her, deciding to just love her as she was, and pray to any god that was listening that that would be enough.

Paris had been an excellent move for Peter as he pursued his dream to become a chef, but the longer they stayed, the less he was sure Karen would survive it. As he rode the Metro to the restaurant each day, Peter acted as though would it be his last in Paris, drinking in the city, sometimes taking a new route if time allowed.

If he had to choose between Paris and Karen, he knew he would choose his fragile girlfriend, regardless of how that might affect his flourishing career. He could be happy anywhere, but Karen's mental health seemed to be suffering during the dark winter months, only to emerge into the light bright weeks of Summer in a mania that alienated their friends and, if he could admit it to himself, sometimes made him fear for his own safety.

During their second winter in the apartment, he was stunned by the delicate pencil drawings she was making, producing piles of sketches each day that littered the apartment floor. They were spare and elegant, drawn from memory mostly, or furtively made sketches of neighbours if she felt brave enough to leave the house. There were new faces amongst the piles of drawings and each day he would ask her about them, to tell him their story. It was a game she liked for a while but as she became more withdrawn, she resented his questions and hid the artwork in piles under her desk.

He had also given up asking if she had approached a gallery.

One particularly cold day after Christmas, Peter rolled towards her as they lay bundled in their bed, him reading a trade magazine, she mesmerised by Albert Camus. He held up an exquisite antique diamond ring, asking her to marry him with his eyes. She choked back tears and nodded, and he slipped the ring on her finger. It had been a stroke of genius, he thought. Karen seemed to glow with inner fire for the weeks afterward. They were lost in each other again. It almost seemed as though the girl he had fallen in love with back in Bondi had returned.

She turned a few of the little pencil sketches into beautiful paintings over those happy months; beautiful portraits of Agnès, Peter and Jan, a distinctive combination of pen and ink, with watercolour and gouache unlike anything Peter had seen before. Jan's father bought the portrait of his son and Agnès parents paid double the asking price of the painting of their daughter. A gallery enquired; they had seen the portrait of Jan in Olivier's restaurant. A newspaper wanted to write an article. Things were finally happening for her in Paris, Peter had said to her one morning as they talked about visiting the gallery. She was nervous about showing her art in Paris, convinced she would never measure up. She loved each piece passionately and lived in terror of any criticism or rejection.

'Do you feel that way about each dish you prepare?' she asked him one day.

He couldn't tell if she was joking. 'Of course, I do," he replied. She threw a pillow at him, so he figured it had been a joke.

Agnès planned a surprise engagement party for the first day of Spring. She hired a private room in the Louvre, although Agnès could have chosen a better time to announce she was returning to Australia. Her work visa was approved, finally, and she was excited to announce she had been offered a position on a cattle farm bigger than Belgium.

Karen told her it was too far away from the beach; she would have to find a cattle station closer to Bondi. Karen wished she would find one closer to Paris.

Agnès' last night in Paris coincided with the opening of Karen's show at the little gallery in the Place de Vosges, the sell-out show establishing her as the next big thing. When the last red dot was placed on the wall to show that every painting was sold, Karen was lightheaded, kissing cheeks and shaking hands. It was her hands that were shaking. Night became morning and the whole entourage traipsed out to Charles de Gaulle airport to send Agnès off in style. Hugs and tears and promises to write daily flowed between the two girls and the whole group posed for a photograph with three pilots who had flown in from Japan. It was a fitting bon voyage for Agnès who had brought so much colour and depth to Karen's life.

'Don't be mad at me for going. I'll come home and we will drink gin at the Ritz,' Agnès whispered, her face buried in her friend's hair.

Karen nodded. 'I'll wait for you here, forever.'

Life went on in Paris; Peter working in the restaurant as a Chef de Partie, Karen selling paintings as quickly as she could paint them. As promised, Agnès wrote every day and Karen organised her wedding with her best friend though they were separated by thousands of miles and various oceans.

The letters stopped in June, although the one that arrived from the Northern Territory police department broke the monotony of the empty tray on her father's desk. Georges flew to Australia and stayed for the southern winter.

Peter and Karen's wedding date came and went.

Agnès had walked into the desert one night, taking her camera to photograph the stars, never to be seen again. No letters. No body.

Georges came home emptier than he had ever been, and they moved from the embassy to their home south of Munich and waited. Karen and Peter's apartment, it turned out, was owned by Agnès' parents. Could they stay and wait, please? In case she comes home to Paris. Karen had to wait. She had promised.

Forever.

Peter made Sous Chef. Karen, moody and volatile again, stopped painting the delicate gouache and ink portraits. The intricate drawings and collages piling up around the apartment were now all skulls, death and anger. There was a new hardness in her work. Karen could not remember being angry before, had never missed anyone before, but she missed her friend like a missing limb. She was angry that Agnès had left her, angry that Agnès had been so irresponsible to let the desert take her. She hadn't missed her parents when she moved to Paris, well maybe her father a little, and the dog. She had missed the dog, but not like this. She had known where the dog was. How does a force of nature simply disappear?

Peter took longer to realise that he had also lost Karen. Exactly when she started using cocaine was unknown. One of the gallerists had taken some of Karen's work to New York and life quickly became a blur of concord flights and five-star hotels. Later as Peter was putting the pieces of the puzzle together, the Director of the gallery confessed she thought the drugs would help with the grieving process after Agnès disappeared. Peter was broken by the confession, but he had to admit that the coke had helped at first. It was the heroin that was her undoing, he had explained to the shocked gallerist.

The gallery was still selling the works on paper. Karen's notoriety increased after her 1995 show in Rome that involved a painting in human blood. Her own.

His own professional success aside, Peter decided it was time to go home. To Australia. They would go to the outback and find their friend if that was what Karen wanted to do. Then they could go back to how things were, before Paris, before his sheltered, nervous girlfriend could sell a painting and make enough money to go on a month-long bender on the proceeds. Karen said she had to stay and wait for Agnès. Peter said he had to leave.

Rachel

Versailles, April 2005

The spring morning was clear and cool, perfect conditions for visiting the Palace of Versailles, Rachel explained to her excited clients. Mostly in their 60s and 70s, they were members of various writers' groups from all over the world. Their booking enquiry told Rachel that the groups 'got together once a 'year to 'go somewhere pretty, drink wine and complain about their health, and maybe do a little writing.'

Despite their advanced years, they were like school children during the mini-city tour, all speaking over one another, and jumping from seat to seat to get a better view. The driver, rolling his eyes at Rachel more than once, took to the microphone to ask his passengers to please take their seats, his broad Northern accent proving incomprehensible to most of the passengers. This only sparked a new wave of excitement as they asked those around them if they understood what the driver had said.

Once on the road to Versailles, the driver relaxed as the passengers settled back in their seats and took out their notebooks apparently ready for the commentary. She prided herself on her knowledge of the area but felt herself blushing as the passengers took notes, the entire bus seeming to hang on her every word. Along with the history of the palace itself, she gave tips on visiting the town of Versailles, and peppered the commentary with scandalous titbits about the royal inhabitants of the chateau and the Revolutionaries, much to the delight of this light-hearted group.

Arrival at the chateau was often frantic as the coaches disgorged their excited passengers, but this group filed out neatly. The group seemed single minded, eager to get indoors as quickly as possible; all obsessed with the history and dramas of the palace, testing even Rachel's extensive knowledge of events and characters involved in the revolution.

They trekked the vast cobblestone forecourt towards the chateau, stopping intermittently to snap photos and ask questions. As groups went, they were quickly endearing themselves to a sometimes-jaded Rachel. Gwen, a writer and her partner Bill, a retired engineer stood patiently with her as the rest of the group took frame after frame of the exquisite architecture, mist rising behind the building, coming from the fountains behind, Rachel explained.

'You're terribly young to be a tour guide,' Gwen remarked.

'Oh, thank you,' Rachel laughed, 'that makes me feel fantastic, considering I'm about to turn 30.'

'How lovely! I remember 30...' she sighed, nudging Bill in the ribs. 'I'm 71 and Bill is 68. He's my toy-boy.'

They all laughed as they continued their march towards the entrance, the guard waving to Rachel as she ushered her clients through the narrow VIP gate and the metal detectors. A hush fell over the exuberant group as they entered the chateau, and made their way through the rooms, awestruck at the interiors and artworks. Rachel was in full swing, thoroughly enjoying discussing the magnificent interiors with such captivated clients, and then there he was, standing in front of her, the tall handsome tour-guide who somehow knew her name, as their respective groups crossed paths in the Queen's bedroom in the Palace of Versailles, of all places. In true romance-novel-style their eyes met across a shiny parquet floor.

'Rachel?' he said, squinting at her as if to see the girl she had been 10 years before. She would discover later that he needed to wear glasses, but his ego wouldn't let him.

'Hi,' she said.

Rachel smiled and searched her memory for his name, his gorgeous face was so familiar. Both tour groups watched the exchange, alert to the electricity between them. Lost in her thoughts of who this man was and how he knew her, she realised that he was still speaking to her. He was suggesting they 'catch-up', and they arranged to have a drink in the garden while the tour groups had their hour of free time wandering about the chateau.

Rachel nodded when he gave her the meeting place. She turned and watched as he continued his tour with his group. She almost went weak at the knees when he gave her a little wave as he disappeared through the ornate doorway.

Jean from Illinois, ("writing historical fiction is not as easy as it sounds,") took Rachel's arm conspiratorially as they continued on their own tour.

'You have no idea who he is, do you dear?' laughing loudly enough that the tourists in the next room turned and peered at her.

Rachel, horrified at both herself and Jean, could only turn red and shake her head.

'Find out his name before you get too in-depth in the conversation, dear. He looks like your future husband,' she said, her eyes twinkling as though she truly could see the future.

Distracted as they all were during the final thirty minutes of the guided tour, Rachel ran through her spiel about the Hall of Mirrors as her charges snapped hundreds of photos and made notes in their ever-present journals. She directed her charges to take a break in the café, wander the gardens or simply sit and enjoy their hour of free time, their knowing smiles making her blush.

'Alex!' Rachel said, under her breath, retrieving his name from the depths of her memory. Freshening up in the restroom before heading to their 'catch-up', the memories flooded back as she touched up her makeup. Happy with what she saw in the mirror, she was relieved she had worn her beloved white designer turtle-neck sweater and black pencil skirt with boots. Alex was a good-looking man, with a smattering of grey hairs and laughter lines around his eyes and she had no intention of letting on that she hadn't remembered him at first.

Aware that he was watching her as she made her way down the stairs from the chateau, she looked up and smiled to see him waiting for her at the Neptune Fountain. They exchanged the usual double air-kisses, and she felt the slight rasp of stubble and inhaled his incredible scent, wondering if her knees were going to buckle under her. The view was breathtaking as always as they walked down the Royal Way towards the Apollo Fountain and the little concession stand selling chocolat chaud beneath the horse chestnut trees. It was perfect weather for hot chocolate. Rachel smiled and tried to ignore the members of her group who had placed themselves at various vantage points along the gravel path to watch their exchange; Jean, notepad out and staring into the distance. Rachel considered patting herself down to check for listening devices.

Alex handed her the steaming hot drink, put his own cup to his lips and continued walking slowly, his broad back to Rachel as she took a moment to gather her thoughts and followed. He wore a navy jacket, pale blue linen shirt, chinos and stylish tan shoes, elegant Burberry umbrella hooked over one arm: his weapon of choice. Rachel had always resisted carrying a totem for her tour groups to follow, preferring a simple clipboard and setting a pace that made it easy for her clients to keep up. Her tours were relaxed and thorough, never rushed or superficial. In other words, she felt there was no need to hold a sunflower or umbrella over her head to wave around for her clients to follow like lost sheep.

'Still using the clipboard, I see. How many people do you lose each year? They are probably still wandering around in the palace.' He laughed; lines crinkled around his eyes.

She poked her tongue at him, but then smiled. She was well known for her inability to embrace certain aspects of the professional Tour Guide's arsenal, including her stubborn Australian accent, which seemed to cling to every syllable she uttered, whether it was in French or Italian.

'You don't really remember me, do you?' he asked, smiling and looking at her over his drink. Rachel's face was bright red before he'd finished the sentence and she threw her head back, laughing.

'We worked together, I remember that much,' she protested, 'I did a lot of drugs in the 90s. No, I didn't, I didn't! That was a joke,' kicking herself at her awkwardness.

'Alexander,' he said simply, and smiled.

'Of course, I bloody remember you, Alex.' She immediately regretted the crassness and cringing at her broad accent. He laughed and somehow managed to look even more gorgeous, as he chatted Rachel found herself staring at him, not really listening, letting his curious accent wash over her as though hearing it for the first time.

'You still sound as Australian as ever! Do you go home often?'

'I have only been back there a couple of times. It's a tough accent to kill. Alexander,' she mused, 'Are your parents Russian?' she asked.

'My father is yes; my name is spelled with a k and seven e's. Why do you ask?' he joked.

'I can hear it in your accent. It's sort of tucked behind the French,' she laughed. 'I love accents, it's kind of a hobby, picking accents. It must be because mine is so terrible!' She heard herself and wanted to die. Who says that kind of thing, she wondered?

'Oh yes, most of my groups are Russian these days so I spend half my life as Aleksandr. It's confusing for my kids, growing up with French, Danish and Russian.' He pronounced the consonants crisply, the 'r' rolling off his tongue.

'Kids? Wow. So, you're like a proper adult?' Rachel laughed, feeling about seventeen, and hiding the sinking feeling that had shown up with the 'k' word; kids usually meant there was a mother involved. A Danish mother obviously.

'Yes, three boys, Noah is 8, William is 5 and Emil is the baby. He's three.' His eyes shone at the mention of his kids.

They continued walking along the gravel path, surrounded by statuary and awestruck tourists, chatting about everything and nothing. Rachel, never one to be lost for words, let Alex talk, entertaining her with tales of his often-fascinating Russian clients, including a famous writer who had been obsessed with Versailles, believing himself to be a reincarnation of Louis the 16th.

A natural storyteller, Alex told her the famous story of the two English spinsters who, in 1911 published a book saying they had passed through a time-slip and saw the Queen, Marie Antoinette herself, sitting on the grass in her hamlet, wearing a white hat and summer dress. Alex's general knowledge was amazing, extending even to the weird and sometimes pointless, but always entertaining.

Their hour of free time flew by; it does when you're having the time of your life, as they say. Although the mention of the children seemed to change the dynamic of the conversation a little, they kissed each other's cheeks and he hugged her, holding her close, a rare exchange in France. Flushed and laughing from the public display of affection, they exchanged business cards, promising to 'catch-up' again when they had more than an hour.

They turned to find both their tour groups milling about, waiting for their tour of the gardens and set off, Rachel with her clip board waving in the air, Alex stylish umbrella held aloft. The remainder of the afternoon was a blur, Rachel encouraging her group to find a nice spot and write in their journals, a brilliant idea that enabled her to dissect and obsess over every part of her conversation with Alex. It was entirely possible that he had mentioned a wife, ex-wife or at least the mother of his children, in those first minutes while she was lost in his accent but unless she could travel back in time like one of those English spinsters, she would never know.

Lost in her thoughts Rachel had caused her own group to run late for their return trip to Paris. The morning's cohesive group had become a loose assortment of weary people, with a few eager beavers rushing ahead, keen to grab the front seats, and the stragglers at the back straining and sweating despite the cool air. The driver had texted numerous times, but she could only herd her poor clients so quickly. He was grumpy by the time the exhausted passengers filed into the coach, checking his watch and tutting.

Rachel felt awful for making her clients rush to the coach, going to extra effort to be lively, her running commentary becoming little more than nervous chatter including anecdotes detailing the construction of the ring road surrounding Paris like a moat. The exhausted writers' group didn't care one bit about le périphérique and how long it had taken to build.

'Tell us about your meet-cute!' a voice called from the rear seats.

Rachel sighed. As they neared their hotel, she relented and hurriedly told them everything.

Well, almost everything. She conveniently left out her constant gaffes and any mention of his children. The entire coach hung on every word, their eyes brightened, and tired faces lifted, nodding at each other with knowing smiles. Aware it would all end up in a novel, short story or poem in some form or another Rachel took a little license with the truth and added a few hand brushes and a lingering stare or two. The passengers swooned on cue. Sometimes she really loved her job.

She left her group at their expensive hotel despite their appeals to join them for a drink in the bar. Thanking them profusely for the enormous envelope full of tips she popped in her shoulder bag after giving the driver his share, she set off on foot. The sun had set on a moody sky, low clouds threatened rain, and Rachel found herself in a mood to match the gloomy sky. After what had been a perfectly successful day, that included a lovely group of clients and a chocolat chaud shared with a good-looking man, she had decided to sulk. Declining the bus driver's offer of a lift home, Rachel wanted to walk, even though it looked like rain, and she had no umbrella.

As the thunder rolled on the horizon, Rachel began to recall all the ways she had messed up her life. It was completely irrational, but she was convinced she had taken a wrong turn somewhere.

'I was too ambitious,' she said under her breath. 'Always chasing the next promotion.'

Continuing along the theme of unfounded self-criticism, she kicked herself for taking the job with the barefoot yacht rentals in Greece. Sure, she had made plenty of money and had heaps of free time to write for travel publications, the one thing she had dreamed of, but at what cost, she asked herself. Was it worth being successful if the love of your life has slipped through your fingers?

Rachel stopped to cross the intersection, Au Bon Marche to her left, glowing as the sun set. 'Rach, pull yourself together,' she mumbled to her reflection in the shop windows. She wasn't sure why she was so convinced that this man, a stranger really, was the love of her life. She'd had her chance with him. The weird feeling in her stomach may have been hunger not lost love.

Wandering the streets of Paris, she knew so well; Rachel made a detour past Saint Sulpice church. She stopped and looked up. The clouds seemed to touch the spires. She was hungry but the feeling in her stomach was more than hunger; the connection between her and Alex had been undeniable. She shook her head. Why now? Could it be a past-life thing, she asked herself, thinking of his bizarre tale of the two women teachers at Versailles. Fat drops of rain fell on cue, and she berated herself for not carrying an umbrella. She asked the sky; do you know who carries an umbrella?

'Alex, that's who,' she mumbled.

She ran to the Metro where she tried to avoid dripping on people. Miserable, cold and wet, she pondered why she hadn't snapped up the gorgeous Alex when she had the chance? They could have been her three adorable children. No, she argued with herself; she wouldn't have had three. Maybe one? Then she could have still travelled, still written for magazines.

The rain had set in by the time she emerged at her stop, so she trudged through the puddles, startling the pigeons under the awning above the empty street. 'I could have done both. Glamourous travel guide by day, sexy earth mother by night,' she said to herself. 'Women do that all the time, don't they?'

Her own mother had managed it. How hard can it be? She pictured Alex's unknown wife as a stunning supermodel juggling toddlers and photo shoots. Who knew why she had decided she should be a super model? Soaked to the skin, Rachel was shivering by the time she reached her building, taking the steps to avoid a telling-off from the building manager; using the elevator while dripping wet was punishable by death in her building. The steps were slippery, and she was shuddering and muttering under her breath.

As she turned the key in the door to her own cosy apartment and saw her gorgeous view across the roof tops of Paris, her cat Beau, and the bottle of wine she'd been given on a recent cave visit, she realised that her life was what she'd made it, and it was pretty great. There might not have been a sexy man waiting for her at home, but she had achieved exactly what she had set out to do.

She was confused about how empty it suddenly felt? Of course, he was married. All the good ones are, she thought a little too bitterly, considering she hadn't given him a second thought in ten years. She'd barely given him a thought at all.

Peeling off her water-logged coat and shoes, she shut the door firmly behind her and stripped naked in the hall, dumping the pile of wet clothes in the bathroom, grateful she didn't have a flat mate to worry about. The shower was hot, and her towelling bathrobe was fluffy. She brushed her hair and twisted it under a towel and padded out to the kitchen. Pouring herself a glass of wine and shaking her head, she marvelled that she could have been blind to the perfect man standing right in front of her.

Cringing inwardly, she thought of the many times Alex had asked her for a drink or a bite to eat. Why had she always found an excuse not to go? To be fair on her past self, she had been busy with study, working, friends coming from abroad constantly, or 'famils', the travel industry term for organised visits to potential locations for tours destinations and accommodation. If her memory served her well, she recalled she and Alex had been on a few trips together, in a large group who partied a little too hard considering they were supposed to be working, and cradled heads all day through countless hotel and restaurant stops.

She leaned on the window frame and watched the pouring rain. 'I must buy an umbrella…' She pictured herself and Alex carrying matching Burberry umbrellas. She sipped her wine. My life is awesome, she thought as Beau the cat rubbed against her legs. She picked up the big ginger cat and carried him to the kitchen to get his food, talking to him and scratching under his chin.

'I don't need a man, I've got you, big guy.' She poured kibble into Beau's polka-dot bowl. 'Everything is purr-fect,' she said, rolling her 'r' and laughing at her own joke. She stood back and watched the purring cat eat. Grabbing her glass, she sat on the sofa and flipped on the television. A documentary about Rome was playing and she sat back and watched, recalling her two years in the ancient city. When she'd been offered that job in Rome the company had thrown a bon-voyage party for her and she remembered Alex telling her he would miss her, which she had thought was sweet. In the days before social media, widespread use of email and cell phones, it was far more difficult to keep in contact. This happened, she realised, mainly because it hadn't actually occurred to her to keep in contact. Putting down the empty wine glass, she lay back on the sofa. My life is perfect, she thought. I'm being infantile about this guy. He's the one that got away, but there are plenty more fish in the sea.

We meet again....

True to form, it took Rachel and Alex three months to get together for a drink. He had phoned a couple of times to say hi, casually suggesting they meet for coffee, but Rachel had always been busy when Alex was free, and free when he was busy. Just like the old days. Not seeing him didn't stop her dreaming of him, though. Every other night she felt as though she was talking to him, walking the avenues of the gardens at Versailles, their eyes meeting across the crowded parquet floors. Convinced she would run into him at the chateau, she took great care getting ready in the mornings, her clients began commenting on how elegant she was, how very French.

In the end it was Versailles that got them together again, both taking a private group through the chateau. Alex's group included a couple of Russian politicians and what seemed like forty secret service agents. Her own group consisted of two Hollywood stars and their families, but even they craned their necks to see who the gun-toting guys with dark glasses and earpieces were protecting. Alex had nodded in her direction, not making eye-contact, obviously under strict protocols, as she knew well, having shown her fair share of celebrities the sights of Paris. Her all-time favourite client had been the gorgeous Sharon Stone. Miss Stone had loved everything, claimed Paris as her own. She had been a delight.

A strong desire to run to Alex and throw her arms around him threatened to overwhelm her, but the fear of being shot by Secret Service guys and bleeding out on the marble stopped her in her tracks. Ushering her own group towards the now empty chapel, she welcomed the silence that descended when the entranced, architecture-loving stars took their children's hands. They walked slowly around the space, marveling at the intricate stone inlays and speaking in hushed voices about the significance of the design, while the nannies bribed the tired, uninterested little children into sullen compliance.

Heading to a local bar to avoid the rain, Rachel had declined her clients' offer of a lift, explaining that she lived close by, intending to catch a train after they were whisked away in a convoy of five black 4x4s. After the intensity of her group and seeing Alex, she was relieved to be outside in the cool air, even if it was raining. Again.

Taking out her new little black umbrella, she opened it against the grey sky and slowly ambled towards the cosy little bistro on the edge of the village. She had taken to hanging her umbrella on the back of her front door and as the rain began to pour in earnest, she was glad she had remembered to bring it for once.

What would her sisters say when she told them about declining a lift back to Paris with her clients, two of the hottest stars in Hollywood? She laughed at the thought of her sisters shrieking at her over the phone. Before they had wives and children, she would have fallen over herself to ride back to Paris with these two stars. Not that she had anything against children but being stuck in a car with one complaining of 'needing to poop', another that had cried on being told she couldn't go to Disneyland, again, was not Rachel's idea of a relaxing ride back to Paris.

'Hi,' a voice said, its owner falling into step with her and stooping under her umbrella. Startled, she lifted the too-small umbrella to accommodate his height.

'Hi,' she replied, as Alex slid his arm around her waist, pulling himself closer.

'What's so funny?' He was instantly familiar, but it didn't bother her.

'Oh, nothing, thinking about something my famous wealthy client said to me.' She winked at him.

'How was the reunion?'

Their previous employer had held a party, bringing together current and ex-staff, an idea borne of a small impromptu gathering a few months prior, too much alcohol and dancing convincing everyone that a reunion for the entire company was a brilliant plan. Faxes and emails began to fly across Europe and the world, and as with every event Rachel planned, the party had taken on a life of its own.

'Yes, I was there, life of the party,' Rachel said, rolling her eyes, 'I was roped into helping organise the thing, so I thought I'd better go! You know how much I love a party!' They may have lost contact for years, but Rachel had always been known for her ability to get a party started and to keep it going.

'Yes, a few people emailed photos. That was some red dress you wore!'

She blushed. 'Oh, that old thing…Um, yes, it was an amazing night.'

'I couldn't make it. Family. You know?' He shrugged.

'Mmm, yes, of course.' Rachel smiled at him. Of course? Rachel didn't know a thing about family responsibilities. She was footloose and fancy free, and had always thought she was happily so, but now she wasn't so sure.

After a drink at the too-crowded bistro, they made a dash for the Versailles-Rive Gauche station just making the train, the ride they had both done countless times now taking on a life of its own as they talked and laughed in the empty carriage. It seemed like only minutes had passed and they were off the train and standing in the entrance to the RER station, talking, completely absorbed in each other as the rain continued to pour outside.

The rain didn't appear to have any intention of letting up, so Alex suggested a nearby place he knew. They ran through the drizzling rain to shelter in the bar that turned out to be under a bridge in a slightly questionable neighbourhood.

'How on earth did you find this place?' she asked as she took in the shabby décor that may have been fashionable sometime in the 80s.

'It's a famous bar, Hemingway drank here, but then Hemingway drank everywhere!'

Hours passed as they covered every topic they could think of until the bar closed, Alex finally discussing his marital status as they gathered their jackets. Rachel feigned polite interest while slowly dying inside. His wife was a flight attendant. A beautiful Danish flight attendant with three angelic children. Rachel had seen the photos. What was Alex doing here with her when he had this gorgeous family at home?

Intending to grab a taxi to their respective suburbs, they'd emerged from the subterranean bar into a cool night as the rain was clearing. Without discussion, as though they did this all the time, they bypassed the taxi rank and kept walking. They walked across Paris until the early hours. Rachel had no idea where Alex lived but eventually, he had walked her to her door in the 18th arrondissement.

Was she misreading Alex's signals or did he just like walking all over town? He didn't hint that he'd like to be asked upstairs, to take things further. For her part, she would have thrown him over her shoulder and carried him up the stairs; she'd been weak at the knees the minute his arm had encircled her waist while walking in the rain in Versailles. Yes, he was trying to stay out of the rain, but surely, he could have used the fancy Burberry umbrella that always hung over his arm.

The rain had stopped, and Alex stood back in the empty street, arm raised in a goodnight wave, leaving her in no doubt that he didn't intend asking for a night-cap. She wished him a good night, quickly making her way up to her flat, where she caught sight of him as he turned the corner.

It's a crush, nothing more, she told herself. He was a friend, a colleague and a married man. Embarrassed and annoyed at herself, Rachel knew she was smitten; she hadn't felt this way since her crush on the gym teacher at high school.

A few days later, a group of tour industry people met for dinner. Rachel arranged it ostensibly to make up for Alex missing the reunion, but the reality was she desperately wanted to see him again. Apologising, he explained that he'd been unable to make the party, having to get home to care for his children, his flight attendant wife working a late flight. Every woman in the group swooned visibly, Rachel suspected Alex had no idea his attentiveness to his wife and children just made him more attractive.

The group had met in front of the building that housed their original employer, some of them still worked in the building; Alex and a few of the others had taken positions with the new company that had moved into the space.

Walking towards Alex, she felt that familiar queasy feeling you get when you have a crush on someone combined with an incredibly strong feeling of déjà vu. She laughed out loud as she recalled seeing him in the street, standing in almost the same spot on the wide sidewalk, on possibly her first day of work, in that building 10 years earlier. He'd laughed too, perhaps recalling the same moment, and kissed both her cheeks. He did his usual thing of standing back, holding her shoulders as he looked into her eyes, smile on his face, oblivious to the rest of the group. It felt so good to be held that way, to be really seen, but she wondered if perhaps he felt as though he were simply catching up with a bunch of old workmates, including her, and she should be embarrassed for fantasising that he would gather her into his arms and kiss her the way French men kissed their girlfriends.

Alex made his excuses straight after dessert, reminding Rachel that he was her lift home. Their friends laughed knowingly and he, to her horror, blushed. It turned out that he hadn't even driven into the city but had wanted to walk with her again. The night was clear and crisp; no need for umbrellas, she thought, although she could have done with a scarf.

'Are you cold?' he asked. He didn't wait for a response. He took off his scarf and wrapped it around her neck. He stood and looked into her eyes, before taking her hand in his and continuing along the pavement. Rachel only heard half of what he said over the pounding of her heart. Time seemed to slow down, and she was shocked back into reality when they arrived at her door. That familiar feeling of wanting to drag him up the stairs returned but she smiled and blushed and he left her with a friendly double-kiss and walked off into the night. Again.

Closing the front door, she stepped into the foyer and leaned on the wall.

'Oh…' she said softly. She was smiling. But she felt ridiculous. The guilt she felt for wanting him showed up as a sick feeling in her stomach, a feeling she had initially mistaken for love. This man was married with three little children, she had no business being anywhere near his business, so to speak. As she climbed the stairs to her apartment, she shook her head. So much for the perfect life, she thought, so much for the pep talk she had given herself a few days before.

After years of feeling she was in control of her destiny, feeling powerful and independent, she felt like a teenager again with her first crush. She didn't know why she hadn't felt this way about him years before; he was good looking, charming and, from memory, he had been very interested in her. What's more, he had been available then. Why hadn't she noticed how lovely he was? In truth, she had been enjoying her life and wasn't interested in having a relationship that would tie her to one place. She pushed the door open and Beau was sitting in the hall, waiting for his dinner. Again, she watched the big ginger cat eat, purring happily.

'Why can't I be happy like you?' she asked the cat.

Unable to sleep, she sat on her tiny balcony looking over Paris. The tea was soothing and, wrapped in a blanket, she eventually drifted off. She woke hours later with a cramp in her leg and Beau, on her lap, curled in a ball. He opened his eyes and yawned, hopped down, stretched and disappeared over the balcony. Rachel stretched too and uncurled herself slowly from the chair. The glow on the horizon told her sunrise was less than an hour away. Perhaps it was the discomfort of sleeping squeezed into a garden chair, but she had once again dreamed of Alex.

Rachel shivered. Leaning against the railing, head in hands, she tried to recall the dream but immediately regretted it. She and Alex, swirling in water as though they had fallen from a boat. They had tried to reach for each other, but he had gone under. It was only a dream, she told herself, but the feeling of dread would not leave her.

Stepping back into the apartment she wandered from bathroom to kitchen, images of the dream swirling in her mind. She missed him, even though they had been together until only a few hours before, walking the quiet night-time streets of Paris, could still feel his kiss on her cheek as he left her at the front door. The image of him going under the water made her shiver again. Stopping short of slapping her own face, she reminded herself that it was pointless to be obsessing about this married man with small children, much less freaking out about a stupid dream she had had about him.

She jumped as her cell phone buzzed signalling a text message.

Please be from Alex, she found herself wishing like a schoolgirl. 'Oh, for fuck's sake. You're being ridiculous,' she mumbled to herself. A text at four in the morning was probably her mother.

'Great conversation. I love talking to you. Miss you right now…See you soon?' the text read. It was from Alex. She pictured him hiding in the bathroom, furtively texting her when he should have been with his wife. A wave of guilt washed over her.

'Oh God, why do I feel guilty?' she seethed out aloud at the phone. In frustration she tossed the Nokia across the room. It hit the side of the coffee table and shattered, startling the poor cat who had come back in search of breakfast.

Annoyed at herself for breaking her brand-new phone, she poured food for the cat and gathered the plastic pieces of the phone from the carpet.

Had she lost grip on reality?

She felt as though she was going crazy; madly in love one minute and just plain mad the next, then feeling depressed a moment later. She and Alex had spent a couple of evenings walking all over Paris, discussing everything from the devastating tsunami in Asia, 9/11, the terrorist bombings in London and

Bali. She enjoyed talking to him, too. None of her friends seemed interested in world events, she felt she and Alex were soulmates, if there was such a thing. Tonight, especially had been incredible; their connection undeniable, and she was definitely attracted to him, but he was definitely married.

It's a text, and probably meant nothing, she told herself. Although he was telling her he missed her right now, at four in the morning. That was different from saying he missed her at lunch time. Surely. Feeling exhausted again, she curled up on the sofa, risking dreaming of Alex.

That's all it will ever be, she thought, a dream.

As much as she desired him, wanted him in her life, and in her bed at that moment, her heart was breaking. Rachel made a commitment to herself that she could never see him again. Or at least never let him walk her home. So, what if they would be good together? He was already with someone, and good people don't go after other women's husbands. It's the sisterhood. She would have to avoid going to Versailles. She didn't trust herself to be near him again.

Unable to sleep, she slowly dragged herself to the shower. An early breakfast and a walk around Ile St Louis would make her feel better. A walk. Alone.

Fancy seeing you here.

October 2005

Avoiding a man that you are in love with is excruciating but Rachel knew she had to do it. Taking groups to Versailles was out of the question, so she began accepting jobs destined for the theme parks instead. Attempting to avoid someone that the universe is determined you run into is like trying to catch sunlight; impossible to do and even harder to keep doing once you've realised how ridiculous you're being.

A new tour firm had head-hunted her, asking her to put together premium day tours for high-end clients. Visiting the elegant offices near Palais Royale to drop off some paperwork, she physically bumped into Alex as she left the ladies' room.

'What the hell are you doing here?' she demanded. If he was startled by her aggressive tone, he didn't show it.

'Ah, this is my new office. This is the company my friends, Gustav and Estelle, started. Have they asked you to do some tours?'

He was his usual charming self, completely unaware that she had turned her life upside down and was going quietly mad since receiving his 4am text months before. He kissed both cheeks, asked how she was and commented that he hadn't seen her at Versailles.

'Oh, I've been doing high-roller theme-park tours, long hours.' Rolling her eyes, suggesting that it was not her choice to escort spoiled rich brats while their parents go shopping, and not realising it was preferable to running into him in the Hall of Mirrors at Versailles.

'Oh no, your worst nightmare!' he grimaced.

Rachel was starting to think she had over-reacted to his text. 'Who did you upset to get that gig?'

'Oh, I was getting sick of all that magnificence and grandeur at Versailles. Did you recommend me to your friends?'

'Er, no I am embarrassed to say that I did not. But I wish I had. I think we will work well together. You look very…relaxed. I don't think I have ever seen you wearing…jeans?'

'They are Kenzo!' Rachel could have said au revoir at this point and gone on her way, or they could have worked together again, colleagues and friends. They turned to walk towards the offices.

'Oh, I'm not sure if you've tried to text me, my phone smashed, and I had to get a new one. Drama.' She rolled her eyes for effect.

He looked at the floor and drew a deep breath. 'I did text you, that morning after we walked home. I missed you, silly I know, sorry. I shouldn't say that. And I didn't hear from you, so I…'

'I dropped my phone down the stairs that morning, so don't stress!' She tried to sound casual and wasn't sure if she had succeeded. 'What did you text?'

'Oh, nothing really. I was sitting on the balcony. Couldn't sleep. I had been…er, thinking how nice it had been walking all over Paris with you. And talking. I can't talk to anyone the way I can talk to you.'

'Same, I'm so glad we're friends,' she said, deciding against giving him a playful punch on the arm and calling him buddy.

'Friends? I'd like to think we're good friends.'

She sighed. He reached out and took her free hand and held it for a moment. She hadn't misread his text at all.

'Alex, you're married,' she whispered, stating the obvious.

'I don't want to hurt anyone,' he said flatly.

An office door opened, and she pulled her fingers away like she'd been stung. Estelle, her new boss, popped her head out and said hi. She looked from Rachel to Alex smiling warmly.

'Do you know each other? How nice.' She smiled. 'We're ready to go through those tours now if you like. Alex do you want to sit in on the meeting?'

The weeks flew by, the new tours became popular, and she and Alex began working together more and more. They had an excellent working relationship that would probably have continued to be excellent if they hadn't started sleeping together. Rachel had managed to convince herself that they weren't doing anything wrong because they were just work colleagues. Alex rarely mentioned his wife, who was apparently sleeping with her tennis partner's husband, a cliché relationship if ever there was one. He seemed unfazed by the news.

She desperately wanted to tell her friends about the whole thing. It was fantastic gossip. If one of her friends had a juicy tidbit like that about someone and didn't share, she would have been ropable. As much as she might have revelled in the sordid details of Alex's perfect wife Hanne shagging her friend's husband, Rachel felt it would be disrespectful to discuss it. It may have had something to do with the fact that discussing Alex's home-life may shine a light on her own indiscretions.

She had always detested people who had affairs, judging them harshly regardless of the circumstances. She wondered if there were ever mitigating circumstances when it came to extra-marital sex? Her mother had told her in no uncertain terms, that the answer to that existential question was no. Her mum had also, somewhat callously, pointed out during their weekly skype call that Rachel was in fact, a mistress.

'Oh mum, that's a horrible word,' she whispered as though someone would overhear. 'It's not like that.'

'What's it like then? Is he your soul mate? Or what do they call it now? Twin Flame?' This was intended to be a little sarcastic but came out a little nastier than her mother had intended.

'I'm sorry, darling.'

'It's okay mum, I wouldn't expect you to understand. You and dad have been together for what, 100 years now?'

'Ha, ha,' her mother said flatly. 'What do your friends say? Marie is a smart woman, what does she think?' Rachel could only sit silently in front of her laptop. She shook her head.

'Oh love, if something has to be kept a secret, then it's probably not a good idea. Do you love him?'

Although she could only nod at her mother on the computer screen, for the first time in her life, Rachel believed that she was in love. The problem was that she couldn't shout it from the rooftops even though she knew rumours were swirling around the tight-knit Parisian tour industry. She had become two different people; one rapturously-in-love woman with dreams of the future and her head in the clouds when she was with Alex, but when she was away from him, she lived a strange kind of half-life where nothing felt real or worth doing. She kept the guilt tucked away in a corner of her mind that she rarely visited.

Eventually the knot in her throat dispersed. 'Yes mum, I do. I love him but I hate that it is all on the down-low, that we must hide. It feels so right, but I've always hated women like me.' The tears were flowing now.

'Tell him darling. If it's meant to be it will be. He must either make up his mind or you have to do it for him. You can't keep going on like this. People are going to get hurt. His children will get hurt.'

A week of sub-zero temperatures did little to improve Rachel's mood following the conversation with her mother. There were few tourists around; most guides preferring to take vacations in warmer climates or head over to the ski-fields of Italy or France. Rachel didn't feel like taking a vacation and hunkered down instead to write the articles she had promised for a new online magazine. She also found time to think about work for the coming year. She couldn't continue with Estelle and Gustav; she would have to find another job. She had to break things off with Alex.

He was never far from her mind. He was busy caring for his boys while his wife worked on long-haul flights. Rachel found if she didn't reply straight away to his texts, he would go days without contacting her. It hurt like hell, but she knew it was for the best. She found herself musing over how things were going with Alex's wife and the tennis partner's husband. Surely that would be difficult to maintain in winter. Tennis was a summer sport.

Christmas loomed and between the weather and her self-loathing, her friends were not quite sure what to do with her. The tipping point came when Alex called her to say he had been 'unable to avoid going to the Maldives with his wife and kids'. The ridiculousness of the phrase had almost shocked her out of love with him. Almost. Seething with anger she left a message on his phone telling him not to contact her again, not caring if his wife heard the message.

If a guy makes you cry while listening to his voicemails on the Metro, he deserved to be dumped. No, he should be hung, drawn and quartered. No woman should have to sit on a crowded train carriage, sobbing. It had to be over; they couldn't continue this way, regardless of how much he cried, or how many flowers he had delivered by disgruntled florists in freezing temperatures.

Leaving long messages on her voicemail, he declared his love over and over. Like every other cheating husband in history, he kept repeating that he and Hanne were no longer sleeping together. As if that was all that mattered. He said he would leave by Easter.

'What the fuck has Easter got to do with anything????' she texted, breaking her own non-contact rule. The extra question marks would show it was a rhetorical question, she hoped.

Apparently, it had something to do with his wife's long-haul flights, but Rachel was beyond caring. In one particularly long message, Alex told her of a dream he'd had. They were swimming in cool clear water; water so clear they could see the sandy bottom metres below. He loved her, wanted her. He wanted to take a boat out and find that water. Shuddering, she was reminded of her own ghastly dream of them being swept up in swirling water, washed away from each other. She deleted the message.

Once she had made her decision, the crying stopped after a few days and by the end of the week was almost back to her old self. Denial and self-absorption could be fun to visit for a while, but it didn't do any good to move there permanently and build a house. She called her friend Steph to tell her that it was over, spilling the whole story. This time she included a delicious twenty-minute rant about the wife who was screwing her tennis partner, or the husband slash coach, or whatever.

Suddenly anger felt good.

'We're going out. To dance,' Steph announced. 'We will go out to the Marais. Rachel, you can't wear jeans.'

'Okay…' Rachel responded a little confused. 'What's wrong with jeans?'

'My friend Rachel doesn't wear jeans, even if they are Kenzo, or Hilfiger! You know how to dress! I see now how you have let yourself go since all this nonsense started.'

As much as she hated to admit it, Steph had a point. They arranged a meeting time and Rachel hit the shower. She dried her hair, scrunching it up into loose waves and carefully applied her makeup. She had forgotten how much she enjoyed getting ready to go out. Turning to her groaning wardrobe, she ran her hand over the gorgeous dresses, most of them bagged to protect the delicate fabrics.

When was the last time I wore this? She asked herself, pulling a black sequined sheath dress from its calico cover. She held it up to her body and decided she would wear it, even if it was a tad over-the-top. Her long black leather trench would keep her warm and the black boots would be perfect for dancing.

Some hours later, their quiet night out ended at 4am in a bistro frequented by market workers and lorry drivers on the outskirts of town. They drank steaming hot chocolate and sucked on their cigarettes while quietly singing along with the radio to Alanis Morrissette's song Ironic, to the amusement of the staff. That song had been a huge hit during her first year in Paris. She laughed as she sang the lyrics. She had met the man of her dreams, and his beautiful wife.

The old house

December 2005

After years of living in Paris, Rome and Greece, this would be Rachel's first Christmas alone. By alone she meant that none of her family would be travelling to Europe for the holidays, preferring to enjoy the summer at home in Australia.

Steph, relieved to have her friend and always-up-for-a-night-out-partner-in-crime back in action, assembled a group of other 'orphans'. Settling on a theme of Red at the Ritz: dinner at the Ritz with everyone wearing something red, for those playing along at home. Rachel's red velvet and tulle dress the perfect remedy to the crippling homesickness that engulfed her on the 23rd. She toyed with the idea of jumping on a plane but the arm and leg the airline wanted in return for a ticket wasn't worth it. Her parents had offered for her to use their frequent flyer points, but she decided to tough it out and stay in Paris.

'As long as you're not sitting around the flat moping,' her mother said.

They had an agreement not to mention you-know-who. 'Oh mum, I'm definitely not moping. Love you.'

Dinner was exquisite, and they danced the night away at a club in the Marais. At midnight Steph went home to husband and children in the suburbs to get ready for a visit from Père Noël. Rachel had arranged to stay the night with her friend Marie at her exquisite townhouse. The next morning, waking to the Christmas Day bells of Notre Dame to walk through the quiet streets to attend Mass, something she had never done before.

They had met years before when Marie was maître'd hotel at Entre Amis, the famous Michelin-starred restaurant. She had children, worked long hours on her feet, and always had a smile on her face. All of this was achieved while looking like she had just stepped from the pages of a fashion magazine. It might sound cliché, but this French woman made glamour and class look truly effortless. She had a wicked sense of humour and a very sharp mind. Rachel felt instantly frumpy standing next to both Marie and her stylish daughter Sara, regardless of how much effort she put into dressing. But beauty and wealth became unimportant after spending five minutes with these warm and generous women in their beautiful home that had been in their family for over one hundred years.

A quiet week was spent reading and sleeping between Christmas and the New Year, with two job offers coming out of the blue to lead high-end overnight tours to the chateaux of the Ille de France and a permanent position as a staff writer for the online magazine Take Flight. She felt her life was getting back to normal again and found herself only thinking of Alex once a day. Approximately. It was a start.

New Year's Eve loomed. Rachel had given up waiting to be surprised by an impromptu visit from a family member and if she hadn't been invited back to Marie's exquisite home for the celebrations, she might have felt lonely. She felt so lucky to be there, enjoying the company, the champagne and incredible food Marie and her children had prepared, the highlight being Ben's triple chocolate mousse. In training as a pastry chef at Hotel le Bristol, Ben was already a genius in Rachel's opinion.

There was singing around the piano just like at home, although these songs were all in French. Laughing and breathless from a round of row-row-row your boat; Rachel had requested a song in English, champagne fuelled phone calls were made to her parents and sisters at midnight, even if it was the middle of the afternoon in Australia.

'I'm calling you from the past!' she announced to her confused nephews. They passed the phone around, everyone talking over each other and excitedly wishing everyone a Happy New Year.

As she said goodbye to her twin nephews for the tenth time the phone rang again. If she had checked the caller identification, she would have known it was Alex. Perhaps she wouldn't have answered. She breathed in deeply when she heard his voice, deciding she would be cool and calm, which after copious amounts of champagne was always going to be a challenge. She dissolved into tears as she hung up. For the third time Alex had told her he was leaving his wife for her, for the third time she told him she didn't want that. She had bluntly told him that he needed to leave on his own terms.

'Do it for yourself!' she said breezily, trying to be non-emotional about it.

'You haven't been single for 10 years. You need to prepare your own meals, iron your own shirts. Don't just jump from her bed…to mine.'

He hadn't left his wife the last time she had said this. And now he was in the Maldives on a family holiday and Rachel was the mistress at home waiting for the phone calls. Correction. She was the Ex-mistress. Everything converged at that point in time. The teary-happy phone calls to her parents, the too-much champagne, the man in the Maldives leaving the kids playing in the pool to phone his mistress. She hadn't realised he was a player. He hadn't looked like a player, she thought.

Marie put her to bed in one of the guest rooms, promising to send one of the boys over to check on the cat.

'I don't want to be alone anymore,' she sobbed, 'I don't want to be the other woman either. I won't steal someone's husband.'

Marie sat on the bed and patted her back like she was one of the children. Gerard had been dispatched to fetch something to help her sleep, but had returned with paracetamol, water and a calm voice. A doctor-husband could be so convenient when your friend is verging on hysteria.

Rachel was so grateful for her wonderful friends. She took the proffered capsules and settled into the pillow. Smiling at the concerned faces hovering over her, she lay back on the cosy bed and fell into a deep snoring sleep a minute later.

Waking sometime the next day to a parched throat and burning embarrassment, she tested an upright position for any signs of headache, and seeing a carafe of water, a glass, a folded pile of clothes and a fluffy towel, she thought that perhaps she had died and was now in heaven. Looking around the sumptuous bedroom she smiled as she thought she would like to go to heaven if it looked like Marie's stunning home.

Grateful to have such kind friends, she padded to the ensuite bathroom, guzzling the water straight from the carafe. After having what felt like the best shower she had ever had, she made her way upstairs, feeling sheepish and sheep-like, hung-over but happy, wrapped in a woolly fisherman's pullover and leggings, moving silently in the felt slippers she had found in her room. Pushing open the kitchen door, she was embraced by the comforting aromas of coffee and brioche and the sounds of a happy family at breakfast.

'Sit, eat,' Marie said for possibly the thousandth time since they'd met.

If she had been at home in Sydney, her mum would have handed her a Bloody Mary and said 'Put a smile on your dial, hold your head up high and know you're a princess! No man is worth getting upset over!'

If that caring pep talk didn't work, she would've taken Rachel out dancing. Rachel knew well that going out drinking and dancing with your mum, while always entertaining, wouldn't be enough this time. What she needed was warmth and sympathy, hot tea and home-made bread. Maybe it was the snow falling silently outside the window.

As she sat devouring the delicate brioche and letting the family conversation wash over her, she felt a shift. It was odd, but this man did seem worth the pain, ill-thought-out behaviour, and even the possibility that she would burn in feminist-hell for sleeping with a married man. She had wondered if she wanted him more because he wasn't available. God knew she had spent hours wandering winter-time Paris, stopping to warm up in cafes, obsessing over this thought. After a good dose of self-diagnosis, she became convinced of her inability to form a healthy attachment, helped along by the countless love quizzes she noticed in every French women's magazine. Why had she never noticed these high-school-style love quizzes before?

Even though she had never given it a second thought before, it bothered her that she had never had a long-term relationship, had never cohabited. Unless you counted the cat that had moved in uninvited, which most people didn't. Growing up with four sisters she had moved out as quickly as she could, never looking back. The free spirit, they all called her, like her mother. Meanwhile her sisters had married their high-school sweethearts and were doing their level best to over-populate the planet.

Her mother had managed to combine a successful career as a corporate travel specialist, raised four daughters and various dogs, rabbits and cats to adulthood and stay relatively happily married. She was a powerhouse of a woman, but Rachel put the success of her parents' marriage down to the combination of her mother's inability to say a bad word about anyone and her father's superpower; the ability to ignore anything 'of the feminine variety' in the bathroom. Out of the blue, it dawned on Rachel that Alex was indeed 'worth it' when she realised how much her father would like him.

This could have been because Alex was just like her father, kind, gentle, funny and smart.

Unlike her father, however, Alex was cheating on his wife. Until he left Hanne, any relationship was out of the question. But he would have to come to that conclusion himself.

February came, freezing and dark, the soft blue winter sky only occasionally peering out from behind thick clouds. Rachel concentrated on taking weekend tours to the Loire and further afield, knowing it would reduce to nil the possibility she would run into Alex professionally. Eventually he stopped calling too, returning to his perfect life with his perfect wife and perfect kids.

She loved the new tours, the clientele was just as fun and infuriating as they were for the local tours, but she could distract herself with new views from the bus, a new spiel for her to prattle into the microphone.

Regular visits to Marie's picture–perfect farmhouse style kitchen table soothed her soul. That Marie had announced plans to convert her magnificent home into a luxury private hotel filled Rachel with exciting plans for the future. They would be the preferred hotel for her tour clients in Paris. Nights out dancing with Steph had taken on epic proportions, with the two of them taking Marie's daughter Sara out to her first night club. Although she missed Alex every day, the fun returned to her life along with the colour to her wardrobe.

A surprise visit from her parents and three sisters, to celebrate her 30th birthday and her oldest sister's 40th was her reward for surviving the winter. Turning thirty hadn't been so bad surrounded by family and friends. It helped that her sister Claire was turning 40 without a grey hair in sight.

On the morning before her family was to fly back to Australia, sitting at Marie's kitchen table, Rachel looked around at the inspiring women with whom she had surrounded herself. Marie was a goddess in her eyes. Then there was her own seemingly super-human mother and sisters. They blew her mind with their stories of holding conference calls while nursing a baby or finishing their latest project while cutting up the oranges for half-time at the soccer. As much as she admired and aspired to being like these remarkable women, Rachel felt she was more like her dad, good at doing one thing at a time. She loved her work and was grateful that it inspired and challenged her.

'It might not give me the flexibility to breast-feed while I work, but that's not really the problem now,' she shrugged to her sister. At least she could change her schedule to avoid an ex-lover.

No-one at her old company asked why she had stopped working with Gustav and Estelle, they welcomed her back with open arms. Rachel would be heading up specialist tours for clients looking for a deeper experience. One of the new tours took them to a winery near Victot-Pontfol, staying two days to experience wine making in greater depth. Or at least wine tasting in greater depth as she discovered. The wine was sublime and the man who ran the place was easy to talk to and easy on the eye.

Their first date was a day trip to another nearby chateau owned by a famous chef. It was a perfect first date. It was the best date she'd ever been on. It was nice to date someone outside of the travel industry, she confided to Steph. It helped that he always brought the absolute best wine when he came for dinner. He was lovely. Her friends met him one by one. Everyone agreed.

'Agréable,' Marie said when asked to describe him. 'He's sweet.'

'Genial,' Sara said, 'with very nice eyes.'

Her friends began to refer to him, not unkindly, as Mr Nice Guy. She resented that a little. Alex was nice. The fact that he happened to be a cheating rat notwithstanding. Rachel realised one day that she was happy. Mr Nice Guy was lovely, and it was…easy.

That should be the happy ending to this story. But of course, it is not.

Alex called her as they drove back from Mr Nice Guy's family house in Normandy. His parents and elderly aunt had welcomed her with open arms. They loved the gifts she had brought and poured affection on Beau and fed him on titbits from their plates. She had enjoyed a perfectly normal and lovely Easter.

The only sticking point had been Beau the Cat, never one for travel, complaining loudly from the cat carrier on the back seat. Grateful for the excuse to avoid talking to her married ex-boyfriend with her perfectly lovely new boyfriend within earshot, Rachel promised to call Alex when she arrived home.

She hadn't told Mr Nice Guy about Alex. He didn't need to know, and she had convinced herself there was nothing really to tell. Dead relationships shouldn't haunt the living, her mother always said, but their polite conversation eventually stalled like the Paris-bound traffic, the whole story tumbling out of her as they sat in the snarl. True to Nice Guy form, he wasn't concerned about the call. Or the story. He didn't call Alex a rat.

'He sounded a little upset.'

'Holy shit, this guy broke my heart. He's cheating on his wife. Don't feel sorry for him. Not even 'Mr Nice Guy' is that nice,' she said, a slight snarl on her face. She had made air-quotes while saying Mr Nice Guy. He pretended not to notice.

Rachel made it clear she had no intention of returning the call.

Alex called her the next day. Twice. She was on the road again, taking a group to Chantilly. Estelle, her previous employer and Alex's friend called and left a message for her, then sent a text.

'Won't you please call Alex? Please??'

No, she most certainly would not.

A week passed, Rachel hoping Alex had given up. Arriving home late to a complaining cat and twenty-two messages, she knew something was wrong. Pouring a glass of wine, she sat on the carpet in the dark and pressed play. The whole sorry tale came out, a jumble of words and tears. Rachel felt ill as she listened, tears streaming down her cheeks. Did Alex really have cancer? She wondered how the man she loved could have cancer while she ignored him. She felt like a monster.

He wanted her by his side during the treatment. He begged her. His wife had moved out weeks before, taking the boys back to Denmark, leaving the tennis partner and her husband to pick up their pieces, too. She came back when Alex received his diagnosis, to care for him. As much as he appreciated her help and to have his boys with him, there's nothing like cancer diagnosis to clarify what's important in life and Alex knew it was Rachel he needed.

Mr Nice Guy understood. Of course, he did; he was Mr Nice Guy, even saying she should call if she needed any help. Rachel watched him walk away from the bistro she had chosen to break the news to him, and he turned and waved, a tiny gesture that seemed in that moment an incredible act of compassion.

April and spring swept into Paris as Alex moved in to her flat in the 18th. The weather was spectacular, and they spent their time riding borrowed push-bikes all over the city, plotting paths that would avoid the hills, so they could avoid talking about how hard the hills were for Alex. When it rained, days on end passed when they didn't speak to another person after the doctors told them there was nothing more they could do.

He proposed as they walked slowly through the Tuileries one morning. It had seemed impromptu, like the idea had just occurred to him, until they sat for brunch at Café Marley and roses appeared on their table. 'What would you have done if I said no?' Rachel asked, teasing him while twisting the diamond ring on her finger.

The boys visited often, and even Hanne found she was welcome in the light, bright flat with the tiny balcony and the orange cat who seemed to take up the entire sofa. They all found healing and even joy at times, three small boys and three adults linked by love and pain and something that felt like destiny.

'Are you seeing anyone?' Rachel asked Hanne as they stood side-by-side in the tiny kitchen. Rachel considered the craziness of the situation as she and her fiancé's ex-wife prepared a meal for the funny little family.

'Yes…' she said hesitantly. 'I don't want the boys to know. It's Stephen. We've known each other for years…'

'Oh, the tennis player? The husband…?' Rachel whispered conspiratorially, forgetting for a moment that Hanne was not simply one her girlfriends.

'Oh sorry…I am probably not meant to know that…' Rachel said, face burning red.

Hanne stopped chopping the onions and turned to face her. Rachel hoped she wasn't about to be stabbed. 'Yes…I guess Alex would have told you. It's okay, really. It's strange isn't it? We both feel like we were meant to be together. Even though we were both married to other people…' she nodded towards Alex in the living room.

'It certainly doesn't sound strange to me.'

'Because you and Alex felt it too, yes?' Rachel nodded, her eyes welling with tears. 'Life plays funny tricks on us doesn't it?'

Somehow the summer was over and soon they were walking Paris in their overcoats again. The doctors gave Alex clearance to fly to Australia for Christmas, the hot weather would do him good, they said. The children were excited that their dad would see a kangaroo and a koala. Emil, who would be starting school in the spring begged his father to bring home a shark. 'A baby shark,' he said when told that a shark was too big to bring home.

'Alex seems so well. Perhaps there had been a mix up in the clinic,' Hanne whispered to Rachel one afternoon as Alex played with the boys in the living room.

Rachel looked up and smiled at the rough play. She put her hand over Hanne's and squeezed it. Hanne didn't see Alex when he was hunched over, catching his breath. Nor did she see the tray of medicines he used daily.

'Maybe…' Rachel replied softly.

Alex caught a cold, a little tickle in the throat, some sneezing. Nothing, really.

But the doctors changed their minds, and the airline allowed the flights to be given to Hanne and their oldest son, Noah.

In the strangest family Christmas in history, Alex's ex-wife and son flew to Australia and stayed with Rachel's parents, while Rachel, Alex and the two little ones had Christmas with all the trimmings courtesy of special delivery from Marie. Skyping each evening with the family in Australia. The tears flowing along with the laughter. Her father sent emails daily. Photos of Noah on the boat, fishing, snorkelling, at the zoo cuddling a koala. Photos of Noah with sharks circling behind him at the aquarium. Emil and William were too excited to be jealous.

A quiet New Years' Eve was spent with the two small boys sleeping between them on their big bed. Having perhaps made a silent pact about not discussing the past, Rachel reflected privately how different her life was compared to the previous year. It wasn't Red at the Ritz, more like Four on the Floor playing board games. No party dresses or dancing the night away in Montmartre.

To make room in the flat, she had boxed up her party dresses and stored them in Marie's basement. Early January brought the happy traveller's home from Australia, suntanned and joyful, Hanne gushing about how lovely Rachel's family had been, how they had doted on Noah.

'They were so kind to me,' Hanne sobbed.

Rachel's sisters welcoming her like family; her little boy just one of the small sun-kissed grandchildren in the backyard swimming pool that summer. Alex's head cold had abated a little and Hanne organised a surprise weekend away in the South, a special Christmas gift for him and Rachel. The weather was kind. Bright blue skies and crisp days for exploring the town. But the cancer was shockingly stealth-like, death stalked them in Provence. It found them in that little hotel in Gordes.

They say life is about the big moments, but at the end, it's rarely a bang. Rachel found it was little more than a whisper.

One last sigh and he was gone.

Lost

The relentless pace demanded after someone dies can be a welcome distraction. Rachel knew if she stopped, she would crash, so she kept going. The feeling they were being punished threatened to overwhelm her. Had they been so bad they deserved this? It didn't feel like they were bad people, but she had no idea how something so horrible could happen. Alex had no other family, yet it was a full church that said goodbye to him that day. Flowers filled her tiny apartment. Friends called, brought food. It certainly didn't feel as though she was a bad person.

Rachel cried for hours when Hanne left for Denmark with the boys, promising to visit often. Her parents came from Australia for the funeral and her mother stayed on, not offering, not even once, to take her dancing. They did do a lot of drinking and crying. And cooking. Together they took up residence at Marie's kitchen table, learning to shell peas, prepare marinades and roll croissants, and how to grind spices in the mortar and pestle. The diversion was welcome. The help appreciated, even if Marie had to teach them how to do just about everything.

'Everything I know about being French, I learned from this woman,' Rachel announced to her mother, her arm around Marie's shoulder. 'My French mother.'

'And I taught you how to party!' her Australian mother said happily.

Rachel admired Marie to the point of adoration. Marie, and now Sara her daughter, had inspired her to be more French, but after losing Alex Rachel gave up, asking Marie to donate her party dresses to charity. It was much easier to wear all-black and anything more time-consuming than a ponytail was too much bother.

Finally, Spring returned once again to Paris and strangely it was time for Rachel to return to some semblance of normality, and for her mother to go home to Sydney. Life resumed a kind of routine. She was accepting jobs from various tour companies, she was busy, but she still made time to sit at Marie's dining room table, until she noticed the quiet conversations between

Marie and Sara. She was embarrassed when she realised she had outstayed her welcome. She began to visit less. That's what you do when your sadness begins to inconvenience your friends.

The new cell phone buzzed somewhere in the apartment interrupting a dream involving an elevator she once rode in Rome and…. Alex…as always. Not waking her fully, she happily rolled over into his arms only to find the bed empty.

'Alex, can you grab my phone?' she called sleepily to the empty room, her own words jolting her awake. Alex isn't here, she thought, hot tears springing to her eyes, the phone buzzing insistently in the darkened apartment. It was going to be one of those days. 'Damn phone,' she groaned, burrowing back down under the duvet.

Curling back into a ball, Rachel took some comfort from the fact that she could stay in bed all day. She had a rare free day. There was nothing to do, no-one to see. No bored children to jolly along while their parents photographed every painting in the Louvre, no smiling benignly while Jim from Idaho explains his passion for Camus, or how Jill from Dorking feels she truly was Josephine in a previous life. In the still dark room, she stared up at the ceiling, shocked to realise that there were some facets of her work that she thoroughly hated. She sighed. Perhaps it was time for a change of career?

Maybe there was a limit to how many times a person could be enthusiastic about the Eiffel Tower, or the chapel at Versailles. She needed to think about what she would do, the next step in her career, if she was serious about leaving Paris. But that could wait because today she did not have to be nice to anyone, no reason to get dressed, and maybe no reason to even get out of bed. Tomorrow, she thought. Tomorrow I will decide. Tomorrow I will plan, something. Perhaps tomorrow I will plan to leave Paris forever.

The trouble with this train of thought was even though some clients could be finicky, or the weather might alter her tour plans, she truly loved her work. No matter the mess in her personal life, Rachel knew she could get out of bed, dress, ride the metro over to Pont Bir Hakiem and get the same bubbly feeling in her stomach when she saw the Tower rising up over the river. She couldn't help herself. Today I still live in Paris, she thought. Who knows what tomorrow might bring?

Hoping more tears would come she scrunched her eyes and dug her fingernails into her palms. She felt like having a really good cry. Scratching at the window reminded her she did in fact have a reason to get out of bed, and that reason was an over-weight ginger cat who no doubt had various homes on his meal and belly-rub roster.

At least the collar he wore was the one she had given him, she thought as he delicately picked over the dry food for the best pieces, although they all looked the same to human eyes. Not for the first time, she felt jealous of his contentment, wondering when she might ever feel happy again.

The cell phone buzzed again, and she walked around the flat, ear cocked, trying to locate it. She had no idea how to make it ring aloud, it had been stuck on vibrate since she bought it. The phone was a mystery, but it too was a welcome distraction; a new shiny thing which unlike everything else in the world held no memories of Alex.

The fact it had been released after he had died made it the first thing Alex hadn't experienced. Rachel knew this was strange reasoning. The phone stopped buzzing and she gave up the hunt, knowing it was a needle in the haystack that was her untidy flat.

Could she leave Paris?

Packing would have to start in earnest if she was going back to Australia, but at the same time, procrastination seemed a better alternative. Someone had told her not to make any major changes within the first twelve months and moving continents and changing careers would probably constitute major, she figured. Sinking into the sofa, she reached over and pulled the woollen blanket Hanne had brought from Denmark across her legs.

The phone buzzed again underneath her. Sliding her hand under the seat cushion she pulled out the shiny new phone, scratching her head at how it had found its way there. Then remembering the solo effort with the vin rouge the night before, she felt lucky the phone hadn't wound up in the fridge.

Three missed calls and a text from Marie, and a missed call from an unknown number. A message from Marie, in the past a welcome distraction promising great company and excellent food, now felt strangely unwelcome. Her grief had made her terrible company; she knew she was too much of a downer for their happy family home. She had begun dodging their invitations even if she had been unable to avoid the kind 'anonymous' deliveries of pastries and her favourite beef cassoulet left with Pierre, the proprietor of the Tabac at the front of her building.

Lying back down on the sofa she opened the text and found herself hoping it was an invitation for dinner but already worried she would be forced to enjoy herself. The guilt brought on by enjoying herself wasn't worth the effort. It wasn't an invitation. It wasn't like any message she had ever received from Marie. It simply read, "Have a lovely day with your American group, my dear friend. Remember to take your umbrella."

Rachel stared at the unusual text. It was odd and the more Rachel thought about it, the odder it seemed to get. In more than ten years of knowing Marie, she had never given her a weather report, nor shown anything other than cursory interest in her groups. She stared at the screen. It was kind of her friend to wish her a happy day…

'What are you up to?' she said out loud, staring at the phone.

Rachel sunk back onto the couch, trying to decipher the mystery text. She had no plans, with a group or otherwise. She had no intention of leaving her apartment that day, nor possibly the next, so she knew she would not need an umbrella. As for having a lovely day, unless you counted eating mac and cheese on the sofa watching EastEnders dubbed in French as lovely, she wouldn't be having one of those either.

Rachel considered replying to the text, assuming Marie had perhaps sent the message to the wrong number, wondering if perhaps it had been intended for one of her children. No, that didn't make sense. She would not address them as "my dear friend."

Putting it down to being 'a weird thing that happened' and refusing to think any more about it, Rachel decided to go back to bed and stay there but the phone buzzed again in her hand. She stared at the phone. It was an unknown number again, but it was a local Paris caller, so she pressed the button to accept it.

'Oui?'

'Hi Rachel? Unique Paris Tours?'

'Yes.'

'I have a group today if you would like it? You've been highly recommended.'

'Okay, umm, did Marie put you up to this?'

'Er, no, Gustav gave me your number. He said you're fantastic and he felt you would be available at short notice?'

Rachel hesitated. She wasn't sure she was ready to leave the flat, let alone lead a group for a company she had never heard of. It felt weird to get such a text from Marie and then out of the blue a random tour company offers her a job, even if it was just for the day.

'Okay, why not…?' she said into the phone, and instantly regretting it. 'Can you fax me the details?'

After saying their goodbyes, Rachel sat on the arm of the sofa. Never one for looking for a sign, she refused to entertain there was any connection between the two calls she had received that day. She toyed with the idea of calling Marie but checking the time she realised she would have a group waiting for her at the Hilton in an hour.

Half an hour later, showered and ready to show her clients the Best of Paris, as the tour was called, Rachel grabbed the fax from the printer, stuck it to her clipboard, giving it the briefest glance, grabbed her phone and keys and made for the door. She threw her trench coat on and stopped in the hall, Marie's text message playing over in her mind.

Shaking her head, she reached for the compact black umbrella but hesitated when she caught sight of Alex's stylish Burberry umbrella. Ripping the printed sheets off the clipboard she folded them and put them in the pocket of her coat. Smiling as she left the practical one in its place, she hooked the gorgeous plaid umbrella over her arm and bolted for the Metro.

She wasn't sure which had been more surprising; the flash metro strike or the rainstorm that seemed to come from blue sky in the afternoon. Paris put on one of her legendary traffic jams that made Rachel and the group abandon the stranded bus and apologetic bus driver on the Boulevard Haussmann. She took her tour group, Burberry umbrella aloft for them to follow where needed, on an impromptu walking tour through the covered passages around the Opera, ending at Palais Royale just as the storm broke.

The group seemed to love the tour and whooped and ran for cover as the rain came down. Her clients had thankfully been university students; she wasn't sure what she would have done with a bus full of octogenarians. The words "American group" floated around in her mind. She left them enjoying chocolat chaud at Angelina.

Sheltering under the cloistered arches of the Palais Royal, her initial response was one of frustration. The rain showed no sign of letting up and a taxi would be impossible to find as the whole of Paris tried to get home in the strike bound city. The lighter mood she had cultivated over the course of the day began to disappear as she trudged along from awning to awning, dodging as much of the rain as possible.

Just south of rue de l'Opera, a scooter winding its way through the traffic snarl stopped at a red light. The passenger was shouting something to Rachel as she crossed the road, miming something with her hands. Laughing. It was at this point Rachel remembered the umbrella hooked over her right arm.

Arriving home an hour later, she was soaked to the skin and freezing, but with a smile on her face for the first time since losing Alex. She felt lighter, freer, than she had for a long time. Opening her front door, she slipped the umbrella into its slot under the coat rack and smiled. Alex, it seemed, was still looking after her.

Rachel remembered the puzzling text from Marie. She pulled her phone out to read the message. Had it really suggested she take an umbrella with her that day? Perhaps Marie knew the people who had given her the group today. That was the only possible explanation. If Alex was sending messages from the other side via Marie, surely, he could have done better than a weather update in a city where it rains as much as it does in Paris.

Lost in thought, her eyes became accustomed to the dark, the chilly flat seemed colder than it should be. Seeing the drenched curtains, she ran to the window. She couldn't believe she could be so careless as to leave the window open for the cat. The rain had stopped but the damage was done. She looked out at the grey skies, the late afternoon sun trying to show itself. Had it been mere hours before, that perfect morning, the perfect blue sky completely clear, without even a suggestion of rain on the way? Who was she kidding? Rain was always on the way! Australia was looking more inviting by the minute.

Shivering, she slammed the window and dragged the sodden curtains across. They would start to smell if she didn't dry them. She marvelled at how the late summer could end with a rainstorm, and Autumn was giving way to winter without so much as a cheerio. The carpet was soaked, and books stood in puddles of water under the window. She had seen a photo in a home magazine with books neatly arranged under the low windowsill of a chic Parisian apartment. It might have looked cute but wasn't a terribly practical design concept.

A photo of her and Alex that had sat on the sill, was now ruined, lying on the floor in a puddle of rainwater. Beau strolled sleepily out of the bedroom where he had presumably spent the day and miaowed loudly for food, oblivious to the rain, the damaged carpet and the weird day she had had.

'Oh well,' she said to Beau, placing the wet frame in an open carton in the middle of the room, 'fewer books to ship back with us to Australia.'

She fed the cat and took a long hot shower, standing under the stream of hot water, her skin pink, the entire flat full of steam. She still hadn't decided whether to sell her apartment and would rent it to one of her colleagues until she could decide. She loved her home and would miss Paris dreadfully, but Paris held little for her now that Alex was gone, his boys living in Denmark with their mother.

She always felt a little more like her normal self after a day doing what she loved best, sharing this glorious city with her clients. She adored showing them her favourite haunts, the little secret gems. Seeing people's eyes light up with new appreciation of the most famous monuments made all the hassle of living in an often crowded, cold city worthwhile. She loved her job, and she was fiercely protective of the place.

Was there anything worse than a client saying they had been disappointed, that Paris hadn't lived up to their expectations?

She sat and watched the sunset, such as it was through the clouds, leaning on the window frame. She loved this stupid, cold, wet, magnificent city.

To Paris with love

Putting her escape plans on hold for a couple of weeks, she threw herself back into work. One last hurrah, she told herself. Surprisingly, group tours of the Chateau de Versailles turned out to be the perfect and surprising antidote to her crippling grief. It probably wasn't the best way to deal with it, but she found she could pretend that Alex would be just up ahead with the next group and the familiarity of the site meant she didn't need to think too much. Somehow her needy clients were a welcome distraction, not the source of frustration they had often been in the past.

'Thirty camera-wielding tourists following you through a priceless museum would've taken Hitler's mind off Poland,' Rachel observed to a colleague. She had received a blank stare as a reply.

'What, too soon?' Rachel asked.

The poor woman didn't respond.

Her friends were concerned, seemingly taking turns to tell her that living in denial was probably good for a while, but sooner or later she would have to face the fact that Alex was gone. She begged to differ. Denial isn't just a river in Egypt, she had taken to saying, much to the confusion of the French speakers; the play on words didn't translate. She couldn't be bothered trying to explain to them she didn't truly believe Alex was still there at Versailles, that it was just her way of coping with the unimaginable and still managing to pay her mortgage.

Standing on the terrace overlooking the fountains, her group explored the gardens in the chilly late afternoon light. Rachel's phone buzzed in the pocket of her black leather trench coat. She had been deep in thought, the ringing phone sending a shockwave through her whole body, every nerve in her body jangling.

A text from Marie. It was an invitation to dinner. Would she please come? They had a gift for her, a surprise. Her stomach flipped over as a thousand butterflies took flight as she herded her group back towards the waiting coach, the driver stood beside the bus, smiling like a kindly uncle.

The clients filed on board, tired and happy. Rachel took her place at the microphone for the return trip to Paris. Halfway through her spiel she stopped. Some of the passengers noticed but most were either staring dreamily at the landscape speeding by or were going through their photos of the day. Clouds were gathering over Paris, reminding her of that strange day when she had received another unexpected text from Marie warning her to take an umbrella.

Marie is definitely up to something, she thought.

Reverting to her usual return-to-Paris commentary, she started mentally composing a text to decline Marie's kind invitation. She knew Marie wouldn't believe she was busy or that she didn't want to sample Ben's latest culinary masterpiece. The thought of a delightful dessert made her mouth water, but she was torn between the promise of dessert and the threat of the unknown, which made her stomach turn again.

Oh, God, she thought. What if the 'surprise' is a man? What if it's Mr Nice Guy?

Would that be so bad?

She surprised herself as she realised how much she'd love to see her wonderful old flame, but she knew Marie wouldn't be so cruel. She would never assume Rachel was ready for a new relationship, or to pick up where she had left off with an old one, no matter how lovely it had been.

Allowing a calm to settle over the coach, she stared out the window. Her mood matched the late afternoon rain clouds building on the horizon. She watched the clouds surge and pile, jostling for space between Tour Montparnasse and the Eiffel Tower, losing herself in the rolling cumulus. A shaft of late afternoon sunlight burst through the billowing clouds illuminating the skyline and bathing Paris in that exquisite pearly light it did so well.

The passengers oohed and aahed around her, cameras clicking as they tried to capture some of the beauty to take home with them. Despite herself, Rachel found her mood lift, gratitude for her enthusiastic clients' child-like delight in the beautiful city she sometimes took for granted.

Perhaps Marie had found a kitten friend for Beau. She often remarked that the old cat spent a lot of time alone, that he needed a friend. Rachel would laugh and protest that he had the best life a cat could wish for; wandering the rooftops at will, chasing starlings and bringing in the occasional startled mouse, only for it to scramble away the moment he opened his mouth to miaow in greeting. She smiled at the thought of her old tomcat, how he'd adopted her the day she'd moved into her flat. He had popped through the window as soon as she opened it, purred around her ankles, and had been there ever since, draped over the sofa and leaving ginger fuzz all over the duvet cover.

Through the bus window, the dramatic cloud show that seemed to promise a storm blew out to a fleeting rain shower, the sun setting in spectacular fashion as her group alighted beside Eiffel's stunning masterpiece. Cameras whirring as the Iron Lady showed off her first lightshow of the evening. The smiles on the faces around her warmed a little piece of her broken heart as Rachel said her goodbyes to her last group for the year. She had reached a decision.

She would leave Paris while she still loved the city, before bitterness stole even that from her. Sydney and her family would be her first stop for a good old-fashioned Australian summer and Christmas on the beach eating watermelon. She could almost feel the sand between her toes.

Smiling, she began to shake hands and, for the first time ever, hug her clients. Her last group had had a wonderful day. There were tips, and more hugs, and business cards were exchanged. The energy was unbelievable with smiles all round as Rachel nodded at their light-hearted marriage proposals and kind offers to stay in touch, recommend her to their friends, or host her if ever she visited Chicago, Edinburgh or Auckland. Clients hadn't done that when she worked in London or Berlin, Rome or anywhere else for that matter. It was the magic of this incredible city. Everyone wants a friend in Paris.

The complications of time travel

Dinner at Marie's table always calmed her soul. The declarations she was too thin had stopped, only to be replaced by a carefully placed plate of Ben's incredible eclairs any time she visited. She was so grateful for their loving care and the bags of fresh vegetables left at her front door. A handwritten note from Sara had cleared up the source of the whispered conversations she had noticed; they were worried about her, not annoyed by her. Had she really thought they were sick of her? It was probably the grief feeding her insecurity.

Glad to be back in the warm heart of this incredible family home, she sat in the floral upholstered chair by the window, polishing the flatware and listening to the soft conversation floating around her. She wondered if she would ever go through a day, or a week without thinking of him. She hoped not. Rachel looked up from the knife she had polished to a brilliant shine. Sara moved to her side, placing a comforting arm around her shoulders while Marie looked on, concern etched on her face.

'What? I'm okay,' Rachel protested, puzzled by their sudden show of sympathy.

'Darling, you're crying. Sobbing,' Marie said quietly from the other side of the room.

Rachel put her hand to her cheek, feeling the tracks of tears she hadn't even been aware she was shedding. 'Oh…Maybe because I decided today to leave Paris and go back to Australia. Or not. I'm lost. I really don't know what to do.'

'We love you, Rachel. You are part of our family. We hate to see you like this.'

'I'm fine. Well as fine as I'll ever be without Alex, I guess.' Mother and daughter exchanged glances. Marie nodded her head.

'I have a good book for you to read.'

Marie left the room while Sara smiled at her, looking like the cat who got the cream, as though she had a wonderful secret she was about to share. Rachel was rattled by their strange behaviour. She stood up and placed the tray of flatware gently on the table as Marie came into the room carrying an old canvas bag from which she carefully drew an ancient-looking leather-bound book. She laid on the table, pushing it towards Rachel.

'You guys are scaring me.'

'We are sorry, but it's time. You need to read this, chérie. This book will change your life. Literally.' Marie looked at her daughter and back at Rachel.

'Ok, that seems…less scary than I thought it was going to be. What is it? First edition of You Can Heal your Life?' Rachel joked as she took the strange leather journal.

She turned it over in her hands. It was unlike any other self-help book she had ever seen. An old brass key attached to a length of red ribbon held the leather binding together. Gold lettering declared it the property of one Antoinette de la Roche.

She looked up at Marie. 'Your mother?'

'My mother's great aunt. She was born and died right here in the house. There are many secrets here and the best one is unlocked by this key. Please read the pages. There aren't many and it will make you see there is perhaps a way out of your misery.' She and Marie sat and motioned for Rachel to sit, which she felt was as safe enough move considering she had sat at that table many times. She unclasped the lock, surprised to see it was not a book, but a collection of loose papers covered in spidery handwriting, rendered in pencil, but well preserved.

The date on the first sheet read Dimanche, 30 Juillet, 1933. The thirtieth of July. Interested but still confused, Rachel looked at her friends' earnest faces and knew they weren't giving her an inch. She had no choice but to read. Sighing deeply, she slowly read through the astonishing story of the woman's life. The details of their summer holiday to La Rochelle, new puppies, a minor car accident her brother had which led to her sister Marie-Louise meeting the man who became her husband. She went into great detail about her sister's children, the war records of her brother and brother-in-law, her father's patients and his growing interest in Psychology.

There were detailed descriptions of scientific experiments, a long passage about the need for all women to be educated and allowed to vote, and finally two long lists of dates and descriptions completed the writings. One list appeared to be an outline of key dates in pre-war and war-time Paris, with annotations obviously added later in ink. The other, a list of names, with comments and dates added in various shades of faded ink. Rachel finished reading and rubbed her forehead, thoroughly confused. She looked up at their expectant faces. Was she missing something?

'Amazing times. It must have been frightening to live in Paris during the war. We're so lucky to live in this era, I know that, but I'm not sure how you think this will change my life.'

Sara and Marie exchanged glances again. Rachel sighed. Clearly, she had missed the point they were trying to make.

'Can you read it to me? Perhaps my French is not good enough to understand the musings of a mad-scientist-renegade-suffragette from the 30s.'

'Don't you see? My mother's great Aunt was indeed a mad scientist, and a renegade and a suffragette. But she wrote this, the writing in pencil, in 1933. The items in ink were added later but all of this, all,' she swept her hand across the pages Rachel had carefully laid on the linen tablecloth, 'was written in a few hours, on July 30th, 1933.'

Marie waited for Rachel to comprehend. 'But…'

'Exactement!' Marie slapped the table and scared the wits out of the Siamese cat asleep on a chair. Rachel was dumbfounded. In all the years she had known Marie, she had never known her to raise her voice let alone slap a table. She leaned back in the chair and closed her eyes. The three women sat quietly.

'No, this isn't real.' Rachel could feel something bubbling up inside her and worried it was either hysteria or vomit, neither of which would be particularly welcome at this moment. It was madness to think of Marie's Great-Great Aunt traveling back in time, something out of science fiction.

'Okay, so if you expect me to believe your mother's crazy Aunt travelled back in time to before the war, why didn't she kill Hitler?' Rachel sat and stared at her friends, one eyebrow cocked.

'She tried, along with many other members of the Resistance who joined her cause and she certainly wasn't crazy. It is well documented; she risked her life many times during the war. She does not mention any of those deeds in this, this first account of her life.' Marie allowed her words to sink in as Rachel sat staring at the old manuscript.

Sara was next to speak, her admiration for her ancestor obvious.

'It's an amazing story. She was almost dead from an explosion and her father saved her life. That is how she came to be in the tiny room, where the portal is. When she awoke it was the summer of 1933? I love how she writes that she thought she had died and gone to heaven, although she was honest about how confused she was that she would end up there and not the other place! She was a real piece of work by all accounts.'

Marie leaned in, her voice low. 'Yes, it seems she was a real agitator during her…her first life, I guess you would call it. A real troublemaker. But in her…second life, she was much more controlled it appears, focussing her attention on education and mostly keeping her head down. She remained mostly unknown as she knew being too visible was dangerous, of course. There are anomalies between this story she has written and what we know as history now. She led a campaign to try to save the last woman executed in France. She failed, Giraud was still guillotined, but Antoinette tried.'

Marie picked up the delicate journal and lovingly returned it to its protective sleeve. Rachel sat in stunned silence not sure if she should laugh or cry at their peculiar tale.

'How much she was able to influence the outcome of the war is unknown to us, but there are stories of those she helped. One day an elderly woman telephoned my mother and told her the most wonderful tale of her great-aunt and the magical room she used to help her family escape the war. My mother was polite, but we all assumed the caller was a little crazy. We have letters from a few others, too. Found them in a hidden safe in what was the old clinic. I don't pretend to understand. I admit it all seems pretty crazy.' Marie paused to catch her breath and Sara jumped in while Rachel's eyes swivelled between the two women.

'It appears she only went back once, unless we are missing something. She passed away in this house in 1990, leaving this journal still hidden under the boards in her bedroom. Why she didn't tell anyone is another mystery, but perhaps she simply forgot. She writes in the journal that the memories washed away, like her previous life had been a dream. Luckily, we found the journal during the renovations for the bathroom on that level. We searched the house high and low and we think we have found every mystery and hidden thing in it. We found jewellery, letters, even a dagger under the stones in the old carriage entry. The mind boggles.'

Marie and Sarah took matching deep breaths and exchanged glances. Marie cleared her throat. 'We only found this one testimony from Antoinette. We thought for a long time that it was creative writing, you know, someone writing a story, but we did some research, and it all checks out, the dates and times. We almost ransacked the house…thinking we might find another journal, but we concluded it was a one-off event until, until I did it.'

It took a couple of seconds for this information to register with Rachel, her expression shifting from polite interest to disbelief and finally settling on astonishment, to the delight of Marie and Sara who once again, quite uncharacteristically, let out loud whooping laughter and clapped their hands.

'You what?'

'I tried it! Using the information my aunt gives here, to 'use your happiest memories to return to that time' and well, I am so happy often,' she placed her hand on her daughter's shoulder. 'I went to the little room and lay on the bed and dreamed of the beautiful family dinner we had had the previous Saturday. It had been a relaxed meal with my sister and her family who drove in from Amboise for the weekend, and well, I was able to enjoy it again.'

Rachel was dumbfounded, stuck halfway between belief and incredulity. She sat, staring at the journal, the faded red ribbon draped over it.

'Oh my god! That's why you messaged me out of the blue and told me to take my umbrella on Tuesday. I wondered what the hell was going on!' Rachel told them the story of the strange day she had had. The fun group of American students, the traffic jam, and the motorcycle passenger telling her to use Alex's umbrella.

'Yes!' Marie laughed. 'The first time you did that Tuesday…Oh, that sounds so strange!' She threw up her hands, obviously enjoying the freedom to talk about something that had been hidden for so long.

She went on.

'The first time, you ended up drenched to the skin and got a head cold because you are a crazy person who lives in a city where it always rains, and you don't carry an umbrella!'

They laughed for a few moments then sat in silence again. Rachel cycling through every emotion she had as she processed the information. 'What happens when you meet yourself? Oh God, are there two of you wandering around in here now, looking gorgeous and competing for the stove?'

'Well now there's only one of me, but yes, I met myself on the stair. It was strange but you don't go mad. They only say this to make people scared of time travel.'

Marie said this far too matter-of-factly for someone talking about time-travel.

'I said to myself, "it's okay, I'm you in one week." She, I mean, I, laughed and we hugged each other, and she- vous savez? You know what I mean, she, or I…disappeared in a kind of shimmer, laughing.' She made waving motions with her fingers. 'Then I went straight to the office and wrote down everything I could remember from the week, as my aunt had done all those years ago. She makes no mention of having met her-er - other self. She does mention her friend saw her after Mass and also her friend reported later Antoinette had disappeared before she could catch up with her.'

'It's unbelievable. I mean, I believe you. I think. But it's …crazy. How can this be real?'

'I don't know,' Sara agreed, 'but it is real. Maman told me so many things that week before they happened. I was suspicious so I asked her straight out if she had been abducted by aliens.'

'And I said, "no but I am a time-traveller" and Sara jumped up and ran from the room in a panic. It was very funny.'

'It wasn't funny, maman! You scared me!' Sara protested. 'But seriously, I have been reading everything I can get my hands on about time travel. It's amazing the information that is out there. Time is like loops, I believe, not straight lines. The concept of linear time lives in our pre-frontal cortex, the part of the brain that has only evolved in the last million years or so. It's completely fascinating. This has changed my life and I haven't even gone back. Yet.' Sara smiled at her mother who sighed deeply at the thought of her daughter, the time-traveller.

'We will see, chérie.' It was as though they were discussing whether she could take a weekend trip to London, not traveling in time.

'And now it seems like a dream, I mean all the memories are mashed together and I don't recall the event at all, except if I read my little story to remind myself. It appears this is crucial, writing everything down as quickly as possible, to commit it to paper, because it fades, like a dream.'

The three women sat in silence again, all lost in thought. Rachel picked up an éclair and chomped thoughtfully. She swallowed and closed her eyes in bliss.

'Have you heard that story about the poet Shelley? He wrote of meeting himself in the garden, weeks before he and his boat disappeared. He says he fainted when the apparition asked him "How long do you mean to be content?" It makes total sense to me now.'

She hadn't given this anecdote a second thought since she read about it years before, in high school.

Sara nodded enthusiastically.

'Oh, yes! He was in Paris in 1814, when he eloped with Mary. Maman, is it possible he stayed in this house and travelled back in time? Perhaps there are other portals here in Paris? If there is one, then there would be others, of course.' Sara wiggled about in her seat and clapped her hands like a child.

Marie shrugged her shoulders and made that very French sound. 'That's logical of course, but then none of this is logical.'

'I want to do it.' Rachel said. 'I want to go back and right my wrongs. I want more time with Alex. Tell me what I need to do.'

'Perhaps you need to go home and think about it, darling? It's not a decision to take lightly.'

Rachel was still not sure she believed it was possible.

'It's now or never, Marie. If I leave here, I'm going to chicken out, I know it. I need to at least give it a go. I could go back to that night, you remember that amazing party I told you about…oh, that night was the best night of my life! Except I'll say yes when he asks me to go out afterwards.'

Tears were streaming down Rachel's cheeks. The three women sat quietly. Sara toyed with the brass key, running the red ribbon through her fingers. Eventually, Marie nodded her head, pushed her chair back and motioned for Rachel to follow her.

...and a cat named Beau

Summer 1996

The scratching of the pencil on the paper was almost meditative as Rachel's hand moved across the page. Searching high and low for a pen, she had seized on the souvenir pencils she had been given at a tradeshow in London, terrified the tips would wear down before she had completed her writing.

'How is it I don't own a pen?' she asked herself, while still feverishly writing all she could think of. A single tear dropped onto the page. Blotting it with her shirt she carefully avoided writing there, only later realising it had made a poignant feature, a blank space with writing around it. She had never been artistic but was almost overwhelmed by the significance of the single tear staining the page that would literally change her life.

Marie had been spot-on in her description of how the morning would unfold, including the mind-blowing event of meeting herself as she left, or entered the apartment, depending on how you looked at it. She, 1996 Rachel, had rocked back slightly on her heels and put her hand to her mouth and 2007 Rachel had thought she would scream, but only the words "Oh, holy shit, what?" came out in a whisper, as she vanished.

Wasting no time and quickly deciding against freaking out after minutes of inner argument that could have gone either way, Rachel scanned her three-room apartment for a pen and something to write on. It looked as it had when she had first moved in, renting the space from her friend's mother, she bought, or would eventually buy the apartment in 2001. Having problems with the timeline already, she would have to remind herself to pay the rent.

Five minutes later she had ransacked her own apartment looking for something to write on, stopping momentarily to run her hand across the gorgeous dresses in her wardrobe. Feeling a little shallow, she realised she missed wearing pretty dresses. Unable to locate a pen, she had to be content with the Union Jack pencils and a 1995 diary, which turned out to be extremely helpful, the dates providing useful prompts to help her remember events. Thank heavens the pencils were already sharpened, she hated to think what damage she would do if she had to sharpen them with a knife. There was no time to ponder the events in her life as they had unfolded the first time around; she had to record everything she could remember and remind herself not to throw herself into Alex's arms when she saw him.

Her heart almost stopped.

Alex. He was alive. She steadied herself, knowing in a few hours the entire staff would be together at a cocktail party held on the roof-top of the Hôtel Raphael. He would ask to walk her home and she would let him. Unlike the last time' when she had said something along the lines of "nah, we're going dancing, do you want to come," which sounded very much like an afterthought and as though she didn't care whether he joined them or not. Which at the time, to be fair, she had not cared one bit.

That cocktail party had been a catalyst for amazing things in her life. Her other life. The one she had already lived. She sat back onto her heels where she was crouched at the coffee table in the middle of the tiny living room. She had returned to this exact moment because it was one of the happiest days of her life. She rubbed her hand; it was aching from writing, but she continued. The memories were washing away just as Marie had warned. She was confused and her stomach was churning as she realised her knowledge of Alex's cancer diagnosis was vague. They had been apart for months.

All she knew was at some time before 2004 he would need to see a doctor.

How would she convince him of that when the time came? She could always show him these pages although Marie had suggested that shouldn't be the first option, and in any case, as her memories faded, Marie warned her she would possibly forget the pages even existed, let alone had any merit.

Rachel had become a dedicated worrier since Alex's diagnosis, second-guessing every decision and torturing herself for any perceived wrong decision. She put the pencil down and went to the window to let the cat in. Looking out across the roof tops, she breathed in the warm air, remembering again that yesterday she was sitting in Marie's kitchen on a dark December afternoon, and today it's summertime. Marie's great-aunt Antoinette had also travelled back to a summer's day.

Rachel watched the Swallows flick across the blue sky and wondered why anyone would ever travel back in time to winter, as though nothing good could happen in the cold. But then she had arrived in Paris in the winter, and it had been a brilliant time for her. Should she have gone back to a different time? She should definitely have put more thought into it, she chastised herself. This is not something to be considered lightly but she had demanded Marie let her go back before she had second thoughts, and now here she was, having an existential crisis about the finer points of time-travel.

'Geez, woman! It's a bit late now to have second thoughts!'

She could hardly go barging into Marie's house to see if they had a room that would send her forward in time. Not that she would go. Seeing Alex, and saving his life, would be worth any amount of stress.

Retrieving the pencil and paper she started writing again, trying to recall every detail of every job offer and business idea she had ever had, and kicking herself for not taking the opportunity to delay for a day to commit the lottery numbers to memory. She quickly reminded herself this whole insane exercise had been to save the love of her life.

She allowed herself a few precious seconds for staring out the window as her memories bubbled up.

'Beau, Beau. Puss, puss, puss,' she called softly, smiling as she imagined her big fat cat lounging with one of his other families. He was obviously busy somewhere, so she went back to her page. After another half hour of fevered writing, she looked up and wondered where her cat was. She would entice him to the window. He was a free spirit, but he always popped through the window when she called, especially if food was involved. Opening the cupboard that stored the cat food she was surprised to see it filled with various kinds of tea, a crystal vase and an iron. When had she bought a crystal vase? Glancing around the apartment, Rachel realised that Beau's cat bowl was missing along with his blanket, toys and the unused scratching post she had carried home on the metro one evening. Beau preferred to sharpen his claws on the wooden table legs. She bent over and inspected the legs. Slowly she ran her hand over one of them. No scratch marks. They were all perfect.

She entertained the thought that perhaps she was in the wrong apartment, although that wouldn't explain the unforgettable experience of seeing herself standing in the hall, preparing to run errands and…

Oh hell, she thought, looking at her watch, recalling her appointment at the hair salon.

She could feel the old memories of her future life slipping away. Like a dream, she thought, remembering Antoinette's words in the old journal. She grabbed her coat as she ran from the apartment only to crash back through the door to dump it seconds later. It was summer after all. Running down the stairs, she wondered if the coat would be there when she came back, considering she had bought it in 2001. She still had no idea how this time travel thing worked. She was fairly sure her entire outfit had been bought sometime in the 21st Century. She hoped her clothes wouldn't start disappearing.

Taking the stairs two at a time, she fumbled the front door lock, dropping her keys. Bending to retrieve them she hit her head on the shelf that held the mail. The shelf that had been removed in 1997 after too many people complained about hitting their heads on it. Slow down, she said under her breath. She squatted to retrieve her keys and carefully stood to avoid the shelf. Reaching out to open the door, it swung open, revealing a tall woman in a flowery summer dress, large sunglasses and an armful of ginger cat. Rachel exclaimed, putting her arms out for him. He was the young cat she remembered from her early years in Paris.

'Oh, you know my cat. Has my tiger been visiting you?' the elegant woman asked Rachel while rubbing the young sleek cat affectionately on the top of the head. He closed his eyes in appreciation.

'Um, yes, I call him…Beau,' Rachel stammered, reaching out to show her the engraved medallion on his blue collar; the collar that was now red, had a bell, and a medallion that read 'Blake' in fancy script.

Retracting her hand, she mumbled a confused apology, unsure if someone had stolen her cat or if she had destroyed the only life she had ever known.

L'Artist

October 1999

Paris is a big city, but each arrondissement is a town, each neighbourhood is a village. Every day, the same people cross your path, stand in line behind you for the best bread, nod a greeting at the Tabac counter, and ride the metro with you. The tourists came and went, of course, but few tourists stayed in the gritty 18th arrondissement in those days. After her free and easy if somewhat cloistered life on Sydney's northern beaches, Rachel was shocked when she first moved to Paris that each area seemed to play host to their own resident beggars, homeless people, or persons sans domicile, many of them disabled veterans and itinerant folks who came to Paris in search of a better life.

Since she had been living on her own again, Rachel had relaxed a little. When they had been trying…she had become quite particular. The counsellor had said that might happen, especially when she was taking the hormones. Alex had tried to get her to relax. That was easy for him to say, he wasn't the source of their problems. Eventually she realised life would be easier if she only had herself to worry about. The apartment was certainly easier to keep clean with just her there. No man, no kids, no…cat. She could finally relax.

As they passed on the stairs, the thin scruffy woman looked into Rachel's face for the first time, though they passed on the street almost every day. Known in the neighbourhood as The Artist, she would sit in the corner of the salon de thé, writing each day in a journal. Why she was called The Artist and not The Writer was a mystery to Rachel.

The Artist had a nickname for Rachel, too; 'Busy Girl.' The girl who looked as though she was always 'elsewhere.' The girl who was always going somewhere, striding along the pavement. The girl who wouldn't raise her eyes to meet anyone else's although it appeared this was about to happen on this momentous day. The Artist stood on the stair waiting for Busy Girl to lift her eyes. Those eyes, normally fixed on the ground in front of her, were gradually travelling from the scuffed boots, past the grubby trousers; yes, that is paint on the hip. She made an additional scrunch of the brow as she took in the strange vintage fur draped over The Artist's thin shoulders.

Rachel had always felt safe scanning The Artist's shabby clothes, sitting askew on her emaciated frame; the troubled woman always averted her gaze before their eyes met. She was surprised to see the woman she had always assumed was homeless inside her building. Completing her habitual scan of the woman's clothes, to her horror she was frowning deeply as their eyes met, but a smile lit up the other woman's thin face.

Seeing this woman on the street was one thing, but her mind went blank, unsure of the etiquette in this unusual situation. Quickly realising it was entirely possible this woman was not homeless at all, and probably lived in the building, she managed a quick bonjour, changing her expression into a smile. Rachel could feel herself blushing. She knew she had been well and truly caught-out body-scanning and scowling at the other woman. Usually well versed in expected social cues after years of living in Paris, Rachel knew an introvert when she saw one, but here she was looking into Rachel's eyes, smiling, looking for all the world like she was welcoming conversation.

'Hello, busy girl,' The Artist said in French, her yellow teeth startling in her pale face. Rachel noticed she had a strong accent but was unsure if she was Irish or maybe from New Zealand.

'I'm going to climb the towers of Notre Dame today,' she continued in high-pitched childlike French. Rachel knew she had to be in her early forties, so the strange voice caught her off-guard.

'Wonderful! It's a beautiful day for it.'

Back in safe territory, Rachel knew exactly what to say to someone planning a day's sight-seeing. 'Get there early, there's always a queue. Take your camera, the view is magnifique.'

'Yes, it's nice and high. I'm going to jump,' she replied. Her eyes betraying the wild thoughts running through her mind.

Oh, God, Rachel thought. This is not safe territory.

'Um, I'm sorry you feel that way. It might feel bad…now, but things can change in an instant. I - er, felt this way a few months ago, but I'm better now. I got some help.'

Rachel knew very well what it felt like to want to die and she knew she had to keep her neighbour here on the stairs, talking. The woman dissolved into tears, almost collapsing on the landing. She crumpled the rest of the way and sat heavily on the step, her head bowed. Neither woman spoke, but Rachel put her market bags down, oranges rolling across the floor. She sat with the crying woman, wrapping her arms around her thin shoulders. They sat for what felt like an hour, one woman sobbing and the other breathing deeply, as though showing her what she needed to do. Eventually the sobs became further apart, and she began breathing deeply following Rachel's lead.

'I wasn't going to jump, I don't think, anyway. I just wanted to scare myself.' The Artist looked up at Rachel, the fear and pain seemed to have disappeared from her eyes, leaving a sadness Rachel understood only too well. Rachel smiled what she hoped was a warm smile.

'Well, you scared me. Come and have a cup of tea with me?' Rachel asked in English, 'You're Australian, aren't you?

'Yes!' she beamed. 'Surrey Hills!'

'Kincumber!' Rachel smiled back and held out her hand.

'No kidding? My dad grew up in Avoca! Karen, my name's Karen.' She shook Rachel's hand and then pulled her into a hug.

'I think you saved my life.'

'You okay now?' Karen nodded into Rachel's hair as they hugged.

'I'm dying for a cuppa myself.' Rachel sucked in her breath, sorry for the awkward turn of phrase. Karen laughed.

'Yeah, me too. Dying,' she laughed, putting extra emphasis on the word dying. 'I don't want to be a bother, though.'

'I think that ship has sailed, don't you? No, I'm joking, it's no bother at all. I've been feeling quite sad today. A bit homesick. Crazy after all these years to be homesick. I could use the company to be honest.'

'Oh, how I've missed the Aussie sense of humour,' Karen said. She sounded more relaxed. They gathered up the fallen fruit and made their way to Rachel's cosy apartment.

'You'll have to come up and see my flat sometime, it's got super high ceilings, and the light. Oh my, yes, the light. I should paint again.' Karen said this as though the idea had only just occurred to her.

She sat somewhat awkwardly on the sofa, facing the kitchen, watching Rachel put the kettle on, who was in turn marvelling at how comfortable she felt with Karen despite her obviously fragile state, their shared heritage making up for the obvious differences in their later choices. Over countless cups of tea, the two women sat and talked for hours, covering every topic from Australian politics to the cost of oysters in Paris, but both seeming to agree to avoid discussing their personal lives. To Rachel's surprise, the conversation flowed freely, and she found she enjoyed Karen's company, the woman clearly had a fierce intellect and a wicked sense of humour. Rachel felt a sense of kinship with the strange hermit from two floors up, having become somewhat of a recluse herself in recent months.

'I have a huge terrace, but I can't use it... I've got a lot of problems, I'm dealing with them, but I've made a fucking mess of my life,' Karen said quietly. They wedged themselves on to the tiny balcony with steaming mugs of hot chocolate as night fell over the city.

'Mmmm?' Rachel enquired, wondering a little late if sitting on the tiny balcony two floors up was a mistake. Surely, she wouldn't risk falling mere metres and ending up in hospital with a broken leg. 'Tell me your problems and I'll tell you mine.'

'Okay, if it's a competition I will definitely win. I'm proper messed up.' She winked at Rachel and over the following minutes told her somewhat edited story of hopeful arrival in Paris in 1990.

'It sounds like a dream,' Rachel said. 'Living in the German Embassy!'

'It was great, until my mental health began to suffer, my friend disappeared, and my partner left. The drugs. It was a great start with a bad ending. I lost the love of my life. I had everything and I blew it all away. Or more accurately I shot it all into my arms.' Karen rolled up her sleeve, showing Rachel the scars and other marks.

'Okay yes, you win,' Rachel replied quietly, rubbing her own forearms, thankfully smooth and unblemished except for the tiny tattoo of an A on her right wrist.

'What's the A stand for, Rachel?'

'Who…it's a who…' Rachel was unsure she wanted to tell this stranger the story, let alone the crazy suspicions she had after finding the diary. 'The love of my life. Alex. I lost him too.'

'I'm so sorry.' It was all Karen could say. What else could she say, under the circumstances?

'I had an A, too. She left Paris and never returned. They can't find her, they say. Her or her body. Agnès. I miss her.'

Rachel leaned across and held Karen's hand as fat tears rolled down her cheeks, until she looked up and smiled. 'Nothing to be done, no use crying over spilled milk,' Karen said.

'No, but we do, don't we?' Rachel smiled and picked up the empty cups. She stepped down from the balcony and walked towards the kitchen. 'Wine?' she asked.

'Sober,' Karen replied.

'Oh, sorry. Good for you,' Rachel said a little awkwardly.

'And the…?' She gestured towards the scarring on Karen's arms, amazed at how comfortable she felt with her neighbour.

Strangely, an image of the traditional shoemaker's studio opposite Marie's front door flashed through Rachel's mind, then an image of scribbled writing on pages. She stopped, leaning heavily on the kitchen bench, a cup clattering across the laminate surface, coming to rest just before the edge.

Could it be true? Could the diary be real? The one she found wedged between the bedhead and the wall, the scribbled pages in her own handwriting, on sheets torn from a 1995 diary? The pages, scratched out in pencil, accented by what looked like tear stains, or rain drops.

The diary sent chills down her spine.

Perhaps this strange woman who seemed so familiar had known her before. Before… Before what, she asked herself. Before she travelled back in time? Despite the strong feelings of déjà vu, she doubted they had been friends…before. Even if by some bizarre miracle she had travelled back to 1995 to save Alex's life, there was no mention in the diary of Karen or The Artist at all.

Rachel emerged from her thoughts.

'…and I haven't used for two years. Two years, three months and…19 days. Ha, ha,' she said although she was far from joking. 'It was going to kill me and while that seems ironic now, I didn't want to die. You know I probably wasn't going to kill myself today, you have to believe me.' Karen looked up at Rachel's pale face.

'Are you okay? Do the scars upset you? Should I go?'

'No, no. Stay. I'm fine, I tripped and dropped the cup. I'm fine.'

Rachel recovered, trying unsuccessfully to put the image of the diary out of her mind. Karen's eyes searched Rachel's face for understanding and must have found what she was looking for. She took a deep breath and sighed it out, looking relieved. A big ginger cat took that opportunity to scale the railing. Karen let out a yelp, startling the cat in turn.

'Oh, this guy visits me, too,' she laughed, self-consciously holding her hand up to her mouth. 'Is he yours?'

'Well, I like to think he is, but I'm not so sure. I think he used to wear a tag I bought him; I can't really remember. I…I used to deal with the fleas in the summer and take him for his shots but someone else does that now…He's very much his own man. His name's B…Blake.' Rachel poured cat biscuits into a bowl, but he was quite content on Karen's lap, enjoying a rub under the chin.

Beau. She was going to say Beau. His name was Beau.

Rachel smiled, thinking of that strange day she met Blake's owner and the way it had upset her to see the woman carrying the ginger cat. The image of words scribbled on paper flashed through her mind again, only to be replaced by the image of Marie's front door. The blue-painted, double carriage door. Rachel stopped and felt her forehead for signs of fever. She felt fine but confused as a new image floated into her mind. Why was she seeing an upscale art gallery opposite Marie's front door? This was a new mystery for her to ponder.

'Have you ever been to an art gallery in rue de Bièvre?' Rachel asked her.

'Oh, umm, I don't think so. Why?'

'Oh, no reason really, perhaps I thought I had seen you there at a show. My friend owns the hotel opposite…House. I don't know why I said hotel.' Rachel laughed at herself and carried a platter covered in the bits and pieces she had picked up at the local market that afternoon, cheese, salty Normandy butter and small pieces of fruit, the bread under her arm and a bottle of sparkling water.

Rubbing the cat's head, Karen explained she hadn't created much artwork lately as she had gone to rehab in Germany on her father's request.

'So, you know they call me The Artist in this neighbourhood. I was…am an artist. Quite successful, too. I sold a lot of artwork. After Agnès left…I started using, and my art was quite angry. People like edgy shit…My dad came over from England where he lives. He's an academic. He made me an ultimatum; I get clean or he'd have me committed. That word scared the fuck out of me, but I was a mess. I was bad enough before Pete left, but after…I should've been dead already.' She frowned.

'Pete?'

'My fiancé.'

'Oh, I thought Agnès….' Rachel replied awkwardly.

'No, she was my sister…. well not my sister, but my soul sister… When she disappeared, things got bad. I was always pretty intense, but when Agnès…died…well I lost it.'

'And Pete? What happened to him?

'He's happy, I believe… I'm happy for him. I was ready to change though. I've been clean since that day Dad sat in my studio and cried. It's not a good thing when you make your father cry.' Her father had driven with her to Germany, stayed in the town, walked with her every step, both finding solace in poetry; she wrote, and burned, pages and pages of what she called 'word vomit'. Meditation had been an integral part of the rehabilitation process and on returning to Paris she worked her way through the list of suggested groups. Her father went home, his sabbatical over. His daughter would have to take it from there.

'My dad rescued me, because I wouldn't let err, my - Pete rescue me. I pushed him away and he went. I was so surprised when he eventually left. But your dad's not going to go, is he?'

'No, some dads don't bugger off, no matter how many times you tell them to. I think we're lucky to have dads like that.' Rachel had been surprised when Alex left too, even though she had told him to.

'The rehab was pretty intense and when it was over, I was on my own. I was confused about what recovery looked like to be honest. I didn't even know how to make artwork anymore. I was looking for a place to fit in, I couldn't see any of my old friends anymore, and Pete had a new life without me.' Leaning down she snuggled the cat's neck. Rachel could see she was trying to keep it together.

'I was desperate, and ripe for the picking, for a guru type to grab me and brainwash me into their cult, but it was weird. I had to seek out the meditation groups. I actively planned on swapping my addiction to heroin for a shaved head and hours of chanting.' Karen laughed, again covering her discoloured teeth with a hand.

'It's a bit embarrassing but I couldn't find a group that would have me. No one wanted to indoctrinate me! I began to think I was beyond redemption, of course, but a throw away comment from my therapist changed that. He suggested maybe I wasn't as broken as I thought I was, that cults only want the weak-minded ones, not survivors. I didn't believe it at first, but somehow it sunk in. I'm so glad I didn't end up in an ashram or cult, even though it was what I thought I wanted. I wanted someone to do the hard work for me, but in the end, I think I have to be my own guru. I'm a work in progress. I hear Pete married someone else. I blew it. She's a nice person apparently. She would be, because he is.'

Karen was whispering by the time she had finished. She took a deep breath. 'And yours? Alex?'

'Yep, married to the lovely Hanne. Again.' Rachel stopped and put her hand to her throat. 'Oh God, you know that feeling of déjà vu? Isn't it the worst? It's like I've said those exact words to you in this exact location before. Or dreamed it.'

'He married her again?' Karen asked, obviously confused.

'Oh, what? Oh no, I meant…' she shrugged, not exactly sure what she meant, but she had an unshakeable urge to grab the strange diary she had found and burn it.

The cat finally jumped down from Karen's lap and sniffed at the blue cheese on the platter. Unimpressed he padded over to the food bowl instead, before wandering into the bedroom and making himself comfortable in the middle of Rachel's bed as he often had done over the past few years and perhaps in a previous lifetime. The diary spoke of a cat, a big ginger cat called Beau. She considered him her cat, but he came and went.

So much in those pages rang true. Rachel would pull it out again in the morning, when she was alone. It was crazy to even contemplate the idea she had travelled back in time. Maybe she had been to one of those amazing clairvoyants her colleague Emma raved about. In fact, the pages had mentioned Emma. She had…would, create a tour company specialising in visiting psychics in and around Paris and London. In the spring of the year 2000…a couple more months would show if this was indeed true, she thought.

The year 2000, she thought. What a strange concept. Rachel was vaguely aware Karen was speaking, asking if she was okay, did she want to go to sleep.

'Oh no, sorry, I was deep in thought. I was thinking about my…er, friend who goes to a lot of psychics. I think I went to one once. I was thinking about the stuff that came true and the stuff that didn't.'

Rachel finally had an explanation for the scribbled bundle of pages hidden in her bedroom. Relieved, she was able to put the more mysterious aspects of the diary to the back of her mind, at least for a while. In the morning she would think about the part that said she had gone to sleep in a room in Marie's home and woken up ten years before. She would wait a few more days before thinking about the part where Alex had died.

The two women talked into the wee hours wrapped in blankets and laughing as they took turns using the bathroom, the copious quantity of tea taking its toll. Rachel eventually fell asleep on the sofa.

Karen pulled the window shut after ensuring the cat was safely inside. She found a piece of paper and a pencil, and after leaving Rachel a note, let herself out. In stark contrast to the previous morning, Karen had a feeling everything was going to be alright.

The Journal

Disoriented, her bladder almost bursting, Rachel woke wondering why she was on the sofa and why her foot was throbbing with pins and needles? As the brain fog lifted, she remembered the bizarre meeting with the woman who said she wanted to kill herself.

Rachel shook her head.

'Not exactly a meet-cute,' she snorted out loud, 'If you wrote that in a novel, no-one would believe it.'

She tested a little weight on her foot but crawled to the bathroom instead. Her foot had yet to resume its regular duties, but her bladder couldn't wait a minute longer. Sitting longer than strictly necessary, massaging her tingling calf muscle, she tried to remember where she had heard the term meet cute. She rubbed her temples. The memories flashed around the inside of her head like fish in a pond. She shifted her mind to the details of the previous day.

Was Karen still in the apartment?

Reluctant to call out, she hobbled into the hallway and peered into the dark bedroom, but only a drowsy ginger cat lifted his head and miaowed. The apartment was empty. Rachel shuffled back to the bathroom, her leg still tingling. She turned on the hot water and stood watching the steam filling the room. Beau, or Blake or whatever his name was, appeared in the doorway, miaowing. Rachel closed her eyes and enjoyed the hot water on her body, despite the cat's repeated and escalating demands to exit the apartment.

'Okay, okay,' she said, shutting off the water. She towelled off and wrapped herself in her fuzzy bathrobe. She opened the window for the cat and watched as he disappeared over the balcony.

Lost in thought, she collected the cups they had left on the low table and piled them in the sink. She set the kettle on the stove, smiling as she thought of her deep conversation with Karen. She had no Australian friends in Paris. There was such comfort in the shared culture and humour. She couldn't remember the last time she had enjoyed herself as much. The kettle began to wail as she spied the piece of paper pinned to the front door. Her heart sank. She flipped the gas off, silencing the squealing kettle. She hoped this wasn't a 'so long and thanks for all the tea' note.

Rachel seized the folded paper sending the thumbtack flinging across the room. In the recesses of her mind, she knew she may regret that action later. Slowly she unfolded the paper, frightened of what it might contain but it was a sketch, a portrait of Rachel that somehow captured her essence like no photo ever had. Mesmerised, she quickly flipped the paper over but there was no note, just the exquisite drawing and a tiny 'Kx' in the corner.

The tears flowed catching her off-guard. She ran to the bedroom to dress, not letting go of the artwork. She needed to see Karen, to check on her, to make sure she was okay. Rachel pulled on jeans and a shirt, dragged a brush through her hair and wound it up into a messy pile on her head. She took a deep breath and reached into the top of her wardrobe and pulled down an old hat box. She pulled at the loose end of the wide grosgrain ribbon and the bow loosened.

Her heart pounding, she lifted the lid and slid her hand into the lining, feeling for the wad of paper. Pulling the strange diary from its hiding place, she gently lay the pages across the bed and returned to the box for the photo album. She didn't need to open it. The first photo was taken at a friend's wedding, the second on vacation in Greece, the third, sitting on the tiny balcony with hot chocolate. There was another with Alex's friend Gustav, and Christmas with Marie and her family. Alex beamed at her from each picture. The familiar déjà vu came over her and she knew she had to visit the house with the blue door to have a good chat with its owner.

Gently replacing the unopened photo album, she picked up the sheets of paper and stood over her little home fax machine, carefully feeding the pages through, copying each one. Tucking the original in her bag, she gathered the copied sheets into a roll. The brain fog had faded. It may have been the gallons of tea she had drunk the previous night, or the lack of her nightly bottle of red wine, but she had the strongest feeling that everything was about to change and decided she was okay with that.

Climbing the stairs to Karen's floor, Rachel contemplated their meeting on the stairs the previous day. Had it been less than twenty-four hours before? She felt they had made a real connection and somehow, she knew Karen wouldn't harm herself. As she reached the top step her hands were shaking. She stopped to gather her thoughts and take a deep breath. She was nervous of what she might find on the other side of the door.

Loud music pulsed from the apartment causing Rachel to wonder if she had the wrong door. Rachel's hands were icy. She stopped and rubbed them together. What was she planning? They had only just met, and Karen was fragile; what would she think of Rachel, coming up here with her crazy diary? The music throbbed. She would only knock twice. If Karen answered, she would tell her about the diary. If she didn't, then Rachel would go about her day.

Before she could change her mind, Rachel knocked loudly and stood back to wait, shifting awkwardly on her feet, trying to remain calm. The music stopped, leaving the thud of the bass echoing in the beat of Rachel's heart. The door opened and swung wide, revealing Karen's studio and living quarters, the artist herself the only sliver of colour in the apartment. The entire space had been painted white, including the floor. The light was pouring in through huge east facing windows which, Rachel calculated, would have taken in the whole of Parc de Belleville. Dumbfounded by the unexpectedly large and elegant apartment, Rachel nodded hello to Karen who stood back to welcome her. She was obviously accustomed to that reaction, although Rachel was unsure how many visitors Karen received.

Karen had mentioned the huge terrace the night before, but Karen had said she was unable to use it. Reaching the other side of the room Rachel realised the view from the terrace did indeed take in the expanse of the huge green space in the east of the city but it was clear the doors to the terrace had been painted shut by a concerned party, possibly her father, possibly her lost love.

Rachel felt awkward, like an intruder. She looked directly at Karen for the first time properly since she had opened the door. Her painfully thin, bare arms protruding from an ill-fitting t-shirt dress, un-brushed hair hanging in her eyes that somehow looked as haunted as they had the day before. Her eyes were red-rimmed, her hands covered in paint.

'Hi, I thought I'd…' Rachel began, none of the previous night's relaxed mood.

'It's okay, I'm a work in progress. Yesterday I was a mess, then I wasn't. Thank you.' She pressed her palms together as though offering a prayer to Rachel. 'But today, I'm a mess again.' She picked up a remote control and aimed it towards the other room, Massive Attack booming again from the speakers. 'I'm going to come right out and say this. You don't want to be friends with me.' Karen was shouting, her attitude was combative, daring Rachel to declare her position, defend her right to friendship.

'I do. I see you're a mess, but you know what? I was a mess too, and now I'm shut down. I've forgotten how to feel. You feel everything. It's woken something in me, and I think I can help you, too.' Rachel was forced to shout over the music she uncrossed her arms and facing the other woman, she waited for a response.

'Oh, so you want to be my guru?' Karen said.

Rachel was shocked. 'I don't want to be anyone's guru. You helped me last night, more than you can know right now, and I want to return the favour. Simple as that.'

Karen left the door wide open and walked towards her. Rachel felt a pang of guilt realising she was relieved to see she had an easy exit if she needed it.

'I need to go see a friend of mine, but if you trust me, if you want me to, I, she, can help…I think…' she said nervously, glancing towards the open door. She lowered her voice as much as she could and held up the copies she had made of the diary. 'I want you to read something that will change everything. Or at least it might, if you let it.'

'What is it? I've read it all, from Louise Hay to Aleister Crowley.' She crossed the space between them and regarded the photocopied sheets with curiosity. She must have seen something that piqued her interest. 'Okay, I'll read it,' she said.

Karen relaxed, her face and voice changing in an unsettling way that made Rachel nervously question her judgement.

'You make the tea,' Karen said, distracted by the diary. She was sounding more like the carefree Aussie who sat in Rachel's flat for hours the previous day, and less like the anxious woman she had been minutes before.

'Okay, cool…' Rachel was still shouting over the music, 'but you have to read the whole thing and suspend judgement until you finish.'

To her surprise, Karen opened a cupboard along the side wall to reveal a pile of soft colourful cushions she quickly and expertly assembled into a stylish sofa.

'It's an original Hopfer, a Mah Jong.' She sat on a pink and orange striped seat, the effect of the colour in the space mesmerising. 'I told you I was a successful artist.' She smiled her closed-lip smile at Rachel as she nestled into the cushions.

'This day just keeps getting weirder,' Rachel said to herself as she filled the kettle. She was starting to enjoy the booming music, realising it had been a long time since she had turned up the music.

Karen lay the pages' side by side as she read them, keeping them in chronological order made easier by the large black numbers Rachel had added that morning as she re-read them herself. She had wanted to be sure there was no mention of Karen in the diary, so strong was the connection she felt with the woman. When Rachel brought the tea over to the low sofa, Massive Attack still booming from the next room, Karen had carefully assembled the pages she had read. The artist's thin hands trembling as she held the un-read sheets. Rachel was fairly sure her hand trembled anyway, rather than being caused by what she was reading.

Her first question would be a variation of 'are you fucking kidding me?' as was Rachel's the first time she had read it. And the second. No doubt she'd had the same reaction when she read the journal Marie found buried under floorboards in her ancient house. The oddest part was that Rachel couldn't recall reading the original journal. But there it was, in this rambling essay that made so little sense that Rachel would have considered throwing it away if it hadn't been in her own handwriting.

Karen leaned back and closed her eyes, clutching the last sheet of paper in one hand, the other pinching the skin between her eyes. She picked up the remote control and lowered the sound on the unseen stereo system to a low throb. Rachel was first to speak.

'Thanks for the drawing you left. Last night. It's beautiful.'

Karen opened her eyes and smiled. She looked so tired. 'Time and art,' she said cryptically.

Rachel sat quietly sipping her tea, Karen's tea getting cold as she contemplated what she had read. 'So, he died, and you, you decided to go back in time and save him?'

'Yes, and I guess I did. He's happily living in Denmark as we speak.' Rachel shrugged.

Karen made a sound in her throat.

'But I have to think of a way to warn him when the time comes. I obviously thought we would, er, be together,' Rachel said.

They sat in silence for a few minutes until Rachel cleared her throat softly. 'There's no guarantee this will work, but the one thing I wrote here over and over was the importance of writing the memories down. The thing I forgot to do was to read it often. I found this only a few weeks ago. None of it made any sense.'

Rachel finished her tea. She picked up Karen's cup and handed it to her. A soft smile on her face, Karen pulled a pen from her pocket and went to write on the page. 'May I?' she said, without looking up.

'Sure, it's a copy. It's yours,' Rachel said.

With a sweep of the black ink pen, Karen drew a perfect copy of the 'A' tattoo inked on Rachel's wrist. Rachel's hand shot to her throat.

'I'm going to get a tattoo like this. For Agnès,' Karen whispered.

Rachel couldn't speak. A fat tear ran down her cheek. She brushed it away and found her voice.

'Last night, I was sure I had been to a clairvoyant and these were predictions…but this is real, Karen. It's all right there. This is a diary, this stuff happened.' After all her confusion over the diary, Rachel now had never been surer of anything in her life. 'I have the oddest memories of certain things because…apparently, I…travelled back in time.'

Karen closed her eyes and sipped her tea.

Rachel continued. 'Some events didn't happen the same way as described in the diary, but close. Too close for coincidence. I pursued a relationship with Alex this time, last time, well, I built my career instead. It didn't work out exactly as I'd hoped but a lot of this stuff came true. It's eerie.'

The CD had finished playing and the silence in the apartment seemed to hum.

'Do you believe it?' Rachel asked.

'Why not?' Karen said, placing her cup on the table. She lay her hands palms down on the coffee table and looked into Rachel's eyes. 'Do you think I could do this?' The childlike quality had crept back into Karen's voice.

Rachel sighed and lay her hands over Karen's. 'I think you can. I have a few errands to run. This is my cell phone number. If it's what you want, call me.'

Karen nodded, closing her eyes. The room was warm; it seemed to be full of electricity.

'But if you do this, promise me, you will do it for yourself. Do it to stay away from whoever gave you the drugs. Do it for your own sake, for your health, for your parents. But remember, if it's meant to be, it will be.'

Karen was looking up at her, eyes shining with tears. She nodded. 'I will, I promise,' the little girl voice was gone. 'Even if Pete and I aren't meant to be, at least I can do all I can to stay away from the drugs.' She motioned towards her scarred arms.

'And save Agnès,' she finished sadly. Rachel was in floods of tears, as though the well that had run dry all those months before had sprung to life. She got up and walked around the low sofa and embraced Karen. They sat together for a few minutes, although Karen was rigid, not once allowing herself to be consoled.

Quickly gathering up her things she left without looking back. Karen would need time to process the information. This was not something anyone should attempt if they are not in the right frame of mind. It was crucial to be able to think of happier times. Karen had to truly believe she was capable of happiness.

The Hotel

Rachel reached up and lifted the ornate knocker on the huge carriage door in rue de Bièvre, for the first time noticing it was shaped like a beautiful woman holding a clock. She stared, open-mouthed at the bronze ornament until the door opened.

'Have you found your aunt's diary this time around?' she asked as Marie opened the huge front door.

'Er, bonjour Rachel, come in, s'il vous plait,' Marie said quietly, checking up and down the street as though it would provide a clue for her friend's odd behaviour.

Rachel leaned on the marble hall table and handed Marie the rolled-up papers.

'I want you to read this and tell me if I'm crazy…or if this is somehow real. Did I really lose Alex twice?' Rachel was panting, her eyes red, hair hanging in her face. Marie took the wad of papers and motioned for Rachel to follow her to the empty drawing room.

'What's happening?' Rachel scanned the bare room.

Sara, Marie's daughter walked into the room carrying a bucket of paint and brushes.

'Oh Rach, you're just in time to help with the painting!'

'We've got our accreditation; we are becoming a private hotel,' Marie said, excitement edging into her normally calm voice. 'It's going to be busy.'

Rachel stared at both women unsure whether to laugh or cry.

'So, it is all true?'

Marie and Sara both stood and nodded dumbly at her.

'Yes, chérie, we will be a private hotel,' Marie said.

The hotel was another piece falling into the puzzle. 'Of course, it will. It's all here…' Rachel pointed to the roll of paper. She lost her train of thought but shook her head as though coming to her senses. 'The diary, Marie, have you found it?'

Her friend's face dropped, and Sara looked at Marie, intrigued, her worried face so similar to her mother's. 'Do you mean my great-Aunt's diary?' Marie lowered her voice almost to a whisper.

'Yes, that would be the one.' Rachel sat down on one of the tins of paint Sara had placed on the floor. Sara took the other one and Marie took the low rung of the ladder. 'I have my own diary…' Rachel was pointing to the papers Marie was holding.

Sara held out her hand for the sheets and Marie placed them with exaggerated care into her upturned palm, as though they were explosive. She sat, silently reading the scribbled pages, daughter handing the sheets to mother as they painstakingly pored over the journal, if a bundle of sheets torn from a disused 1995 diary could be called such a thing.

'Yes, we have found the diary of my mother's Great Aunt, we found it in…'

'1991, during the major renovations. I know.' Rachel put her hand on Marie's arm. Marie jumped like Rachel had given her an electric shock.

'Oh, mon dieu. Would you like to read it? I mean read it again…'

'Yes, I would. I know now that I lost him, that he…' she swallowed the lump in her throat. 'Marie, he died the first time. Ironic, isn't it? I wondered what could be worse than losing the man I loved to another woman…at least I know now. Now I've lost him again, and I've come to terms with it. It wasn't meant to be, for us.' Rachel looked down at the floor, a tear dripping on to her shirt. 'I'm just trying to work out how to warn him when the time comes, how to tell him to go to the doctor. I have his email address. I guess I'll tell him I went to a psychic with my friend Emma. My mind is swirling. I…I…feel like I'm going crazy, it's bizarre isn't it? He left me, but now I know it could be much worse!'

Rachel stood and paced the length of the room then stood staring but not seeing anything through the ancient mullion windows. They had been sand-blasted, leaving them as clean as they day they were installed, sometime in the 18th century.

'To be fair, he didn't leave you,' Marie said quietly. 'You made him leave. He didn't want to leave you Rachel, but you gave him no choice.'

Rachel and Sara looked at the older woman. 'You spoke to him?' Rachel said, her voice cracking.

'Yes, before they…he…err left Paris. He was so sad.'

Rachel felt like screaming at her friend, but she lowered her voice. 'I had no choice. I didn't want to be the reason he can't be a father, it's all he ever wanted. I felt, I knew, he should have children, it was meant to be. And I couldn't… Then I found this….' She held the loose sheets of paper disdainfully between two fingers as though it was toxic waste, 'and this confirms it. He had three children, and…I went back and changed everything.'

Rachel collapsed on the stone floor. Marie and Sara sat either side of her as she sobbed. Marie, eyes flashing at her only daughter, stood and excused herself to get a hot pot of tea which would no doubt be accompanied by a plate of pastries. The sobs subsiding, Rachel relaxed against her friend's shoulder and sat up, dabbing her eyes with tissues.

'I should just bloody go and do it again!'

'Sweetheart, do you want to…?' Sara said in a whisper.

'No, no….no I don't…I need to talk about it. He's with her again, the one I wrote about in the diary. She's super nice and gorgeous. Apparently, we became…friends last time, if you can believe that! She spent Christmas with my family.' Rachel's face was blank. She was trying to understand the weirdness of the whole mess. 'She's still a flight attendant, and left her tennis coach husband this time around, for Alex. Last time around she was sleeping with the tennis coach or something. How bizarre is that?' Not expecting a response, she sat, calm now, leaning back on her hands.

'It's not surprising. We are attracted to the same people, no matter how many times we try to do things differently,' Sara said, almost matter-of-factly.

Rachel sniffed and regarded her young friend. 'Have you?' Rachel asked in a low voice.

'Yes, but it's a huge secret. I've done it a few times, that's why I was going to offer for you to do it again. You mustn't tell maman. She believes I have only done it once. Maybe twice.' Sara smiled enigmatically, making Rachel forget herself, Alex and Karen for a few moments. She could feel the frustration melting away. Some things are meant to be, she thought, horrible, nasty and sad, but inevitable. She gave a huge sigh and blew her nose.

'I just wish I'd kept this diary in my nightstand and read it every day. It's so easy to forget and then go ahead and mess things up but in an entirely new way.'

The two women sat on the cold stone floor discussing the intricacies of time-travel, both agreeing the crucial step was to write everything they could remember, but both also agreeing some things were out of their control.

'I'm still working at a restaurant and studying even though I have…tried different ideas. Then I had this idea to create the hotel. I think it comes from, you know, repeating….' Sara laughed. 'I had hoped to marry Brad Pitt in at least one of my lives.'

Marie came into the room carrying a tray laden with goodies and the two younger women, laughing now, made their way to the round walnut table covered in a drop-sheet in the middle of the entry foyer, for once bare of one of the enormous flower arrangements Marie loved to create.

'Well, it's good to see a smile,' Marie said, looking from one woman to the other, concern in her eyes. 'You're not planning to go back again, are you?'

Rachel shook her head. 'No, I've given it my best shot, some things are just not meant to be. My ginger cat was truly my cat last time around. His name was Beau. He still visits, but you know, he's not really mine now. He's Blake…'

She pulled a face. Sara and Marie laughed.

'And in - this life - my oldest sister only has two kids. In the last, she had four. I'm not sure she is changed in any other way, she seems happy, but I'm sad for those two kids. I mean, where are they? I feel awful…I must have changed something. It's not to be trifled with.'

Rachel did not dare to look at Sara, lest she give away her secret.

'Would you like to read the diary of my Great-Great Aunt…again?' Marie placed the leather book on the table. It was tied with a length of red ribbon, a brass key tucked into the folds.

Rachel felt the familiar shiver of recollection. 'I haven't read it yet, have I?' She reached across the table to take the little bundle. 'The key? Is it for the…room?' The two women nodded.

They sat in companionable silence, eating the slice and drinking tea, Rachel absorbed in the reading of the fascinating piece of history.

'I am writing a book on this woman, my ancestor, Antoinette de la Roche. Not about the time portal, of course, but about her contribution to science, to medicine, to La Résistance,' Sara said.

Rachel looked up. 'I remember reading this. Oh, it's this amazing feeling of déjà vu. I have it all the time. Do you…?'

Sara glanced at her mother.

Marie rolled her eyes. 'Of course, I know you've been back numerous times. I know you, you're my daughter!'

Sara sighed. 'Thankfully I no longer have to keep a secret from my mother, although I clearly didn't keep it very well. Yes, I have that feeling all the time. In French we also say déjà vécu which means something like "I recall remembering this". Eventually, somehow it all loops over itself and yes, you get those strange feelings of "have I seen this before?" and "Have I met this person before?" It's all quite unbelievable to those who haven't experienced it. Which is everybody, of course! I feel excited about being a pioneer, like Antoinette,' Sara's eyes were sparkling. 'You know, once I decided to study medicine, like Antoinette, like her father, like my father. But I couldn't do it! I wasn't cut out for it. That was the time I discovered just because we can go back in time, nothing is certain, nothing is guaranteed.'

'How old are you? I mean, what's the furthest you've…Oh I couldn't find the English for this, let alone the French!' Rachel laughed.

'I've had my 25th Birthday twice, but I don't think I'll do it again, after the next one!'

'So, you know what's going to happen for the next…three years?' Rachel asked, a little too loudly. A chorus of shushing sounds came from the other women.

'Well yes, and no. I mean, nothing is set in stone.'

Rachel knew that only too well. Throwing caution to the wind, she told Marie and Sara the story of the sad, strange woman who lives in her building, their meeting on the stair, their strangely comfortable conversation over many, many cups of tea. She pulled the portrait from its safe place in her tote.

'I always have the most incredible déjà vu every time I see her. I mean even when I thought she was a junkie. Every time I see this woman, I get the overwhelming feeling that I know her, and I have to help her, even though she doesn't appear in my diary. I thought she was homeless, but she lives in my building. She's an incredibly talented painter. She was successful. Internationally. Shows and the whole shebang.'

Rachel pushed the sketch across the table to Marie.

'I keep having a flashback, or forward or whatever it is, of a gallery across the lane-way here, I see her work hanging in that gallery, oh and she's Australian, like me.'

Marie and Sara both looked towards the street. They both knew there was no art gallery, only a shoemaker with a dentist clinic above.

'Maybe, chérie, you have been back more than once?' Sara said.

Rachel stopped to gather her thoughts, trying to shake the image of the scarring on Karen's arms, the thinness of her shoulders. 'Maybe I have, but no matter what, The Artist needs help and I think she needs the kind of help only we can offer.'

A few hours later, four women made their way to the basement of the old house. Marie was a few steps behind, deep in thought. She quickened her footsteps and caught Sara's arm.

She put her lips to Sara's ear. 'I'm worried. She might be too unstable.'

Sara stopped. She lightly held her mother's arms and whispered, 'Maman, Karen is fine. Remember, your Great Aunt Antoinette did it while she was dying. If you are scared, you'll make her scared. You should go.'

Sara dropped her hands from Marie's arms.

Marie wondered when her daughter had become so tough, but realised it was probably not a good question a mother should ask a daughter who constantly travelled in time.

Sara walked away without looking back.

As the three other women entered the little stone room, Marie shuddered. The room would have been demolished in the renovations if it hadn't had metre thick stone walls. Someone had known about this time portal when the house was built.

'Que sera sera,' Marie whispered under her breath as she left the house.

The Artist writes

Rachel told me some things can't be changed. You sit in this room, and write down, or speak about all about your best time in Paris, the time you were happy, you know? Then before you go to sleep, someone winds the clock back a few times and then you go to sleep. I thought I'd be so excited I couldn't go to sleep, like when you were a kid, and it was Christmas Eve? Rachel said she's done it. And the young girl, Sara, she's done it a few times. You think happy thoughts like Dorothy in Oz, and if you can go to sleep, well, the next day, you're there, where and who you were then.

They said to me 'Can you remember a time when you knew you were exactly where you should be? When you were happy? They said this with such pity I felt a wave of shame come over me.

'I wasn't always addicted, ladies,' I said.

It broke the mood a little bit and we could really talk then. Once they realised I wasn't just a dirty, drug-fucked loser. It was the day he proposed, I said proudly, and they saw me in that moment, I think, as a woman…as a woman in love with her man, thinking everything is going to be wonderful and not planning to destroy her life.

Surely Rachel, with her own story of love lost, knew no-one ever set out to destroy themselves, even if Sara was too young to understand that yet. That day at the end of '92 was the happiest day, I was the happiest person, he was happy, our friends were happy, our families were happy.

Everyone in Paris was so fucking happy.

I know now from all my meditation a happy life is simply the matter of choosing to be so. Pain is inevitable, but suffering is a choice the Buddha said once.

Or was that Yoda?

We'd all laughed at that joke and the mood kept getting lighter and lighter.

'I choose right now, to believe in magic, to change my mind,' I said aloud to the room.

Then I said, 'In my new future, that is my past, I'm going to think of the thing I would habitually do, and then do the absolute opposite.'

We all laughed some more.

They are good people, good women. I want to find them again. I want to be friends with them, instead of befriending the people who helped me destroy myself. Rachel and I talked for hours in the little room deep under that old house, just like we did the day before, the day we met. Perhaps she was my sister in a previous life, or my mother.

I feel like she gave me life.

Then it was late and time for them to go. The young girl, Sara, whispered in my ear.

'When you wake, go home. Go and find yourself. Make a better life.'

Everything sounds more romantic when it's whispered in your ear en francais. In French, even crazy words sound like a love story.

'It will be ok because you will understand, even though you don't think you will, you won't go mad, I promise. They always tell people this because no-one wants you to believe time travel is possible.'

Sara said these exact words to me. She went to the window that was painted over; the room was dark except for the light from the candles. I was worried at first that there wasn't enough air in the tiny room, that the candles would rob me of my oxygen before I woke. Rachel pointed out the gap under the door, the cool night air seeping in.

'Tell me about how happy you were and let's get you back there,' she said in the dark.

Then I told them the whole story of the day Pete proposed. Rachel seemed amazed that my happiest day had happened in winter.

'I remember thinking nothing good ever happened in the winter,' she said, more to herself than to me. Then she shuddered.

Sara laughed at her and just said 'déjà vu?' and they both laughed.

I laughed too, more at them than with them.

Rachel was sitting on the edge of the settee and patted my hand. 'Just wait 'til you experience the déjà vu. It's mind blowing.'

I took their word for it, just like everything else.

Sara lit another small candle and leaned on the mantle where the little broken clock sat stuck in the layers of varnish. 'She loves this stuff,' I thought to myself.

'You're a time-travel junkie,' Rachel said to her, and she laughed.

'Guilty as charged' she said, fiddling with her watch.

'Is it really real?' I whispered to them in the dark.

Sara held out her wristwatch. She'd told me earlier it had been found under the floorboards in the house.

'What is a clock if not a time machine?'

She smiled softly like she was the Mona Lisa herself. Then she turned and fiddled with the hands on the little mantel clock stuck in the varnish.

But suddenly she was serious.

'Remember, write it all down, everything you can recall because it will slip through your fingers like a dream.'

Then Rachel was talking. She kept saying this, really stressing it's important to I write it all down as soon as I 're-set' myself. That was her very un-sexy term for it. Re-setting.

'As soon as you see yourself and re-set, get writing.'

She smiled and smoothed my hair.

'Get paper and pen and write down all the good decisions you're going to make. Because it washes away. Like when you're on the beach and the tide comes in. The beach still looks the same, but it's smooth and the shells have moved to different places, and other things have washed away. Memories sometimes pop up, like remembering a dream you once had.'

'Oh, don't worry, I'm going to do a hell of a lot more than just write,' I said to them.

I was already picturing it. The paintings, the drawings.

I picked up the paper and charcoal sketched Rachel, her hair falling around her shoulders.

'How does it work?' I asked not because I needed to know, but because I really wanted to be lulled to sleep. At University I learned that listening to someone explain how something worked sent me to sleep every time.

'I don't know,' Sara said, 'It's something to do with this little clock… This old room. Paris…'

'This is crazy; it can't be real. Can it?' Even though I said this, I knew in that moment it was real. I just knew.

'It's real, I've done it many times,' Sara said.

I looked at Rachel for confirmation, and she nodded.

'I know now that time is just a kind of space. But if you don't make better choices, if you don't actively recall and seek out a better life for yourself it will be just as hard the second time round. Or third. We humans have such bad memories,' Sara whispered to the dark room. There was that Mona Lisa smile again in the light of the candle.

'Tell us again, Karen, tell us about when he proposed, tell us about how happy you were.'

Peter

Winter, 1992

Accustomed as she was to constant worry, Karen stood at the open door, wondering briefly what she would have done if the door had been locked. She knew the door would be unlocked but it took her a few moments to remember why.

Peter.

He would be home soon, and the door to their apartment was always unlocked at this time, ready for him. He would take off his shoes and leave them at the door. She had told him this was important, not bringing the street into their apartment, and god-knew-what off the floor in the kitchen where he worked. Her exhausted boyfriend would tip-toe, as directed, to the shower in their tiny bathroom, washing off the city and the food smells. Then he would crawl onto the low futon bed and sleep while she 'made art' in the adjoining room, her sacred space, he had called it solemnly at first, and then with increasing cynicism as she descended into her selfish chaos.

Shaking her head as if to dislodge the memories, she knew that was then and this was…well this was then again, she laughed to herself.

Time is of the essence, she told herself. The term now had so little and so much meaning at the same time, considering she had just felt it slip free of its moorings and somehow take her sailing back to a happier time. She took a deep breath to calm her jangled nerves, using the breathing technique they had taught her in rehab. Her heartrate quickly returned to normal. She noticed how calm she was, she truly felt like her old self, the way she had felt before things got out of control.

And by things, she meant the drug use which up until then had only run to smoking weed. She had started injecting later that year, after the show in London.

Remembering her arms, she threw her jacket to the floor, pushed her shirt sleeves up to the elbow and let out a whoop. Seeing the flawless white flesh on the inside of her forearms, she kissed them the way a body builder kisses his biceps.

This is it, she told herself, it's really happening, unless she was having an amazingly realistic dream. She resisted the urge to pinch herself. There's no time to waste, she thought, again laughing softly at the old view of time, but all jokes aside she had to get to work creating a blueprint for a better life. She heard a rustling noise and turned to see herself standing in the doorway to her studio-cum-bedroom door, a look of concern and confusion on her face, her own face.

'Holy Shit. What the fuck?' her 1992-self gasped.

'Because we made a mess. We didn't love ourselves enough.' Karen was confused by the grammar.

'Oh. Where did you come from? When?' she said simply, her sad eyes lowered to the floor she held out her arms to her future self. Karen slowly allowed herself to embrace herself.

'The year 1999. Can you believe that? 1999! It doesn't seem real does it? We stopped using though. Everything. We did it,' she whispered in her own ear.

'Don't start,' 1992 whispered back, quickly fading into memory. She stood alone in the hall for a moment and knew what her second tattoo would be, after the letter A.

'Okay,' she said out loud, rubbing her hands together in the cold apartment. 'Let's get this show on the road.'

The day was bitterly cold and after pulling the curtains closed to keep out the draughts, her priority was to turn up the thermostat. It was something she had feared, had become obsessive about, the idea of change frightening her more than slowly freezing to death. She claimed the cold helped her think. The feeling of power that accompanied that one little action of turning up the heat delighted and spurred her on. Almost gliding on air down the short hallway, Karen dragged her jacket back on until the space warmed up and made a beeline for her drawing desk.

Now grateful for her obsessive buying of art materials with any money she got her hands on, she worked methodically, covering page after page in writing, drawings, portraits. Agnès as an angel. She drew stylised maps of Paris, places to go and those she needed to avoid. Working until she had covered every blank surface in the room, except for the canvasses which were next on the agenda. Once a prolific artist, she hadn't created this much new work in years. She felt, at least for the moment, the insecurity and fear that plagued her for most of her life was just a bad dream.

Catching sight of the fluffy koala toy clinging to the light cord hanging from the ceiling, she realised Agnès would still be in Paris. She would be living in her parents' luxurious apartment, still raising hell all over Paris. She hadn't disappeared yet.

Now she didn't have to.

She had run out of paper, so she grabbed a pen and began a portrait of her dear friend and partner in crime, Agnès, on the wall, filling the contours of the huge portrait with snippets of memories as they came to mind. Agnès could not return to Australia and she would have to find a way to convince her friend of this. If she didn't go back to Australia, go into the desert, she wouldn't….

Karen stopped drawing. She was crying, great sobs racking her body. She had talked and talked to her shrink about Agnès. He said in the end there was nothing she could do about it. She couldn't wait to tell him he was wrong, but then he might think she was certifiable, not just a recovering junkie. Time travel and all…

A click interrupted her confusing train of thought and told her Peter was home. Pete, the love of her life.

Her heart began to pound. She hadn't seen Peter for nearly three years…but had only seen him the night before if you had asked her on this day in 1992.

She stopped drawing and pictured him standing in the doorway, exhausted, trying to remove shoes and socks and peel his jacket off without making a sound. Peter, the love of her life. She smiled for what felt like the first time in years, twisting the diamond solitaire on her finger that seemed to fit her again, not nearly slip off every time she put her hand down because she had become skin and bones.

Today he had, would…ask her to marry him.

'Holy sh…' she said, staring at her hand.

She quickly pulled the ring off and went to the dresser that she knew held the ring box, hidden in the summer clothes they joked they would wear for two weeks of the year. Would there be a second ring there when she opened it, she wondered, amused by the possibility. She was not supposed to know about the ring. It had been, was to be, a surprise as they lay in bed. She stripped off her jacket again, amazed by the warmth that had spread through the room and through her bones through her frenzied journaling and adjusting the thermostat a couple of degrees. It was good to feel some muscle and even fat on her skeleton, the way she had been before drugs had left her an empty shell.

As much as she desperately wanted to run to him and throw herself into his arms, she had never done anything like that before, and he would wonder what the hell was wrong. She immediately had the idea that she would find the therapist she had been working with over the past year, in 1999 that was. The retired professor had been her saviour and she knew she was going to need some industrial strength help to make this change stick, but not the pharmaceutical kind this time.

Slipping through the bedroom doorway she stood in the shadows and watched her man silently strip off his shoes and socks and place them in the plastic tub by the door, as directed. The shame she felt almost made her physically ill. She was a bully, there was no other word for it. Shame was new though, she thought, an emotion she wasn't capable yet of in 1992, so she knew that 1999 memories were still there.

Rachel had been right to tell her to write everything down, the memories were lifting like mist, but she knew she had committed enough to paper that she would be able to constantly remind herself not to screw up again, like Rachel had. Karen was determined to learn from any mistakes she could get her hands on, hers or Rachel's or anyone else's who cared enough to share them.

Peter looked up and saw her standing in the hall, jacket in hand, no doubt with an odd look on her face. This jacket wouldn't be in BHV until autumn of 1998 she mused, looking down, him mistaking her thoughtful look for disapproval.

'I'm sorry babe, I won't disturb you again. I'll just shower.'

He looked terrified, shuffling towards her, almost cowering. What had she done to this strong, loving man? Tears sprang to her eyes. She had abused the man who loved her.

It was the old frog trick. A frog thrown in hot water will jump straight out, escape as best he can and get as far away as possible. But put a frog in cold water and slowly heat it up, and that frog will sit there, quite contentedly boiling to death.

'I love you, Pete,' she said, dropping her jacket and stepping over it and into his arms. Taken aback he stood stiffly in her embrace, no doubt wondering what the hell was going on.

'I…I love you too.'

He put his cold arms around her and rested his head on her shoulder. Then he was sobbing silently into her hair. Standing for what felt like an eternity, she eventually pulled back from him and looked into his eyes.

'Everything is going to be better, I promise. I've been doing a lot of…reflecting, and I know I've been an absolute monster. I'm so sorry.'

As many times as he had heard promises of things getting better, he had never heard her apologise and, lost for words he stood holding her at arms' length looking slightly to the right of her right ear. Completely unnerved he pulled her into another embrace, enjoying the contact that had been missing from their relationship for weeks by this stage, or had it been months.

'I'm sorry, too,' he mumbled into her shoulder, although he wasn't sure why.

'Pete, what are you apologising for?'

'I don't know,' he laughed nervously.

She clung to his neck and he picked her up, Karen winding her legs around his waist, she pulled his sweatshirt over his head, throwing it to the floor, a look of horror on his face.

When had she turned into the control freak that couldn't stand a sweatshirt on the floor or a hot sweaty boyfriend in her bed?

She cupped his chin, pulling his gaze away from the offending shirt on the spotlessly clean parquet floor, kissing his full lips, enjoying the feeling of rough stubble on his chin. Never one to dwell on the past, Pete strode the last few steps into the bedroom and lay her onto the futon, pushing the artworks that littered the whole room onto the floor. He stopped and picked up a couple of the drawings.

'Wow, babe, these are amazing.'

'You can look at them later,' she said, pulling her own shirt over her head.

Arrivals

Gare du Nord, Paris. June 2016

Arriving in Paris should only happen by train, and on a Sunday, Rachel often told anyone who asked, and even many who didn't. Many years of arriving in Paris on weekdays, surrounded by commuters and confused tourists had convinced Rachel of this fact. She stood a little apart from the group to phone the drivers to let them know they could pull the cars around. Catching sight of herself in the plate glass windows she smoothed her pencil skirt and adjusted her sunglasses. Perfect scarf, black boots shiny, and not a hair out of place, umbrella hooked over her arm. Her friend Steph said she was rocking a sexy Mary Poppins vibe, and she was happy enough with that. At forty-two, she would take sexy-anything, even Mary Poppins.

Taking a deep breath, she walked back to the group, tucking her phone into its pocket on her tote. The women gathered in a group on the pavement, shielding their eyes from the early morning sun, beside piles of luggage. Rachel was relieved she had opted for two cars for the arrival, knowing that everyone over-packs. The tour details package sent to each participant always urged them to bring as little as possible. Shopping opportunities would be many and varied, and evening wear available to borrow.

The suggestion that they travel light had clearly been taken as a guide only by everyone except Betty, who had a Kelly bag over one arm and pulled a matching carry-on. A seasoned traveller she knew how to travel light, but Rachel knew Betty had the means to simply purchase anything she may need on the fly. Betty's friend Janet stood behind her facing away from the group.

The women began to introduce themselves, sharing names and small details of their lives. Scanning the cluster of eager, smiling faces, Rachel listened to the excited chatter. She pondered, as she did each time a new group arrived, where the week would take them. There would be plenty of tears and laughter, that was always a given. Occasionally other emotions reared their ugly heads, but Rachel knew she had the experience and the training to deal with anything her charges could throw at her. She had been there too and knew the twists and turns life could take. Paris was a great place to confront your demons and practice some self-care. The City of Light was an amazing place to discover your own light all over again.

As she stood exchanging pleasantries with the group, she wondered, as she always did, who would decide to stay and make a life for themselves in Paris. And of course, who might decide to opt for a total life makeover, so to speak.

One previous client had taken the direction to heart, arriving in Paris with little more than the clothes on her back, so determined was she to create a new life for herself and leave the old one behind. Rachel often wondered about the Stayers as she liked to call them. It wasn't for the faint of heart, and she only offered that extra service to those truly in need. They had to be ready to make a go of it. Occasionally, even in a city the size of Paris, she would run into one of her Stayers. As expected, most didn't remember her although she knew firsthand that overwhelming sense of déjà vu it brought with it. She knew it would make sense to them as time passed. Time heals all wounds they say. Rachel knew this to be true.

One of the clients who had flown into London the previous afternoon from Australia, stood away from the group and seem distressed that her phone wasn't working. Rachel moved towards her to offer some help with the phone when it sprang to life and a torrent of text messages came pouring in. Her chosen ringtone, a little like a clown would choose for the horn on his car, rang out through the early morning air to the stares and eye-rolls of passers-by. She seemed unfazed by the attention, visibly relieved to finally receive her messages again. She smiled and began scrolling through the phone, her manicured nails tick-ticking against the phone screen. She began muttering under her breath while the rest of the group stood silently, embarrassed, as the barrage of text messages continued, ringing out loudly over the noise of the train station.

'Oh, it's my son,' she said, as she looked up and saw the nine other women looking at her. 'He misses his mummy, you know.'

A tall woman in jeans, her messy bun piled on her head cleared her throat. 'How old is your son?' Her voice was calm.

This is Carole, Rachel thought. Carole was travelling with her sister and had left her own small children at home with their father.

'Seventeen,' Paula replied. 'He and his partner are looking after the house.'

Text messages continued to pour in. Rachel noticed side-eye glances and disapproving frowns directed at Paula.

'Nonsense. Seventeen-year-olds don't have a partner. At seventeen it's a girlfriend or boyfriend. Turn that phone off, would you?' Betty looked directly at Paula. She looked bored rather than annoyed.

The rest of the group looked aghast at the outburst but then each woman seemed completely fascinated by the contents of their hand luggage. Rachel took a deep breath, as deep as her tight skirt would allow, and prepared herself to mediate a slanging match in the middle of the Gare du Nord but it was clearly water off-a-Dior-raincoat to Paula. She was already busying herself replying to her son's latest missive.

'So cute,' she gushed, 'He wants to know where the toaster is kept.'

'Seriously, can you please put that on silent or something?' Betty said. Janet was rubbing her temples. The rest of the group stood awkwardly by, but Paula seemed to be made of Teflon.

'Seriously,' she mimicked Betty's tone, 'can you mind your own business?' Paula didn't look up from the phone.

Betty took Janet by the hand and steered her away from the group. The group turned to look at Rachel as two sleek stretch limousines pulled up to the curb. Previous groups had made their own way into Paris and met at the hotel, but Rachel's friends in the tourism industry had suggested the stretch limos. It had seemed like a great idea after a glass of wine or three.

Hire a driver, they said. All together in a limo will be fun, they said.

As the group stood in awkward silence, Rachel mentally cursed her friends and their wine-fuelled 'excellent' idea, quickly calculating how she would get Betty and Paula in separate cars. To be fair, the shiny cars were lovely, and they were certainly attracting attention. The passengers snapped a few photos, standing politely back to allow the lucky passengers access to their vehicles. The lead driver rounded the back of the car and opened the rear door with a flourish.

Rachel took her cue and stepped forward. 'Your chariots await,' she said.

Smiles spread across the face of even the weariest traveller as it dawned on them that the elegant stretch limos were for them. Tick that one off the bucket list, ladies, Rachel thought. Perhaps it hadn't been such a bad idea after all.

The caring driver ushered Betty and Janet in first. Rachel waved Ingrid, Sam and Paula toward the car purring behind, handsome driver waiting by the open door, but it was too late. Ingrid and Sam had jumped into the lead car, laughing like children. Paula followed her friends. There was no more room, so Rachel joined sisters Carole and Wendy, and mother-daughter duo Georgia and Judy in the rear limo. Perhaps Betty and Paula will be best of friends by the time they reach Saint Germaine, she thought. Luggage was stowed, champagne poured, and doors shut, and the cars eased their way into the almost non-existent Sunday morning traffic.

Rachel began to point out various sights as they drove, but the passengers seemed more interested in chatting about a Paris wish-list that seemed quite handbag-centric. She sat back and let the conversation wash over her. Although she had travelled over from London with the group, Rachel had had little time to speak to them before the Eurostar. They all appeared quite relaxed on the train, so Rachel left them to their own thoughts, although she was able to take a little time to chat with each lady, put a face to each name from the applications. Rachel used the information in written submissions to match her client groups. It was essential to have like-minded people in a group where rest and relaxation, and often personal transformation, was the motivation for the vacation. She had toyed with the idea of calling her tours 'retreats' but her friends and colleagues who, like her, had worked with tourists for years, felt the clubbing, shopping, and eating aspect of the tours was the main attraction for many of her clients. They feared calling it a retreat would conjure images of waking at dawn for yoga and drinking green smoothies for a week. Not that there was anything wrong with that, it just wasn't what Rachel offered. Unless that was what the group wanted.

Rachel smiled and nodded at an enthusiastic Georgia who was regaling the others with stories of her few months in Paris as part of a study abroad programme.

This is going to be a great week, Rachel thought, but then realised she had her fingers crossed. She uncrossed them and rubbed the tiny dents where her fingernails had marked her skin. Her tour company tended to attract a diverse group of potential clients who had one thing in common; they all viewed Paris as a restorative place to visit. Some groups wanted to look at museums, others were passionate about cooking, and often the wine that went with the cooking, and some wanted to party for a week, but this group seemed…special. Their booking requests all arrived within a week, the group forming organically each time she checked her emails. Each applicant seemed to have come to a turning point in her life. Some were at the lowest point. An illness, disintegration of a marriage, a bereavement, had literally sent them packing, and there were all looking for a way up, or out.

As she had at the station, Paula had stood out in the application process. In her own words, she already had an incredible life and wanted to use this time in Paris to take it to the next level. She wasn't broken-hearted, divorcing, or sick, she wrote, she simply wanted to return to Paris to have fun and let her hair down and come into her own power as a woman. Rachel wasn't at all sure she could help anyone come into their own power, but as her friends were on the tour, she couldn't really refuse her.

Rachel found Paula intriguing. It was refreshing to encounter such a confident and successful woman. Although she normally only took eight guests, Judy's daughter Georgia was not officially attending the tour, so Rachel felt Paula would be easy to accommodate. She obviously did not intend relocating to Paris or appear to need any special help apart from a few days shopping, time at the day spa, and some nights on the town.

After reading their applications, Rachel was excited about the group. She sent acceptance packages and deposits began to roll in. Then Paula's extensive wish list arrived via separate email.

Bienvenue à l'hôtel De la Roche

Rachel smiled at the eager faces around her, congratulating herself and finally deciding that the stretch limousines had been a good idea. Carole, Wendy, Judy and Georgia were relaxed and chatting quietly discovering that they had much in common. Wendy and Judy even knew some of the same people from their teen years surfing around Sydney's northern beaches.

Rachel wondered how things were going in the other car. Betty and Paula were both what Human Resources departments would call strong personalities. Rachel hated the term. They say opposites attract, but these two successful women were so similar they seemed to repel each other like poles on a battery. Rachel had heard many times over the years that you really get to know someone when you travel with them. Betty was obviously used to pulling no punches, and Paula was noticeably adept at ignoring others' opinion of her.

Lost in her own thoughts, Rachel hadn't realised that all four of the other women in the vehicle were looking at her expectantly, remarking how successful the application process was and how well matched they seemed.

'I'm not sure the ladies in the other car will have the same opinion,' Wendy said, almost under her breath.

Georgia and Judy chuckled, and Carole scolded her sister for being rude.

'My sister would be nice to a carjacker,' Wendy said with a loving smile in her sister's direction.

'Here you go Mr. Carjacker, would you like my purse, too?' Wendy laughed, patting her sister on the leg. 'Sorry, sissy. I'm bitter and old, I know.'

Wendy leaned back and closed her eyes. They were sisters but as Wendy was eleven years older than Carole, according to their applications, they were very different people with very different lives. Carole had filled out her application in a hurry, moments when her children were in bed or playing happily, which, with four children under five, a home-based business and a hard-working FIFO husband, were few and far between. She had simply written 'I'm not unhappy, I'm boring! I want a Sabrina Experience!' scrawled in red pen with three exclamation points. Sabrina was one of Rachel's favourite old movies and she had a great week planned for Carole. A session with a personal shopper to whisk her around the famous shopping districts and department stores, a couple of hours at the spa and lots of time to enjoy Paris with her sister. At the end of the week, some of the other women would join in for a photo shoot with a photographer who specialises in vacation shoots around Paris.

Carole was most definitely not a candidate for moving to Paris. She had a happy marriage and small children, and, like Paula, she wanted to let her hair down and enjoy her week in Paris.

Wendy, on the other hand, was more than ready for a new life. This was probably because her old one had completely disintegrated. Her application had brought Rachel to tears. Her marriage break-up and unfulfilled desire to start a family was a little close to home. To add insult to injury, technically, Wendy was homeless, having left the marital home to her husband and his new girlfriend. A real contender for making a permanent home in Paris, either now or at some point in the future…or past, Rachel thought with a smile. A successful partner in an international law firm, she would have no problem finding her way in Paris and would certainly not be homeless, technically or otherwise.

Wendy's application said she had researched the Louvre and wanted to spend a lot of time there. Under the heading 'secret desire' she wrote of her desire to have a 'rustic picnic on the Champs de Mars with a gorgeous Paris fireman then go out dancing and see where the night took them.' With a handful of exclamation points at the end. Secret desire indeed. Rachel often marvelled at how many people's Parisian fantasies involved the legendary Pompiers of Paris.

Rachel looked up to see that the limos were about to cross the bridge to the Left Bank. The car stopped, the driver smiled at Rachel in the rear-view mirror and gestured at the lead car.

'Tourists,' he said, rolling his eyes theatrically.

Rachel pressed the button, the tinted window sliding silently down into the door. The lead limo was waiting at a pedestrian crossing as a large tour group traipsed after their guide who was holding aloft a bright yellow umbrella covered in sunflowers. Rachel smiled, reaching down to touch the Burberry umbrella that was now a permanent fixture in her daily life.

Georgia took advantage of the pause and, opening the sunroof, stood up with her head out of the vehicle. She took a few quick photos then urged the other passengers to do the same. Each woman stood head and shoulders out of the limo, taking their first photos of Paris for this visit. The inclusion of the young Georgia may help everyone relax a little, Rachel thought.

The women were staring at her again.

'Your turn,' Georgia said.

She could hardly say no, so Rachel stood and popped her head through the open sunroof. She watched another tour group cross the road, led by the same bright yellow umbrella. A drone whizzed over her head. Confused, she looked up and down the street, spying the real reason for the hold up. A common sight in Paris, a movie set had taken over the bridge and surrounding streets. A voice on a loudspeaker bellowed 'Cut' and people running left and right.

Would she be in a movie poking her head through a limo sunroof? Rachel hoped not. Filming seemed to be centred on the bridge with their limousines and the small snake of traffic behind out of shot. A young man with a bright orange vest that said 'C R E W' was talking to her.

'It will be a few more minutes, ma'am, is that okay?' the New York accent asked.

'Sure, of course,' she said, flipping her own camera over to video to get some footage for the website. The lead limo gleamed in the sun. She pressed the little red button to start filming when the sunroof on the other car opened. Perfect timing, Rachel thought. Then a bright pink, bejewelled mobile phone flew from the car, disappearing over the railing of the bridge. Rachel almost dropped her own phone and would not have believed it if she hadn't caught it on camera. Sinking back down into the car she fought the sinking feeling in her stomach.

'Oh geez,' Rachel gulped.

'What's wrong, Rachel?' Judy asked.

Georgia jumped up again and stuck her head through the sunroof. Paula's head could be seen protruding from the top of the lead limousine. She appeared to be talking to the others in the car.

'I can see Paula, she's pointing at the film crew I think, and telling the others in the limo what's going on.'

'Well, mmmm…I think Paula has thrown her cell phone through the sunroof, and it went into the river,' Rachel said hoping that was what happened. Something told her that perhaps that wasn't what had happened at all. What she knew for certain was that someone had thrown Paula's phone from the sunroof. Her heart sunk as she showed the women the video she had taken. Sure enough, the bright pink projectile disappeared over the side of the bridge leaving little doubt to its final resting place. Unless it had landed on a barge it would now be making its way to the bottom of the Seine, to rest among the thousands of rusting keys, shopping carts and bicycles. The group had been together a little over three hours, but everyone knew exactly whose phone it was.

As much as she encouraged responsible tourism, Rachel hoped that Paula had simply decided she needed a fresh start, which included a new phone, in Paris. She tried to ignore the butterflies in her stomach.

Georgia was standing up with her head through the sunroof again. Rachel opened her window, craning her neck to see if anything else would be ejected from the limo, and hoping it wouldn't be one of the other passengers. She found herself regretting the limos again. I'm on a rollercoaster, she thought, not an elegant journey into Paris. She was often surprised she got anything done considering how often she over-thought every decision. The limos were lovely but as luxurious as they were, encouraging the client to arrive at the hotel under their own steam often gave them either a sense of ownership over their fate, or left them reeling at the enormity of the city. Dragging a rolling bag up dozens of Metro stairs and across cobblestones was a great workout plus it taught clients a little resilience. It could also bring out some much-needed vulnerability.

Closing her eyes, Rachel leaned back against the leather seat and contemplated the wisdom of making decisions concerning her business while on a wine tour with colleagues, all of whom ran various unique tour companies in and around Paris. She berated herself for a long list of stupid ideas, starting with the limousines.

Stop it. Stop this minute…Rachel told herself. Clearly someone had to take control of the voices in her head. They were being mean! She could hardly blame herself for a phone being thrown into the river, could she?

Who knew what had been said in that car during the ride from Gare du Nord?

'Ooh, I hope the director caught it on film! Like Andie in Devil Wears Prada,' Georgia said.

'She's making a new start,' Judy said, 'Good on her. I should do it too!'

'Or maybe,' Wendy said slowly, 'one of the other women couldn't take it any longer and threw it for her.' Clearly Rachel wasn't the only one who had come to that conclusion.

'Oh, do you think someone would do that?' Carole asked, looking anxious.

'I would have,' Wendy replied.

Carole had taken her sister's hand, Rachel noted. She was getting nervous. Her application, despite its rushed nature, revealed high hopes for her time in Paris. She clearly didn't want anything to jeopardise it.

'Wendy warned me that being on a tour with other people can be…interesting…' Carole said, looking at her sister.

'I don't want you to get too attached to the outcome. Just take a chill-pill,' Wendy said, rubbing the skin between her eyes.

'I told you I won't take any drugs,' Carole whispered to her sister. She smiled apologetically at Rachel.

Wendy laughed.

'What's so funny, sissy?' Carole said, an edge in her voice.

Judy leaned across and patted Carole's hand.

'Georgie explained that to me one day. There's no pill, it's something people say, like whatever floats your boat.'

Georgia was laughing too, and Wendy had hunched over in her seat, her back heaving with laughter. Rachel watched Carole for any sign she was getting upset. She did not want to come across as a crotchety teacher supervising the bus to camp.

'You can be such a 'B' sometimes, you know.' Carole turned to face her sister.

'Oh, stop it, I'm going to wet myself,' Wendy said, wiping her eyes with a tissue. 'Okay, everyone, take a deep breath,' she said. She inhaled deeply, held it for a second and let it out slowly. The other women followed her lead.

'Wow, that is an amazing trick,' Georgia said.

'Very handy in court, let me tell you…and when your husband is trying to mansplain why he cheated.'

'If I'd known how to stop myself from laughing, I would have avoided so many detentions at school.' Her mother raised her eyebrow at this news, so Georgia jumped up, her head and shoulders through the sunroof again. 'Paris is so beautiful, even if you're just sitting in one spot watching the same people walk across a street over and over.' She called out to the other car.

'Georgia, please don't shout in Paris,' Judy said.

The young woman sat down again.

'The other girls are taking turns popping their heads through the sun-roof, too. Sam asked if there was room for her in here. But then she laughed, so….'

Rachel was about to open the car door to see when they could get moving, but she could see the crew dismantling the barricade.

'My guess is that Betty hurled that damn phone out the window as an alternative to shoving it where the sun don't shine,' Georgia said. Judy looked at her daughter over her sunglasses and Wendy grinned at her sister who was looking anxious again. Rachel took a deep breath, mimicking the technique Wendy had taught them.

This will just be another straight-forward week with a lovely group of ladies, she affirmed under her breath. Her mind, as well as her heart, was racing so she took another deep breath. It had been a strange morning and she really didn't need any drama right now. She'd woken early from an odd dream, drenched in sweat. She had seen her own face, floating in front of her. There was a tiger…no, a cat… She couldn't quite get a handle on all the images, but the old familiar feeling of déjà vu was settling over her.

Just as she had calmed herself enough to leave the house, she had found the embossed invitation under her door. The opening of an art show at a gallery that didn't exist, with a painting of her that she couldn't explain.

She opened her eyes to see Wendy studying her. A strand of hair had escaped her ponytail. Tucking it behind her ear, she felt as though she was falling apart. She smiled at Judy. Dreams mean nothing, and one strand of hair does not constitute a bad hair day, she told herself silently as the cars finally began to move.

They crossed the river. 'On your right, you will see Notre Dame,' Rachel said.

'Yes, ladies, Paris awaits,' Wendy said, a little too sarcastically for Rachel's liking.

I am equal to this task, Rachel told herself, hoping the affirmations would start working soon. Despite Wendy's cynicism, the passengers all swivelled in their seats, oohed and aahed at the ancient cathedral forgetting momentarily about the potential drama unfolding in the other limo. The towers of Notre Dame are the cathedral's most photographed features, but the eastern view of the structure with its flying buttresses and formal gardens, were Rachel's favourite view in Paris. Even after years living and working in the city, she still thrilled at the sights as though seeing them for the first time.

The limo stopped at a red light, tourists stopping halfway across the road to photograph the cars with the cathedral in the background. Judy quickly took the opportunity to play tourist, poking her head through the sunroof. She couldn't believe it herself, that she was standing with her head out of a sunroof, in a limo, driving through Paris. If her husband could see her now, she thought.

Ex-husband, she corrected herself.

Judy rested her arms on the warm roof of the car and took it all in, not wanting to break the spell of the city by trying to capture it on her phone. She could see the lead car easily, but no-one was using the sunroof. She wondered what might be going on in there, grateful she wasn't involved. She had had enough drama for one lifetime. She carefully eased herself back down into the car. Had she made a mistake taking a tour? Should she and Georgia have simply rented an apartment where she didn't have to deal with other people?

'I've been here a few times in my life, but I was always working, I never saw the sights, but I feel like I'm home finally. That's strange isn't it?' Judy said.

'No, I feel the same. It sounds nuts, because I've spent so little time here as an adult,' Carole admitted.

'Yes, well you will see the sights this time and I hope you love it even more when it's time to go home, or make it your home, whatever the case may be!' Rachel said. 'You'll be a virtual local by the time I'm finished with you!'

'Oh yes please,' Georgia pleaded, 'I'm definitely moving here. I love Paris so much. I'm going to write and take photos, and paint and live in a gorgeous apartment. A small one, of course, but nice. With a view. Dad said he'd help me,' she finished, not looking at her mother.

'Perhaps I will become a local, too,' Judy mused quietly.

'Mum, yes! We can be room-mates,' Georgia laughed.

The limousine slowed to a crawl as it made its way down a narrow alley. Finally, they stopped again, and the chauffeur opened the door for the passengers. Smiling as he welcomed each passenger to Paris, reaching his hand out to help each lady exit the vehicle with style, their smiles lighting up as he did so. When the clients were standing in the laneway, Rachel took another deep breath and, taking Myles' hand, stepped out into the bright sunlight.

The women were already tumbling from the other limo, not waiting for the driver to help them from the vehicle. Betty and Janet, were first, followed by Sam. All three were clenching their lips, as though trying to keep a straight face. Paula emerged, red faced, and tear stained. Rachel raced to her side, placing a protective arm around the woman's shoulders. Ingrid scrambled from the car, immediately going to her friend's side, making soothing sounds, like she was trying to pacify a toddler.

'Stupid old bitch,' Paula hissed at Betty as Janet held her friends' shoulders. Rachel wasn't sure if she was holding her back, or upright.

Sara, their host, stood in the shadows of the carriage entrance, unseen by everyone but Rachel. Having worked in her mother's private hotel for years she was used to highly strung clients arriving for their 'retreat', but Rachel suspected today's events had taken things to a whole new level. Ingrid moved forward and took her crying friend's hand. The rest of the group held back to give Paula some space.

'Oh, screw it,' Betty said, scanning the faces that were desperately trying to avoid eye-contact with her. 'Aren't we all here to enjoy ourselves, to leave our old lives behind for a bit. Maybe even to start again?'

'Betty, please…stop,' Rachel interrupted.

'No, I won't stop. That damn phone beeped and shrilled the whole way here. I asked you to silence it. Everyone did.'

Paula's tear-stained face blushed red, while Ingrid and Sam stared at the cobblestones.

'We're all here to have a good time and we owe ourselves a little bit of self-love, ladies. You can't move forward if you're looking backwards, well you can, but you'll probably fall flat on your arse. Your son will be fine,

Paula,' she said, placing herself in front of Paula. 'Give him the opportunity to miss you, or at least to have to find the toaster or make do with bread. Woman let it go,' she said, now standing in front of Paula, looking directly into her eyes.

'Let it go,' she said again. She took Paula's hand and held it.

Paula stood staring at her own hand, gently resting on Betty's own tiny hand. Paula appeared to be traveling through a full spectrum of emotions, no doubt wondering how to extricate her hand from this crazy woman in front of her. Rachel towered over both, her boots making her at least twenty centimetres taller than them. Two petite women would be easy to pull apart if there was a catfight in the street.

'Leave me alone. I don't need you to tell me how to behave. I am a surgeon!' Paula hissed.

Betty put her hands up in surrender. The sounds of Paris seemed to drop away as the group stood in the lane, unsure what to do next. Rachel looked over Paula's shoulder and gave Sara a look that said, "Get your butt out here lady, and help me." At least she hoped that's what the look was saying.

Sara pretended to step back into the foyer and close the door, silently laughing the whole time. Rachel shot her another look that hopefully said, "don't you dare."

Sara took a deep breath.

'Welcome to Paris, Mesdames, Bievenue à l'hôtel De la Roche," said a voice from the shadows as their stylish host stepped out of the old carriage entrance and into the bright sunshine.

Lunch at the Hotel Déjà Vu

The scene in the laneway was a first for the hotel, somehow managing to operate for ten years without guests screaming obscenities at each other in the quiet street. Sara was glad her parents were not present to witness the scene. Quickly regaining her composure and politely waving at the neighbours, she stood welcoming each lady in turn as they walked through the enormous doorway and into the cool dark foyer.

Young and effortlessly stylish, but with a wisdom beyond her years, Sara often sat listening to a crying client well into the early hours of the morning and had seen her fair share of bad behaviour from drunken guests. She had a nonchalance about her that came with youth, but she cared deeply for her clients, and showed it in very practical ways. Singling out the distressed Paula, she put her arm through hers and led her to the elevator that whisked them to the top floor kitchen. Leaving the rest of the clients to mill around in the foyer while she paid special attention to Paula could have seemed antagonistic, but no-one begrudged Paula a little special treatment.

In truth, they were relieved, glad to be spared any more drama, making themselves comfortable in the spacious foyer, sinking into chairs and sofas, grabbing magazines from the huge coffee table. Rachel waited for the luggage to be unloaded, the drivers leaving it neatly stacked in the carriage entry. She thanked them and confirmed with Myles the collection time for the next morning. He would be their driver for the next week. Ten in the morning and not a minute before, she reminded him, experience telling her that no-one would be ready to leave the hotel before mid-morning.

Rachel had only two important tasks on this introduction day before she could have a well-earned dinner with Sara and Marie. The first thoroughly enjoyable task was the tour of the magnificent private hotel they would call home for the next week. As they walked through the stunning building, each guest gushed appreciatively at the luxurious bedrooms, the comfortable living rooms complete with library, music room and inviting over-stuffed couches piled with feather-filled cushions. The group, one-short while Paula was being fussed over by Sara, made their way down the carved stone steps to the basement. They were gobsmacked by the sparkling swimming pool in the cavernous area; dipping their toes and splashing each other. Not one woman glanced in the direction of the gym equipment which made Rachel laugh.

'Paula and I will probably go running each morning. Like we do at home. If anyone wants to join us…' Ingrid asked, looking at Sam, who screwed her nose up at the idea.

'There is a great gym-club just off Boulevard Saint Germaine. It has an indoor running track,' Rachel explained. 'I suggest people use this as a safer alternative to running on the street. A previous guest had a nasty fall on a slippery cobble-stone, so if you're running, please make sure you take care, and take a companion with you, and of course there is the gym equipment here.'

Two-by-two they made their way up the stairs to emerge at the fourth-floor landing. Tall glasses of sparkling water waited for them on the terrace with views towards the towers of Notre Dame and each lady took turns posing for photos in the beautiful space. They turned at last to enter the heart of the home, even though it was on the top floor, the incredible farm-house style kitchen and dining room where they would meet each morning for brunch.

'Brunch at nine,' Rachel reminded them. Shoulders relaxed and deep breaths were taken. She winked at Sara.

'We believe that nothing worth talking about ever happened before nine in the morning,' Sara said.

Paula looked up from her steaming cup of tea and seemed restored to her previous poise. Ingrid went to her and hugged her shoulders.

'So, Mesdames, welcome to my home, and yours for the next week. This house has been in my family for more than one hundred years. My great-great grand-Père was born in this house in 1889, the year that the Eiffel Tower was built. My ancestor was a prominent physician, his wife who I have been told I resemble, an artist. Many of the paintings you see on the walls here are her work, including the self-portrait on the landing that many believe is moi,' Sara said. She walked over and stood under the ornately framed painting. She struck a pose to mimic the artwork, to murmurs of surprise and amusement. Well-rehearsed at her spiel she could have done it in her sleep. She loved her home and loved to share it and its history with her guests.

'You are welcome everywhere in the hotel, except of course for the maintenance rooms near the pool and the third floor, which is my family residence. My mother and father, and my brothers live here also. Ben is a chef and Sebastien, or Bas for short, is in IT. They help with the hotel sometimes, but they work in day jobs too, so you probably won't see them at all. Bas is home today so he can help with your phones or laptops if you have any problems with the Wi-Fi. You can simply ask Rachel and she will organise it. We have Claudine who helps us with the housekeeping. I think you will find everything you need in your rooms, in the living room and here in the kitchen, but if you need anything at all, please let us know, or once again, ask Rachel.'

She looked over and smiled at Rachel who took her cue.

'Thank you, Sara. And thank you for hosting us over this week in your unique and beautiful home. I welcome you all officially and express my deepest gratitude that you chose to spend this week with me, to re-discover what makes you smile, what is truly important to you and what turns your light on!'

A polite round of applause followed, and Rachel waited, a small smile on her face. She never really knew what to do while people applauded as they always seemed to do at this point, so she stood awkwardly, looking at Sara. She made a mental note to change her introduction speech to something less likely to inspire spontaneous applause.

'Thank you. It's going to be a lot of fun. Sam and Ingrid, could you please show Paula your room and give her the quick tour after lunch? Here are your keys.'

Rachel handed antique iron door keys each with a different jewel-coloured ribbon attached. She stressed the importance that the keys stay here in the hotel as they were almost impossible to replace.

Sam, Ingrid and Paula were sharing the only triple room; a large space with its own kitchen, which they all vowed to avoid using for anything more taxing than making a cup of tea. Carole and Wendy, Judy and Georgia took the three rooms on the second floor overlooking the walled garden, mother and daughter sharing a room. Wendy, having paid for her sister's trip, had splurged on separate rooms for them knowing she would welcome the space and her sister would welcome the novelty of a King size bed all to herself. Janet and Betty had spectacular adjoining rooms in the original attic of the home with private lift access. It had once been servant's quarters, but now housed a luxurious suite with a private bathroom and views across the roofs of the arrondissement to the Pantheon.

'In your tour documents you have been given a time slot this afternoon. This is your special opportunity to sit with me and discuss the week, how you are feeling, and if there is anything you have forgotten that you would like to do here in Paris. I will give you the phone numbers you need, including the contact number for Myles, our driver for the week.'

There were smiles all round. The limos had been a huge success after all, and Myles was such a sweet young man.

'I will answer any questions you have, in person or via text, during the week, you can also make suggestions and we will endeavour to make your dreams a reality. A point of housekeeping, none of the antique clocks here in the house are functioning. Sara and her family keep them for sentimental and decorative reasons. There is a digital clock here in the kitchen, one in the lift and one by the pool. It can make for some confusing times, but please don't try to adjust the clocks. You don't know what might happen in a magical old house like this. You might end up in the 19th Century!' She winked theatrically at Sara to laughter all round.

'Let's get washed up for lunch and then, when we are all finished, around 4.30pm, we will synchronise our watches and phones, and you are free to go crazy and take in the sights of Paris. Tomorrow morning is our first day-spa session, and the car will collect us here at 10am.'

The buzzing group moved away to their respective rooms to freshen up before lunch. They hadn't eaten since breakfast in London, hours before. Paula chattered noisily about how much she loved the unique space the three women would share over the coming week. She threw herself on the fluffy duvet on her bed and rolled around. She seemed happy to shake off the frustrations of the morning. Splashing water on their faces and running fingers through their hair, they all but raced back up the stairs, meeting the rest of the group on the landing. It seems they had all decided to make their way back to the dining room quickly. The traffic jam on the stairs forced them to admire the paintings and the smooth stone steps.

'Imagine the stories in a house like this,' Carole said to hums of agreement all round.

'Lunch is served,' Sara announced.

The group made their way from the landing through the cosy sitting room and found their places at the enormous table, exclaiming all at once about the food and the setting. The view through large plate windows was dominated by the ancient building opposite. Sara explained a little of the history of the street but only Carole seemed interested. She sat giving Sara her undivided attention while the others were focussed on the delicious meal.

After lunch, amid offers to help with the dishes that were declined by Sara and Claudine, the guests headed to their rooms to settle in. Rachel sighed, grateful for the opportunity to stop smiling for a few minutes. Sara left Claudine to clean the kitchen, coming to the table to hug her friend.

'How are you? How's your mother?' she asked Rachel.

'Got the all-clear, apparently. She's feeling much better but I hope she wasn't saying that so I would be back in Paris in time for this tour, but she insisted.'

'And the doctors? How are they coping?' Sara asked, a cheeky grin on her face.

'You know my mother! She wasn't impressed with the diagnosis and told the doctors she would recover fully within the year, and well, she did. Even cancer can't keep that woman down. I thought I was going home to bring her back here for some much-needed Paris-time, but she's fine. Miraculous really,' Rachel explained.

'Are you okay?' Sara asked.

'Yes, I'm fine. I hated leaving her. I can relax around mum. Being in Australia was so weird though. I was overdressed everywhere I went. Mum thought it was hilarious when I took her for physiotherapy in vintage Dior. She laughed so hard the doctor thought she would hurt herself. She's always cheering me up and she's the one with cancer!'

'She is a touch cookie,' Sara said.

'Tough,' Rachel corrected, laughing. 'She's a tough cookie. Yes, she is!' She hugged her young, but somehow old, friend tightly and they both laughed.

'I will never understand those silly sayings. All our sayings in French make sense.'

'Oh, like Aller se faire cuire un œuf?'

'Oui! This makes total sense. You are annoying me, so go and cook yourself an egg, instead of annoying me!'

'Bon, tu a un pet de travers,' Rachel replied, triumphant to Sara's look of surprise. 'Telling someone they are farting crooked. Now, that makes no sense!'

Sara laughed until she couldn't breathe. Rachel had lived and worked in Paris for years and still struggled with the more complex aspects of the language at times, but she had worked out every idiom, curse word and insult known to the average French dock worker.

'I will go so you can do your work with your lovely ladies, so then we can go for a drink, you Aussie Legend.' Sara loved using Australian, English and American idioms as much as Rachel loved the silly French sayings whose origins were now lost to time. 'Do we have any free nights this week, chérie? Can you find time to have a nice meal?

'Of course. There's Thursday night while the ladies are going to the clubs with Stephanie…but first I'm going to…an art show. I think. It's across the lane here. There was an invitation slipped under my door today. Will you come with me? And then we can go to dinner…' She was rambling and her heart was racing.

Rachel placed on the table a creamy white folded card with the words Mère du temps in matt black lettering and what appeared to be splashes of watercolour paint across it. She pushed it towards Sara. Sara looked up at her friend's face.

'Déjà vu?' Sara said, eyes sparkling, her hand lifted for a high five.

'Déjà vu!' Rachel confirmed, laughing, slapping her friend's hand.

Sara looked down at the gallery invitation. 'Oh, it's you! With your hair all loose, like you used to wear it,' Sara exclaimed, delighted to see a portrait of Rachel that was simple in its style but rendered such an instantly recognisable likeness.

'That's beautiful work. A friend of yours? Oh, this is going to be across the street. In the old shoemakers. That's a bit - weird.'

'No, it's very weird. Very, very…I always… saw a gallery there…remember? I don't know the artist, but they obviously know me,' Rachel said.

She lay her hands flat on the table as though examining them.

'At first, I was creeped out, I thought I had a stalker. But I did a little online stalking myself. Mère du temps, is the nom de plume she uses. Do you call it a nom de plume when it's a painter? Her pseudonym, I guess...' She trailed off unsure whether to continue with Claudine, the Housekeeper, in the room.

'Mother Time...' Sara said. They both sat staring at the card.

'Sara, I think it's Karen. You know...the artist that had the...the drug problem...? She went... back...?' she whispered, raising her eyebrows at Sara and motioning towards the stairwell.

'Ah, mon dieu! I have that memory too. Do you think it is her? Have you never met her? I mean, again?'

'No, but she knows me on some level. She put this under my door, at least someone did,' she said, pointing at the gallery card portrait. 'You know how strong the feeling of déjà vu is? We live it every day...I told her to write it all down. As Marie told me. Just like you do every time you go...back,' Rachel whispered.

Her eyes were glued on Claudine at the sink for any sign that she might be listening, although the headphones firmly planted in her ears and the tuneless humming suggested Bruno Mars was the only thing on her mind. Sara put her finger up to her lips and tilted her head signalling a move to the cosy sitting room off the kitchen. They shut the door behind them.

Rachel felt as though she had been holding her breath again. 'It's been years though. She wanted to go back to...was it Christmas, 1992? That's 25 years ago! Look at the photo on the back. She's absolutely covered in tattoos. It's strange, I recall so much of that night, the first time she and I met, on the stairs...in, was it 1999? Who knows what's changed? Oh, it's hard to remember. Anyway, I remember showing her my little 'A' tattoo. She was horrified at the idea of the needle, of getting a tattoo, even though she was all scarred from the drugs. I think her husband is a chef, not that those things are related, but he's just taken up as Chef de cuisine at Entre Amis...' She laughed awkwardly staring again at the invitation to the exhibition that stared back at her with her own eyes. 'I'm rambling again...'

'Yes, you are...so he's at Entre Amis, where maman worked all those years! That's a funny coincidence, isn't it?'

'I know, right? It's all too weird. But I know it's her now. Speaking to you like this, I can feel it. If only she had put her name on the invitation and not just the pseudonym. It's puzzling why she waited this long to contact me,' Rachel said.

'Maybe she found her notebooks again. You lost yours for years and forgot all about it…remember?' Sara crossed her eyes and laughed. The grammar of time travel was, is, always tricky.

'What do I do? I can't just waltz into the gallery and say 'hey, this portrait looks exactly like me. Is this a neighbourly thing or were you a drug addict in an alternate time-loop and I sent you back through a time portal and well, you seem to have made a better go of it second time around!'

They both laughed.

'No, this isn't something that happens every day,' Sara said.

'Are you worried she might…tell people…' Rachel made circular hand gestures.

Sara copied them. 'I don't know what this is.' She waved her hands around in circles, 'But no, I'm not worried. Who on earth would believe in time travel?'

All roads lead to Montmartre

Judy and Georgia were first to sit at the vast farm-house style table with Rachel, excited to see what was in store for them over the following week. Judy was a picture of style as she almost glided into the kitchen in a gold Camilla kaftan. The former model was stunningly beautiful but had a quiet sadness to her that made Rachel want to cry.

On her application she touched on the cloud that hung-over her, the depression caused by her on-going and bitter divorce. She seemed fragile, like she was made of tissue paper. She had phoned Rachel from Australia late one evening to ask for the special favour of bringing her daughter, as an honorary member. 'I need her with me, to keep me from doing something…unforgiveable,' she had whispered into the phone.

'That's perfectly fine, Judy. It will be a pleasure to have you both. We will work out the costing for meals, that kind of thing and email it through. Are you okay tonight?'

'Yes, I'm fine. Georgie is here with me. I hate that I lean on her so much, but I've just received the divorce papers and…'

'I understand, Judy. I've been through a bad breakup.'

Soft sobs came from the other end of the line.

'Rachel, I have to find something to live for, other than my daughter. It's too much pressure for her. She has her own life ahead of her.'

The conversation had begun awkwardly but within half an hour she and Judy were chatting like old friends. Rachel wondered if Judy would take up the option to stay in Paris, to make a new life, make up for lost time. Or go back and do it all again… When the time came, she would make the offer, although no-one with children ever chose to go back. It would be her first and after that conversation, she knew it was a long shot.

The week in Paris was Judy's fiftieth birthday gift to herself and she was enchanted that the events planned for the week would include dinner at Jules Verne restaurant on the Eiffel Tower for her special day. Along with day-spa visits and a makeover, mother and daughter would be enjoying a photo shoot in various locations around Paris. They would also be making time to enjoy each other's company, wander the streets and take a personal shopping tour. They pored over the glossy brochures and itinerary.

'I want mum to let her hair down, laugh and have fun,' Georgia repeated which was met by an eye-roll from her mother.

'I can't let my hair down, it's too short.' Judy stuck her tongue out at her daughter. 'And can you stop fussing over me, please? I'm fine. I just need to relax.'

'I know, mum, but you've been so sad, and I want to hear you laugh again. She's got the best laugh,' she said, looking at Rachel.

'And of course, I know I'm not part of the tour, but I just want to find a nice apartment and a job and fall in love with a cute French boy. One with a family farm and a beach house!'

'Just that,' Judy said, making little speech marks in the air, 'do they have bridal registries in Paris? And knowing you, George, it will probably happen,' she said hugging her smiling daughter.

'Oh, mum, no bridal registry yet, but I do have my sights on some new shoes.' She whipped out her phone and showed Rachel the shoes and boots she had been researching.

'You can show the personal shoppers those photos and they can take you to the high-end stores, but I always go to the stores up near the university. They are well priced, and you know the sales are on now?'

'I saw that on a few of the blogs I read. Thanks so much Rachel. I'm going shopping tomorrow while mum is at the spa. I will meet you late for the walking tour, if that's okay. So much to see.'

Her enthusiasm was contagious, and made Rachel fall in love with her job all over again.

'What are you planning to do this afternoon?' Rachel asked.

'We're heading up to Montmartre. I'm told that's the place to be on a sunny Sunday afternoon!'

Rachel used the minutes between appointments to skim the other applications. Janet's had been filled out by hand and scanned, her graceful handwriting an insight into her artistic nature. Betty's, on the other hand, was short and concise. She was familiar with Paris and had many friends here in the city, having lived and worked here over the years, but had recently sold her apartment. Janet and Betty were up next, but Betty came alone.

'Janet's taking a bath and a nap, so she can be fresh as a daisy for dinner tonight. She's a bit self-conscious about her illness. She was so vibrant; you should have seen her when she was twenty. She was magnificent. And now…she's very shut down.'

'Yes, well I hope we can help her. I know what it's like. Paris, and being shut down are my areas of expertise,' Rachel replied, a wry smile on her face.

Betty reached out and patted her hand. 'Come out with us tonight, I'll have you and Janet up on the table and dancing!'

'Oh, did I mention I have plans tonight,' Rachel laughed, looking at her watch. 'Where are you heading?'

'We'll take a taxi up to Montmartre. A lot of memories for us there. The three of us…Janet's husband…all lived there many moons ago, so it will be fun to see the old haunts, if they're still there.' She paused briefly, a flicker of something across her face, quickly replaced by that big smile. 'I'm sorry. About the phone thing. I feel awful. Not about the phone, that was inevitable. I'm sorry for making everyone feel uneasy.'

'I understand what you're getting at, but it was a bit over the top. You'll need to apologise to Paula,' Rachel replied, looking Betty in the eyes.

'Yes, I know. I've already ordered her a new phone. The latest one. It will be delivered in the morning.'

'That's a good start,' Rachel smiled.

They sat in silence for a few moments, both reading the tour documents and brochures spread out on the table. Then Rachel ran through Betty's and Janet's wish-list coordinating some key events with some of the other clients.

'We're both excited to be part of this group,' she began, 'and we hope to be able to enjoy all of the planned events, but we are older, so we'll enjoy them in our own way. I hope that's okay?' she asked, the Boss-Lady façade falling away, showing a little vulnerability for the first time that day. Rachel assured her it was perfectly fine and couldn't resist the urge to hug her. Not a hugger by nature, she couldn't explain it. Betty seemed a little surprised by the impulsive show of affection, but all the self-help books and counselling courses had told Rachel that she should go with her gut, and her gut, strangely enough, had told her to hug. Her gut had never done that before.

They both laughed a little awkwardly as Rachel helped Betty with the phone numbers that would keep them connected over the week.

'Is it my imagination, or has Janet not uttered a word since she arrived?' Rachel asked.

'Yes, well, that is a bit of an issue. She's fine with me of course, but she hasn't spoken to a soul since her husband passed. Not even the kids. They're freaking out, of course.'

'Wow, okay. That makes it interesting, but we can accommodate anything. Call me, any time. If you or Janet need anything, remember Gerard, Marie's husband, is a doctor, a General Practitioner. You have his number,' she said, patting the documents. 'Don't hesitate to call if you need him. He is the most beautiful man.'

'I will keep that in mind. Janet is loaded up with enough medication to fill a hospital, so I think we will be fine, but it's reassuring. I have a physician here in Paris, though. And a plastic surgeon,' she finished, discreetly pointing at the various body parts she had had work on, to an increasingly amazed Rachel.

'Why don't you organise Myles to take you to Montmartre this evening?' Rachel asked her.

'It sounds funny, but we want to take a taxi. That's how we arrived the first time. Our car broke down at the bottom of the hill. It had brought us three all the way from London. Phillip stayed with the car and luggage…such a good man….and Janet and I took a taxi up to find our lodgings. I want to re-create that moment of arriving. A limousine wouldn't be the same.'

Betty had disappeared into the lift when Sam, Paula and Ingrid climbed the last step, tumbling into the kitchen, laughing. Sam was panting lightly from the stairs.

'Maybe I should take you up on the offer of going for a run with you,' she said to Ingrid.

A fleeting look of annoyance crossed Paula's face. Rachel made a mental note that there was some animosity between Paula and Sam. Paula sat down and opened a leather travel dossier. With a click and a swipe, she opened the itinerary for the week on her tablet.

'Can we please go over my wish-list….err, our wish-list? Lists…' Rachel was having trouble getting a read on the mood between the three women. She pulled Paula's application from the pile. It was certainly well-researched and lengthy. A first for Rachel, she had a long list of things she absolutely did not want to see in Paris, the Louvre being one of them. She had written, "regular visits as a child ignited a passion for all things French, but I have simply visited that museum too many times. I have no intention of being bored!!!" A couple of extra exclamation points drove the point home.

Sam and Ingrid had sent their applications on the same day, Ingrid from Australia and Sam from the UK. Childhood friends, Sam had given the trip as a gift to Ingrid for her recent 52nd birthday. No-one had said as much, but Rachel had the distinct impression that Paula, Ingrid's friend and employer, had invited herself on the vacation. Her application had arrived the following day. Ingrid and Sam stood at the windows. The view always drew people in; the ancient façade of the building opposite seemed to change colour and shape as the light shifted during the day. Even at night, the lights from the surrounding buildings gave it life. Paula had taken the chair closest to Rachel. 'So much to do, so much to see,' she said.

Rachel smiled and took a deep breath. The other women took the seats opposite. Rachel ran through the details of the week. 'Of course, the tour of the Louvre can be skipped if you like, you can window shop, or…'

'We don't want to skip the Louvre,' Ingrid and Sam said in unison.

Paula sighed. 'I've just been there so many times…'

'I've never been there,' Ingrid said, almost apologetically.

'Paula, you can do the walking tour with me. We'll go on to the wine tasting and the others can meet us, okay?' Paula looked at Ingrid for a few moments. Was she trying to get Ingrid to change her mind about visiting the museum? Ingrid seemed to be avoiding catching Paula's eye.

'Fine,' Paula said, although it didn't sound fine at all, but then she brightened, 'All the other plans sound great though.'

'Great,' Rachel replied, gathering up the documents and handing them to each woman. 'Is there anything extra special that you want to add?'

Ingrid and Sam looked at each other and then at Paula. 'No, really Rachel, it all sounds amazing. We just want to wander through Paris arm in arm,' Ingrid said. Once again, she was being careful with her words, careful whose eye she caught. She kept her face trained on Rachel's.

'That should be easy to accommodate. Where are you going tonight?' Rachel asked.

'Montmartre,' the three women said and laughing they said their goodbyes as Wendy and Carole arrived at the landing. Carole was gripping her chest and breathing hard. Ingrid hovered around her, concern etched on her face.

'Sorry, I'm joking, those stairs are so steep,' she moaned.

'Take the lift,' Paula said. Her tone was unreadable but fell somewhere on the aggressive side of condescending. Each woman in the room turned to face her. She looked puzzled for a moment. 'What? It makes sense to take the lift,' she said. 'If she's struggling so much…'

'I'm fine, I just need to get used to it. I've got little kids, I'm pretty unfit…' Carole said.

Wendy glared at Paula. The lift doors opened. Sam and Ingrid rushed in while Paula gathered her things.

'I'll meet you in the room. I'm going to take the stairs,' she said.

Wendy stared after her as Carole took a seat at the table and picked up one of the glossy brochures.

'She's a piece of work,' Wendy said.

Rachel cleared her throat and Carole patted her sister's hand but said nothing. She was obviously the peacekeeper of the family.

Wendy sat at the head of the table. Rachel found people endlessly fascinating. None of the other women had sat at the head of the table, instead choosing the seats either side of Rachel. The sun had dropped lower in the sky, the softer light of the afternoon filling the kitchen with a warm glow.

'Oh, I could live here…' Carole said softly.

'It's a special place isn't it?' Rachel replied.

Running through the wish list, Carole became more and more enthusiastic, but Wendy seemed distant. Like Judy's, her application had brought Rachel to tears. Here was a woman who had been screwed over by her ex-husband and needed…time. She and Judy, who'd experienced similar heartbreak, would find each other over the week, she knew from experience. Rachel didn't have to bring them together; it would happen.

'Of course, your shoot is booked for Thursday,' Rachel said.

'Shoot? What shoot?' Carole asked. Rachel looked at Wendy. The photo shoot had been her idea.

'We're doing a photo shoot, sissy. Fancy clothes, makeup, camera…the whole nine yards,' Wendy explained.

'Oh…My…God, sis!!! Thank you. It's a dream…'

Wendy rolled her eyes as her sister hugged her excitedly, but she had a huge smile on her face.

'So, you're all set. Where to for dinner?'

'Carole read in the guidebook that Montmartre is the place to be on a sunny Sunday afternoon in Paris. So, Montmartre it is.'

...a little too much Champagne

All roads led to Montmartre that evening. Sunday in Montmartre is magical, and each small group made their way in search of some of that famous magic, and perhaps some champagne. Sam, Ingrid and Paula bumped into Georgia and Judy, chatting and getting to know each other better on the journey. They stopped the taxi near the Pigalle Metro station and went hunting for the gelato store Georgia had raved about. Strolling in the late afternoon heat, licking their ice-creams, Judy spied Wendy and Carole waiting at the Funicular.

'Yoo hoo,' Ingrid called, waving her arms around to the delight of the elderly gentleman walking towards them. He hesitated in front of her and smiling, took her hand, kissed it and continued on his way. They all stopped in their tracks and stared after him. Ingrid put the hand up to her heart.

'Only in Paris, eh?' Sam said, nodding her head in the direction of the elderly gent.

They caught up with Carole and Wendy and laughed and hugged like old friends. As many people as there are in Paris at any given moment, and as many cafés, bars, restaurants and bistros found in the city, the group found a table at a touristy bistro just down from Place du Terte, as Betty and Janet emerged from the taxi. Georgia jumped up and threw her arms around them as if they were her much loved aunts, not women she had met just hours before. Forgetting her plan to exude Parisian polish and style at all times, the young woman practically dragged them to the table, excitedly asking them about their plans for the week.

'I love your jumpsuit,' she gushed to Betty.

Betty could tell that Georgia was comfortable around older people and managed to speak to her and Janet respectfully, minus any patronising. She was grateful for the enthusiasm and energy Georgia brought to their group.

The waiter hovered and Betty took charge, ordering charcuterie and champagne for the whole table as a busker wandered towards them with a violin and held their rapt attention. The sun slipped down behind the low buildings and the sky took on that perfect blue that Paris does so well. Meals were ordered, and the drinks flowed. Sam and Judy were in deep conversation, Wendy and Betty telling travel stories while Carole and Georgia listened intently. The violinist, who had now been joined by a puppeteer, played.

Ingrid took a deep swallow of the last of her champagne and hiccoughed. 'Betty, where did you buy your outfit?' she asked a little too loudly.

'This is a Young British Designers' piece, the girl who does these is just out of college. Amazing talent,' Betty called across the table.

'Oh, don't you think it's a bit young for you?' Paula asked. She glared at Betty.

Betty didn't flinch. 'I don't' think clothes have an age or a use-by date. I love vintage Chanel as much as I love Matthew Williamson.'

'Oh, but people have a use-by date though, surely…'

'I don't use people, Paula, so I am left wondering what you mean.' Betty didn't look away. Janet's hand gripped Betty's arm.

Paula pulled her tablet from her tote and turned her back on the group. She held up the tablet to video the busker. A ripple of chatter went around the table and each woman glanced at Paula. She stood and clicked a few buttons on the tablet. She seemed oblivious to the tension she had caused at the table and began a loud video-call with her son.

'You should come to Paris,' she said smiling into the screen. Others in the busy restaurant were turning to watch her. She held the tablet up to show him the view.

'Mum, I have to go…it's morning here. Text before calling in future,' he said, and the screen went blank. She stood staring at it.

Wendy shook her head. 'Paula, come for a walk with us,' she said brightly, pulling an already tipsy Carole to her feet. Carole reached out and patted Paula's arm. Paula shrugged it away and took her seat at the table. She opened an app on the tablet and began to type.

Carole looked at her sister for guidance. Wendy shrugged and took Carole's arm and steered her towards the market stalls. Most were packing up for the day and were quickly being replaced by wine sellers and oyster bars. The daytime buskers giving way to a band that was setting up on a purpose-built stage.

Betty waved a hundred euro note at the violinist. He took a deep bow as though he had just finished to a standing ovation at the Opera House. The young puppeteer pretended to refuse the money unless he received a kiss and blushed on cue when he bent to gently brush cheeks with her. Betty smiled up at him. He bowed and tucked his puppet up onto his shoulder and melted into the crowd.

'Only in Paris…' she said to Janet. She had tears in her eyes. Janet took out a clean tissue and pressed it into her friend's hand.

The band were belting out 60s classics and groups of people were rock and roll dancing like professionals in the square. Wendy and Carole wandered back towards the table. Georgia jumped up.

'Let's dance.' She held out her hands to them.

Wendy smiled and shook her head slowly. 'I need a lot more champagne if I am going to dance,' she said and sat back down.

Carole grabbed Georgia's outstretched hand and they joined the spinning couples on the dancefloor. Six-foot tall with long flowing hair, Georgia quickly became the centre of attention. Sam got up and Judy joined her. They had no idea how to do the moves that everyone on the floor seemed to know, but soon they were being spun all over the dancefloor by far more experienced dancers.

Paula held up her tablet to video the festivities. She felt ridiculous holding up the huge device but as her phone was at the bottom of the Seine it would have to do. She opened the group chat she had created especially for the trip and posted the video. Only Ingrid had joined the chat. Oh, and Sam, she thought.

The barman called last drinks. She looked at the time.

Thank goodness, she thought, feeling weary. She had been awake for more than 24 hours. She lowered her eyes and stole a glance at Betty and her friend Janet. Janet had not introduced herself and Paula felt that kind of thing was unforgivable. It doesn't take much to say hello, no matter how sick or tired you were. As a surgeon, Paula knew that well. She began packing up her things. The manager was talking to Betty about the bill. Paula leaned across and slid a fifty euro note towards her.

'Oh, that's okay, duckie, it's my treat,' Betty said, sliding the note back.

'Duckie? Really?' Paula glared at Betty. The manager went to the bar and returned with another bottle, this time whiskey, and a tray of glasses. Paula looked at him, then the tray, then across at Betty. Betty arched her eyebrow. Paula quickly looked away. Ingrid was reaching for the glass Betty was holding out to her.

'Ready to go?' Paula said to Ingrid.

Sam and the others had sat back down. Betty passed the pretty cut-crystal glasses along the table, their contents glowing in the candlelight.

'Salute' Betty said, and the group raised their glasses.

Paula rolled her eyes at Ingrid. 'I think we should go now,' she said, but loud enough for the group to hear. No one seemed to have any intention of going anywhere.

'Just have a drink and enjoy yourself, dear,' Betty shouted over the music. She held up a glass for Paula to take.

'I'm not your fucking dear, and I don't need you to tell me to enjoy myself,' Paula took her tablet out again. She opened up the App store to see if she could download the Uber app.

'I can throw that tablet out into the square for you if you like?' Betty said through gritted teeth.

Paula kept her head down but felt her heartbeat in her throat.

'You know, I am already tired of trying to be polite when you are obviously determined to ruin your own time in Paris along with everyone else's,' Betty said lightly.

'Oh, so throwing my phone into the river and offering to smash my iPad is you being polite? God help me if you start really trying to upset me,' Paula said.

Shaking her head, she shoved the tablet back in her bag. She pushed her chair back and walked over to where Ingrid had begun swaying in time with the music. She grabbed Ingrid's hand, dragging her reluctant friend into the square. Ingrid draped herself over Paula's shoulder.

'I didn't pay all this money to come to Paris, leave my family to fend for themselves, and be intimidated and insulted,' she said quietly to the night.

'Mmmmm?' Ingrid said.

They walked slowly around the square. The crowds had thinned dramatically, and the still-warm night air stirred with a cooling breeze. They reached the opposite side of the square and turned towards the Sacre Coeur. They could still hear the party going on behind them. Paula was fuming.

'She's rude and obnoxious and thinks she can flash her money and people will do whatever she says.'

Ingrid pointed at the lit domes of the church in front of them. 'Paula, ignore her. Yes, you came all this way to have fun and enjoy. Stop worrying so much about your kids. They will be fine. You need to concentrate on you.'

'I know, I never put myself first, do I? I need to learn to be more selfish, I think.'

Ingrid stood and stared at the white domes of the church glowing in the dark sky, swaying slightly. 'I'm a bit drunk...'

'She gets under my skin...' Paula said.

'I feel a bit...sick...' Ingrid said.

'We've worked together for years. You know me, Ingrid, better than anyone. You know I always find the best in everyone.'

'Let's keep walking...' Ingrid said.

'Are you even listening to me?' Paula said.

'Yes, of course...I'm just a bit...tipsy. But yes, I agree. You are very good at finding people's faults and then pushing just about every button they possess. You have strong opinions and that's okay because you're a doctor and that's import...ant...' Ingrid hiccoughed and held her hand up to her mouth.

Paula stared at her friend and colleague.

'What?' Ingrid said. 'You've just got your nose out of joint, Paula. With this group of women...they're successful, educated...beautiful women. Judy, Georgia and...Wendy...stunning women, even in Paris...You're always the smartest person in the room...like that poster on your wall says.' Ingrid draped her arm across Paula's shoulders and smiled into her face. 'Betty has been a bit mean, though,' Ingrid conceded. She gave Paula's shoulders a light squeeze and set off down the street. 'Let's go see the view...' she called back at Paula who was still standing in the middle of the lane.

Ingrid's words were still ringing in her ears. She turned and set off after her friend who seemed to have picked up speed. Ingrid turned the corner and disappeared, so Paula broke into a light run. She rounded the corner and saw Ingrid ahead, leaning against the fence, with all of Paris spreading out before her and the magnificent white stone church towering behind them. Paula stopped in front of Ingrid; her arms folded across her chest.

'I don't feel well. I think it was the oysters,' Ingrid said.

'It was all the booze you drank. How could you say such a thing to me?'

'What did I say?'

'That rubbish about me being jealous.'

'That doesn't sound like something I'd say,' Ingrid said, a look of genuine confusion on her face. 'Betty probably said it, I don't think she likes you very much.' Paula stared at Ingrid; her fists clenched.

'We should get back, Paula, I've left my bag on the table.' She set off towards the square, leaving the late-night crowd and Paula behind her. Paula wondered how she was going to get through the week now that that awful little bird of a woman had managed to turn her best friend against her. She turned and ran after Ingrid again. It wasn't difficult to catch her, despite Ingrid's long legs, she was tottering on heels and had obviously drunk far too much. Paula fell into step, still seething.

'Paula, you're a good friend,' Ingrid slurred.

Paula smiled at her and nodded. Yes, I am, she thought, too good a friend to get upset about drunken nonsense. Ingrid was drunk and had a tendency towards moroseness in that state, but Paula had never been the brunt of her friend's drunken words; she usually reserved those for her husband. Ingrid's life had been stressful for a while and she had tried to do all she could for her friend without being condescending. It was clearly a case of jealousy, but Paula knew Ingrid was the one battling with the green-eyed monster.

'You're a good friend, too, Ingrid. And you're a great nurse. I love working with you.'

Ingrid smiled and took Paula's arm. 'I am a good nurse,' she said firmly. 'We should go and have another champagne. Where's Sam? Sam's a good friend, too.'

Paula stopped but quickly took a little hopping step to catch up. Sam, the third wheel.

'You know we met at high school, me and Sam? But she's not tied down, like we are…' She stopped. 'Did you want to get married, Paula?'

'Uh, yes…come on, we gotta get back. I'm tired.'

'No seriously, did you want to? Did your husband get down on one knee and…?'

Place du Terte had become quiet and the band had finally stopped, packing their instruments away and melting into the night. Paula continued walking towards the rest of the group but stopped to see if Ingrid was still following her. She could see her friend in the middle of the square, looking at the smooth old cobblestones as though she was searching for something. She walked back to help, but before she could ask what she was searching for, Ingrid spoke.

'He never asked me,' she whispered.

'Who? Who never asked you what?'

'Joe. He never asked me to marry him. He just bought a ring and we set a date. He didn't ask, he just…assumed…' She trailed off. 'I got married by default.' Ingrid laughed. 'I don't want to get in the taxi, Paula. I always go with the flow and I'm not doing that anymore.' She turned and began to walk back towards the onion domes of the basilica glowing in the night sky.

'Oh no you don't, Ingrid Maurer. I'm tired but I'm not going to let you get mugged in Paris and I'm not walking all the way back to the hotel, so you will get in that taxi willingly or I will carry you over and throw you in the trunk!'

Ingrid put her hands on her hips and bent over, her shoulders heaving. The rest of the group tumbled from the restaurant in a pack, heading towards two waiting taxis. Sam stopped and pointed at Ingrid standing in the square. She held up Ingrid's bag and then gestured towards the taxis. Paula ran back, took Ingrid's hand, steering her towards the group.

'Hurry up, Ingrid, I need to pee,' Georgia called.

'So much for the Parisian poise,' Judy said.

Ingrid took her bag from Sam. 'Ok, I am going to get in the cab. Only because, only because,' she wagged her finger at Paula, 'only because I want to, and because Sam's here…and it's a bloody long walk and my feet are sore. I might be a little bit tipsy. I just want you to know I am making a conscious decision…because Georgia has to pee…'

She finished this speech by gently poking Paula in the forehead with her finger.

'Oh, so it's because of Georgia's bladder, not because I asked you,' Paula was too tired to be properly angry. 'Let's go.'

As they walked towards the taxi Ingrid leaned on Paula's shoulder.

'You're lucky I decided to get in the taxi. I don't think you could pick me up if you tried. I don't even think you could piggy-back me…'

Paula laughed. The thought of her piggy-backing Ingrid along a cobbled street in Montmartre was just too ridiculous. A minute later, they were both doubled over laughing, with the rest of the women watching on, wondering what on earth was happening. They walked together to the waiting cars and everyone piled in, all laughing now, although they had no idea why.

'It's good to see you laughing,' Betty said.

Paula's face fell. Ingrid had already squeezed in next to Sam. Judy, Wendy and Carole took the other seats.

'Come with us,' Betty said, holding the door open.

'I'd rather walk,' Paula growled, but climbed into the car.

UNIQUE PARIS TOURS

Please tell us a little about yourself! Betty Edwards-Grey. Google me!

The first time I saw Paris… 1948. I have memories…snippets… my hand held by a nanny in the Luxembourg Gardens. It's like a photographic image in my mind and watching my parents walk away from me, hand in hand. We were a close family, but my parents had that kind of love that outsiders couldn't penetrate, not even their children. My father loved to tell everyone that I invaded France on the same day as the Germans. There is a photograph of my extended family standing in front of the clinic where I was born, in Perpignan and my witty father had labelled it 'The British Invasion of France'. We were lucky to live in Andorra. It was safe and a very good way to grow up. We visited Paris on route to London after the war.

Is there a song that reminds you of Paris? I saw David Bowie at the Olympia in 2002 – he was remarkable. Or anything by Jacques Brel. I was at that concert too, in '66…

Is there a scent that takes you back every time? Sadly, whenever someone blows cigarette smoke in my face, in the street, I am transported back to the city of light. I am really not the romantic type!

What's on your Must-See list? Must see list? Just want to see my dear friend Janet enjoying herself, I want to sit on a terrace and drink a good Cognac. I want to visit Fontainebleau, but if that doesn't work in with the schedule, Janet and I will get there under our own steam. I want to relax and have fun.

Do you have a secret wish for your time in Paris? To travel back in time to the Paris of my youth! Hahaha

UNIQUE PARIS TOURS

Please tell us a little about yourself! Janet Walker… Age? A lady never tells!

The first time I saw Paris… You will have to forgive me if I cry a little too often. I've been unwell, and I lost the love of my life very recently, although any length of time would be recent. I still refuse to believe he is gone… We arrived in Paris together and Betty too and lived in a studio. We lived and painted in that tiny studio. My husband's work especially was very popular with the Americans who flooded Montmartre. We did very well. They were brilliant years. Betty's father owned an apartment in the centre of the city, and we moved there when I fell pregnant with our eldest. That was 1968 and the riots and everything, we moved back to Australia. It wasn't the same. Montmartre is special.

Is there a song that reminds you of Paris? Anything by the Beatles. We drove up to Hamburg to see them perform at the urging of a friend whose name is lost to time… The snow was heavy, and we made it back to Paris just before midnight on Christmas Eve.

Is there a scent that takes you back every time? My husband had no sense of smell, very handy for an oil painter, so I would come home to a very heady smell each day and throw open the windows. I painted watercolours, en plain air, out in the countryside with a group of women painters. We thought we were so avant-garde, all wearing men's suits and hats. Pretending we were starving artists, when we were all collecting money sent by our parents. A long answer to your question…paint thinners and the smell of oil paint.

What's on your Must-See list? That's easy, Montmartre and Fontainebleau.

Do you have a secret wish for your time in Paris? I wish my husband was still alive and waiting for me in that little apartment in Montmartre.

Monday

Judy glided into the sunlit breakfast room on espadrille clad feet with Georgia following, sunglasses pushed back onto her head. Carole was cradling a mug of steaming coffee, but she raised her hand in greeting. Georgia dropped the sunglasses down over her eyes.

'Good morning, Judy, Georgia. A little birdy told me that Montmartre will never be the same again,' Rachel said.

'I'm never, ever drinking champagne again,' Georgia said, pressing her fingers to her temples.

'Rookie…' A voice from the elevator chimed across the room as the door hissed back to reveal a very put-together Betty, and Janet who was looking tired but happy. There were a few quiet chuckles at Betty's joke. Georgia hugged Janet and Betty and asked them about their plans for the day.

'This…is for you,' Betty said, plonking a small white box in front of Paula. Before Paula could respond Betty continued. 'We're heading to the spa with all of you, of course. Lately, when I'm in Paris, I've been going to the Anne Sémonin over near Galerie Vivienne, I've been a regular at Le Meurice for years. Will you be joining us, Georgia?' Betty asked.

Paula rolled her eyes. 'When I'm in Paris…' she muttered and pulled a face. Ingrid choked down a laugh. Betty ignored them but Georgia took a deep breath and flashed her eyes at them. Paula glowered at the young woman, but Ingrid lowered her gaze and picked up her coffee cup.

Paula opened the box. It was her new phone. Betty had already moved on to breakfast, but Paula wasn't looking her way. She held the shiny new phone up for Ingrid to look at, but Ingrid seemed completely absorbed by the task of eating her croissant.

Georgia cleared her throat. 'I won't go to the day spa, Betty, but I will hitch a ride in the limo. I'm going shopping and hopefully to get my nails done at a place I used to go to when I was staying in the Marais. I'll meet up with you all for the walking tour and,' she stopped to take a deep breath, 'the wine tasting.'

The room gave a collective groan at the mention of the word 'wine'.

Rachel poured the coffee and quickly explained that she had taken the liberty of shifting the wine tasting to another evening.

'Tonight, instead, it will be dinner at a quirky restaurant after the walking tour. Champagne optional.'

She ran through the day's itinerary. A light lunch would be served at the spa and afterwards, Rachel explained, they would make their way on foot to the restaurant over near the Eiffel Tower, weather permitting. They should all bring their umbrellas and wear sensible shoes she reminded them, lifting her own red Burberry high-top sneakers from her tote.

'No booze for me tonight. Thank goodness we'll get some exercise, and our livers will have some recovery time,' Carole said.

'Speak for your own liver, lovey,' Sam said, putting on a Groucho Marx accent.

'It would make more sense to do the walking tour, then go to the spa? We'll be all…sweaty…' Paula said. The rest of the group looked at Rachel.

'We are going to stroll in the quiet of early evening, not lace on our Nikes for a run. There will be no…sweat,' Rachel said, screwing up her nose for effect. She laughed and the rest of the women realised she was joking.

Paula shrugged.

The group enjoyed a relaxed breakfast, relishing the peace and quiet, the delicious food and her own company. Little was said, each one either lost in their own thoughts, reading or perusing maps and guidebooks. Sara's brother, Ben, came in to help Paula sort out the new phone, leaving her grinning. She tucked the phone into her skinny jeans.

'It fits perfectly, don't you think?' she said, wiggling her backside at Ben.

The young man blushed and looked at Rachel, his eyebrow arched exactly the same way both his sister and mother did when puzzled. Rachel jumped up from her chair.

'Great phone, Paula…and you look great today…not to mention fresh as a daisy. You didn't get into the champagne last night like this lot, then?' She crooked a thumb at the table to laughter all round.

'No, fresh juice and water for me. Not that I'm judging, I prefer to keep my head straight. I have a lot I want to accomplish this week.' She smiled in a way that could be construed as smug if one was being picky. Rachel was still hopeful that a slightly more relaxed Paula would make an appearance soon.

'I like the new rose-gold phone, Paula,' Georgia said.

'I've been thinking of getting one of those,' Wendy said, picking up her own phone. She handed it to Betty. 'Can you do mine today…?'

The group erupted into laughter. Everyone except Paula. Ben grinned and stared at the floor as he left the room with the discarded packaging.

Paula took a deep breath and turned to Georgia. 'Thanks, yes, it's the same model I had, until yesterday,' she paused and glared at Betty, 'but it's the new colour.'

She pulled the phone out of her pocket. 'And I have a new ring tone…' She pressed the button and a tinkling bell sounded. She nodded towards Rachel who smiled.

'That's wonderful, Paula. Remember, ladies, phones on silent at the spa.'

Everyone nodded. Betty studiously avoided making eye contact with anyone but had a smirk that would have made a schoolgirl proud. Rachel made a note that she may need to have a quiet word with Betty to see if she had offered Paula an apology along with the shiny new phone, perhaps give her the old 'life's too short' speech, but she figured Betty should already know that. Performing a quick head count of who would be joining her at the spa, Rachel texted their driver to give him a time to meet them in the street.

That first Monday morning at the spa usually set the tone for the week, quickly pinpointing those who were keen for a transformative experience, and those who were in need of a break from their daily routine, an opportunity to focus on themselves.

'Enjoy the facials, ladies, I…am going back to that comfortable bed,' Wendy said. 'I will meet you later for the walking tour?'

Rachel nodded. Wendy bent and kissed her sister on the cheek. 'Have fun.'

'Fun! Are you kidding?' Carole said. 'I can't remember the last time I even had a haircut without at least one child hanging off me, let alone spent hours in a day spa at an international hotel being indulged. No bed is that comfortable!'

Rachel's phone trilled. 'Okay, driver's here in five…'

Ten minutes later Rachel, Judy and Georgia, Ingrid, Sam, Carole and Paula waited in the stretch limousine for Betty and Janet.

Paula sighed. 'Once again we're waiting for Lady Elizabeth.'

Sam and Ingrid glanced back and forth between themselves, but Georgia couldn't contain her frustration.

'I expected someone of your profession to be more compassionate.' The teenager glared at the respected surgeon. 'You know Betty is in remission from cancer and she's had a double mastectomy, right? And Janet's sick, too. And she hasn't spoken a word since she got here. Have you noticed that?' the young woman demanded.

Paula was lost for words, dropping her gaze into her lap. Silence descended on the plush car as Betty and Janet emerged from the enormous blue carriage door. Myles helped them into the vehicle and shut the door.

Betty looked around at the blank faces. 'Okay, who died?'

Rachel turned the dial on the air-conditioner. Cold air blasted them. 'It's hot today, isn't it? she said with a nervous laugh.

'Actually, I was thinking it was already pretty frosty in here,' Betty said.

As Myles drove along the busy Paris streets the tension in the car dissipated. Rachel dialled back the air-conditioner as the passengers put the windows down and snapped photos of the city, glorious even with Monday morning traffic. Cameras clicked and Georgia caught Rachel's eye and nodded towards the sunroof, silently asking Rachel if she could open it.

'Georgia is going to open the sunroof, ladies, hold onto anything not bolted down.'

Rachel laughed, hoping it would further lighten the mood in the limo and to her delight the group visibly relaxed. Only Georgia and Carole took turns to pop their heads through the roof, the fun having worn off for the others. The two younger women were thoroughly dishevelled and decidedly un-Parisian by the time the car stopped in the rue de Rivoli. Each lady seemed enchanted to find the gloved, outstretched hand of the dashing young driver assisting their exit from the limo. There was something in that small gesture by the young man that made each client smile. Rachel thanked Myles who bounded back to the driver's seat with a renewed spring in his step too. Rachel noted that there was something about kindness that benefitted even the giver, always an unexpected bonus. Then she realised the young man was probably happy to be acting as personal driver for the gorgeous young Georgia who waved to them from the back of the limo.

Rachel directed the group to follow the young attendant from the spa who met them on the curb. She watched the women walk into the spa, mouths open in awe, Paula snapping photos with her new phone. Rachel waited back to give a few last-minute directions to Georgia who was thrilled to have the limousine to herself. Once the car drove away Rachel snapped a few photos of her own for her socials. The sun was shining on the stunning façade of the old hotel and red geraniums tumbled from stone planters as the doorman helped a guest with his luggage. Some days she loved her job more than others and this was one of those days.

The staff stood in a tidy line to welcome the group, small smiles on their perfectly painted lips. Betty, the last to arrive in the softly lit foyer, was greeted small cries of delight and delicate air-kisses by each beautician. Paula stood rigid, her back pressed against the wall, clutching her bag to her chest.

'Don't mind me…' she mumbled.

Rachel picked her way through the gathered ladies and gently prised Paula out from between the upholstered easy chairs. 'I will introduce you to Charlize, she is a miracle worker,' Rachel said but immediately regretted her choice of words.

'You think I need a miracle?' she said, glaring at Rachel.

Rachel didn't miss a beat. 'She gives the most incredible massage,' she said, steering Paula towards the passageway where a woman stood waiting with a fluffy robe and a bottle of sparkling water. She left Paula with Charlize and made her way back to the foyer.

Some of the beauticians had dragged themselves away from Betty and approached their assigned client. Betty introduced Janet to the two remaining attendants, in her flawless French. Janet was her dearest friend, she told them. Could they pay particular attention to her as she was unwell? Rachel knew Janet was ill of course, but only from Betty's disclosure; there had been nothing in Janet's application about her illness. Understandably Janet wanted to keep her illness private, although it was obvious to anyone paying the slightest attention that she was not well. Rachel had assumed it was a result of the long-haul flight and the aftermath of her late husband's slow demise from cancer. Experience told her that people usually had good reasons for keeping secrets. Her own mother had refused to tell anyone outside the immediate family that she was ill.

Betty appeared to be relishing her role as caregiver to her oldest friend, as Rachel's own father had stepped into the role of carer during her mother's illness, although his own health had suffered a little in the process. Betty however, appeared to be a picture of health, which was incredible considering the nightmare of breast cancer she had endured over the past year. Mother hen one moment and teenage-style bad influence the next, Betty was determined that she and Janet have the time of their lives in Paris, but Rachel wondered if Betty had told her friend about her own health challenges.

Standing to one side Rachel nodded her head at Betty as she and Janet made their way to the massage rooms, though deep in quiet conversation they hardly registered her presence. She wondered if she would have a friendship like that in her own life, if it wasn't too late.

Satisfied that each person had a treatment plan and had been paired off with a beautician to dote on her, Rachel relaxed a little. While she would have previously sat in the business centre of the hotel, working on emails or checking her social media pages, Rachel decided on a rare treat. She had booked a manicure and facial in the luxurious spa, feeling it was well-earned and long overdue. She took so little time out these days, she sometimes forgot how it was done. She sat in the plush leather chair and the manicurist handed her a warm scented towel.

An hour later, enjoying her post-facial ginger tea and admiring her newly polished nails, she overheard Betty entertaining some of the staff with her version of what she was calling the Flying-Phone incident. Obviously used to the spotlight, Betty was now poetically referring to it as the moment she jettisoned an unnecessary anchor for Paula, adamant she had done her tour-mate a favour for which she should be eternally grateful. Fortunately, the whole story was told in French and while it did not pay to assume anything in life, she was fairly confident that Paula did not speak French and would not understand if she did happen to overhear.

The staff hung on every word Betty said, quietly laughing at the brazenness of it, though she figured that somewhere in the building, Paula was telling her side of the story, attentive Charlize nodding sympathetically, scandalised by the offending behaviour.

The fact that Betty didn't appear to care one way or the other what Paula thought of the situation possibly irked Paula more than the thought of her phone at the bottom of the river. Despite the stories told over breakfast of fun times had by all at Montmartre the night before, Paula seemed as fixed in her opinions as Betty, and Rachel knew she had her work cut out for her if they were to all enjoy their week. She hoped they could move past their differences; they were similar people and could be wonderful allies if they could both stop trying to be in control. She was grateful for Georgia's reproach in the limo. It seemed to have some effect on Paula, but Rachel had to convince Betty to keep her opinions to herself.

Rachel found herself chuckling as she listened to Betty regale the staff with a story about the antics of the various interns that had passed through her publishing house. She had developed a professional distance over the years but found herself enjoying Betty's company. Betty reminded her of her own mother. She was a woman who seemed to live life on her own terms, but Betty had that je ne sais quoi; incredible personal style, impeccable grooming and a sexiness that most women half her age would love to exude. In her tour application she had written that she lived life with no regrets.

Rachel wished she could say that herself.

UNIQUE PARIS TOURS

Please tell us a little about yourself! Carole (Wendy's sister!)

The first time I saw Paris… oh, that's a song or a movie or something, isn't it? See, distracted already! Okay, so the first time I visited Paris I was a baby, my sister was twelve. I am so keen to see Paris again. My memories of my first visit to Paris come from the photos of my sister holding me on her hip standing in front of the Eiffel Tower, the view from a hill somewhere, eating ice-cream, riding a carousel. There's a great photo of us standing under the gorgeous little arch in the Tuileries. I know now that it's called Arc de Triomphe du Carrousel but when I was a kid I would fantasise that it was a magical gate. hahaha!

My second time in Paris was a couple of crazy days in the summer of, now I have to think. It was 1999?? I just had to go and find the photos to check. I was on a bus tour and we were arriving in Paris for our first night. We had three nights in Paris! I thought it was way too long at the start. My boyfriend had just broken up with me, right there in the bus! And he was already moving in on a new girl, right in front of me. Mortifying. I was travelling with him, and now he had broken up with me, and I had to spend three whole days in the city of love while he got with someone else (she ended up dumping him for the driver! Ha!). And it rained, the whole time! It rained for three days and three nights straight. On the tour of Notre Dame Cathedral, one of the guys dropped to his knees and started praying out loud for an Ark. It was funny then but now I think of how rude it must have seemed to the actual worshippers. Double Mortifying.

Is there a song that reminds you of Paris? On that tour, I will never forget as we drove up to the Eiffel Tower, the music blaring in the bus. The song was Un-Pretty by TLC. That was our break-up song and when I hear it, even now, I can picture the tower, all of us piling out to take photos in front of the clock on the tower, the one counting down to the Year 2000! It wasn't a great start to a 21-day trip (!) but I had a great time. Actually, it was amazing. So what if my boyfriend dumped me as we drove towards Paris? I wasn't going to let that stop me from enjoying the trip I'd saved up for! It was a mad couple of days in Paris, and to be honest, I fell in love with about five different guys during those few days. The city is intoxicating. I was a different person when I came home, I was a different person when we left

Paris to head for Amsterdam, if I'm being really honest. And the boyfriend. I have no memory of him on that trip at all. He's there, in a few of the photos… I'd like a new song to remind me of Paris, I think.

Is there a scent that takes you back every time? That's a funny question…. Impulse, that spray cologne. There must have been a different variety on that bus for every girl.

What's on your Must-See list? Wendy and I want to stand under the little arch again, and pretend it's a magical gate… I would love to go to Montmartre, have dinner at a swanky French restaurant and go SHOPPING! A bistro! I want to have my hair done and nails done…

Do you have a secret wish for your time in Paris? Is it too much to ask for that? Can I have a Sabrina Experience? Can you send me home to my gorgeous hubby and my wonderful kids a completely different person…? Can't wait!

UNIQUE PARIS TOURS

Please tell us a little about yourself! Wendy Carpenter - I am a lawyer first and an academic second and woman somewhere at a distant third.

The first time I saw Paris... The first time I saw Paris, I love this questionnaire! It's so sweet! That first visit to Paris was just my parents and me, in a tiny apartment tucked behind Gare St Lazare. It was 1978 and the only thing I can recall from that visit that isn't tied to photographs was the smell and sounds of the train station. The diesel, the smoke, the whistles. I'm sure the smells and sounds that I fell in love with no longer exist, now that everything is electric... I was ten years old. Still young enough to enjoy the playgrounds but old enough to notice that all the nannies were African. I wanted to be a train driver, but the nanny told me that little girls didn't drive trains. I should be an air hostess instead...

My parents were journalists and we travelled through Europe for a couple of summers. We would wander the streets, sit in café's, go to protests, regular tourists...and then they would write all night and submit articles to all sorts of magazines and newspapers. It wasn't easy to do back then, without the internet, but life on the road was fun and cheap. My sister, (Carole who will be writing her submission while hiding in the bathroom with a glass of wine and a bag of M&M's), was there on the second of those trips. She was nearly 12 months old and kept me fascinated and busy for hours. How lucky for my mum that all I ever wanted was a baby sister and she was able to give me one. I was 16 before I truly realised that Carole wasn't a gift to me, and that my parents had had sex to create her. What a shock that was. I didn't look dad in the eye for a few days, and when he found out why he had laughed till he had a coughing fit. I laughed too. Eventually.

Is there a song that reminds you of Paris? oh it's so cheesy, but I loved that song Woman in Love by Barbra Streisand. It was the second trip to Paris, when Carole was a baby, which stands out in my memory. That old song...mum and dad would sing it to each other if it came on the radio. My dad would waltz a little around the room and we would all laugh, even Carole. So, when you ask, what songs remind me of Paris, that song, most definitely!

There's another song. The other song is one that I can't even listen to anymore. 'All I want to do is Make Love to You' by Heart makes me feel violent, homicidal. I need to heal that because it breaks me. It was 1990, during my very short, whistle-stop honeymoon and this song played everywhere. Everywhere! You could even hear it in the metro. Often enough I was unable to find the source of it and began to wonder if it was in my head, so in love was I (gag). Not.

Is there a scent that takes you back every time? No not really. I can't wear Anais Anais anymore but not because of Paris…

What's on your Must-See list? I want to see the Louvre. I didn't get to see it on my honeymoon. My husband said we didn't have time. We had arrived in Paris on a rare day that it was closed, and although we toyed with the idea of staying an extra day, we had a ferry to catch. I have avoided visiting the Louvre, I could have flown to Paris, at any time, but there was something that stopped me. And Carole would love to have a photo shoot…together. That sounds like hell to me, but I'll do it for her. She is my baby sister after all. We want to visit the little arch near the Louvre too, the Arc du Carousel, or something like that…I should Google it, but I'm sure you know it well. We have some old photos of us standing under that, she was a baby… It seemed like a magical gateway to me then.

Do you have a secret wish for your time in Paris? Then I come to the most difficult question. You want to know my secret wish? This is something I have never told anyone but my husband. For many years my secret wish was to have a child of my own. Helping my mother to raise my sister was so rewarding and my sister and I are so close. I dreamed of having that kind of relationship with a child of my own. It's tough for me to voice my secret wish. My whole adult life has been about ignoring my heart and going with whatever my head was telling me to do. I don't know if having a baby is on the agenda for this week in Paris (I joke!) so I will tell you my second secret wish. I want to picnic on the Champs de Mars on a blanket, with cheese and wine. That's all. Just a lovely group of people, a warm summer's day, to laugh and be free…

Wendy

Wendy burrowed into the huge plush bed and pretended to be sleeping. Carole had been so excited about the day-spa, but Wendy knew herself well, and knew she needed some space. Her alone time was for everyone's safety, she liked to joke. It wasn't a joke, though. She hated that she was jaded and bitter and would wallow for a few more hours before putting on her big-girl panties and starting her new life. Carole had told her the first thing they both needed to change was their preference for actual big-girl panties.

'If you're going to bag a sexy fireman, you're going to need sexy lingerie!' Carole had laughed as she began tossing Wendy's sensible knickers at the window. If the window had been open it would have been hard to explain to the garbage truck driver emptying the bins in the laneway below.

Carole told Wendy she had dodged a bullet. No man to answer to, no children to worry about, an amazing career, and plenty of money. It sounded like the perfect life to the stay-at-home mum of four. Wendy wished she was able to look at her own life that way. On paper, she had it all, but wondered why it felt empty and wrong without the man who'd treated her worse than anyone had ever treated her in her whole life. She'd interviewed serial killers who'd been more honest about their life choices.

The truth was she was enjoying feeling sorry for herself, bizarrely relishing the pounding hangover and the dry throat. God knew she had no more tears left. She'd tried to cry the previous night, with two bottles of champagne under her belt, reading the text messages Jim had sent her over the past year but she was cried out.

Images of the night before played out in her mind. Betty had stood up at the end of the table and made a little speech. She urged the group to forget the regrettable and remember the critical, or something like that. For a tiny woman, Betty could sure put away the champagne and still inspire the troops like a miniature Churchill. She'd pointed at Wendy and told her she was beautiful and intelligent and any man who couldn't see that wasn't worth crying over. Wendy knew she was right but had given the tears one last shot.

She lay under the fluffy duvet and considered writing a list of all her good points, something her therapist had said would help. She'd read enough self-help books lately to know but knowing the wildly expensive psychologist had also suggested it helped. A little voice in her head kept her from grabbing her journal and pen. Everyone knew what Einstein had said about madness: doing the same thing and expecting a different result. The flip side of that was the much more positive 'if you want something different from what you've always had, you have to do something different from what you've always done'.

Cliché and all, the words were still true. And powerful.

So, Wendy lay in the soft bed and fell asleep until midday, something she had never even managed as a university student. Then she stood under the huge rain-shower and told herself all the good things about herself that she could think of, including things Carole said that she didn't truly believe. She wished she could be the person her sister thought she was. To Carole, Wendy had freedom, money, prestige and a certain glamour, an aura that made people do whatever she asked them to do. This irritated Wendy. Carole knew how hard she had worked to achieve all she had and how it had cost her the love of her life, her self-respect and her youth, not necessarily in that order. Carole had said herself that Jim had always been threatened by her success. Wendy had worked her ass off to get where she was, while Jim was forever 'finishing his novel' and Carole was partying her way through an Arts degree then raising her children, Wendy was studying and working long hours and kissing ass. Countless days spent unpacking dusty boxes of papers, researching and finding answers to questions. Carole had enjoyed family holidays while Wendy had travelled to remote communities, helping people protect their land from unscrupulous developers and governments.

That had been her life in a nutshell. Looking after everyone else. To be fair, Carole constantly reminded her, and everyone within earshot, how many people Wendy had helped, saying she was Wendy's fan-club president, that she deserved her 'corner office' and her art collection. She deserved her success.

What she hadn't deserved was the way her husband had treated her. Leaving her was one thing, she could put that down to growing apart. Marriages do that, she'd told herself. It wasn't her fault and she'd even forgiven Jim, knowing that he'd struggled with his writing career and felt he'd failed, despite his success as a teacher and lecturer. It was that one little lie that stole her future. You can't miss what you never had; she knew that. It's simple logic. But she couldn't forgive.

The whole family had been charmed by Jim. He was always the guy helping wash the dishes after the party. Carole had told Wendy that while she was away for work, he would visit her and their parents for meals, play with the kids and often spoke about her work and how proud he was. He would give the 'behind every great woman speech' so often it elicited good-natured eye rolls and yawns from the other men in the room. Jim had been a gentleman and a scholar, literally, even during their breakup.

He had told Wendy that she was even beautiful in her grief. This had earned him a slap which Wendy knew now he had been wanting all along. He'd wanted her to get angry, to punish him, but she'd been stoic and silent as though struck dumb by his betrayal. Carole had assured him in various emails, phone calls and social media posts, that if he had been her husband, he would have felt the wrath of a woman scorned.

When Wendy had not fought for the house, Carole had lost her mind, but it had been his mother's house after all. Carole had protested that it was an old house and Wendy had spent thousands on it. It wasn't fair, but then Wendy had always known life wasn't fair. She'd researched enough crimes to know that life didn't discriminate, and sometimes awful things happen to good people and good things can happen to the truly awful.

Emerging dripping wet from the best shower she had ever had, Wendy grabbed her phone and let Rachel know she would be keeping her hair appointment after all. She had needed the sleep more than she'd needed a spray tan. She chuckled to herself as she recalled Sam and Ingrid drunkenly discussing very, very seriously how much they needed a spray tan as if it was the most important thing in the world. Betty had told them all she hadn't had a tan since the '70s and they'd all laughed like it was the funniest thing they'd ever heard. Champagne did that sometimes.

Wendy looked at her body in the full-length mirror. She was athletic and tall with a thick mane of chestnut hair. There were a few greys in the mix, but she knew she could still turn heads if she wanted to, the thought of which made her smile and roll her eyes at her reflection. Suddenly she felt different. This day felt strangely like a watershed, a turning point, although she had absolutely no idea why it should. She felt she was at a crossroads but perhaps it was what true freedom felt like. Perhaps she felt it was the first time she had ignored life's itinerary and done what she felt like doing. She bunched her hair on top of her head, then pulled it back severely the way she did when she was in court. Pulling faces at her reflection, she thought, I could become a nun today, or a prostitute. Or both.

She laughed at her own joke and felt something dislodge in her back, but it only made her laugh harder. Laying back on the plush bed the reply came back from Rachel that the car would collect her in 10 minutes. The champagne was waiting.

UNIQUE PARIS TOURS

Please tell us a little about yourself! Judy Rotherham. 49 – I turn 50 while we're in Paris!

The first time I saw Paris… My aunt lived in Paris and we visited every Christmas. It was beautiful – a magical time to be in Paris. I had modelling assignments there in my teens which sounds far more glamourous than it was. I love Paris…but I'm sure everyone writes that.

Is there a song that reminds you of Paris? I love all those cute little buskers playing piano accordion. That's Paris to me.

Is there a scent that takes you back every time? Most definitely, roasting chestnuts! That is unmistakable. Crepes…fresh bread…rotisserie chicken in the market. Yes, the food of Paris is a huge attraction, but considering I have been trying to lose weight I might need to find some new smells…perhaps the smell of the river as I walk along it each morning, but then I only think of the croissant I could have after the walk! There are no diets in Paris!

What's on your Must-See list? To have my birthday dinner somewhere special, to climb the Eiffel Tower, to take a boat ride, to see the Louvre. As you know my daughter Georgia will accompany me, but she won't be part of the tour as such. I will cover her expenses as discussed. She spent the autumn in Paris last year for University, and she loves it. She has told me the song that reminds her of Paris is Hotline Bling, whatever that is! The smells she says remind her of Paris are cigarettes and Chanel Coco Mademoiselle perfume and sweaty boys, but I think she said that to tease me!

Do you have a secret wish for your time in Paris? To celebrate my birthday with my daughter and perhaps find a reason to smile again. Yours, Judy

The cute-French-waiter-cliché

Georgia was embarrassed, to say the least. To add to her horror, her face was warm, and she knew her cheeks had turned a vibrant shade of red. Even her ears burned.

The salesgirl had been very sweet and explained her error.

'Non,' she said patiently, 'the word soldes means it is on sale in French, not that somebody has already bought the shoes. It's not the same as sold in English,' she finished, almost in a whisper.

She was being kind not to add to Georgia's mortification.

'Would you like to try them?' the funky salesgirl added, smiling. Georgia nodded and sat on the leather bench. Her mother had told her about the famous twice-yearly Paris sales, and Georgia had set out with plenty of cash and high hopes, only to be constantly confronted with what she thought were 'sold signs'. She was relieved now that the redness on her face had softened into a more attractive pink as she looked down at the gold gladiator sandals, wondering how life could ever be complete without them.

'Oui,' she declared, 'I'll take them.'

'Oh no, these are already soldes,' the clerk joked.

Georgia laughed as she paid and waited for the girl to box the sexy gold sandals, her first successful purchase. She couldn't wait to get her hands on that glossy white bag with the ribbon handles. She asked the girl if she knew where she could get a decent cup of coffee, hoping she might offer to join her. Her dream of living in Paris would be easier with a few cool friends, especially one who worked in a shoe shop.

'Oh yes, right next door has the best coffee in the Marais,' the girl said, finalising the sale.

Hiding her disappointment that she hadn't just made a new friend, Georgia thanked her with a gushing merci, her feeling of fitting in like a local evaporating again. She said her goodbyes and thanked the girl again.

'À bientôt,' she added with a wave.

She made her way next door to the café, tripping on the uneven footpath. The couples sitting at the sidewalk tables stared at her. Georgia tried to cover her embarrassment by peering into the crowded café as though looking for a friend. The place was packed. She was about to give up when she noticed a hand waving her towards a table, two elderly gentlemen moving over so she could sit. Embarrassed all over again, she tried to convince them that they didn't need to move. They simply smiled and motioned her towards the vacant seat. The waiter, gorgeous in his long black apron and slicked back hair, waited for her order, as she practiced the phrase in her head.

'Un Café au lait, et une bouteille d'eau,' she said, taking her seat.

She had practiced the phrase in her head countless times and now managed to say it as though she had been born ordering coffee in Paris. Her French was improving daily but sometimes it gave her a headache just ordering lunch. Cute-French-Waiter-Guy flashed a smile and asked her in rapid-fire French if she had been shopping, as he gestured towards the carrier bags.

'Oui, les soldes,' she shrugged, as if powerless to resist a bargain.

She had seen a woman do this the previous day, eliciting much laughter from her friends. Now that Georgia understood the phrase and its connotations, she used it to full affect. Cute-French-Waiter-Guy laughed, his eyes shining. Georgia smiled back and relaxed a little. The elderly gentlemen at the next table smiled warmly at her.

Paris was a rollercoaster. One-minute she felt she could be a local and the next, like the proverbial fish out of water flapping, floundering and gasping for air. Sometimes she literally stood there gaping like a fish her mouth opening and closing as she struggled to find the right French word. She knew the effort would be worth it, but it was tough. After graduating near the top of her year, how annoying it was to feel like a beginner again.

The journalism course at university had been fun but she had not put in enough work. Still trying to find magazine work six months after graduation, she had naïvely thought that having been a model would give her a foot in the door, but the opposite seemed true. Frustratingly people assumed she was just a pretty face and when they looked at her university results their suspicions were confirmed. University had been a lot of fun and her modelling assignments had mostly consisted of weeks in Bali modelling bikinis, partying on islands and boats. She'd had a great time but now it was time to 'hashtag adult'.

She was determined to make Paris her home. She knew that her surfer-girl looks wouldn't get her work in Europe, but she wasn't interested in modelling anymore. She wanted to do something challenging. At last, she had a passion and a goal, and it made her work harder than she ever had in her life. With the aim of working for a great magazine, she had created a blog and was hash-tagging, monetising and posting everything in sight.

Georgia had fallen in love with Paris while on a school trip. How lucky she was to be able to attend a school which offered trips to France and Noumea. She wondered what her passion would be if she had never fallen in love with Paris, but she knew deep-down that it was fated; her love for Paris was something that was rooted in her soul somehow.

Cute French-Waiter-Guy brought her order on a silver tray and placed it with a flourish on her table, along with a serviette and cutlery. Was he hoping she would stay for lunch, she asked herself, smiling up at him. Her mobile phone trilled as he was about to ask her a question, and she panicked when she saw it was her mother. Georgia wasn't ready for a Cute French-Waiter-Guy to realise that she wasn't a local. Luckily the phone stopped.

'Ma mere,' she shrugged again, and was rewarded with another brilliant smile. He wished her "Bon Appetit" and went to seat a couple at the only other vacant table.

Georgia saw her mother had sent her a couple of texts, but she put her phone aside and drank her coffee, watching the pantomime of the Cute French-Waiter-Guy trying to seat the couple, who appeared to speak only Chinese. When they were comfortably seated, he patiently helped them order cold drinks and salads. He was a rare sight; a waiter, seemingly the only one, in a crowded bistro in a busy city who would take the time to help a couple order and smiling all the while. The elderly gentleman to her right noticed her admiring the waiter.

'Vous etes Americaine?'

'Non, je suis française,' she lied, feigning surprise that he would think otherwise. She smiled and said 'Je suis Parisienne.'

'Ah, oui. Bien sur,' he smiled, tapping his nose with his forefinger. 'And I wish I was 20 years old again.' He rose to leave, and Georgia laughed and blew him a kiss, which he caught and put in his pocket.

She relaxed against the woven seat-back and read her mother's texts. Georgia was happy to see how positive her mum was; the day spa was magnificent and the treatments 'to die for'. Even Georgia was stunned by the selfie her mother sent. She wore a white turban and robe. It was fabulous. She added it to her newsfeed. "Hashtag beauty-in-Paris" she wrote and tagged her friends.

Her mother had been a real beauty as a young woman, she was still striking but her beauty had somehow been eclipsed by the terrible sadness since Georgia's father did what he did. This smiling photo had none of the sadness, her brown eyes sparkling, a broad smile on her face. For Judy, coming to Paris was a last-ditch effort to find something to be happy about. Georgia didn't want to admit to herself that her mum was literally looking for a reason to go on living, not just a figurative raison d'etre. Georgia signalled the waiter for her bill, but he explained that the elderly gentleman, Monsieur Canard, had paid for her coffee.

'Vraimant?' Georgia asked. 'Really?'

'Oui, Il est vraiment appele Mr. Canard,' the Cute-French-Waiter Guy said animatedly.

Georgia forgot all about trying to be a polished Parisienne and doubled over laughing. She was oblivious to the smiling faces all around her, as she wiped her eyes and caught her breath.

'Oh, my goodness, that's the first time I've understood a joke in French,' she giggled, still trying to regain her composure.

'So, you're Australian?' he smiled. 'I thought you were, I mean look at you,' he gestured at her, by which she assumed he meant her height, her suntan and her long, surfer-girl hair, 'but then you seemed so French'.

Georgia beamed. She had fooled a Cute French-Waiter-Guy into thinking she was French. 'Wait. You're Australian?' she asked a little too loudly. 'I thought you were French! How long have you lived here?'

'I've been in Paris three months, but I travelled and worked a lot in France before that. On farms mostly. I'm trying to get a visa; I want to stay. It's not cool for a guy to admit, I know, but I love Paris,' he finished his sentence looking down at his shoes.

'Well, your French is amazing.' She was rambling but didn't care.

'So is yours,' he said.

'No, I put on a good show, but there's lots of holes in my understanding. It's impossible to practice though. No-one wants to speak French to me if I don't pretend, I'm a local, and then as soon as they discover I'm not, they speak English to me. I can't blame them though; most French people's English is way better than my French!'

'You can practice here any time,' he replied as he prepared to seat another group of diners.

'À demain?' he said, raising an eyebrow.

'Oui,' she stammered, 'à demain.' See you tomorrow. Cute-French-Waiter-Guy was no longer French, but he was offering to help her with her French. And he was still very cute.

She made her way out into the bright sunshine, tripping again on the same step. This time she laughed and didn't care who saw her.

The streets of the Marais felt a little like home to Georgia. She retraced her footsteps to the gorgeous apartment she and her friends had stayed in during their semester abroad. Standing in front of the ornate entrance, she toyed with the idea of trying the code she had used the previous year. She looked around to see the prim gentleman from the bakery next door striding towards her. Would he remember her, she wondered? He barked at her in rapid French. She took a few steps backwards. She asked him politely to "répétez, s'il vous plait," before resorting to a sheepish "parlez vous anglaise?" He turned and walked back to his shop.

'Rude,' she said quietly, confused as to what exactly had just happened.

Unsure whether to wait for him to return, Georgia crossed the street, horrified that she felt unable to even perform the basic social niceties. She would have to learn the language, that was a given, but she would also have to be prepared to humiliate herself, a lot, to learn how things worked here in Paris. Head down, she was no longer interested in shopping or finding the nail salon she had been to in the past. She would have to develop a thicker skin if she was to realise her dream of living in Paris.

After walking for what seemed like an hour, she looked around and realised she had no idea where she was. Following the sound of heavy traffic close by, she found herself on a huge intersection surrounded by cars and standing on an unromantic bridge overlooking an unromantic train line.

Sighing, she headed away from the traffic in search of the dreamier Paris that she had lost back in the Marais. She wondered if she was being too idealistic about the move to Paris, and was she having second thoughts about her ability to pull it off? Quickly putting any negativity out of her mind, she pulled her phone out and texted Myles to rescue her. How lovely would it be to have a gorgeous limo driver to squire you around Paris? She felt a little guilty and knew she should grab the metro. Rachel had said it was fine, she told herself.

'Just this once,' she said out loud as she texted him her whereabouts, which by this stage was a tiny café attached to a fruit shop.

Cold Orangina in hand, she scrolled through her Socials to see what her friends were up to. Clicking on her account, she noticed that her mother's photo already had 180 likes.

Taking a screen shot she sent it to her mother and then sent numerous photos to her dad, throwing in one of Judy looking relaxed and happy the night before in Montmartre. She couldn't resist showing him what he had so carelessly thrown away, although she knew it was cruel. He would be back by her mother's side in the blink of an eye given half a chance. It made her so sad to think that something so good as her parent's marriage could be ripped apart in a moment's weakness.

The sleek limo purred alongside the curb. Georgia grabbed her shopping as Myles ran around to open the door for her.

'Thanks Myles, you're a lifesaver!'

'Hi,' a voice said, before she could take a seat.

Georgia entertained Wendy with the story of the cute Australian-French-Waiter-Guy and Wendy in turn described her sleep-in and the best shower in history. They asked Myles to reveal some stories of Rachel's previous tour groups, but he explained that theirs was the first group to use the limo service. They pulled up in front of the Le Meurice and he suggested she leave her new shoes in the limo and he would deliver them to the hotel. She didn't want to be parted from her new shoes but didn't want to drag the bag all over town.

'You'll be careful with my new babies, won't you?' she pouted a little. She thanked him profusely and waved goodbye as he drove away.

'You're waving goodbye to your shoes, aren't you?' Wendy dead panned as she walked into the hotel for her hair appointment.

A summer storm was brewing as the group met on the pavement for their walking tour, Rachel assuring them that Myles would rescue them with the stretch limo if a downpour interrupted their afternoon. Clouds continued to build over the course of the walk providing a dramatic and memorable back drop for their photos. They headed up past Maxims, Hotel Crillon, and along the length of rue du Faubourg Saint-Honoré, oohing and aahing at the luxury flagship stores. They continued through the neighbourhood that held embassies and luxurious apartments, stopping for a cocktail at a swish joint behind the Arc de Triomphe as the storm rumbled overhead.

The opportunity to climb the Arc de Triomphe was taken up by half the group, the others enjoying the spectacle of the traffic circling the huge monument. Although part of the tour was encouraging the clients to tick items off their must-see list, Rachel was determined to show her clients parts of Paris they had possibly never seen before, taking them along tree-lined residential streets quiet in the cool afternoon air, only to emerge blinking at the view of the Eiffel Tower from the terrace of the Palais du Tokyo. More photo opportunities followed from the Trocadéro before they continued strolling through the leafy suburbs, arriving at the quirky little restaurant that was once a suburban train station.

A little footsore and thirsty, they filed in snapping pictures of the architecture and the stylish fit-out. Dinner was delicious and a gentle hum of conversation washed around the group. Rachel sometimes had to organise the groups to swap seats half-way through dinner, but this group was so organic and inclusive she was able to sit back and relax, watching the women interact and enjoy themselves.

Georgia excitedly showed off the now hundreds of likes on her mother's photo on her pic sharing sites. 'My bikini shots don't get that many likes!' She pouted at her mother.

'Just don't put a picture of me in a bikini on there,' Judy said.

The hours seemed to rush by and soon the restaurant was closing, so they made their way out to the street. The city was clean and fresh from the rain. Myles was waiting with the car to take Janet and Betty back and it was a unanimous decision to grab a lift to the Seine. There was only so much Rachel could say about the 'leafy' residential suburbs that surrounded them.

Stopping near Pont Alexander III, the gold dome of Les Invalides rising behind them, Myles opened the door for those who wanted to walk. He said he could not understand why anyone would want to walk when they could ride in luxury and soon, he was suffering rounds of double- kisses from the slightly inebriated women. He managed to tear himself away before whisking Janet and Betty away in his limo.

'Would you like a bit of a tour around, before heading back?' Myles asked.

'Myles, we would go anywhere with you!' Betty said. She looked at Janet who had her hand on her chest. Betty reached over and took her friend's wrist to check her pulse.

'I'm still alive,' she said, pulling her wrist away but smiling at her old friend. 'I look like death, I know, but I feel better than I have in years.'

'Good! Drink?' Betty asked, moving towards the chilled champagne that seemed to be a constant fixture in the limousine.

'Sure, why not!'

The most famous bridge in a city filled with famous bridges stretched out in front of them. Cameras clicked and flashes lit up the night. Crossing the river on Pont Alexander III they oohed and aahed at the Eiffel Tower putting on its sparkling show once again, cameras set to video capturing the moment for friends and family back home. After doubling back across the bridge, they continued walking along the Left Bank.

'I think it's easy to forget that Paris is a busy city and home to more than two million people. Twenty-nine of the world's largest companies listed in the Fortune Global 500 have their headquarters in the Paris region, ranking it third in the world, after Beijing and Tokyo. And it's number one in Europe.' Rachel talked to the group, slipping easily into tour guide mode.

'Oh my god, I forgot you're a tour guide!' Georgia laughed. 'You're more like a cool Aunt who happens to live in Paris!'

'Why, thank you.' Rachel laughed.

They continued east along the quai enjoying the cooler air after the rain shower and the view across to the Place de la Concorde and the Louvre, finally arriving at the Pont des Arts. The group fanned out across the bridge, snapping dozens of photos and watching Paris revolve around them. Rachel stood at the end, leaving the women to enjoy it in their own way as they disappeared into the crowds of tourists on the famous bridge.

'A penny for your thoughts,' Judy said, quietly slipping beside Rachel.

'Oh, you know, thinking about love and loss. That's all,' she joked, shrugging her shoulders like they weren't the two most important subjects in the world. Paula joined them. She was grinning.

'I put my lock on the bridge,' Paula said.

Rachel pursed her lips. 'I do wish you hadn't, I am very clear about my position on responsible tourism on my website and in the itinerary.'

'Come on everyone we'd better get back; I can hear the chilled champagne calling us!' Judy said, as Sam, Ingrid and Georgia walked towards them. She took her daughters arm and steered her away from the conversation.

'I didn't think that applied to me…' Paula said, 'I,' she said slowly as though speaking to a child, 'was very clear about my intention with this lock. It was engraved specially…' She put extra emphasis on the words "clear" and "my." Rachel could feel her pulse in her temples.

'As long as you understand that the city is spending an awful lot of money to clear them away. I'm sorry, but your lock won't be here long, engraved or not.'

Paula looked as though she'd been slapped. 'They can't…'

'They can and they will,' Rachel said. 'What's done is done.'

'I'll go and get it back.' Paula turned around and peered back along the length of the bridge.

Rachel could see Paula wasn't sure exactly where her lock was. She sighed and stepped forward, putting her hand on the other woman's shoulder. 'I'll help you find it.'

Paula brushed Rachel's hand away. 'There's no point, I'll never find it, plus the key is…' she mimed throwing it into the river. 'It's with my phone, I guess.'

Rachel suppressed the urge to say all the things that were running through her mind. Instead, she nodded her head towards the Left Bank and smiled at Paula.

'As I said, what's done is done. Shall we?' She gestured along the bridge.

Paula walked ahead of her. 'You know that is a really annoying turn of phrase?'

Rachel nodded her head slowly, walking a few paces behind while the rest of the group waited a little way along the road. Once they were all reunited, they made their way slowly along the Seine in the warm night-time air. No one spoke and Rachel was grateful for the chance to gather her thoughts. She truly did not know how to talk to Paula without upsetting her. She was grateful that everyone had worn comfortable shoes. Too many times she had had to call taxis for clients who chose fashion over comfort for her walking tours. Everyone hears how walkable Paris is and misjudges how tough it is to walk on cobblestones all day, let alone in heels. Besides, unless you are a movie actor or royalty, no one truly cares what you wear on your feet.

The Seine was busy with tourist boats and the streets seemed to be filled with partygoers and tour groups. Rachel led the women along the quai, pointing out the famous and not-so famous landmarks, including her favorite Irish pub, the pharmacy with the cute English-speaking pharmacist, the famous Shakespeare and Co bookstore and the green boxes belonging to the bouquanistes or booksellers, along the quai. Paula trailed behind the group, taking photos of Notre Dame, having appointed herself unofficial photographer of the group. Ingrid wandered back to where her friend and boss was standing, leaving Sam with Judy and Georgia as they waited for the lights to change.

'I'm going to move here,' Paula blurted as Ingrid got within earshot.

'Really?' Ingrid was surprised by the announcement, thinking only how this would affect her job. She was a little embarrassed by her own selfishness.

'I've been offered a job here. Can you believe that?

No, Ingrid thought. I really can't believe it.

UNIQUE PARIS TOURS

Please tell us a little about yourself! Dr Paula Grange

The first time I saw Paris… I am thrilled to be joining you on this Unique Week in Paris! I have frequently visited Paris over the years and am looking forward to spending time with my dear friend and colleague Ingrid Maurer. The first time I saw Paris…? My parents visited regularly so it is entirely possible I was conceived there. They had told me that I was to be named Paris, which would have been preferable to Paula if you ask me. I named my own daughter Paris.

Is there a song that reminds you of Paris? It doesn't get any more Parisian that Edith Piaf!

Is there a scent that takes you back every time? A scent that reminds me of Paris? Roses from the gardens. Fresh bread baking. So many wonderful smells!

What's on your must-See list? This list is extensive, and I have forwarded it to you on a separate pdf. I am not interested in museums as I have seen all of them.

Do you have a secret wish for your time in Paris? What is my secret wish? Oh, la la, my secret wish is to have an affair with Jamie Foxx, but I don't think that's going to happen! A Paris themed secret wish would be to have lunch or dinner at a Michelin Three Star restaurant.

Tuesday

Rachel was deep in thought, working through the schedule for the day. Sam, Ingrid and Paula, were to go with Rachel to shop in the Marais. Judy and Carole had booked out the whole day with the personal shoppers. Georgia went along for the ride, while Wendy was planning to spend a little time with her sister before going walking with a photographic group.

Betty and Janet were on route to Fontainebleau with Myles as their personal driver and guide. Rachel had been floored to discover that the young driver had virtually grown up in the chateau, his father the chief gardener. He would not be an official guide as he didn't have the proper documentation, but he would accompany the clients and ensure they had everything they needed. He had told them he would be the thorn between two roses, to which Betty had replied to a puzzled Myles that he could be her Benjamin Braddock any time.

Paula was being difficult about the private shopping tour. Rachel had re-organised the schedule twice but there were still clashes. She had also wandered into the family's private quarters and asked to use the washer. Rachel was frustrated. She would have to sit down with Paula and run through the tour documents. The assumption was that clients would read through things in their own time, but it was obvious Paula hadn't, considering the information covered everything including laundry and locks on bridges.

'She has no idea,' Sara said matter-of-factly to Rachel on Monday morning as they waited for the group to come up for breakfast.

'I am so sorry. She means well, but she doesn't realise it's not a good thing for Paris. So many tourists believe Paris is an over-grown theme park here for their entertainment,' Rachel said.

Sara was shaking her head. 'Ah, no, I was speaking in general. She is forthright but doesn't think before speaking.' Sara finished with that typical puff of the lips that only the French seem to be able to pull off. Sara could be quite forthright herself, Rachel mused.

'She is very firm in her beliefs.' Rachel tried to defend her client.

'Yes, but all of them are wrong!' Sara said flatly. 'Sometimes the smartest people can be the most ignorant.'

Rachel had been in the business of making people happy for over 30 years if you counted all her years in Paris, proving time and again, to be an exquisite judge of character. Something told her that while Paula talked a big game, there was an undercurrent of trouble brewing for this incredibly talented woman although she was unsure exactly what form it would take. Rachel had been around people long enough to know that no one can go through their whole life being right about everything, and the people who have to tell you how perfect their families are, are usually hiding something.

The day unfolded in the typical mayhem of the second day in Paris. Rachel and Sara laughed that they could almost set their watches by it. The limo was on its way east with Betty and Janet, so they had the option of walking to their various appointments or catching taxis. Everyone milled around in the elegant foyer. Tuesday was always the day when the reality set in that this was just one week, and they really needed to make the most of their time. Carole, Judy, Wendy and Georgia shared a taxi to the offices of the personal shoppers while Rachel set out on foot with Ingrid, Sam and Paula. Pulling the door shut behind her, Rachel turned and bumped into the three other women who stood transfixed on the pavement in front of her.

'Rachel...?' Sam stammered.

Hanging in the enormous picture window of the art gallery opposite the hotel was the painting from the exhibition invitation. A six-foot-high portrait of Rachel's face, the same style as the little sketch she found in her hatbox the night before. The hat box was full of mysteries, but it was unmistakable. This had to be Karen's work. The Artist. Although it was not yet open, various staff milled around in the huge white space as they hung the delicate canvasses and framed drawings, most showing faces, but the other imagery was uncanny. Ink drawings, black with bursts of tattoo-like coloured drawings of flowers, skulls, clocks and guttering candles, applied directly to the walls soared to the vaulted ceiling. Canvases leaned on the wall waiting to be hung, ethereal portraits, lettering and clocks the other dominant features of the works.

Rachel stood rooted to the spot until one of the staffers saw her, obviously recognising her from the portrait. Sam and Paula had their cameras out and were videoing the exchange. The young man stylishly turned-out in gold skinny jeans and a tight black t-shirt opened the door and walked towards the little group. He held out his hand and shook Rachel's somewhat limp right hand. Ingrid reached across and touched Rachel lightly on the chin. She obviously had no idea her mouth was hanging open.

'Pietro,' he said, his accent a mix of New York and Rome.

'Ra…Rachel.'

'I know who you are. It's amazing to finally meet you. Will you come on Thursday night? Everyone is dying to meet you. You're all welcome,' he said smiling at the three transfixed women standing beside their guide. The only response Rachel could muster was a nod.

Georgia held up an off the shoulder, gold sequined top, raising her eyebrows suggestively at Carole as if to say, "you want to try this?"

'Ah, I don't think I'd be doing the school run in that!' Carole replied.

It became obvious to Georgia and Wendy that they were superfluous to the shopping experience as the paid professionals swooped into action. Wendy said her good-byes and hit the pavement in search of photo opportunities while Georgia snapped a quick series of photos of her mother looking incredible in everything. She sat down to post some of the images.

'Mum, your last pic has over 300 likes!' Georgia said a little too loudly, earning herself a scowl from Fabien as he laced Judy into a bustier.

Judy tried to look interested in her daughter's news but was concentrating on breathing at that point. 'Perhaps…a…little…looser…?' she suggested to Fabien who smiled but shook his head.

'Take a photo of this look. She will get over 1000 likes!' he said.

Georgia snapped a pic of them both pouting, his perfectly manicured hands pretending to lace her tighter, foot on her derriere. After gaining their approval and adding the filter Fabien suggested she hit the share button, kissed her mother, air kissed everyone else and made her way out the door. Destination? A coffee or glass of wine in a tiny Marais café with a cute Australian-waiter-guy.

The morning in the Marais with Paula, Ingrid and Sam had passed pleasantly enough, but Rachel was having trouble convincing Paula that she should be happy. Here they were, four women, shopping, in Paris and Paula was complaining to anyone who would listen. The other women took turns to fawn over Paula, help her choose outfits or tell her she looked gorgeous, but she was still miserable as they sat down for lunch at Le Dôme du Marais. Rachel left the table to take a phone call and Paula continued to complain.

'Paula, seriously, you haven't smiled all day! We're in Paris!' Ingrid said softly, gently gripping Paula's hand. 'Paris!'

'Oh, I'm sorry. I'm missing the kids and hubby. You know how it is?' she replied.

Sam picked up her water glass and put it to her lips, willing herself not to roll her eyes.

Paula had originally declined a personal shopper to spend the time with her friends instead, but it became increasingly obvious over the course of the morning that she would have enjoyed it far more, while Ingrid and Sam were happy to wander the streets and window shop. Paula was unhappy with the selection available in the Marais, Rachel pulled a few strings with her friends at Galeries Lafayette to get her in at such short notice for the VIP treatment, Rachel stressing to Paula how special it was to be given such access.

'They're sending a car for us. Here to the restaurant. Keep your eye out for a silver E-class Mercedes,' Rachel said, her tone of voice implying that this was a very special treat indeed.

This, Rachel had figured out, was the key to working with Paula; she had to feel it was special, unique and exclusive. True to form, Paula tried to encourage Ingrid to go with her, completely ignoring Sam's existence.

'I think we'll walk back slowly,' Ingrid said, not daring to look at Sam. 'You guys have fun. How exciting to be chauffeur driven to Galeries Lafayette!' she enthused, hoping it would soothe any hurt feelings, although the entire group seemed to be becoming a little too accustomed to being chauffeured around Paris in the limo.

They were miles from the hotel, but Rachel didn't dissuade them from walking, knowing it would give the friends some time together. Paula always seemed determined to exclude Sam from anything she or Ingrid wanted to do, although Ingrid was just as determined that Sam would be included. It made for something of a tug-of-war, with Sam acting as the rope, and Rachel constantly running interference to mitigate any hurt feelings.

Amazed that no matter a person's age, insecurity could rear its ugly head, Rachel also knew that Ingrid had scrimped and saved her spending money for the trip, preferring to spend it on experiences rather than things. She had enjoyed the brief shopping trip, choosing an elegant blue silk shift dress and a white peasant top, and although she seemed to enjoy helping the others find perfect outfits, the exercise seemed to have exhausted its pleasure for her. Sam had a great eye for fashion and was already weighed down with bags from every store they had visited. Ingrid smiled at a slightly indignant Paula as they left her and Rachel. Once the girls at GL got their hands on her Paula would forget all about Sam and Ingrid.

'She'll be fine,' Ingrid said to Sam, ushering her away from the bistro, although she was trying to convince herself.

They crossed the street and took a narrow passageway, determined to wander the back streets that the limo could not navigate. Laden with their shopping bags, the warm afternoon air made their walk into something of a bar-crawl, as they stopped at various cafes on the way. They had seriously misjudged the distance but didn't care one bit. Taking a wrong turn, they found themselves standing behind the Centre Pompidou, confused and just a little tipsy. Calling Rachel for suggestions for where they went wrong, she laughed when they said they were standing behind a giant Lego power station. She directed them back towards the river via the Hotel de Ville, suggesting they stop at the quirky Kilo shop if they see it on their journey, and reminding them about dinner that night, her tone implying they might not make it back in time if they were as drunk or lost as they sounded.

The Kilo shop was closed by the time they arrived, but they pressed their noses on the glass, vowing to return the following day to grab some vintage goodies. Foot-sore and grateful to see the river again, they crossed Pont d'Arcole, Sam excitedly pointing out the Maison Heloise et Abelard, and telling Ingrid of the doomed love affair.

'It's amazing how women were shunted off to the nunnery as soon as their usefulness was exhausted or for their 'safety',' she sighed, as though having suffered the same fate herself.

They walked in silence, enjoying the cooling breeze coming off the river. Ingrid felt like pinching herself, being here in Paris after all these years, and wondering why she waited so long to come back. Perhaps it had something to do with children, and parents, and schooling, mortgages and braces for crooked teeth. She thought she should stop thinking about all that and simply enjoy the view.

'Have I said thank you? For this amazing gift?'

'Only about a thousand times, babe,' Sam laughed. 'Hey, let's get ice-cream,' she said, pointing to the winding line outside the Bertillon store. They stood, leaning against the railing enjoying their glace and the entertainment from the buskers on the bridge, their feet surrounded by shopping bags.

'I miss playing music for the fun of it,' Sam said.

'I miss dancing for the fun of it. Hell, I miss having fun for the fun of it! When did it all get so…' she trailed off, not knowing what she was trying to say? 'We thought being adults was going to be this great big adventure, but it's just pay bills and die, really. Isn't it?'

'And don't forget the heart break and leg-waxing,' Sam added, smiling.

'Fuck it, babe, we're in Paris. Let's tell Rachel we want to take up the option of going clubbing on Thursday night and have some fun for the fun of it, and dance for the hell of it and I'll get up on stage somewhere and play something until someone chases me away.'

'Sounds like a plan,' Ingrid replied licking the ice-cream that was running down her hand.

They slowly made their way back to the hotel intent on fitting in a swim in the basement pool and a nap. The evening's festivities featured dinner at Jules Verne on the Eiffel Tower to celebrate Judy's 50th birthday. A hair stylist, make-up artist and a rack of gorgeous clothes were waiting for them at the hotel. It was like a dream. They would make themselves beautiful and a stretch limousine would whisk them across Paris.

UNIQUE PARIS TOURS

Please tell us a little about yourself! Sam Clements – musician and teacher.

The first time I saw Paris… Like lots of English kids I'd visited Spain on the holidays but had only passed through Paris. I've had a few visits as an adult. I love it. I fall in love a little more every time.

Is there a song that reminds you of Paris? Anything by Sibelius. The Swan. The Violin Concerto. Swoon…

Is there a scent that takes you back every time? The smell of the Metro, the smell of the rain on a hot summer's afternoon, horses in the Bois de Boulogne.

What's on your Must-See list? I'd love to have dinner on the Eiffel Tower. Window shopping with my dear friend. Bertillon! The Louvre…

Do you have a secret wish for your time in Paris? Perhaps to loosen up and have a little fun. Drink too much champagne in a gorgeous frock!

UNIQUE PARIS TOURS

Please tell us a little about yourself! Ingrid Maurer, 51. Bored housewife.

The first time I saw Paris...oh I'm getting excited already. For Paris, of course, but also because I will be spending time with my gorgeous friend Sam, whose application you should have by now? But back to the first time I saw Paris...

It seems like a different life now, but when I was a young dancer, I was offered a job at the Moulin Rouge. Believe it, or not! It does truly seem like it happened to another person and perhaps I simply read about it in a book or saw a movie once. I can't remember too much about those glorious two weeks in Paris, when I was a dancer at the Moulin Rouge! I lived in Paris! It was magical but, to tell you the truth, I haven't spoken about it with my children. Until this week, my children didn't know I had lived in Paris, even if it was only two weeks...!

Is there a song that reminds you of Paris? I fell down the YouTube rabbit hole for hours looking for the name of a song! So many songs! Papa Don't Preach, isn't that weird? And Sledgehammer. But there was this French song that I just couldn't recall, but after spending all that time on Youtube, I know it is L'Aziza by Daniel Balavoine! How the memories flood in when I listen to that song! And the sound of a steel drum takes me to Montmartre on a Sunday afternoon. I cannot wait to see that place again.

Is there a scent that takes you back to Paris every time? What a question! Cigarette smoke, Nivea hand cream (that sounds crazy!). Fresh bread, of course.

Believe it or not, The Moulin Rouge itself isn't on my must-see list. I want to spend time enjoying Paris. I want to go to Montmartre, because this is where I stayed, but really, I want to take a book and sit in a café and people-watch. There was a restaurant we used to go to that had a pay phone cabinet in the corner, so if I see that it will be amazing, but I can't even remember where it was.

What's on your Must-See list? Oops, I didn't see this question and answered it above! So that's my must-see. Sitting in a terrace café, scribbling in a notebook! I'm such a cliché! The Louvre, of course, and all the major monuments. I want to window shop, to stroll, to eat ice-cream and take photos. It will be enough to simply be in Paris. I don't have a lot of spending money, because, as you know, my dear friend Sam is paying for me to go on this trip with her. She and I are truly soul sisters! I have had a rough couple of years, and she has always been there for me.

Do you have a secret wish for your time in Paris? That's a great question. I need to forget about day-to-day life for a while, where I'm wife, mother, nurse and grandma. I love all those things, but it'll be nice to just be Ingrid for a while. Maybe a fancy dinner in a fancy dress!

Looking forward to meeting you! Ingrid Maurer xx

Heartbreak at la Tour Eiffel

Judy smiled softly at her reflection. She liked what she saw for once. The text from her soon to be ex-husband had been expected, but not welcome. Happy 50th birthday, love of my life he had texted. No cruelty or irony intended. He simply had no idea that this would break her heart all over again. All her hard work, undone in seconds.

Georgia read it and reacted without thinking as usual. 'He's such a child, mum,' she said, almost under her breath. 'I should send him the photo of you being laced up by Fabien today. A screen-shot to show him how many likes it has already.'

She checked her account on Judy's phone.

'432 likes. That's crazy. In just a few hours, and Fabien shared it too.' Georgia lay back on the bed in her silk sheath dress, taking selfies. Judy envied her daughter's free spirit.

'Dad would have zero clue about the pain this is causing. He's emotionally stunted. He's a fucking emotional bonsai.' She threw the phone on the bed and continued lacing up the gold gladiator sandals. The phone buzzed. Judy clenched her teeth wondering what her husband had texted now. Georgia checked the phone but there was no text. She snatched her own phone from her bedside table. It was from Julian, aka cute-Australian-waiter-guy. Her mother arched an eyebrow at her.

'It's from a boy,' Georgia said in a stage whisper.

'A French boy?'

'Well…no, not exactly…' She told her mother the story of how she and Julian met, and the details of their fun French lesson that afternoon.

'It's nothing, mum. He's not French, so no deal!'

'Oh Georgia, you think…everything is nothing! A cute boy sends you a text. It's nothing! Your father is a moron. It's nothing.' Judy was exasperated but she knew her daughter was onto something.

As they made their way down to the lobby, she put the unwelcome text from Grant out of her mind. Georgia was right. Her soon-to-be-ex-husband had no idea how to 'adult'. She hated the fact that her heart had leapt at the sight of the text, an old habit that was hard to overcome. Try as she might, Judy couldn't help thinking about the life they had had together. He'd called her the love of his life on their second date when he was a young, broke medical student working and studying long hours. She was a busy model in the way models were busy in the 80s; long gruelling photo shoots for the big department stores and standing in inappropriate clothing in all kinds of weather waiting to 'get the shot' for photographers who were wrapped in coats and scarves.

Judy had even worked twice in Paris, although the schedule had been so tight, they'd only managed to see the sights through car windows on the way to locations each day. One night, Grant had turned up at her hotel and whisked her away for the night. They had eaten in a traditional restaurant overlooking the river, drunk cocktails in a tacky tiki-themed bar under-ground somewhere, and made love in his cheap room near Gare du Nord, serenaded by the trains that reminded them he would be back in London by midday to start work.

Paris does that to people; makes you forget the day-to-day and tells you to just feel, like a beautiful but cruel lover. When the fun is over, when there's only sadness and hurt, the relentless beauty is still there, always pulling you in but pushing you away at the same time.

Judy looked down at her smooth hands. Although she had trouble accepting it, she was still a beautiful woman, if you asked the French. Back home she was an over-weight has-been but the longer she stayed in Paris, the better she felt about herself. The plan to move to Paris was the first real decision she had made in years. She and Georgia would announce their plans at dinner, so it was crunch time. Judy was horrified to admit that until the moment they had decided, she was still considering taking her husband back. She had given herself until the end of the week to decide if she would go back to her old life. What was left of her life anyway? She couldn't believe she had been approached by a model management firm who were following Georgia's posts of her week in Paris.

Paris, as they say, is always a good idea and she knew she could be happy here. She also knew she could say the word and her husband would be back by her side. They could have their old happy life again. He was remorseful. Truth be told, he was more devastated by his own behaviour than she was. She thought it would be easier if he didn't want her anymore, if he had wanted to leave. But meeting Wendy had put that idea aside.

The women milled around the lobby looking gorgeous. Silks and satins glowing in the candle lit room. Judy was thrilled to see Betty and Janet would be joining them for dinner despite their day at the chateau. A photographer had a tripod set up in front of the grand piano and each lady posed, and then they posed in groups. Finally, a photo of the whole group was taken, and they filed out to the laneway. Myles was waiting with the limo in front of the enigmatic portrait of Rachel smiling at them like a modern Mona Lisa.

The limousine took them to the eastern leg of the tower and a red carpet showed the way to the elevator designated for the Jules Verne restaurant. Tourists stopped to photograph the group, no doubt speculating about who these glamourous women were. It was fun to pretend to be someone else for a while, Paula had said to the group.

Dinner at Jules Verne was spectacular. The conversation was the best part; phones banished to their clutches. They talked about new books they were reading, the films to see, trips they were planning and bucket-list items they were ticking off. No-one mentioned ex-husbands, or divorces, reality TV shows or the latest post on their social media. Rachel chalked this evening up as the zenith of her career.

Georgia mentioned the lovely young man she had met, keeping the story vague, and the group had differing opinions on how she could proceed. It was interesting to see the various courses of action that the women prescribed, all tainted or informed by their own journeys.

'He's just a guy. It's nothing,' she said, but they had all heard themselves say that at one stage in their lives and they had known that it wasn't nothing.

Judy and Georgia announced their plan to move together to Paris and the group applauded. Georgia had been offered an internship at a magazine and Judy wanted to finally learn French and do some painting courses. There were toasts all-round to celebrate their new life in Paris. A beautiful cake was delivered to the table for Judy's birthday and a trio of waiters sang to her. She beamed but Rachel and anyone else paying enough attention could see the sadness behind the smile. The cake was delicious, and the champagne flowed. Then, it was time to leave.

This proved more difficult than they had expected. Drinking too much and sitting for too long was always a problem, and more than half the group was a little worse for wear. During the meal, Carole had maintained that there was no such thing as too much champagne, but when you fall over your own shoes after taking them off for safety's sake, you have had too much champagne. They managed to leave the restaurant with their dignity intact, but Carole was complaining loudly now they were out on the terrace, that she may vomit on the Eiffel Tower.

Paula made a beeline for Judy and began asking about her plans to relocate. She cleared her throat and walked to the centre of the loose circle they stood in.

'I'm excited to announce that I'm moving to Paris, too. As I told Ingrid yesterday, I have decided to accept the position I've been offered. It's a step back financially, but I don't care because I simply want to work in Paris. They don't care that my French is basic, it's my surgical skills they are after.'

Everyone congratulated Paula and asked her about her plans which she was more than happy to talk about. Georgia suggested they all find a grand apartment together, and Judy smiled but made no commitment. Paula could be shrill and overbearing at times, but Judy could see a deep desire to be loved, which is all anyone really wants but it didn't mean she wanted to be flat mates with the woman.

Ingrid stood quietly to one side a smile fixed on her face.

'Do you want to come for a little walk with us?' Wendy said as a very drunk Carole pulled at her sister's hand.

'We need more champagne,' Carole called, to a chorus of laughs but Wendy held her sister's arm and kept walking. Ingrid didn't follow. She seemed frozen to the spot.

Paula looked over at her and put her hands on her hips. 'You won't have trouble finding another job; you're the best nurse in the world. I'll write you a great reference,' she said.

The women stopped talking and looked at Ingrid who now had to deny she was worried about her job. And this was the precise moment that the entire evening turned to merde. Ingrid started to cry, turning on her heel to walk away from Paula she tore the hem of her dress. Carole pulled her phone out to take photos and saw that she had a lot of missed calls. Wendy's soon-to-be-ex was calling.

'Hello, asshole,' Carole said into the phone.

'Carole I've been trying to call Wen, is she with you?'

'She doesn't want to talk to you, Jimmy.'

'I've just sent you an email, I've got news and…and I didn't want her to find out in…in a bad way…'

'I didn't read your email because we're at the Eiffel Tower having an amazing time so you can f…'

Wendy took the phone from her sister.

'What do you want?' Wendy said, looking spectacular in Vera Wang, holding the phone at arm's length.

'Wen, I wanted you to hear it from me before you went on Facebook or something.'

'Let me guess. You're getting married? Having a baby?' The phone went blank and Wendy thought he had hung up but seconds later the face of Jim's new fiancé filled the screen. The rest of the group huddled around Wendy.

'Yes, we're getting married,' the fiancé said. She was holding her left hand up to the camera. The phone went blank again and then Jim was back on the screen.

'Yes, Wen, I'm sorry…can you just…no, please let me talk…' he looked back at Wendy. 'Sorry, I just wanted to tell you.'

'Great, thanks, yes, that's lovely. I see she's wearing your mother's ring. That's great. Great…how lovely. It fits her finger well,' she said sweetly, 'did you have it enlarged?'

Everyone cringed. The next few moments were a blur both on screen and for Wendy as Jim and his fiancé seemed to be grappling for the phone at their end. In the chaos someone mentioned a baby and Wendy seemed to freeze. Judy's heart almost leapt from her chest and she rushed to Wendy's side to hold her new friend up. Before anyone could disconnect the call, the face of Jim's young fiancé appeared on the screen.

'You heard right, we're having a baby, and felt we should be the ones to tell you.' She pulled a reluctant James into view. 'I may have his dead mother's ring on my finger, but I have his baby in my belly. I guess some men can't breed in captivity.' The final line sounded like she had been rehearsing it for a while. The screen went blank and the only sound they could hear was the wind and a moaning sound coming from Carole as she attempted to keep her dinner down. Paula walked forward and took Wendy's free hand, and between her and Judy, they guided her away from the railing. No one spoke.

How cliché can one man get, Paula wondered. She knew her own husband wasn't happy in their marriage, but he certainly wasn't shagging a uni student. She hoped. Standing with one arm around Wendy's waist in silent support, a little voice somewhere in her head was trying to suggest that perhaps her husband may be shagging a uni student, but she didn't know. How would she know? They barely spoke and when they did it was to indulge in what her horrid son referred to as 'hallway sex'. For those playing along at home, hallway sex is saying Fuck You as you pass your partner in the hallway. Yes, she had just referred to her son as horrid.

Not only had her once-happy marriage disintegrated, she had to face the truth that her children were spoiled, materialistic and insensitive. Her son was rude and lazy, and her daughter had a lot of followers on Snapchat but few real friends. Paula knew she was a brilliant surgeon, professional success was obvious to anyone, but she could see that everything else in her life was merely a thin veneer of respectability, she had failed as a mother and a wife. She leaned against Wendy, who put her arm around her in a rare show of emotion. Paula looked out silently into the night.

'I feel, weird. Like, strangely – elated,' Wendy said quietly. 'I feel like I can do whatever I want now. For the first time in years.'

Judy turned and hugged her new friend. She had a smile on her face, but tears in her eyes.

'You Okay?' Wendy asked.

'Me? I'm fine. You?' Judy said.

'I'm great. I mean it's not as if any of this came as a surprise.' A huge smile spread across Wendy's face. 'She's welcome to him.'

'But doesn't it make you want to kill someone? I mean, he's having a baby…' Paula said. Everyone turned to look at her.

'I mean yeah, if Wendy can be strong in the face of this…I mean…then she can do anything. What a mess.'

Judy put her hand on Paula's arm. 'If this is your idea of empathy, you should probably keep it to yourself,' she said.

For once, Paula had the sense to look shocked. 'I didn't mean…'

Wendy was so grateful to the wonderful women standing there with her. Receiving this kind of news, in the worst possible way, may have sent her mad if she hadn't the support of these women. She looked over towards her drunk sister who was now making her way to Wendy's side. This was new territory for both of them; Carole had never had to support her sister. Wendy had always been the rock, a second mother, and now when she needed her, Carole was fall-down drunk, wearing a hire gown worth thousands of Euros that had a tear in the knee area and at least two small vomit stains, her long hair tumbling across her face. Carole stood in front of Wendy and tried to speak, but a choking sound emerged. Once she was convinced that Carole wasn't going to throw up on her, Wendy laughed and hugged her sister.

'It's okay, you idiot, I'm fine.' Wendy realised that she was now holding her drunk sister upright.

'It's all good, ladies. I think we should call it a night, don't you?' she said, looking at the group over Carole's hunched shoulders. It reminded her of when she would carry her toddler sister to her bed, so many years before.

As they made their way to the elevators, Judy stopped to look out over Paris as the silent tears slid down her cheeks, but she smiled regardless. To be standing here on the Eiffel Tower, on her 50th birthday, dressed to the nines with her daughter, dinner at the world-famous Jules Verne restaurant. It was a real bucket-list moment. As tactless as Paula could be, Judy had found Wendy's poise inspirational. If she could handle that conversation with such dignity surely Judy could handle a thoughtless text from Grant. Pulling a tissue from her clutch she daintily dabbed the tears while her daughter mocked her, mimicking the dainty hand movements. They both burst into laughter, the wind plucking the tissue from her hand, it disappeared into the inky black Paris night.

'See mum, Paris is telling you that you don't need to cry anymore!' Georgia said hugging her mother. Judy pushed her now windswept hair behind her ear.

Waiting at the elevators another group of tourists snapped photos of the group in their glamourous gear. Georgia ran over and took selfies with the group and they all laughed when she told them she was Angelina Jolie. After his big day at Fontainebleau trying to keep up with Betty, Myles was having a night off and in his place beside the limo stood an impeccably dressed, good looking, silver-haired man.

'Do you think he might actually be a stripper?' Carole ventured in a stage whisper to much laughter from the group as they walked towards the car.

'No, I am not a stripper, but I can do a dance for you.' His sexy French accent making some of the women weak at the knees, he performed an accurate Elvis impersonation, eliciting whoops of excitement from the now unruly group.

The women piled into the car, their demeanour more 'bachelorette party' than 'successful women on retreat'. The return journey to the hotel was, in a word, raucous, with champagne overflowing onto elegant silk pants and skirts, their wearers having obviously decided to make the dry-cleaning bill worth it. Rachel suggested to Henri, the driver, they take a little drive around Paris to view the monuments lit up, but it was probably to avoid heading back to the hotel with a rowdy bunch more reminiscent of Ibiza than the 5th arrondissement. Touring the usual monuments, they stopped at the Arc de Triomphe, Place de la Concorde and Pont Alexander III for more photographic opportunities. Decorum had gone out the window by the end, breasts were bared, and woos were wooed.

Henri, the epitome of Parisian charm, politely declined Carole's offer to take over the driving so he could sit in the back with the group.

Cognac and Tea

As midnight approached the limo crept down the narrow street coming to a stop in front of the elegant doors, the mysterious portrait of Rachel luminous on the other side of the street. Both Rachel and Henri were holding their index fingers up to their mouths to keep the group quiet. Rachel found she was holding her breath as she tiptoed into the entryway. She drew her finger across her throat to show what would happen if they made any noise. The entire group made their way up the stone stairway, only Betty and Janet, arms around each other's waists, rode the elevator to their attic penthouse.

'I need tea. Does anyone else want tea?' Carole whispered into the darkness. She couldn't make out any faces but pools of light around their feet showed the way.

'Feel free but please, very quietly. I'm going to hit the sack,' Rachel whispered. She took the turn at the top of the stairs and padded away. The silent group made their way to the dimly let kitchen, Carole busying herself boiling the kettle. Wendy supervised, concerned her drunk sister might burn herself but she seemed to be back in control of her faculties.

They arranged themselves on the comfy terrace, the towers of Notre Dame looming silently in the middle distance. Teacups were passed around wordlessly, each lady enjoying their own thoughts or trying to sober up a little before going to bed. Wendy placed a tray of nibbles, that always seemed to be sitting ready, in the middle of the table. Betty, having seen Janet safely to bed pulled the glass door shut behind her. The group let out a collective sigh.

Georgia said, 'It's so hard to be quiet when you're tipsy.'

'Tipsy?' snorted her mother, to quiet laughter.

Ingrid and Sam grabbed the lighter and one by one lit the huge pillar candles in their glass hurricanes. The scene glowed; conversation and tea flowed. They had all lost track of time and as the lights on Notre Dame's towers were switched off the entire group seemed to draw a breath of wonder. The evening seemed to be winding down when Betty disappeared then came back through the door with a bottle of cognac.

'I was saving this for a special occasion, but this seems as special as any other time I could think of,' she said, taking glasses from the tray she had brought from the kitchen.

Georgia got up to hand out the glasses. 'I've never tasted cognac before,' she said eager to experience something new and oh so French.

Glasses were swirled in palms, the golden liquid glinting in the candlelight. Georgia threw her head back to down the liquor, but Betty gently laid a hand on her arm and signalled that she should swirl as the others were. After a few meditative moments as they all watched their glasses, one by one they lifted it to their lips and sipped, appreciating the warm liquid. Georgia drained her glass and looked about expectantly, instantly blushing both from the warmth of the liquor and the fact that no one else had drunk their cognac as though it was a shot. She muffled a laugh and held out her glass for Betty to re-fill.

'Henri was dishy, wasn't he? I'd love to find a good man…' Wendy said before Carole began coughing.

'Oh, my goodness, Wendy, don't say something like that just as I'm taking a sip of this fire-water!'

'Fire water?' Betty protested.

'I didn't mean it; I just have never had anything like this before. I'm not worldly wise like all of you,' Carole said blushing.

'You didn't let me finish,' Wendy interrupted. 'I was about to say, I'd like to find a good man like him…in my bed!'

The women laughed and choked on their drinks with nods all round.

'I'm celibate. I wouldn't know what to do with a man if one landed in front of me naked,' Judy said.

'I think you would! I know I would,' Wendy interjected, relishing the look of shock on her sister's face. To more laughter.

'I haven't been out with anyone for so long. It's time I got on eHarmony or something,' Sam said.

'Do they have that for you, er…?' Paula asked. If anyone else had asked she might have found it refreshing but with Paula, there was always an agenda.

'Ah, lesbians? Yes, we do. I've been doing a bit of research…'

'Research,' Ingrid laughed holding her fingers up and making speech marks in the air.

The glass door to the terrace opened again and Janet appeared, almost floating in her floor length satin night dress, taking the seat next to her old friend. The women all greeted her quietly.

'What's the topic?' Janet asked. Betty poured her a glass of cognac.

If the rest of the women were stunned to hear her speak finally, they didn't let on. 'Um, let's see…we've covered lesbian dating sites, good men and, ah…celibacy,' Wendy dead panned.

'Fascinating! Heard of the first, tried the second and the third…highly overrated, wouldn't recommend it,' Janet shot back to laughter all round.

Georgia's couldn't believe her cheeks were burning at Janet's mention of sex. She was having trouble seeing Betty or Janet as a woman rather than a grandmother or an elder. They were both older than Georgia's own grandmother, and grandmothers aren't supposed to think about sex.

'Sex isn't everything,' Judy said gently, sensing her daughter's discomfort.

'Oh, don't be silly,' Betty retorted, 'of course it is!' The whole group laughed, louder than they probably should have considering the hour.

'Well, no guy ever looks twice at me…everyone thinks I'm a lesbian, even though I'm married with two kids!' Paula said.

'Aren't you? And what does marriage have to do with it?' Betty laughed. 'What does it matter if the guys don't look at you? You are married, with two kids. Remember?'

Everyone bristled a little, worried that the Paula-Betty war was about to launch another battle. Ignoring Betty's comments, Paula continued, dropping her voice.

'I know I'm among friends here, so I need to tell you ladies something,' Paula continued, ignoring Betty. 'I think my husband is trying to have me killed. For the Money. For the kids.'

Silence met this little confession. Betty was first to recover. 'Honey, while I would believe that your husband could be trying to have you killed, it's probably not about your kids from what I've heard. He probably just wants out.' The group froze, while on cue a siren whined somewhere across the river.

'Shots fired,' Wendy said to no one in particular.

'Why, thank you, Betty. I don't think anyone has ever said anything quite so cruel to me,' Paula said softly.

'Now that I find hard to believe!' Betty quipped back, mimicking Groucho Marx.

Paula made a strangled sound in the back of her throat that may have been a laugh.

'This might be the cognac talking but, I'd love to have an affair. I can't even get anyone to flirt with me. The good-looking doctors never give me a second glance; they're all terrified of me. I'm hot though, right? I mean I work out, my boobs cost a fortune…' She looked at Ingrid. 'Everyone says I'm in love with Ingrid. Which I am of course, but not as in love, you know? I don't want to sleep with her.'

Ingrid placed the back of her hand on her forehead and pretended to cry.

'I'll sleep with you, darling,' Betty said, winking at Ingrid. The group laughed.

'So much for my big confession. Thanks for your compassion, everyone,' Paula said, downing the last of her drink.

'You need to lighten up a little. Getting a divorce isn't the end of the world. People do it every day,' Wendy said.

'On that light note, I think we might take our leave,' Betty said. She handed the almost empty bottle to Georgia and blew a kiss to the night sky. Janet waved shyly and said good night. There was a chorus of whispered 'good nights' and 'bonne nuits'.

The group sat in silence for a few minutes each alone with her own thoughts. Carole leaned over and hugged her sister. 'I'm out too,' she said, waving a good night to the group.

Georgia jumped up. 'I'll walk down with you,' she said, taking Carole's arm protectively.

'I'm only 36 you know, I don't need help on the stairs,' Carole said, a little too loud.

'I didn't mean that…I just…I don't like the dark, okay,' Georgia huffed. 'This house is old and scary at night. I think I've watched too many movies about haunted houses.'

Silence descended on the terrace, the only sounds coming from the night-time city. Judy and Wendy sat together in comfortable silence, both grateful for the peace and quiet, but both aware that the other was experiencing almost the same pain. It was oddly comforting knowing the man they loved was having a baby with a much younger woman.

'Mine's pregnant too…and adamant it's his,' Judy began, out of the blue. 'I mean, my husband's…unbelievable. We were married eight years before Georgia saw fit to grace us with her presence, but this girl's…like…bam. Knocked up. She came to my house one night; I think she was trying to find him.'

'Jim's girlfriend did the same thing,' Wendy laughed softly and took a sip of her drink. 'Was your husband home at the time?'

'No, he'd been sleeping at the surgery. They're not together. They had that one night that destroyed everything, but they didn't have a relationship. I have to admit, it helped me immensely knowing that she was looking for him, and she was suffering, that she thought he might have moved back home. I haven't spoken to him at all. He rang when we got back from Florida, from seeing my parents. Grant, my husband, was busy at the surgery, and he called between patients. The last thing I ever said to him was "hi honey, how are you," and it all just blurted out, right there, over the phone. I listened and then hung up. Nearly thirty years together and I got a phone call. I took a nap then got the financials out. I was determined not to be a victim. I'm not sure what came over me. I was a woman scorned I supposed and, well, hell hath no fury.'

The silence settled over them again. Wendy swirled the last of the cognac in her glass.

'Me too. I made him suffer. It sucks, doesn't it? What we turn into? Fucking hard witches. The little bitch came to our place so many times while Jim was trying to decide if he was staying or going. She stalked us! But he chose her, so he had to pay. He'll have a hard time paying for the lifestyle to which he's become accustomed.'

Judy laughed. She was enjoying talking with Wendy, despite the unpleasantness of the topic. Sam and Ingrid dragged their chairs close, grabbing blankets from the huge wicker basket in the corner. Paula appeared with a bottle of wine.

'Are we bitching about our exes?' Sam asked the group. 'Anyone want to hear my tale of woe?'

'Misery loves company!' Judy raised her glass to the group.

'My ex stole my job and then settled down with the guy next door, literally.' She took a gulp of wine and paused for effect.

'He left you for a man?' Wendy asked.

'She left me for a man. We were both music teachers working at schools in a large village. She was at the elementary school; I was at the high school. I thought we were happy, I loved her, and I really loved my job. We had been together for eleven years. We were a couple; you know?'

Sam looked around at the group to see if they wanted to hear her story. 'She always got home first and would feed the dogs, check the mail, start dinner, that kind of thing. She must have opened the letter asking me to apply for a full-time position at the school, and I don't know what transpired but from what I can piece together, she applied for my job, and because I never received the letter, I didn't. Apply, that is.'

'And the guy? What the fuck?' Paula prompted, interested in something Sam was saying for the first time in their long acquaintance.

'I moved away. I got a job at a private college. To be honest, my ex, did me a huge favour. My new job is amazing, and I travel a lot with the college orchestra. It's my dream job.' Sam smiled.

Four fascinated faces implored her to tell them about the guy. Now. Sam threw her head back and laughed. 'She had never had a boyfriend, and I guess she wanted to see what it was like. It didn't work out and last I heard she was dating a dentist. Gender unknown.'

'So, it doesn't matter really. Gay or straight, the wrong partner is the wrong partner,' Ingrid said.

'No, the moral of the story is people are assholes and will screw you, then screw you over!' Wendy said. 'I'm a lawyer, believe me, people are the worst.'

'It's like Sartre said, hell really is other people!' Sam said.

A collective sigh was interrupted only by the gentle tinkle of crystal as the group clinked glasses toasting themselves for their brilliant insight.

Wednesday

The morning dawned misty and soft, perfect for staggering hangovers. The breakfast room was full of regretful drinkers desperate for coffee and vegemite on toast, a tough call in Paris. Carole was dumbfounded when Ingrid plonked the tiny black bottle with the bright yellow lid on the creamy white tablecloth in front of her.

'Where did you get this?' she asked, opening the lid and breathing its salty scent.

'I bought it at the airport in Sydney. It was going to be a little gag gift for Rachel, but I think your needs are greater,' Ingrid said, seemingly untouched by the drinking the night before.

Carole reached for the toast as her memories of the previous night flooded back in. 'The dress I hired is ruined,' she cringed, putting the piece of toast down and burying her head in her hands. 'I can't afford to pay for it. I'm 36 years old and my sister is still fighting my battles.' She picked up the toast and ate, the agonised look on her face giving way to ecstasy as she bit into the dark goodness of the spread.

'I'm sure it will be fine.' Ingrid said, pouring coffee for both of them as the elevator hissed open revealing a large pair of black sunglasses that were propped on Betty's nose, her face pale, bed-hair standing on end.

'Betty!' Carole exclaimed. It was the first time anyone had seen Betty anything less than glamourous.

Betty put both hands up and sat wearily in the chair opposite, pushing an empty coffee cup towards Ingrid who was closest to the coffee pot.

'Coffee. Please,' she whispered, and to Carole, 'Dear, please use your inside voice.'

Carole mouthed 'sorry' as the three sat in companionable silence.

'I am so glad the photo shoot is tomorrow and not today,' Carole said quietly, putting her forehead on the table. 'Although after all that puking, I think I lost the last kilo I've been wanting to shift.'

'We probably wouldn't have drunk like teenagers on Spring Break if the photo shoot was today,' Betty pointed out unhelpfully. 'You don't look hungover at all.' Betty observed lifting the sunglasses to peer at Ingrid and flinching at the bright sun pouring through the windows.

'I didn't drink that much champagne,' she explained. 'To be honest I had a few at dinner, but I didn't feel like partying after Paula dropped that bombshell about moving here. I need my job. Things are not great, money-wise, for us at the moment.'

'Do you think there's a job? I mean, it doesn't make sense, she doesn't even speak French. Is she that good a surgeon?'

'She's great…but I didn't think…I shouldn't say anything.'

The words hung in the air as the elevator hissed open again, Paula emerged as Sam, Judy and Georgia stumbled from the stairwell sunglasses wedged on their faces.

'You look as fresh as a daisy,' Judy said to Paula. 'I don't know how you do it.'

'I take small sips and drink a glass of water between each alcoholic drink. I don't like feeling out of control. My mouth tends to get me into enough trouble when I'm sober, you imagine if I got drunk.'

'Yes, you make an excellent point.' Betty said.

Paula stuck out her tongue. Betty put her sunglasses back on and returned to her coffee. Silence fell over the room as the newcomers took their seats.

'Is that Vegemite?' Georgia shrieked.

Sara popped her head back into the kitchen, alerted by the commotion, looked around the room and said 'More Coffee? Croissants?'

Breakfast was almost over by the time Wendy ventured into the kitchen, unable to avoid the inevitable comforting words and hugs much longer. Georgia was the first, throwing her arms around her and dragging her to the table, asking her what she would like to eat. The young woman knew how her father's infidelity had almost destroyed her own mother's world and seemed determined to try to comfort women in the same position any way she could. Each lady made soothing sounds and tried to be quietly supportive of Wendy, but no-one knew quite what to say.

'It's okay ladies, I'm fine. I was already well on my way to over him before I got that phone call. I'm moving on. We're all moving on,' she said, one eyebrow cocked, daring them to continue fawning over her.

Everyone relaxed. It would be a good day to visit the Louvre, a must-see for most of the guests although Wendy confessed to being more excited than she could ever recall being, and just a little nervous. She told the group she was wondering if she could finally put aside the resentment at her husband for not visiting the Louvre on their honeymoon. She wanted to let it go, she had been carrying it around for years.

Rachel would lead the group on a tour of the main sights, then they would have the option of a private tour of the museum laboratories, or a wine tasting over behind St Eustache church. Wendy had been fascinated by the option of taking a tour of the museum's laboratories, but she had yet to interest anyone else. Despite nursing hangovers, the group seemed more excited by the idea of learning about French wines. Paula had been reluctant to visit Notre Dame and the Louvre, saying she had seen both so many times during her childhood. She suggested a morning spent doing her laundry might be preferable, but Rachel had gently talked her around. Surely, she could leave the laundry for a few hours.

Meeting at the end of the ancient street near Pont de l'Archevêche, the group milled around and waited for the last few stragglers. The women snapped photos and admired the view of the cathedral's flying arches.

Betty stepped forward as Rachel and Paula approached. 'Paula, look, I just wanted to take this opportunity to formally apologise about the phone and I realise that simply buying a new one and writing a cheque are not the same as an apology, so I hope you can forgive me.'

Paula looked at Rachel as though waiting for her to translate. 'Fine,' Paula said, and kept walking.

The group stared after her as she strolled along the bridge with her phone in front of her in a selfie stick.

'That went well,' Wendy said.

'Fuck it,' Betty said and turned to the group. 'I tried. I've done all I can. It's no longer my problem.' There were a few nods and some murmurs.

'So that's that, then,' Rachel said. She walked through the group and onto the bridge. She had arranged for them to meet on the quai rather than in the foyer to avoid questions about the art show opposite the hotel.

The group wandered across the bridge, posing for photos and enjoying the very Parisian busker, an elderly gentleman on a piano-accordion playing classic French tunes. Rachel was still deciding if she would attend the opening of the art show, but she would try visiting Karen in her studio. Sara couldn't believe how terrified Rachel was of the whole situation. They had tried online-stalking Karen but found that she had no private profile, just the page for her pseudonym Mère du temps, that had hundreds of thousands of followers. Never a fan of mysteries, Rachel had taken to pretending the whole thing was not happening, although this was proving difficult with a very inquisitive group who saw her portrait every day and an intrigued Sara who said she wished she had a portrait, too.

Rachel signalled for the group to wait to one side of the entrance to the gardens as Rachel pointed out the French Deportation Memorial on the eastern tip of the Ile de la Cité.

'This memorial is dedicated to the 200,000 French Jews, homosexuals, gypsies, political opponents; men, women and children deported from France to Nazi concentration camps between 1940 and 1944 and did not return,' she explained. 'We won't be visiting the memorial as a group, but I urge you all to go in. Sara's ancestor Antoinette de la Roche was a scientist, a suffragette and a member of the Resistance. Of course, the family is proud of this fact. Sara is writing a book. You can ask her about it if you like.'

They stood in quiet contemplation for a few minutes, slowly moving away one by one towards the river. Rachel wished for once that she had a sunflower to hold overhead. She kept losing track of her clients as they continued along the Left Bank. They reached the busy Pont du Carrousel and regrouped before crossing to Right Bank, the arches of the Place du Carrousel beckoning. As they passed under the arches Rachel reminded Wendy and Carole about their bucket-list item. She pointed to the elegant little Arc de Triomphe du Carrousel from the photos taken when they were kids. Wendy pulled a small black book from her handbag and unzipped it to reveal a handful of faded Polaroids and snaps of them standing under the arch.

'And there's the tears!' she laughed as Carole tenderly inspected each image.

The group milled around as Carole and Wendy re-enacted their childhood photos, although Carole drew the line at letting Wendy hold her on her hip much to everyone's disappointment. Georgia asked if she could post some photos, proudly showing the group the huge number of likes her mother's images had garnered.

'Oh Georgia, it's embarrassing,' Judy protested.

'No mum, it's not. It's incredible! You're so beautiful! Four thousand people can't be wrong!' she said, waving the phone at her mother.

The rest of the group gathered around Georgia's phone, amazed by the gorgeous images she had been posting and the huge number of likes and comments they had. Wendy asked Georgia to explain to her how the whole social media thing worked. Georgia confessed, out of earshot of Judy, that she too had been surprised by the popularity of her mum's photos.

'Surely there is a way to leverage that kind of popularity?' Wendy asked. Georgia responded with a wink as they made their way down the stairs.

Rachel had decided against engaging an official guide as the group said they wanted to simply wander the museum. Afterwards everyone would gather at Café Marley while Wendy and Paula toured the labs where the artists and curators restored and researched the artworks. Paula seemed to have forgotten all about her reluctance to revisit the museum. It was a pleasure for Rachel to see her so excited to see a section of the Louvre she hadn't known existed and that few other people visited. To visit the main museum, Carole, Sam, and Ingrid stuck with Rachel who created a mini tour of her favorite artworks and entertained the small group with fascinating information about the palace and collection.

An embarrassed Carole had deep regrets about questions relating to Dan Brown's novel, The Da Vinci Code. Where was the body found? Have the damaged paintings been restored? Rachel had to explain that the book was a work of fiction. Carole was mortified. Ingrid tried to pacify her but couldn't stop laughing.

After hours of walking all over the museum into the afternoon, the exhausted women slowly made their way to the stunning café overlooking the spectacular Pyramid, the setting sun casting a golden glow over Paris.

As they sat and sipped their drinks, each lady lost in her own thoughts, Rachel contemplated a potential meeting with Karen, The Artist, the following day. Judy and Georgia sat on the low ledge around the fountains that surrounded the Pyramids, talking to a tall, dark haired man who handed Judy a business card. He made a 'call me' gesture with his finger and thumb to his ear. The whole group watched from their table at the Marley, riveted on the action unfolding.

'Do you think Georgia has been approached by an agent?' Sam said.

'He handed Judy the card, what makes you think it wasn't her that was being approached?' Betty teased. 'Are you being ageist?'

Then a young man approached, this time greeting Georgia with a double kiss and then politely shaking Judy's hand, while the group watched on, intrigued.

'And here's Bachelor Number Two,' Ingrid said.

Georgia leaned across and kissed her mother's cheeks, turned and walked towards the river with Bachelor Number Two while Judy lifted her camera to take a photo of the pair from behind.

'Wow…Okay…' Sam said.

'Oh, to be young again, eh?' said Betty.

The entire group swivelled as one in their seats to watch Judy walk towards the table, a small smile on her face. 'Spill!' Sam demanded, before she even had a chance to order a drink.

'Georgia has a date with a young man,' she replied, making a locking gesture on her lips.

'Is he French?' Ingrid asked. Judy made the locking gesture once more and mimed throwing the key over the railing.

They had thirty minutes to reach the little wine bar that was hosting the group for a degustation. Setting out on foot, Rachel gave each group a different route to follow on their phones, all roads leading to Palais de Vin. On arriving at the quaint but lively wine bar, they took a seat at the outdoor tables for aperitifs and compared photos of their evening stroll, there was much oohing and aahing while hunched over cameras and smart phones, Rachel fielding lots of questions about various buildings and monuments.

'Paris has more to see than you could see in a year, visiting a new site every day. There are still places I haven't visited in this city and I have lived here for so many years…' she trailed off wistfully.

'It's wonderful that you are still so in love with this city. How long have you lived here?' Carole asked.

Rachel pondered the question. How long had she lived in Paris? Technically she had lived here since 1995 but she had done 12 of those years twice, hadn't she? She had lived in Rome…last time, for 5 of those years, and London for a couple of years on and off this time… This was definitely a trick question; addition was completely out of the question after a couple of glasses of champagne.

'Half my life really, on and off,' she said.

The group seemed happy with the answer, discussing at length how 'French' Rachel appeared, how elegant she was after all these years living in Paris, or had she always been stylish, they asked.

'Oh no, I was down-right scruffy when I arrived in the city with a backpack and dusty Doc Martins on my feet. Fashion had never been important to me as a teenager, and it hasn't been until...' She was having a minor insight that would warrant further attention later, she decided. 'Until the last few years.'

After years of trying to emulate Marie's effortless chic and grace, she realised she may have achieved it to some extent, but it certainly wasn't effortless. She had become extremely fashion-conscious in recent years, and as she turned and glanced at her reflection in the bar window a flash of a memory: walking with a group towards the palace at Versailles, chatting happily to her clients, while wearing jeans and a pullover. She shuddered. This memory could not have been from her 'current' life, she would not have been seen dead in a pullover outside of her apartment, especially not at Versailles with a group. Was it Karen's presence in Paris that was causing memories of her previous existence to resurface? This was a good question for Sara.

The waiter appeared at the door, cheerily inviting them to take their place in the wine room as Paula and Wendy appeared at the end of the street, Wendy walking about ten paces ahead. Rachel's heart sank.

What has Paula said slash done, now? she thought to herself, ushering the rest of the group into the bar as quickly as possible. She signalled to the owner, a good friend, with a wave of her hand that somehow was meant to convey the message that he would have to look after her group for a moment. She ushered the ladies through the door, closing it quickly behind them; she did not need anyone else to be involved in whatever was the latest drama with Paula. Wendy's face was like thunder as she arrived and greeted Rachel with a quick peck on each cheek. She's mastered the French greeting, Rachel thought and was just about to tell her so.

'Keep that crazy woman away from me. Please,' she said through gritted teeth. 'She ruined...ruined that tour, because...' Paula had caught up with them now, arriving her face impassive. 'She ruined it because she was too busy flirting with the man…the gay man, guiding the tour.' There was a heavy emphasis on the word 'gay'.

'He even said you were 'barking up the wrong tree' but you wouldn't listen. Ugh.' Wendy threw her hands in the air and, eyes wide, marched into the bar, still shaking her head.

'Are you okay?' Rachel asked.

'No, I'm not. Apparently, I'm an idiot,' she said, looking Rachel in the eye. 'I'm sick to the back teeth of these rude, judgemental prudes.'

'You're not an idiot, hun, just trying a bit too hard. You're a wonderful person, and people will see that if you give them the chance.'

'In my defence, he flirted with me first…' Paula replied, her chin lifted. She pulled the door open and went into the bar.

Rachel had ever met anyone as resilient as Teflon Paula.

Thursday

Rachel stood inside the closed lift, willing someone to press the call button to save her from what lay just feet away on the other side of the doors. The last time she had visited this floor had been in what felt like a different life. She had given up trying to understand the science of it all, as if it could be called anything but magic. She inhaled deeply and let the air out slowly, now willing her heart to stop trying to gallop out of her chest.

The last time she had visited this floor she had climbed the stairs. The lift had been installed in 2009 when prices started to rise in the neighbourhood. Lost in thought, she realised to her horror that someone had opened the outside door of the lift and any opportunity for escape had gone. Any second she would find herself standing face to face with someone from this floor and that could only be Karen, or someone linked to her. The Artist had bought the neighbouring apartments on the floor according to the gossip around the building.

Rachel glanced down at her handbag, pretending to rummage in it as the door opened to reveal the good-looking young man from the gallery. His eyes smiled, as he peered over what could only be a painting wrapped in brown paper. He waited for her to open the door and leave the lift. Rachel felt rooted to the spot, her arms glued to her tote which she clung to like a shield. His smile turned to confusion as he carefully leaned the parcel against the wall and reached out for the internal door. It opened with a soft sigh of air.

'I'm so sorry, I was deep in thought,' Rachel stammered.

'That's fine,' he replied warmly, holding his hand out to shake hers.

'Rachel,' she said, shaking his hand.

'I know,' he laughed. 'I'm Pietro, Karen's son. We met…'

'And…this is my sister, Sofia.' He pointed along the landing towards a willowy figure. She was also carrying painting-shaped parcels wrapped in brown paper. She leaned them against the wall and held her hand out to Rachel who was feeling trapped in the lift.

'Rachel,' she said out of habit, shaking the young woman's hand.

'I know,' she laughed, showing a mouth full of perfect white teeth. The three of them stood for a moment smiling at each other, Rachel fantasising about the lift coming free from its cables and crashing to the ground floor.

'You know what, I am so sorry. I must have pressed up instead of down again. Do it all the time. Must. Pay. More. Attention,' she said, awkwardly chastising herself.

'Oh, that's fine, it was actually perfect timing! Can I put these in the lift with you and we'll meet you in the lobby?' Pietro said.

Rachel could only manage a nod and a weak smile as he slid the three parcels into the lift with her and closed the glass door, giving her a little salute and pointing at the floor as though saying 'see you down there'. He shut the outer door and Rachel leaned across and pressed the down arrow.

They have no idea how nuts all this is, she thought. Perhaps they had been told that Rachel knew their mother all those years ago. Okay, I knew their mother years ago, that's a simple way of looking at it. Was she over-thinking the whole thing? God knew she usually over-thought everything so it wouldn't be a surprise. Of course, they could say they had known one another in Paris back in the day. Pressed further the holes would appear though. This time, according to her bio, Karen and Peter had moved to Italy before Rachel had moved to the building. She could hardly say they met in Paris in 1999 when Karen had been living and working in Italy. Rachel was sweating profusely even in the air-conditioned lift.

What will be, will be, she thought, sighing as the lift touched down. She jumped slightly at the soft ding made as the outer door unlocked. Karen's gorgeous offspring would be waiting on the other side of the lift, smiling, welcoming her into their lives, their inner circle. Rachel didn't do inner circles, preferring to stay on the periphery even with close friends and relatives. It was safer that way.

The best part about the time travel, she realised, was that people would forget, she could tag and release them back into the wild. Unfortunately, one of those injured wild animals had found its way back and Rachel was terrified that her life would be ripped to shreds by these well-meaning people.

The door opened once again with a soft exhalation, Rachel returning their smiles, hoping it wouldn't come across as a grimace. The two young people stepped forward as the door opened, arms extended, Rachel worried they were about to group-hug, but they were merely reaching towards the parcels in the lift. She felt herself blush.

'We will see you tonight?' Pietro asked.

'Yes, yes…of course,' she stammered, not knowing what else to say. She couldn't lie to these people even if she wanted to. Her apartment was downstairs from theirs and her group was staying opposite the gallery. She was trapped, and not just in the lift.

'And Sara? Marie? Everyone is welcome.' Sofia had stooped to look directly into her face. This girl is an Amazon, Rachel thought.

'Ah yes, I think so,' Rachel replied, feeling as though she was being probed by aliens. Very tall aliens.

'Great!' Sofia enthused. 'It's going to be awesome. Mom and Dad are so happy they found you still here. And the hotel. Can you believe it's right across the street from the gallery space? Dad can't wait to meet you. He's flying in shortly.' She checked her watch. 'Would you like to ride with us to the gallery?'

Her brother was on the curb loading the paintings into a sleek black SUV, the first splats of rain hitting the pavement. Rachel could hardly decline the offer and then arrive thirty minutes later at the blue door, soaked to the skin. She put her discomfort aside for a moment and thanked them. Sofia opened the passenger side door for her, and Pietro jumped in the back. The ride passed pleasantly, Rachel encouraging the young ones to tell her as much about themselves as possible. Born in Italy, raised in the U.S, their father a celebrated chef, their mother a successful artist and vocal campaigner for the decriminalisation of illicit drugs. Rachel had been allowing their words to somewhat wash over her but was interested in this piece of information.

'Mom is very anti-drug and has campaigned tirelessly to make addiction a medical issue, not an issue for the justice system. Things are bad in the States and Italy. So many young people in prison because they have an addiction or because of a minor offence. It is an unfair system and more often than not, they come out of prison worse than when they went in. So sad,' Pietro took a breath. 'She does these great talks in high schools and colleges. She's so passionate and she goes from speaking English to French then Italian and she does a painting while giving the talk.'

'Which is then donated to the school,' Sofia interjected.

'Yes, they are happy to have a Mère du temps painting for their collection or she is happy for them to sell it, to use the money however they like for the school,' Pietro finished.

'The paintings are filled with imagery, showing how good life can be, but it's short and fragile, so lots of skulls and candles dripping, flowers wilting. It's very clever.' Sofia was speaking again.

These kids are so passionate about their mother's work, Rachel thought, strangely proud herself. The world would have lost this passion and goodness if she hadn't helped Karen all those years ago. She thought of the small group of people who she and Sara had taken 'back'. She wondered if any others had made such great improvement with their lives. It was too bad she had managed to make such a mess of her own life second time around. There was a woman who had terminal leukemia, another one with a prescription drug habit that was slowly taking over her life and that of her husband, the one that felt she had married the wrong person. Rachel was shaken from her reverie by the words time travel.

'Excuse me?'

'It's all part of the talk. The message is that drugs ruin your life and staying away from drugs is easier than trying to find a time portal and going back to clean up the mess,' Pietro explained. 'Mom stands in front of packed auditoriums and keeps them so engaged. It's a gift. She then takes the group through a visualisation of what their life would be like on drugs, what it would do to them and their families, their future.'

'It's dark. At first some of the schools were a bit freaked out by it. Thought it was too heavy,' Sofia said.

'The darkness is followed by the light, like in all her paintings. In the visualisation she takes them right into the feeling, kids are crying, sobbing. But then she has them retrace their steps back to that point, sitting there in the auditorium, going back in time to when they made a choice to stay away from drugs and have a healthy, joyful life. It's ingenious and beautiful. And it works. After just 12 months, the data they started collecting from the local social workers, police and hospitals pointed to this being successful. Even in areas of high drug crime.'

When he finished speaking, Pietro's eyes were sparkling with tears and Rachel realised she had tears of her own making fresh tracks through her carefully made-up face. Rachel couldn't remember the last time she had cried. She would have to fix her face before the group saw her and started asking questions.

Thursday morning brunch was to be held at the local market. Rachel saw her group walking towards their designated meeting point on the corner as the black SUV crept down the laneway towards the gallery. Thanking Sofia and Pietro she gathered her things, promising them she would make it to the show. She smoothed her long skirt and made her way up the street to catch up with her clients. Her head was spinning but at least she had resolved to go to the art-show, if not the opening. She needed to see Karen but wasn't sure she could deal with a huge crowd looking on.

At the market, the group milled around, cameras snapping away.

'Is there anything more photogenic than a French marché?' Judy asked as Rachel stood waiting for everyone to gather around.

Moving from stall to stall, Rachel chatted to the owners and staff like old friends and, translating to the group, handed around produce, bread, cheese and meats to try. The group was astounded that most of the farmers were able to suggest recipes and even wine pairings for everything from mushrooms and truffles, even certain breads.

After the informative, and filling, tour of the market they found a café for coffee and spent a lovely hour chatting amongst themselves, comparing photos and purchases. At precisely midday, the car would collect the group for their much-anticipated photo shoot. Those who hadn't opted for the shoot were free to roam Paris until Myles returned to take them clubbing that night. Rachel felt sick at the thought of clubbing and was amazed that even Betty and Janet had taken up the option. She thought back to her younger years, always the life of the party. She knew every cool club in town, but she had happily left those days behind.

The group stood almost as one and slowly moved back towards the hotel. Ingrid and Wendy had both opted out of the shoot, along with Betty and Janet, but Georgia was busily trying to convince them all it was the best idea in the world. Ingrid waved her book at the group and bade them farewell. She was heading to Montmartre, alone, to spend the afternoon with herself, she had explained.

Betty and Janet said they would be having an 'arty day' intending to visit the Musée d'Orsay and the L'Orangerie but thanked Georgia for trying to include them. Wendy, on the other hand, changed her mind and decided to join her sister for the 'frivolous and silly' fashion shoot, much to Carole's excitement.

Myles was waiting in the laneway talking to one of the gallery staff and Pietro, who all turned as the group approached.

'You didn't tell me you were famous,' he said to Rachel, nodding at the portrait. Rachel smiled at the men, shooing her group into the limo. Behind her dark glasses, her eyes were scanning the gallery for Karen.

'See you tonight!' Pietro called as Rachel climbed into the limo and shut the door.

Myles crept the limo down the now-crowded laneway and turned onto the quai, watching Rachel in the rear-view mirror, no doubt thinking what everyone thought when they saw the portrait, 'when did you become so serious?' She was wondering the same thing.

She became aware that the group was peppering Georgia with questions about last night's date, but the young woman was deftly fending off all enquiries. She changed the subject, scrolling through her Instagram feed.

'We were approached by two agencies,' Judy said.

'No mum, you were approached. The first contacted us through Fabian's Insta.' She looked at her mother and smiled. 'And the second… I was taking photos of mum at the Louvre and voila as they say in Paris, they found us in real time. The agency has been following the photos on my Socials all week. Mum's going to be a model again!'

The car erupted into screams and poor Myles nearly ran a red light. Judy had her hands up, protesting that perhaps she wasn't going to sign with an agency, but the smile on her face told a different story.

London Calling

The exquisite dresses glowed in the spot-lit dressing room, and the wall of shoes caused the group to draw a collective breath. Each woman seemed to gravitate towards her favorite colour although Fabien had made it clear that he would choose the outfit most suited to the client's colouring. No discussion would be entered into. Rachel loved and trusted Fabien and would normally leave her clients in his capable hands, warning them that Fab was a genius and could be quite temperamental, but with Paula present Rachel had decided to stay. She had become quite sarcastic with the other ladies and Rachel knew Fabien was a gentle soul who would not take kindly to being baited.

Each lady was paired with a stylist and disappeared into the salon. Rachel stood at the huge panoramic window watching the river silently sliding by, so lost in thought, she didn't realise her phone was buzzing. Seven missed calls and a few texts from Sara requesting information on her car ride that morning with Karen's kids. She fired off a dozen long messages to give the juicy details and promised she would fill in the gaps later. She was so engrossed in the texts she didn't notice that Carole was standing on the raised platform in front of the mirrors, transfixed by her own appearance. Rachel checked her watch. Had she really just spent an hour messaging Sara? She was supposed to be on Paula-Duty, but she had been absorbed in her phone. She realised she was sweating in the air-conditioned space and wondered if she was about to have an anxiety attack. Finding the plush sofa, she sat and breathed slowly in and out.

'Rachel, are you okay?' Carole asked from across the room, watching Rachel in the reflection.

'Oh yes, I'm fine. Thanks, just felt a little, warm, hungry. Warm and hungry. Hot and Hangry,' she laughed. 'Carole you are stunning,' she finished, giving a little round of applause to Fabien who had created a smoky-eyed film star look for Carole, her long hair falling down her back in loose curls.

'Even on my wedding day, I didn't look this good,' Carole said. She looked at her reflection from every angle and turned to look at her sister who had emerged from the salon, dark hair piled on her head, smoky eyes like her sister's.

'Oh, Wen look at you!' she squealed, somewhat ruining the old-time Hollywood allure Fabien had been aiming for.

'Don't cry lovey, you'll ruin your makeup,' Wendy said, unable to turn her head, her own hair being given its final spray of lacquer but knowing from the break in her sister's voice that she was about to cry.

'I just wish you hadn't told me this morning that you're moving to London. I've been on the verge of tears ever since. How could you just tell me like that?'

Rachel was amazed by this news.

'How should I have told you? A singing telegram? A hand-written note?'

Fabien's studio overlooked the river and the Eiffel Tower on avenue de New York. If the weather was bad, clients could still have their shoot done in the safety and privacy of the studio, with the plate glass windows offering an uninterrupted view of the tower and the river. But the perfect days, like today, they would do a few shots in the studio but then they could go out beside the river, after make-up and hair. Fabien led Carole to the glassed-in alcove and began to position her for her first shots. He pressed a black button on the wall and the huge plate glass window began to move back into the wall, bringing Paris into the studio.

Carole stuck her tongue out at her sister as the photographer started to shoot, prompting a very French outburst of, "ooh la la," from him, followed by tutting from Fabien. Later they would all agree that the photo with her tongue out was very funny.

Wendy had made her decision by her second day in Paris. She hadn't considered for a moment that Carole wouldn't support her choice or somehow feel betrayed by it. Her sister hadn't seemed to have an opinion when she was living her dull as dust existence, married to a man who never wanted anything more in life. As it turned out he had wanted more, but not with her, she thought ruefully. Carole had even urged her at the outset to forgive Jim and 'work it out'. Work what out? she had asked her sister. He left, for a much younger woman and had no intention of coming back, so what would you like me to 'work out?' Did Carole think she was going to 'work things out' with a husband who had so brutally broken her heart and her confidence, and taken away her chance to have a baby?

She had thought Carole would be happy for her but apparently Wendy was being selfish. There had been raised voices. I am quite tired of being the one who makes all the good choices, the smart one in the family, she had said and received a slap from Carole.

Wendy had cried. The tears coming as a surprise to both her and Carole. You never cry, Wendy, Carole had whispered. I'm sorry. I can't believe I slapped you. Wendy had turned away. Not usually given to tears, she took them as a sign she had made the right decision, along with the terror that had taken up residence in the pit of her stomach. Carole would have to learn to live with the new Wendy.

Carole turned this way and that for the camera, the river Seine sparkling in the background while another fat tear rolled down Wendy's freshly powdered face. Carole would be fine. Their parents, too. She looked in the mirror as the stylist held up different shoes. She pointed at a pair and the stylist screwed up her nose. Wendy shrugged. Wiping the tear and letting the make-up artist powder her again, she decided to stop thinking about her life-altering decision.

Big deal, she thought. I'm moving to London, not the moon. I'll get a job and a flat, and if I hate it, I'll go home again, or I'll go somewhere else. She would make the move to London with or without her sister's approval. You can do that in your forties.

The photographer was signalling to her to join Carole in the shot as some tourists stopped to watch the proceedings.

'Why did I sign up for this?' she asked as she stood next to her sister.

Carole, who was having the time of her life, gave her a sideways glance. Originally planning to forego the photo shoot in favour of a day at the Musée D'Orsay, she changed her mind in order to spend the extra time with her sister. She could visit the museums any time, now that she had decided to re-locate just across the pond. She smiled at her sister and struck a pose straight from Madonna's Vogue video.

One by one, the women emerged from the salon cocoon as beautiful butterflies to stand in front of the photographer. They were awkward at first, but within minutes each lady was smiling and relaxed, striking poses that would make a supermodel proud. Fabien and his team had outdone themselves this time, Rachel told him. He begged her to let him 'have his way with her' and winked. She knew he meant he wanted to style her. She winked back but declined, promising that next time, she would let him do whatever he wanted. Fabien loved a bit of innuendo. In fact, innuendo was one of his favorite English words.

A change of outfits and they made their way across the road to Passerelle Debilly taking over the timber foot bridge while other tourists gawked in the background and took selfies. Rachel stood in the shade of the umbrella that had been set up. She certainly wasn't dressed for summer in her Ellie Saab jumpsuit, no matter how amazing she looked. Myles arrived with the limo and, after another outfit change, afternoon turned into evening as the ladies were photographed in some of the most picturesque parts of the city. The final shot was taken as the sky turned that particular shade of blue that Paris does so well, with the tower just beginning to sparkle.

Too soon it was time to head back to the house to get ready to go clubbing with Stephanie. They each chose an outfit from the rack to wear for the night out, striking one more pose as a group, with Rachel in the middle. On the ride back to the hotel, Rachel looked at the image that the photographer had kindly snapped on her phone for her. The ladies gorgeous in their designer outfits looked like a group of brightly plumed tropical birds with Rachel, a black-clad raven in their midst.

Art and Life

In preparation for the art show, the narrow street had been closed to traffic. The normally quiet alley was a hive of activity, pools of light showing tables laden with polished glassware and bottles of wine. Huge banks of pillar candles filled the street along with incredible bouquets of flowers. Rachel stood four stories up in Sara's darkened kitchen with her face pressed against the windowpane, trying to see the comings-and-goings in the laneway below, wondering if she would gather the courage to come face to face with Karen. Clearly Karen remembered her, the house, Marie and Sara. Clearly Karen, unlike Rachel, had followed their instructions to record everything and read it daily, to the letter.

Obviously, the timeline had changed but Rachel's recollection of those few intense hours in 1999 seemed to be getting stronger by the day. Even the gallery opening across the laneway was strange. What had been a shoemaker's workshop until recently was now an up-scale art gallery. Rachel had known that night with Karen that this was going to happen.

Had she had a premonition of this exhibition? A niggling thought had been working its way into her brain over the past few days; was her vision of the gallery and the exhibition actually a memory? Would she go back again and give it all another shot...or had she already.

The loop of time was a tricky place to get stuck thinking. The daily bouts of déjà vu were an indication she had gone back more than once according to Sara, but she couldn't be sure. Even Sara, who had lost count of the number of times she had gone back, was vague about how the timelines could loop back over onto themselves. Dreams became confused with memories from the past life and the current one.

Something she did know, or at least thought she knew, for sure, was that she had only one memory of finding herself already at home and that was enough to last many lifetimes. There were too many questions and she wasn't sure anyone had the answers, although she knew the woman who had painted those incredible portraits may hold some clues.

Becoming aware that someone was standing beside her in the dark, she turned to see Janet's profile watching the action in the laneway, the blue hour making her pale face glow. Quite used to Janet's reluctance to speak, Rachel simply nodded hello and was surprised by the spoken reply. 'Do you think you'll go to the opening?'

Startled by the sound of Janet's voice she temporarily lost the use of her own. 'Um…err…yes, I'll pop in.'

Rachel realised that the suspense was killing her. She wished she had been able to visit Karen at her studio, to speak to her in private, away from her children who seemed to accept all too easily that their mother had gone back in time. Karen's lined face floated into her memory, along with her scarred arms, her sad smile.

'Who is she? The artist? I mean, who is she to you?' Janet asked. 'Do you know her, or did she just paint you?' It seemed that after weeks of not speaking to anyone other than Betty she had a lot to say.

It was strange to hear her say 'the artist', the name Karen had been known by before. Before. The Artist, without the sneer, or the pity, it came out of Janet's mouth sounding elegant and proud.

'Betty and I went in, to enquire. She's a collector, Betty, you know. I'm an artist so I love to see beautiful work, but I can't afford to collect in the way Betty does. I bought one of the little tattoo paintings.' She paused looking down into the street. Rachel followed her gaze to see the unmistakable figure of Karen disappearing into the gallery.

'She told us you saved her life.' Janet turned to face Rachel. 'That you talked to her for hours, stopped her killing herself, helped her to go back and sort things out.' Janet used quotation marks in the air with her fingers when she said, "go back."

She handed Rachel a thick glossy folder containing the catalogue from the art. The artist had signed the front page, Mère du temps and then underneath she had also signed her real name, Karen Jones. An invoice was stapled to the back cover, but the lighting was too dim to make out what it said. Placing the dossier on the table Rachel went to flip the light switch on.

She pored over the catalogue, fascinated by Karen's use of imagery and portraits, apart from the fact that it was obvious to her, as it would be to Sara and Marie that this body of work was all about travelling through time, mortality and an homage to those who had helped her during that time. There were many faces she didn't recognise, but she, Marie and Sara all featured in the collection. There was an elfin young woman whose image appeared over and over. She realised that this must be Karen's 'A'. Her lost friend Agnès. Finally reaching the last page Rachel read the invoice. Twice.

'Oh my -' she said slowly reading the enormous sum of money recorded.

'Betty bought it. Your portrait. Mère du temps, is highly collectable, legendary in the United States. Very charitable, gives more art away than she sells, but still the prices keep going up.'

Janet went on to tell Rachel about the artist, filling in the blanks between what she knew from the car-ride that morning with Karen's children. After her encounter with Rachel and Sara, the artist had set herself on the right path. After years of success and happiness she had only returned to Paris because her husband had been offered a partnership in the restaurant Entre Amis. They were staying with friends, but Sofia and Pietro had moved into the apartment to make things ready for their mother to resume painting in the studio again. While unpacking the cartons stored there, they had found notebooks, canvasses and walls covered in drawings.

'Rachel, the woman is undeniably talented, and she's famous, both for her artwork and for her work with young people, her anti-drug message, but I was a little concerned about her, to be honest.'

Rachel stopped staring at the enormous sum of money printed on the page in front of her and looked up at Janet's concerned face. She waited for Janet to continue.

'She seems to think she literally went back in time. From '99 to '93. From a room in this hotel, or house as it was then.' Janet's face was impassive.

The thousand responses to Janet's statement jostling for position in Rachel's head were interrupted just as they were about to erupt from her all at once. Excited voices filled the room as the rest of the group filed in, dressed to the nines after their photo-shoots and pumped for their night of clubbing with Stephanie. Janet melted away like a ghost as the room filled, leaving the dossier from the art gallery on the table. Dragging her attention away from the paperwork, Rachel gave a little cheer as the ladies twirled and admired each other's outfits. Sara appeared with a tray of champagne glasses but almost dropped it, distracted by the catalogue on the table. Rachel decided she would let Sara drag her to the show; it had to be done and now she found herself wishing the group would just drink their champagne and leave so she could get it over-with.

The elevator door sighed open and Paula struck a pose, eliciting a cheer from the hyped-up group. The black lace bra wasn't exactly revealing as bras go, but considering its intended role as an undergarment, it definitely revealed more than your average blouse, which seemed to be missing from Paula's otherwise beautiful ensemble. The other women tried to cover their shock or amusement, all avoiding eye contact, with each other, and the wearer, who had obviously intended to shock given the grand entrance. She twirled the stunning red silk and tulle skirt and flashed her pink suede stilettos. Everyone oohed and aahed and studiously avoided mentioning the absence of a top layer.

Rachel surveyed the room and did a quick head count. Janet stood on the far side of the room looking towards the towers of Notre Dame, quietly drinking her champagne, but Betty had yet to enter the room. Shuddering, Rachel realised Betty would walk out of that elevator at any moment and humiliate Paula.

No, she would destroy Paula.

Marie, who had been away visiting her mother bustled into the cosy lounge with a tray of hors d'oeuvres, smiling and greeting her guests. Sara took the tray from her, placing it on the table she leaned over to take a better look at the gallery dossier, eyebrow raised. The chatter died away as the cathedral bells chimed for the hour. Marie made a beeline to Rachel's side and wrapped her in a hug while Sara stood transfixed by the folder on the table. Marie looked from Rachel, to Sara, to the dossier and back to Rachel, eyebrow arched the same way her daughter just had, prompting Rachel to snort with laughter as the bells fell silent. Marie smiled and Sara raised both eyebrows this time, causing a full-blown fit of nervous laughter from Rachel. Quickly gathering herself, she was mortified that Paula would think they were laughing about her missing top layer, but she seemed completely oblivious as she discussed her new shoes with Wendy.

'Ladies, it is my extreme pleasure to introduce to you, Marie, famed maître d' and hotel owner, mother of three, including Sara, and the most elegant woman I know,' Rachel said proudly, holding Marie's hand.

'It is lovely to have you all here in my hotel and home. I look forward to getting to know you a little better over the next few days. I have been away visiting my mother, who is the most elegant woman I know,' Marie said.

The ladies gave a polite round of applause and Marie made her way around the room introducing herself and making small talk.

Sara walked with her mother, topping up champagne and making introductions. Marie typified French elegance even while cooking breakfast or sweeping the foyer and as her eyes finally arrived on Paula, she blanched visibly.

'The car will arrive in five minutes, perhaps everyone should finish preparing for the evening?' Marie spoke to the room, but everyone knew the comment was meant for Paula.

'Well, I'm ready. This ensemble is a la mode, very in, according to my personal shopper at Galeries Lafayette,' Paula said sweetly, looking Marie directly in the eye.

Smiling her most charming smile, Marie shook her head ever so slightly. 'Yes, it is very in at the moment, for the young girls, but not really intended for 'les femmes d'un certain age.'

Paula feigned shock. 'Clothes have an age? Betty would disagree! I couldn't afford clothes like this when I was young. I'm slim and have great boobs that cost a fortune, so why shouldn't I enjoy them?'

Heads nodded all around and Marie put her hands up in defeat.

The elevator dinged softly, and the doors slid back. Betty emerged in a stunning white pants-suit and black patent stilettos, a huge crystal at her throat and a gold Chanel clutch. Her eyes scanned the room to ensure Janet was there, happy, drink in hand, and she walked forward smiling at Marie, arm outstretched in greeting. Having shaken their host's hand, she turned and gave Paula a once over while everyone held their breath.

'Chop, chop, girls,' she commanded. 'Paris isn't going to paint itself red!'

Mère du temps

The group filed into the laneway, now filled with glamourous people, waiters with trays and arty types dressed in black, a photographer snapping away. The once-empty, stark white gallery space looked incredible; the portraits spot-lit, a DJ playing dance music while everyone stood admiring the works. Rachel and Sara played sheepdog, herding the distracted group towards the end of the street where Myles waited with the car. Rachel just smiled enigmatically when asked if she was going to the art show, which Georgia remarked made her look even more like her portrait. Piling into the limousine, a smiling Myles opened a bottle of champagne, his eyes carefully avoiding the scantily clad Paula who was desperately trying to get a reaction from the young man.

'How do you think we all look tonight, Myles?' she asked, feigning nonchalance.

'Well, I can say you are the most beautiful women in Paris tonight, and I am French so I can be trusted. We understand beauty in all its guises,' he said, poetically, avoiding eye-contact as he handed out glasses of champagne before retreating to the safety of the driver's seat.

'Oh no, not more champagne…' Carole joked, rolling her eyes. 'Well, only if you insist.'

The group raised their glasses to Judy for her birthday, despite her protestations that they had done that enough already. After toasting each other in turn, they toasted Paris, the limousine, Rachel, Sara and Marie. Ingrid suggested they toast Paula's breasts. They were all eager to meet the mysterious Steph who knew Paris nightlife better than anyone, according to Rachel. For good measure they toasted the hotel, Paris again, and finally Myles.

'I love the limo,' Georgia gushed, 'But I'd better not get used to it. I'll be catching the Metro when I move here.'

'Unless you snag yourself a rich guy, a 'Sucre daddy',' Paula said, matter-of-factly, 'to keep you in the manner to which you've become accustomed.'

'I'm not a prostitute, Paula!' Georgia snapped.

'Georgia, she was joking,' Judy interrupted, hand on her daughter's arm that had flown up in disgust.

'Things aren't working out the way they're supposed to. He's from Brisbane, Mum! I didn't come all this way to meet a guy from Brisbane!'

'So what?' Judy said quietly. 'He's lovely. Just enjoy his company.'

The other women looked around at each other, intrigued. Were they referring to Bachelor Number Two? It was obvious to everyone that poor Myles was besotted with the lovely young Georgia, but he certainly wasn't from Brisbane, so who was this mysterious man?

'You never know! What does it matter where he's from if he's Mr Right?' Carole was already slurring her words.

'I'm not even going to get married. I'm my own woman! Like Rachel, I want a career,' Georgia protested.

'You're 22. You don't know what life will bring, darling,' her mother said calmly. 'And Rachel had a husband, you know. You just don't know the turns life can take. There's plenty of time for you.'

Georgia turned to her mother. 'There's time for you too, mum. You're only 50 and you're still beautiful! You still have your best years ahead of you.' Mother and daughter embraced, as well as two women can embrace in haute couture with a full face of makeup. The group murmured their agreement, still trying to figure out who this mysterious man was.

'Stop it you two, you're ruining my make-up,' Carole sobbed, dabbing her eyes with a tissue.

Wendy put her arm around her sister and reached out and took Judy's hand. Looking around the car at the faces surrounding her, she knew the tears would come if she spoke.

'For fuck's sake, you ladies need to lighten up! Drink some more champagne.' Janet raised her glass and laughed.

Ingrid grabbed the champagne and filled each glass in turn, they toasted Paris once more. Janet timidly standing up to put her head through the sunroof for the first time as they crept along rue de la Huchette in search of their first stop.

Marie and her husband, Gerard, stood in the now crowded laneway, clutching glasses of wine. They were both staring up, captivated by the portrait of Rachel, her long flowing hair and relaxed smile showing a side of their friend that they hadn't seen for some years. Sara joined them as a gallerist was making a beeline for them but stopped in her tracks when Rachel came through the old blue carriage door. The staff member lifted her arm and made a signal to Pietro who was standing with a group of people at the back of the gallery. He signalled to someone standing out of view in a back room. This little chain of events resulted in Karen and Rachel coming face to face across 100 feet of polished concrete gallery floor. Rachel looked away, self-consciously asking Marie a question. She took the glass of wine the waiter handed to her, drinking it in one gulp, before realising she was now standing in the middle of the gallery with Karen facing her.

'Holy shit, what happened to you? You look like a dominatrix!' Karen laughed, throwing her arms around a shocked Rachel.

'What? A what?' she stammered.

'Darling you were so soft and lovely when I knew you last time.'

'I'm still…'

'Yes, you're still beautiful. Here,' she handed Rachel a dossier like the one Janet had given her.

'I was going to say, me. I'm still…me.' She looked down at the glossy white folder. It contained a half-dozen drawings and photo-copied pages of notes, stapled together. She looked up at Karen who was standing a little too close, her heavily tattooed arm resting on Rachel's shoulder. Time hadn't made Karen any less intense than she had been as a recovering addict.

'A copy of some of my journal, from that first day. Like the one you gave me. Oh, the déjà vu, the recollection, is so strong. It's so crazy, isn't it?'

Rachel nodded, intent on the artwork, unable to read the journal in the dim lighting but desperately wanting to. She edged her way over to the brighter lights above the bar area.

Karen was still behind her. 'Do you remember everything?' she asked.

'Everyone retains certain memories, like we do in our…err, regular life,' Rachel whispered. She continued to pore over the photocopied sheets of paper. Finally, she located the name she was looking for.

'Karen, what happened to your friend, Agnès? Is she…?' Rachel looked around the room.

'Here.' Karen pointed to the end wall of the gallery. Above the space, a huge portrait loomed; a young woman with a pixie-cut and a gleam in her eye. The label next to the artwork had a red dot.

Rachel looked up, her mouth hanging open. 'Agnès?'

'Yes, of course, you didn't meet her. She's beautiful.' Karen stood in front of the artwork now, her palm pressed against the painted surface.

'Yes, she's beautiful.'

'She was the main reason my life has been so…amazing. She gave me so many gifts, believed in me completely. Loved utterly.'

Rachel could no longer hear Karen over the music, but she stood, lips moving, as though speaking to the painting, then closed her eyes, slightly bowing her head. Was she praying? Rachel wondered.

'We met in Australia. She loved it there, only came back to Paris to get her visa sorted. After I - met you…after Pete, she was the one I had to sort out. I didn't have to tell Pete; he was just happy to be happy. Very uncomplicated.' She looked over at her husband. He was in the process of telling an animated tale, his arms flailing, eyes intent on his audience.

'In the end I tried telling Agnès the whole story, the portal, the drugs, everything.'

'And she didn't believe you?'

'Oh no, she believed every word. That was the problem. She said if it happens again, well, it's meant to be.'

Karen turned to Rachel and took her hand. She turned Rachel's wrist over, revealing the faded "A" tattoo, a matching one adorning her own wrist. A large tear made its way down her cheek.

'She went to Australia. Went to the same farm, miles from anywhere, went wandering off into the desert with her camera. I sometimes picture her, lost and dying out there in that brutal landscape, and telling the sky that she was sorry, that she should have listened. But I know she probably just flipped the sky off and laughed joyously. I asked her to at least leave a note about where they could find the body. She didn't, so that didn't change. She's still lost.'

Rachel stood hand in hand with Karen, the A's on their wrists pressed together.

'Some things are just meant to be,' Rachel said, leaning in so Karen could hear her. She only nodded.

'I wouldn't change anything. It's made me who I am today,' Karen said smiling.

'A few days later, after I,' she gestured with her thumb, pointing backwards. 'I went to your apartment door, but a young couple lived there. When did you come to Paris? To live in the building?'

'1995,' Said a voice beside her, Sara had joined them.

'Sara,' Karen breathed, enveloping the young woman in her arms. Sofia arrived at her mother's side, handing a similar dossier to her.

'Is the time portal still there? Does it still work?' Karen asked, not lowering her voice. Instinctively Sara looked around for eavesdroppers, only to see every eye in the gallery on their little group.

Sofia held her hand out to Sara, introducing herself and leading her over to the delicate colour-pencil drawing of the blue carriage door. It had a red dot. Sara looked around at the sea of red dots. It appeared the show was completely sold. Everyone was talking about the time portal, the blue door, the symbolism.

Yes, people, it's all just symbolism, Sara thought, but she was worried about what might happen next. Would she have hordes of people showing up at her door?

Karen's husband Peter, the famous chef, joined the little group in the middle of the gallery, wrapping Rachel in a hug. A photographer began snapping away, a stunned Rachel in the centre, looking like she was about to faint, cry or vomit. Everyone wanted to shake Rachel's hand as she stood smiling stiffly like a lottery winner outed by the local media on her doorstep while still wearing pajamas.

Sara walked back to the group and took Rachel's hand, feeling her relax a little as they circled the space to admire the artwork, trailed by the photographer.

'Thanks for rescuing me,' she whispered before explaining the story of Agnès.

Pietro, Sofia, Karen, and Peter joined them at various times, and introduced themselves to Marie and Gerard, who seemed to be the only one from the house across the street who was enjoying himself. Sara put her father's enjoyment down to ignorance. He was blissfully unaware of the portal for starters. And because he didn't use Social Media, he had no idea that the story of the time-portal had gone viral in the past hour. Checking her social media accounts, she saw eight friends had already messaged her with a variation on the theme of "Isn't this your front door?" or "I hear you have a time-portal in your pool shed."

Spying Rachel's friend Stephanie, Myles stopped the limo in the middle of the cobblestone laneway. He ran around to open the car door, the passengers waiting for their turn to take his hand. Inquisitive tourists stood aside snapping photos, unsure if the passengers were famous or not. All safely out of the limo, a self-conscious Myles continued the slow crawl along the one-way street.

Stephanie stood over six feet tall, an electric blue pant suit and sky-high patent leather shoes ensuring she was unmissable on the street, her brilliant smile welcoming the group to the first club of the evening. Rachel had briefed them on how the night would run. It was basically a glorified pub-crawl. They would have one hour in 4 different clubs, meeting on the curb, on the hour, to move on to the next location. They were to stick to their buddies so everyone was safe, but if they weren't at the designated meeting point on the hour, they would be left behind, and a text sent to Rachel for safety's sake. They were to also send a text to Rachel to let her know they were okay, or if she should launch a search and rescue. No-one was to be left alone. Paris was a beautiful city but could be filled with danger after dark for the unsuspecting and the drunk.

The first club was low-key, fun and stylish and they all met on the curb as planned, piling into the limo like clockwork. The next clubs were not to everyone's taste, Georgia loving the first, young, hip club and hating the next that was thoroughly enjoyed by everyone over 35. The last club was the highlight of the night. It was a huge dance-club with top DJs and incredible singers. Previous groups would dance into the wee hours then venture back to the hotel with tired smiles on their faces, but these women were feeling the effects of too many late nights and too much champagne. They were happy to sit and enjoy the music and the spectacle.

It was late, and Steph was enjoying the slower pace. The group seemed content to talk from the comfort of their plush booth. She was about to ask if everyone was ready to go home when Paula grabbed Ingrid's hand and dragged her away. The rest of the group sat and watched the ensuing argument with increasing concern. Paula's behaviour had become erratic over the course of the evening. Insults directed towards, and often reciprocated by Betty were expected by the group, but Paula had upped her game. Even Steph had come under fire, but she simply held her hand up and turned away from Paula. Betty and Janet decided to leave. Waiting for a taxi on the midnight streets of the 17th arrondissement seemed less frightening than spending any more time with Paula.

Ingrid and Paula were obviously shouting at each other now and could just be heard over the loud music. Security circling them like sharks, Ingrid pulled her arm away from Paula and walked back towards the booth. Paula was at her heels. Georgia stood up to let Ingrid sit with Sam, but she stood in front of the group, tear-stained face held high.

'Can we go?' she said. The question was directed at Sam but included the rest of the group. 'I'm sorry Stephanie, I'm tired and Paula, well, she needs to go too.'

Paula now stood bristling at the edge of the group, arms folded, jaw set. 'Oh my God, you are wet blankets. The clock strikes twelve and the princesses have to run to the carriage, or they'll turn into pumpkins.'

'Yes, I think it's time to go.' Stephanie stood, signalling for the bill to sign. 'Ladies?' she looked from face to face, ensuring Paula was not left out of the invitation. 'I think it is time to go and get our beauty sleep.'

'It's going to take more than sleep for this lot.' Paula sneered at the group.

'Ok Paula, that's enough,' Sam said, offering Paula her hand, the other one in Ingrid's.

'So, you want to hold my hand now, but you wouldn't dance with me before.'

Sam blushed. She had been mortified when Paula had tried to kiss her as they danced together earlier. Paula had never attempted a civil conversation with Sam, rival for Ingrid's friendship in her mind, and now she was trying to pash her on the dance floor.

'Let's just go?' Sam said, ever the diplomat.

'No, I'm not going anywhere with you. Or you. Traitor.' Paula turned to Ingrid.

Judy tried to intervene but was insulted for her trouble, Paula remarking that she might buy her a copy of the famous book 'French Women don't get Fat' for a moving-to-Paris gift. Satisfied with the looks of horror on her tour-mates faces, Paula lifted her chin and glared at Judy.

'You are all so fucking…. nice! It's so boring! I miss Betty, at least she would have told me to shut up,' Paula spat.

'Ok, well I will not be so nice. There is a saying 'ere in France, perhaps you have heard it? Actually, you may have heard it tonight…shouted at you from a distance. 'Elle s'habiller trop jeune pour son âge'? Non? Perhaps I can translate it for you? In England they will say mutton dressed as lamb, have you heard this one?' Stephanie put her hands on her hips.

Paula laughed hysterically, although no-one else joined her. The waiter stood awkwardly by while Stephanie signed the bill, kissed him on both cheeks and calmly took out her phone to call Myles. It wasn't even midnight, but everyone was on their feet, ready to leave. A security guard approached Stephanie and quietly enquired if she needed any help. Paula stopped laughing.

'Screw you all!' she yelled and attempted to storm from the room, as well as a very drunk person in heels and a tulle skirt can 'storm' from a room.

Ingrid and the security guard followed her. They were miles from the hotel and Ingrid had no intention of letting Paula out of her sight in the state she was in. Paula had talked her down off the figurative ledge in Montmartre on Sunday and now it was her turn to help. As she pursued a determined Paula, she realised that it had only been five short days since their arrival in Paris, since she had had her own epiphany at the Sacre Coeur. That too had been fuelled by too much champagne. It had been a full week. They had all done so much in such a short period of time and the cracks were appearing. Paula had seemed to be faring well, ticking her bucket-list off each day, she had appeared well rested and enjoying herself. She had rarely been using her phone, which now that Ingrid thought about it probably wasn't a good sign, meaning that her family had likely stopped replying to her messages. Her bossy, passive-aggressive messages.

At a signal from the security guard who was following at a discreet distance, the '6-foot-tall, 4-foot-wide doorman stopped Paula from leaving, gently suggesting she wait for her friends. Stephanie and Rachel regularly brought groups to the venue, and the doorman was not about to allow one of their clients to wander around Place de Clichy on their own, especially one wearing only a brassiere, silk and expensive shoes she was now trying to take off.

Despite the rage pulsing through her head, Paula stopped and listened. A large man was offering to sit on her if she didn't behave and Ingrid was at her side, panting and puffing. Admitting defeat, she chose to take the kind advice from the man-mountain in front of her. The doorman allowed Ingrid to lead Paula away to the side of the entry, but he wouldn't let them through the door. Paula could see she was trapped and sat heavily on the steps leading to the cloakroom, her face in her hands. Ingrid sat next to her, attempting to soothe her but Paula lifted her head and asked her to stop.

'I don't want your pity, Ingrid. Leave me alone,' she said, her voice impassive.

'You helped me in Montmartre. I wasn't going to let you run off into the night, never to be seen again! So, you got drunk. Big deal. We've all done it.'

'Well, you didn't pop a pill and make a complete ass of yourself, did you? No, but I did! Of course, I did,' Paula said through her gritted teeth. The group crowded the foyer.

'Did you take one, Paula?' Ingrid asked in a harsh whisper, horrified. 'You should know better.'

'It was perfectly safe; I used a pill tester. I am a bloody doctor you know! Just because you lot wouldn't join in…I wasn't going to miss out.' she said, crying now.

The doorman discreetly ushered newcomers away from the scene on the stairs and signalled to Stephanie that the car was waiting in the street. Myles quickly changed his usual joyous expression to one of concern, holding the door of the car open as they filed morosely from the club into the limo. The return trip to the hotel was silent for a change. No champagne was poured. Stopping in the now deserted laneway, no sign of the crowded art show held there a few hours before, the portrait of Rachel still watched from the darkened gallery, unnerving in the eerie silence. The limo crept down the lane.

Avoiding eye-contact, the group made their way silently to their rooms. No tea and cognac on the terrace tonight, Carole thought.

She clutched her sister's hand as they negotiated the dark stairwell. She had been approached by Paula too, with the offer of a party-pill. Come on Carole, it will liven things up a little, Paula had said to her. Carole had never been so fast to say no. She'd taken ecstasy once with a boyfriend. It had been scary and if she was honest, fun at the time, but she had been back home, in a club they knew well surrounded by friends. Carole shuddered. Who knew what Paula had taken and where she had got it from? Everyone has done stupid things in their life, but Carole was happy she had put such things behind her.

Wendy went to her room to shower and Carole did the same. She peeled off the slinky dress and lay it lovingly over the back of a chair. Her room was a mess. Being with her sister seemed to take her back to childhood. She showered and removed her makeup and stood in front of the mirror.

Had they only been in Paris for mere days?

It seemed an eternity since she'd seen her kids. She put her pajamas on and climbed into bed with her phone, scrolling through photos of her children. She'd made a deal with her husband that she wouldn't be in contact all week but that didn't mean she couldn't fall asleep every night looking at the photos.

There was a quiet knock on the door. Wendy had two bottles of water, and a plate with some bread and grapes. Carole smiled at her sister who sat on the edge of the bed and handed her a bottle. Wendy put the plate on the bedside table and handed Carole some grapes.

'That was an interesting night,' Wendy said.

'It would have been even more interesting if I'd taken the pill Paula offered me.'

Wendy looked at her over her glasses and shook her head.

'I think I understand why she's a mess because I could have so easily gone the same way these last few months. You spend your teens and twenties studying, your thirties and forties building a career…and in her case raising ungrateful children and stitching people back together, and now she wants to party.'

Carole nodded. 'Do you think I'm going to be like that in my forties?'

Wendy shook her head. 'You're a great mum, your kids are amazing, and your hubby is the kindest sweetest man in the world.'

'Wend, that's the nicest thing you've ever said to me.'

'Oh, and you didn't spend your twenties studying and you're not building a career, so you'll have no excuse if you do,' Wendy said, ducking expertly to avoid the grape her sister hurled at her head.

They drank their water and lay in the dark the way they did when they were young girls. They fell asleep joking about how quickly one sobers up when someone in the group loses it although they doubted Paula would be laughing right now.

Friday

Brunch was a small, disjointed affair. The group drifted in and out as the morning wore on. Paula hadn't shown her face, choosing to remain a lump under a duvet that Ingrid monitored for signs of life during the course of the morning. Sam had left her to it, suggesting a pillow over Paula's face would not be a bad thing as she left to meet Carole and Wendy at the famous flower market.

Rachel had texted the group various options and meeting points they could take up and a reminder about the traditional dinner that night near the university. She had entertained them with stories of the two brothers who owned the old restaurant, their great-grandfather's original business opened in 1922 that still used the Provençal menu brought by him to Paris all those years ago. The tiny bistro had survived the war, the riots of 1968 and the influx of phone wielding tourists who all fancied themselves food critics.

After the art show, Rachel stayed at the hotel. She thought she would be emotional, but she was on a high, talking into the wee hours with Sara and Marie on the roof-top terrace. They read and re-read Karen's incredible journal, captivated by the beautiful artworks she had generously given them. Betty and Janet joined them after leaving the club early, but they didn't mention Paula's antics. Betty pored over the gorgeous drawings Karen had given them.

'So, it's all true then?' Janet asked, quite matter-of-factly considering she was enquiring as to the existence of a time portal.

'Of course!' Rachel, Sara and Marie all said at once, smiling.

'No, don't be ridiculous!' Gerard said in unison with the three women.

'Shame,' Janet said, squeezing Betty's hand but not looking at her old friend. Rachel expected the rest of the group to join them on the terrace post-clubbing but hadn't even heard them arrive home. She was blissfully unaware of Paula's behaviour until receiving Stephanie's text the next morning as she sipped her coffee.

'Bloody hell, Paula!' she mumbled under her breath. Her head was still spinning from meeting Karen and the response on social media. It was only a matter of time before the mainstream media started talking about it.

She sat back at the table and tucked a loose curl behind her ear. She was horrified that Karen thought she dressed like a dominatrix. Pretending she was looking out for someone, Rachel stood, and checked her reflection in the windows of the café. White skinny jeans, red tank top, black denim jacket, scarf…nothing out of the ordinary for a stylish woman in Paris. She had decided to leave her hair out today. The jeans could be a little more relaxed, she thought, but the wedges are perfect for the flower market. Dominatrix, indeed.

Judy appeared beside Rachel, looking cool and calm in Camilla, her hair slicked back.

'Do you think my look is too severe?' Rachel asked a surprised Judy as she joined her on the street to wait for the rest.

'Err, perhaps I am not the best judge. A frumpy house-wife, or house ex-wife from Sydney…'

'Frumpy! You are so not frumpy!' Rachel snorted.

They waited until the designated time, quickly realising it would be just the two of them as text messages began to come in from the other women.

'Just us then? Still happy to do the flower market?'

'It's on my must-see list!' Judy enthused.

They wandered through the Île de la Cité flower-market enjoying the cool morning air, waving to Wendy and the others as they enjoyed a drink at the café in the square. Rachel was bursting to ask Judy about her plans with the agency, Georgia's love interest, and the goings on at the dance club. Judy for her part, had received a cryptic text from Georgia, was desperate to ask Rachel about the art show and now the sudden concern that her look was too severe, but they wiled away an enjoyable hour drifting through around the Île de la Cité, making small talk and in not so much indifference but a mutual desire to avoid gossip.

Janet and Betty approached as the designated hour to meet on the quai for the Mystery tour. Wendy, Carole and Sam strolled over from their table as Ingrid and Sara came around the corner from the rear of the hotel, Paula conspicuous in her absence. Obviously, none of them have been online, or they would have been asking about the show, Rachel thought. She directed the group to wait beside the bridge and they were soon distracted by the view of Notre Dame.

'My father has checked on Paula,' Sara said to Rachel. 'She is fine, but she has a very big headache, and she is embarrassed, as you can imagine. I talked to her for a while. She's coming to dinner. I told her she must come.'

Rachel laughed at her friend. She certainly had a way with people.

'Have you seen the news? Ben says we 'broke' the internet!' Sara said, waving her phone at a stunned Rachel.

'Oh no…' was all she could manage as she scrolled through the feed.

'We had to use the old exit…' she said arching her brows. 'It was strange…I get the shivers every time I walk through that door now!'

Tourists stood back clicking cameras madly as a line of vintage cars filed along the quai in front of the group, faces lighting up with recognition and delight when the women were told the cars were their mystery transport for the afternoon's tour. They piled into the cars excitedly snapping photos and the little convoy set off, past the Conciergerie and towards the Left Bank. For two hours they circled the city going as far west as the Bois de Boulogne and north to Montmartre, the cars attracting much attention as they wound their way along the winding hilly streets.

The convoy of tiny vintage cars delivered the group to the Bassin de la Villette for the final leg of their mystery tour, the passengers breathlessly thanking the drivers and making their way up to the canal boat. Georgia and Bachelor Number Two were standing beside the canal, waving madly to her mother and ran to meet her as though they had been apart for years, not hours. Bachelor Number Two, Julian, greeted Judy warmly, waved to the rest of the group and got back on his scooter. Everyone wanted to know what Georgia had done with her day, but Georgia had just one question on her mind; why was the online world melting down with a hoax post about the artist Mère du temps? And what the hell did it have to do with Rachel and that portrait? Once she had boarded the canal boat, she made a beeline for Rachel.

'Okay Rachel, you've won the internet today. It's that 'blue and white dress picture' all over again but this time it's your face! P.S. I love what you've done with your hair today,' Georgia said. She was breathless and smiling. She held up her phone and scrolled through the feed. Everyone had shared the post. Rachel was mortified, glancing across the deck for support from Sara, who was deep in conversation with Janet and Betty.

'What can I say, Georgia, other than it is all true.' Rachel held her hands up in defense.

'Yeah, right, and I'm the queen of England,' she said, taking her mother's hand and doing a little spin.

'You're looking happy,' Rachel said, relieved that Georgia had already lost interest in the subject. As Sara had suggested, if they stuck with the truth, they might just get away with it.

'I had the best day. I think I'm going to love living here in Paris.' She hugged her mother. 'Mum's going to be modelling and I've got an internship with a fashion blogger who's mega.'

'And you've met a lovely young French friend, I see?' Rachel arched her eyebrows and took a sip of her drink.

'Well, yes and no. He's lovely, but he's not French. He's from bloody Brisbane, but he lives here. For now.' She shrugged her shoulders.

Rachel was pleased for Georgia and Judy. It was her favorite part of the job, seeing her clients happy at the end of the week. She looked around at the chattering, relaxed group, wondering if she had indeed made a mistake including Paula in the mix. She had never had such a turbulent week, and each drama connected to the same person. Today had gone off without a hitch and everyone was smiling, laughing and dancing, enjoying the gorgeous warm summer evening.

The noisy group hushed as the tour boat disappeared into the tunnel as they approached the end of the line at Port de l'Arsenal, the music bouncing off the illuminated walls. Emerging from the tunnel as another perfect day was ending with a stunning sunset, the group raised their glasses to the musicians and to Paris once more as they docked. Disembarking, the group was on such a high, Rachel considered taking a less direct route to the restaurant to dissipate some of the energy before they entered the tiny space. Like children on the last day of school everyone spoke at once, except Rachel and Sara who strolled arm in arm.

'I'm so glad you decided to spend the day with us,' Rachel said. 'After the emotion of finally plucking up the courage to go to the gallery last night...To come face to face with Karen was amazing, all those memories flooding in...'

'You're famous, the tours will be busy.'

'And the hotel will be full!' Rachel laughed.

'Do you think anyone will take it seriously? Time travel? People might believe that the Da Vinci Code was non-fiction, but a time-portal? We don't believe it and we've gone through it.'

Rachel told her about the conversation with Georgia.

'I'm just going to keep doing what I have always done with my clients and if the time is right and we believe someone will benefit from that little stone room behind the pool then we will do what we have always done.'

The restaurant glowed like a welcoming farmhouse. It was tucked away near the university, between a green-grocer and a tiny wine shop that was like something out of a Harry Potter book. A lone figure stood outside the restaurant looking down at her phone. Paula. Sara had told her she would be missed if she didn't attend the dinner but had completely left it up to her to get there. The little bit of tough love had worked, and she smiled a thin-lipped smile as she looked up to see the group approaching. Rachel empathised with how hard it would be to show her face with the group again, but Paula's resilience and strength had shown through. Or it could have been a complete lack of self-awareness. Teflon Paula, Rachel thought, as the group welcomed her with hugs.

The brothers Milo and Pierre welcomed the group to take their seats, both making a great show of their affection for Rachel, her face blushing crimson as they both dropped to one knee to propose, a playful fight broke out when she placed both gaudy, plastic rings on her finger. Marie and her husband Gerard appeared at the door.

The food arrived immediately as a set menu paired with wines was to be served. Conversation and wine flowed, smiles and cameras flashed. The night went by in a whirl with the two brothers flirting and singing, pouring wine and serving at table, their love for their restaurant obvious. The night was winding down and half the group wished to go dancing, the other half wished to go to bed, Milo offering to join those who wanted to dance, while Pierre volunteered to join anyone in bed to a laughter and a sea of waving hands.

They began the slow walk back along the quai.

'A perfect day,' Rachel said to Marie.

'A perfect day? We had to go out the back way,' Marie said, 'so many people were in the street.

'Oh dear, I'm so sorry,' Rachel replied. 'Sara suggested we go with the story but be a little sarcastic about it, so people will think they are a little silly believing it…it's working so far.'

Sara fell into step with them. 'Maman, it will blow over. At least you had an excuse to tell papa all about it,' Sara said. Gerard was walking behind with Paula.

'Oh, he doesn't believe a word of it and he refuses to let me send him back a week to prove it. He says he's a scientist, but I tell him Antoinette de la Roche was a scientist too and she did it,' Marie said.

'I can hear you, you know. You are all completely crazy,' he said catching up with them and leaving Paula with Ingrid. 'It's a gimmick the artist thought up to sell her paintings. Speaking of completely crazy,' Gerard said, lowering his voice, 'Paula told me she had been offered a position at the hospital where I have my rooms. I took her word for it, but I very much doubt they would hire a surgeon who does not speak any French. I gave her the benefit of the doubt, but I think it is highly unlikely.'

Rachel shook her head slowly, disbelief and sadness vying for position. She would have a word with Paula in the morning and ask if she wanted to 'go back', that the time portal was real and give her the option of using it. For such an intelligent woman, she had made a mess of things. Rachel hoped she was well behaved while out dancing; she didn't think the group had much more forgiveness left in them.

Saturday

The rest of the house was still sleeping when Rachel and Paula sat opposite each other in the cosy study. The room had been the clinic of Marie's great-great grandfather. Rachel was cradling a huge mug of milky coffee, trying to wake up. She had stayed up half the night talking with Sara and Marie, but Paula looked fresh.

'How was your night?' Rachel asked.

'Great. I did all my washing and packed.' Paula sat back in the seat and crossed her arms.

Rachel looked down at her coffee and blew on it. It wasn't terribly hot, but she wanted to buy herself some time before responding.

'I thought you went dancing?' She took a sip and closed her eyes.

'No, I don't want to take a bag full of dirty laundry home. I need to hit the ground running when I land.'

Rachel took another sip. In all her years she had never had a client stay in to do their laundry. 'So, you can prepare for your new position here at the hospital?'

Paula looked away from Rachel, turning in her seat to look around at the book lined walls. 'Uh huh. Yep. Do you think there are ghosts in here?' Paula asked. 'I'm used to dealing with corpses on occasion, but this room feels different. Do you feel as though you're being watched?'

Well done changing the subject, Rachel thought. She took a breath and placed her cup on the table. 'I'm so comfortable here, this house feels like a second home to me now, but yes, there is something here. A presence I think you'd call it,' she said, 'but a kind one.'

Rachel sat back in the chair. Paula was still looking around the room. It seemed that she wanted to look anywhere but at Rachel.

'I've been worried about you, Paula,' Rachel continued. 'You've not been…err… yourself the last couple of days. Would you like to talk about it?'

Paula shifted her gaze to look directly at Rachel.

'I'm going to start by saying you don't know me at all…but if you mean I've been a bit crazy then yes, I have. I realised that I've done everything wrong in my life. How I managed that is anyone's guess. I got everything wrong,' she said. She placed her palms down on the leather inlaid desktop. 'My kids hate me, my husband hates me and my staff hate me. Even Ingrid hates me, but she's too kind to say so.'

'I'm sorry you feel that way, but I know for a fact Ingrid doesn't hate you. She cares deeply about you. She asked me to speak with you.'

'My life is a mess and I'm going home to see my children who, did I mention, hate me, and I'll come back here and start again. There's nothing for me at home now.'

She continued to stare at Rachel and crinkled her nose. 'Dammit,' she said 'I can't even cry. I really wanted to cry, but the problem is I don't care.'

Rachel stood and moved around the desk and put her arm around Paula's shoulders. She had endless patience for crying. Marie often joked it was her super-power, but she didn't know what to say next.

'I'm fine, I'm fine,' Paula said, 'at least I will be when I sort this mess out. I wish I could go back in time like the artist said and…and un-do it all, you know? I'm still baffled as to how I got it so wrong. No, I do know that I married the wrong man; it's his fault the kids are the way they are. Bad genes, you know?'

I wish I could go back and do it again…

Rachel had heard those words often and knew she had the means to help Paula do exactly that. Paula didn't suspect that the time portal truly existed; who would? Regardless, Rachel wondered how Paula would fare, travelling back to a time when she believed she was happy. She could start again, armed with the knowledge of what not to do the second time around, like marrying a man with 'bad genes.' She worried that Paula lacked that essential trait for someone contemplating going back, humility.

Rachel went to the bookshelf. She wasn't looking for anything in particular, she was again buying some thinking time. Even if she could send Paula back, she knew it wasn't that easy. She had visited the city as a child, but Rachel racked her brain to recall if she had mentioned a time in Paris as an adult.

'There's always a way to sort these things out,' Rachel said softly. 'And remember, nothing is wasted, no experience, regardless of how horrible it is when you're going through it, is without its lessons.' She sat on the edge of the antique desk.

As much as Rachel feared for her clients who decided to re-do things, she couldn't help but get a shiver up her spine thinking about it. Things hadn't really worked out exactly as she had thought they might when she went back, but she had finally come to enjoy her life as it was, as she had made it, rather than thinking about how it could be.

'I know. I need to change everything. I'm going to ask Judy who handled her divorce. She got her fair share. I won't ask Wendy; she got screwed and she's a lawyer.' Paula rolled her eyes. 'You know, I've forgotten what it's like to enjoy myself, what it's like to smile and be happy,' she said.

Rachel smiled but her mind was racing. Enjoying herself? Was she referring to the racy outfits, dancing on tables, and public displays of unwanted affection? Could she tell Paula the portal was real? Offer to help her go back? She could change her life, but Rachel had no idea how that would affect her children. She took a deep breath.

'Happiness. It's the key, isn't it? Were you happy last time you were in Paris?' Rachel asked. She always led with this question as they had always believed the portal would take you to your happiest time in Paris.

Paula stopped smiling. She was thoughtful for a moment, then a stunned expression crept across her face. 'I lied,' she said, and then jumped a little as though the words frightened her. 'I lied to you. I'm so sorry.'

'What about?'

'Ingrid and Sam had both been here and well….' Stopping mid-sentence, Paula shrugged, her lips thinning, cheeks turning red with embarrassment. 'At least the mystery is solved. We can both see how I've made such a fucking mess of my life!' she announced, sitting stock still in the seat.

'Oh… You've never visited Paris, before? It's okay.' Rachel was shocked but covered it quickly. 'Paula, stop beating yourself up so much. You expect so much of yourself, no one can live up to the standards you set for yourself.' Rachel leaned on the desk, a smile fixed on her face. She had been about to convince Paula that the time portal indeed existed, that she really could travel back in time and try to sort out her crazy mess of a life. Rachel wondered what would have happened had they tried.

Paula sniffed and looked around the room. 'You won't tell the others?'

'No, certainly not. Would you like to come to Versailles today? Everyone is going.'

'I would love to come! It's on my list. I want to see the gardens. I've downloaded an app, so if you don't mind, I'll just take myself off for a self-guided tour,' she said as she made to leave the room.

Teflon Paula was back.

Standing in the foyer waiting for the tired group to gather for the drive to Versailles, Rachel considered that at the very least she could have sent Paula back to the beginning of the week. She could have thought about how happy she felt to be in Paris and armed with the information she need not make such a mess of things. Rachel remembered that Paula hadn't seemed terribly happy on the Eurostar. This was followed by problems and frustration with her phone…and the day only went downhill from there. The phone flying from the sunroof and the screaming match in the laneway was still fresh in her mind. Rachel had a feeling that Paula had needed things to come to a head in some way, and anything else was just avoiding the inevitable.

Returning to Versailles was always difficult for Rachel, but at least the hot weather would take her mind off the nostalgia. She fanned herself, grateful she had chosen the white Maticevski sundress instead of her customary pantsuit or pencil skirt with boots. Smoothing the silky cotton under her hand appreciatively, she smiled. She might be relaxing her look, but she wasn't going to be sacrificing style. The windows and sunroof firmly closed, the air-conditioning was a welcome addition for the passengers, most of whom were nursing another hangover.

'You ladies have certainly made the most of the week,' Rachel said to the group.

This phrase, spoken at the right time, typically at the commencement of the drive to Versailles, caused much thought and introspection. Would anyone go back and do it all again? She watched their faces as they quietly relaxed against the car's leather seats. Let's get down to business, Rachel thought, smiling at the pensive group. She knew the kinds of thoughts that were probably racing through their minds now that the week was almost finished.

Heat was radiating from the cobblestones by the time they reached Versailles and it wasn't even nine. Emotions were running as high as the temperatures as the tired, mostly hungover group reached the entrance, all trying to push through to get out of the sunlight. Recent terrorist activity had tightened security at Versailles, restricted vehicular access to the palace forcing the over-dressed party to sweat their way to the cool of the security check point.

'Can we get a cold drink before we start, Rach?' Georgia begged, to a chorus of nodding heads and groans of agreement.

'We will be starting our visit to the Chateau de Versailles with morning tea at Ore, the Ducasse restaurant,' Rachel said to the relieved group, who obediently followed her to the gloriously cool space.

Rachel made sure everyone was seated and had ordered and then sat quietly to one side and took out her phone. As usual for this stage of the tour, the conversation was subdued and many of the women were deep in thought. Paula was standing at the bar with an espresso and after drinking it, tucked her headphones in her ears and left the restaurant without looking back. Rachel sighed. The phone buzzed in her hand, startling her.

It was a text from Wendy. 'Can we have a chat about coming back to Paris?'

Rachel's head snapped up and she found Wendy in the busy dining room. Wendy smiled and tapped her watch. Rachel nodded. She knew exactly what Wendy wanted to talk about.

An hour later, refreshed and refuelled the group were eager to explore the chateau. Rachel was looking forward to it; the castle was her true passion. The group made their way slowly through the growing crowds, stopping at each room to huddle in and hear Rachel's commentary. The Queen's rooms were Rachels favourite places in the whole chateau, but it was closed for renovation, so she stood in a quiet place and described the space. She was in full swing, explaining the significance of the rooms and noticed no one in the group was looking at her. She had been so engaged with her spiel that she hadn't looked around and read the mood of the group.

'I'm so sorry, I'm just so passionate about this space. You'll all have to come back to see it when it opens…in three years! Let's keep going. The Hall of Mirrors awaits,' she said, turning on her heel.

They waited for a group to move along the corridor before heading into the next large apartment. The light was dim, and the space was cooler than the rest of the palace. The ladies fanned out enjoying the luxurious space, as another group entered from the opposite direction.

'I know it's lovely in here, but we have to keep moving if we want to see the gardens,' Rachel said.

'No one seems terribly interested in the gardens,' a voice said.

She turned. She knew that voice. Standing ten feet away across the shiny parquet floor, as he had all those years ago, was Alex.

'Hi,' he said. Their tour groups topped admiring the ornate room to watch something far more interesting.

'Alex…'

He walked towards her. 'How? Why are you here? Are you back in Paris? Working, I mean?' She blinked as though fearing it was a hallucination or worse, a coincidence.

'I arrived in Paris last week. Gustav has me working already.' He gestured to his group. 'I went to Marie's last night, but no-one was there. A photographer was standing in the street with some tourists then I saw an enormous portrait of you. It seems a lot has happened since I was last in Paris.' He laughed softly.

'I went back to Marie's this morning and she said you would be here. It is fitting, don't you agree. Like déjà vu.'

Rachel nodded. 'More than you know.'

'I'm staying, Rachel. I'm staying this time; you can't tell me to go.'

A quiet sob escaped from her lips as he took her in his arms.

Betty and Janet

'Once again we find ourselves in a fancy limousine headed to an exotic destination,' Sam quipped.

Little ripples of laughter went around the car. It was their last hurrah in Paris and all eyes were shining with a mixture of excitement and emotion as they pulled up to the curb in front of the luxurious old hotel. A lone paparazzo stood sentry in front of the building in case someone famous should arrive. The screen dividing Myles from his passengers had rarely been up all week, as the women had insisted on making their dashing young driver an honorary member of the group. He turned and raised his forefinger to his lips.

'You must pretend you are fine ladies tonight,' he said in a stage whisper.

Snorts of laughter followed. Although all were silent with wonder as the young chauffeur opened the door to reveal the impossibly elegant Plaza Athénée. The iconic red awnings glowing, huge bouquets of flowers giving off intoxicating scents, and every light shining in the early evening light. The paparazzo sprung to life, but quickly saw he was wasting his time on regular people. He went back to playing with his phone.

Myles held out his hand one by one to his passengers, each woman mouthing thank you or merci in turn. The normally chatty group were speechless as they made their way along the red carpet to the entrance of the building. Rachel, light-headed but smiling radiantly, dressed in an elegant white pantsuit, stepped forward to welcome her group as the doormen opened the doors.

The concierge gave the slightest of bows and welcomed them to the hotel, ushering them into the foyer to clear the sidewalk. Rachel smiled at them and mimed putting her hand under her open mouth and pushing it shut, suggesting that they should follow suit. 'Welcome beautiful ladies, to the Plaza Athénée and our final dinner all together.' Rachel looked at a sea of smiling, curious faces.

'Will Alex be joining us this evening?' Carole asked.

'He's parking the car,' Rachel said, smiling as her shiny hair fell in soft curls around her shoulders.

The maître d' showed the awe-struck group to their table in the ornate dining room. Rachel was distracted, looking out for Betty and Janet. Alex appeared at the doorway. Her heart skipped a beat as she lifted her hand and waved to him. She wanted to take his hand and ask for a suite upstairs, but she knew this final dinner was unmissable. She knew she had had that feeling before and she closed her eyes, waiting for the déjà vu to pass. Her reverie was interrupted by Ingrid and Paula arguing near the front door. A doorman hovered as their voices rose. Rachel hurried to the scene and ushered the two women into the large foyer, Alex standing to one side.

'Quiet, please. Please,' Rachel said. She held a finger to her lips. 'What's going on?'

Paula, tears in her eyes, turned and ran from the hotel. Alex pointed at the door, a question in his eyes, but Rachel shook her head. She turned to Ingrid. 'What happened?'

Ingrid's face was red, her fists clenched. 'I just…just called her on her bullshit. She was lying to me. About her Paris job offer.'

Rachel wasn't surprised.

'I was upset. Last night I asked her what I was going to do about work, and she was so dismissive. I was seething so I asked Marie's husband to phone the hospital this afternoon. He confirmed my suspicions.'

Rachel put her hand on Ingrid's arm.

'She thinks I'm stupid. She thinks we're all stupid.' Ingrid shook her head and walked slowly back to the table, taking a glass of champagne from Sam.

Rachel took Alex's hand and quickly filled him in as they headed towards the ladies' room. She unlocked her phone to call Betty. She didn't want anyone to miss this dinner, after the week they had all had together. She wanted to introduce them to Alex. Janet's outlook on life and her prognosis had improved over the week, receiving news that she was in remission from cancer. Betty, the little firebrand from London, successful, wealthy, no-punches pulled, was now a symbol of strength for Rachel. Early in the week, she had received very different news; a call from her doctor to tell her that her cancer had metastasised. She had only months to live, at best. She had sworn Rachel to secrecy, not even Janet was to know. Rachel had seen others do this, hide all manner of illnesses for one last week in Paris. She had broken her own rule and offered Betty the use of the time portal, before Karen had told the world. To her credit, Betty had taken the information in her stride; both the terminal diagnosis and the crazy news of a time portal in the basement.

The tone sounded in Rachel's ear. At the same moment she heard the muffled sound of a cell phone ringing in the ladies' room behind her. It interrupted a heated conversation, the words "time portal" drifting unmistakably through the closed door. Rachel held on to the call, thinking it was an amusing coincidence until she heard Betty answer as the voices went silent. Rachel moved as far from the ladies' room as she could lest Betty hear her.

'Hi Rachel,' Betty chirped, her voice high and thin.

'We're in the bathroom, we'll be right out.' She didn't wait for a reply.

'Okay,' Rachel said awkwardly to her phone. She grabbed Alex's hand and pulled him towards the waiting group. A small round of applause came from the table as Rachel officially introduced him to the women. They ordered wine and starters. She let the conversation wash over her. Her mind was still on the snippets of whispered conversation overheard in the ladies' room and she wondered where Paula had gone. Alex leaned across and kissed her cheek. She sighed and kissed him back.

Rachel had told Betty about the time portal in confidence. It was not to be discussed. Period. Although in light of it being all over the internet at present, that rule had gone out the window.

Oh, what does it matter? She willed herself to relax and enjoy the company, the wine, the exquisite surroundings, and Alex sitting by her side. She had spent years hiding something that didn't need to stay hidden any more. The media was already losing interest. The little stone room at the back of Marie's house would continue to help those who needed it and continue to stay hidden from those who didn't. How short people's attention span is these days, Rachel thought.

Janet appeared at the back of her chair and tapped Rachel gently on the shoulder.

'Can we speak? Away from the table?' she asked, smiling at Alex and squeezing his shoulder lovingly. 'Alone?'

Rachel followed Janet back to the bathroom where she found Betty sitting on a sofa, handkerchief dabbing delicately at her eyes.

'Betty won't go back so I want to. I told her I will choose her, I'll change everything. I want more time.' Great sobs wracked her thin body as she stood wringing her hands.

Betty shook her head sadly.

'No one is going back, Janet. We've had our fun,' she said softly. 'You remember what Hemingway said?'

'Can't we have one conversation without you quoting Hemingway at me?' Janet retorted, exasperated. She sat down and sighed. 'Okay, I'll bite. What did Hemingway say?'

'He was my father's friend, so no, I can't. He was much wiser than both of us and he drank. A lot. If he hadn't been such a boozer, he would have been a genius!' Betty stood and took Janet's hands in hers.

'Darling, Ernest said, "see Paris and die" and that's what I intend doing. It's my time and going back isn't going to do anything. We all die, and we've had a good life, lovey. You have your gorgeous kids. We've done some things, haven't we?'

Janet nodded, hand to her throat.

'Promise me you'll stay with me for the rest of my life?' Betty asked.

Janet nodded again, fat tears rolling down her cheeks.

'And you won't try to change things?'

Another nod. Rachel handed them both tissues from the sleek counter-top box, keeping one for herself. Betty dabbed under Janet's eyes then her own. 'Now, let's fix our faces and go chat up the famous Alex.'

Sunday

Myles inched along Place Joffre. The stretch limousine came to a stop in the dusty parking bay, the École Militaire looming above. The women were dressed in jeans and t-shirts or flowing summer dresses. Everyone smiled as they filed out of the car and carefully made their way across the road. Myles followed with a picnic basket and handed it to Rachel.

'Enjoy your last meal in Paris, for this visit. I'll see you next time you're in town.' He gave a little bow.

They begged him to stay but he had work to do. He explained that he was collecting a couple from their hotel for a guided tour of the chateau and gardens at Fontainebleau.

'Thank you, Rachel, for organising my accreditation with your friends. I am so happy to be more than a driver today,' he said, blushing.

'Oh, you're so much more than a driver to us, Myles!' they all chorused, laughing and hugging the sweet shy young man.

He stepped forward and took Georgia's hand. 'I would like to take you out for dinner when you are living in Paris. I know some very good places, cool places,' he said shyly.

The rest of the group stood back.

'Thanks Myles, that'd be mega,' Georgia said, pulling him into a hug. His face blushed crimson. She had no idea the effect she had on the poor guy.

He bid each lady farewell with the obligatory air-kiss to each cheek, finishing with Rachel.

'I'll see you next month, so we can do it all again,' she said quietly. 'I hope you don't become too famous for your tours that I can't work with you anymore.'

'I will always work with you. You are very special. I am so happy to see you are happy. You look like your portrait today. Relaxed and beautiful.' He smiled and kissed her hand before turning and making his way back to the car waiting in the centre of the road.

The group walked under the trees catching little glimpses of the Eiffel tower through the lush green foliage. Emerging into the bright sunlight they stood and watched some tourists playing Boules. No one seemed to know the rules and they had already lost the jack, so they simply bowled the balls from one end of the open space to the other between sips of wine directly from the bottle. They seemed to be enjoying themselves. Alex and Sara stood under the trees ahead waving to the group.

When they caught up, Rachel handed the basket to Alex. He bent to kiss her. The group gave a little cheer, then followed the pair through the trees to a long trestle table. It was set with a pale-yellow tablecloth, mismatched white crockery and glasses, and simple wildflower centrepieces.

'Your picnic awaits,' Sara said, as Claudine began placing crusty baguettes on the table. Long platters of charcuterie, simple salads and breads, bottles of wine and tall bottles of sparkling water dotted along the table.

'We thought you had the picnic, Rachel,' Carole exclaimed.

'So much for bread and cheese on a blanket,' Wendy laughed, rolling her eyes, but smiling at the gorgeous provincial style setting before them.

'We have blankets. You can take what you like and go and lie on the grass.' Rachel pointed to the blankets, but the women were already taking their seats under the trees. Paula took the seat at the end of the table and angled her chair to face away from the others. Alex, Sara, Claudine and Rachel poured wine and showed them how to tear the bread.

'Oh, I'd love to go back and do this week again…' Georgia said wistfully.

No one spoke. They had all arrived at different conclusions about the rumoured time portal, most believing it was a ploy by the artist to sell her work. Rachel had stayed up all night explaining everything to Alex, among other things.

'I'd like to go back to buy some Bitcoin,' Alex said, breaking the tension. Sara and Rachel laughed, followed by the rest of the group.

Ignore it and it will go away, Marie had wisely said. Most people on the web were already treating it as a joke or a marketing ploy. Who would believe it anyway?

'So, what's in the picnic basket, Rach? Or is it empty, just a prop to throw us off the scent?' Carole asked, to change the subject.

'Oh, it was a prop,' Rachel replied, sitting at the head of the table and pouring herself a glass of wine.

'To all of you,' she raised her glass to a chorus of 'to us' and 'salutes'.

'To Paris,' Georgia toasted, to another round of echoes.

'Oh no, I can feel another hangover coming on,' Carole groaned.

'Actually, the basket is not empty, there is a surprise in it,' Sara said in her usual mysterious way. Alex approached Rachel with the basket, placing it on the empty chair.

'Yes, there are gifts in there from all of us,' Betty said.

'Oh, no you shouldn't have!' Rachel protested. 'You all paid me a lot of money to come here,' she said to laughter and applause.

'Don't get too excited, chérie, there was a rule. The gift had to be from the heart, and it had to be something already owned, or found while here in Paris,' Sara said.

'I would've given you my old phone, but I didn't bring my diving gear,' Paula said. She wasn't smiling.

The other women looked at the table, or the sky.

'I'm sorry, Paula…' Rachel wasn't sure what more she could say that hadn't already been said. Paula had had a lousy week and there was nothing she could do about it. In the back of Rachel's mind, she knew there was a terrible review coming and there was nothing to be done about that, either. She would refund Paula her entire tour cost. It meant she would make nothing on the whole week's work, but it would be worth it.

'On the bright side, you got a new phone out of it,' Georgia said.

Everyone was smiling at Paula, as though willing her to smile back.

Sara cleared her throat. 'Let's see what's in the basket.'

The first item was a slim journal and a silver pen. Rachel picked it up and opened it. At the top of the first page, someone had written "Paris Summer 2016" but otherwise it was empty.

'That was the travel diary I bought at the airport. I thought I would write all about the week, but as you can see, I haven't had time. I've been too busy having the time of my life,' Carole said, tears already welling up in her eyes. 'Thank you, Rachel, for the most amazing week. Thank you, ladies, for making this the best week of my life. Please, don't tell my husband I said that! Wendy, my sister, thank you for this incredible gift. I don't know how to thank you enough except to say I am so happy that you are moving to London. I will start saving my pennies as soon as I get home to come and visit you.'

Everyone was crying now, but they were tears of joy as Wendy hugged her sister.

Alex laid a tiny silver Angel pin on the table and everyone stopped and looked around the table.

'That's from me,' Janet said. 'My grandson gave it to me when Phillip went to hospital and it clearly doesn't work so I'm giving it away.'

No one knew what to say but then she laughed. Janet had been such a surprise package this week, a sparkling wit and a fierce intellect shielded from view by her sadness.

'No, seriously, it brought me back to the city I love. To old friends and new.' She lifted her glass of sparkling water and toasted the table.

Alex's face reddened as he placed the next item on the table. A pair of women's full briefs, white with rosebuds, price tags attached, size 12, sat folded on the table. Rachel looked around at the group.

'Me,' Wendy said, raising her hand. 'Don't worry, they are brand new. I bought new underwear for this trip. A lovely little selection of full briefs with little blue and green dots, daisies, sunflowers, and rosebuds, as you can see. My sister convinced me that we needed to err, change our undies to change our lives. So, we went to Etam yesterday morning and bought some sexy, some silky and even some saucy. Look out London!'

'I bought some too, look out Canberra! Well, my hubby, at least…' Carole said.

'Thank you so much. I'll put them aside for, err…'

'Washing the car,' Alex said, making polishing gestures.

The next item was a usb stick in the shape of a treble clef.

'That's from me. It's music,' Sam said. 'I brought it with me because I take it everywhere. My own compositions that I have, just this morning, finally clicked the button to allow others on the Web to hear. I had a producer work on them and had the files ready to upload months ago, but I have never had the courage to press the button. So, this morning, I finally did it.'

Another little round of applause rippled around the table. Sam drew a deep breath. 'I love working with kids, teaching them to love music, but this is something I have always wanted to do.' Everyone applauded again. She blushed and Ingrid leaned over to give her hand a squeeze.

Alex pulled a delicate silk scarf from the case and carefully placed it on the table. 'That's from me,' Georgia said, raising her hand apologetically like a schoolgirl. 'I had no idea what to give you, but when I saw that portrait and it was so soft with the pastel blues and greens, it reminded me of this scarf I had in my bag and well…'

'It's beautiful, Georgia,' Rachel said, lightly tying the scarf around her hair. She turned to Alex who gave her a peck on the cheek.

'Oh, you two are so cute!' Betty said, making a gagging gesture while Janet pretended to shoot herself in the head with her finger, to more laughter and smiles on sun-dappled faces.

The next item was a book. A mystery novel set in Paris.

'Me,' said Ingrid, raising her hand. 'Like Carole, I bought this book at the airport thinking I would have all this free time for reading, and well, I didn't! I bought a book in Montmartre for the flight home, Paris by Edward Rutherfurd. It's about five hundred pages, so it should be enough for the flight back to Australia!'

Ingrid and Carole groaned.

'Let's see if we can get upgraded,' Carole said, Ingrid nodded her head.

Judy cleared her throat and stood up. 'I didn't have anything to give you that would reflect what you've done for me this week. I would have to give you the world…' she said. She raised her glass and toasted Rachel who came around and hugged her. A small round of applause rippled around the table.

'For crying out loud…' Paula was shaking her head.

Once again, the group turned to look at her. This time the fake smiles were not quite as bright. She looked down at her lap and the group held their breath. She stood, reached for a baguette and a bottle of wine and after giving a curt bow, turned and walked onto the Champs de Mars towards the Eiffel Tower. Rachel pulled away from the embrace with Judy and called after Paula. Everyone watched her go but no one followed. They had done all they could do for Paula.

'She will be okay, I'll make sure,' Sara said, but didn't attempt to follow her.

'Right then, that leaves my gift,' Betty said, nodding at Alex. He handed her the white glossy dossier from the Mere du temps art show.

'Oh no, I can't accept…' Rachel said, her hand to her throat. 'No! What am I going to do with a huge portrait of myself?' Rachel laughed as she opened the dossier.

'Sell it. It's worth thirty thousand euro. Probably more now with all the brouhaha around it,' Betty said.

'I guess I could hang it in the hotel, if Marie agrees,' Rachel said. She looked up to see Sara's shocked face.

'Oh, wow, are you serious?' Sara said. 'Of course, we'd get insurance…it would be quite the talking point.'

'Would you mind, Betty?' Rachel said.

'It's yours, darling, do with it what you will.'

Rachel looked at Sara and nodded.

'Would it be weird for you? Seeing it every time you are there with a group?' Sara held up her gift for Rachel. A pair of polished keys on a red ribbon. The larger ornate key to the carriage door and the smaller one, for the old servant's entrance. Rachel held out her hand and Sara draped the red ribbon over her palm. The keys seemed to shine in the dappled sunlight.

'Like déjà vu, you mean?' Rachel said.

Sunday…again

Paula's phone was searching for Wi-Fi, but that wasn't what she wanted. She wanted her roaming to kick-in. Desperately. She hit the phone with her hand as though that would somehow help. A drop of sweat ran down her back. It had been a long journey to get here but she wondered if leaving the children unsupervised had been a good idea. Their father was there, but no doubt he would be…busy.

She had to see what her kids were up to. She wanted to check their statuses, their photos, their check-ins, and she was anxious to log into the closed-circuit cameras she'd had installed the previous week. The installer had told her that she must, by law, install a sign to let people know they were on camera, but she would do that when she got home. Right now, she needed to know what they were doing…and with whom.

She closed her eyes against the bright morning sunshine and the rising panic in her mind. Her stomach was churning. I need to eat, she thought.

Paula Grange was well versed at ignoring her feelings, especially the strong ones like fear, rage and if she was being honest, love. Love wasn't safe anymore for Paula; her husband had forgotten she existed; her staff feared her. Then there were the kids. She had given them every bit of love she had, and they had taken it, jumped all over it, then taken a selfie to post it on their social media. The caption would read something like "here's my mother's love for me that I have shat all over." This was not an exaggeration.

The rest of the group seemed very together, but it was easy to feel like an outsider when your whole life was falling apart. She rearranged her matching luggage and took a deep breath. One of the women smiled over at her and gave her a little wave. It was Carole. They had met at the airport in Sydney and kept bumping into each other. Paula had been waiting to board the

Eurostar when they had met again, along with Carole's incredibly stylish sister Wendy. They chatted, finally realising they would be in the same tour group.

She went back to her phone, deciding to turn it off and on again.

While waiting for the phone to re-start, she watched Ingrid and Sam deep in conversation next to the luggage pile, oblivious to everyone else. She hoped it wouldn't be like that all week. She sighed and closed her eyes, trying to use one of the relaxation techniques her therapist had taught her. Giving up, she opened her eyes, realising that Carole and her intimidating sister were walking her way.

'Paula! Can you believe we're in Paris?' Carole gushed. Carole was lovely, and about as threatening as a dandelion.

Wendy smiled serenely. Carole had told her that her sister was a famous human rights lawyer who was married to a writer. They lived in London with their two children and a couple of Labradoodles. She turned heads everywhere she went and had completely monopolised Rachel, the tour guide, on the train journey. They talked like old friends, laughing softly, their heads close.

A taxi pulled up and a petite woman jumped out, hugging Rachel on the fly, kissing her on each cheek, twice.

Paula's phone sprang to life and a barrage of texts flooded in, her quirky ring tone attracting the attention of the group and passers-by. Relief and dread fought for supremacy in her gut as she scrolled through the texts from her son. How she had managed to raise such a selfish, lazy child she had no idea, although the fact that she still did everything for him probably had something to do with it.

Her heart sank as his texts became increasingly aggressive. She slowly deleted them one by one, and taking a deep breath, replied as succinctly as she could without getting emotional. The link to the CCTV cameras didn't appear to be working, but her daughter's Snapchat, which she followed under an alias, was working overtime. Her daughter Paris and friends were scantily clad and dancing on tables. She regretted naming her daughter Paris, but also regretted telling her daughter she wasn't classy enough to have the name.

She shook her head, and her hand went involuntarily to her throat, more messages coming in from her demanding son. How on earth had he run out of money already? She would have to tell him where the secret stash was.

Through her veil of disgust and fear she became aware that Rachel and the petite woman were standing in front of her, talking to Carole and Wendy.

'Sara, this is Carole and Wendy. Wendy knows Paris well, has a lot of déjà vu when she's here.'

Sara's face lit up. 'How lovely! We will have a glass of wine and a conversation about that, I think.'

They smiled at each other as though sharing a delicious secret. Paula blinked at the two women. Two sleek limousines swung into the concourse, stopping in front of the group. Rachel grabbed Carole's hand and lead her towards the cars, beckoning Wendy to join them. The French woman still stood in front of Paula, smiling.

'Paula? You are Paula?' Sara's calm demeanor and soft voice was like Valium to Paula's adrenalin saturated body.

'Ah, yes,' she replied putting her hand out to shake the stranger's offered hand, but her phone was still in it. Paula laughed nervously. Her shoulders ached from holding them rigidly. She shuffled the phone into her other hand and shook Sara's.

'It is so lovely to see you a-…er meet you. I am Sara, the host of the private hotel here in Paris where you are staying. I have come here specially to meet you. And to give you this.'

She handed Paula a piece of paper.

Sara lowered her voice. 'I wanted to welcome you to Paris. This is going to sound crazy, but if you read that, and follow the suggestions you're going to have a great week. Trust me?'

'O…kay…?' Paula said, not understanding anything the young woman was saying.

She ran her eyes over the page. Nothing made any sense, except for the first line that read "put your phone on silent and keep it in your bag if possible."

The second line made her bristle. "The kids will be fine, stop stressing, monitoring and face-timing. They will do what they will do anyway."

'How dare you. Where the hell did you get this list? Is this some kind of joke? Did my husband put you up to this?' Paula was seething, her voice a harsh whisper and dripping with venom as she said the word "husband."

'No, it's very complicated…' Sara stopped and looked around to make sure no-one was listening. 'I've come back…in time…from next Sunday to give you this. To stop you from having a bad week. You had a bad week…er…last time…and now you get to do it again. I've never tried to help someone else like this, but because you had never been here before and the thing happened in the limo and well, will you trust me?'

Paula stared at the rambling French woman who grabbed Paula's hands and looked into her eyes, imploring her to listen.

Finally, Paula found her voice. 'Stop, please…you're freaking me out. I don't understand.'

'I've come to help you…'

Paula put her hand up. 'You must have me confused with someone else. I haven't even set foot in the limo yet.' Something made her look back down at the list. Her shoulders dropped. 'There's information on this list that no-one knows. Stuff I haven't even admitted to myself.' Her face flushed red.

'The third line…but how?' She looked up at Sara. 'You're right, I've never been to Paris, I said I had because it was a condition, and I really wanted to come…'

Sara smiled and held Paula's hands in hers. 'We're going to do this week together, oui?'

Paula nodded. The group was now piling into the cars. The young driver came to collect Paula's luggage.

Sara turned to her. 'This is very important. You need to read the list each morning and night and don't show it to the others. Use it to remind you to relax and enjoy Paris.' Sara's voice was low and hypnotic as the two women walked to the waiting car. Rachel signalled for Paula to travel with Sara, Ingrid and Sam.

As they waited to climb into the limo Paula's phone honked again. Sara hid her grimace with a smile. 'One last thing, Paula. Let's put that phone on silent and leave it in your bag. I'd hate anything to happen to it.'

About the author

Christine Betts is an Australian writer who left her heart in Paris some years ago. Most days she can be found at the beach.

Christine writes about Paris in all kinds of genres which is probably not helpful for search engines or 'also boughts' but the heart wants what the heart wants.

You can catch her on Facebook by searching Paris Time Travel and she writes about art, creativity and personal development over at www.writerpainter.com.

Like everyone, she is a work in progress.

Thank you for reading Hotel Déjà Vu.

If you enjoyed this story, a positive review would be incredibly helpful and very much appreciated. You can also find more of my writing at www.writerpainter.com.

Some notes about the story

The new edition of the novel resembles the original eBook the way twins look alike. There are too many similarities to count but the editions are different in all the ways that matter. The beginning has been completely re-written. The doomed Antoinette, the original time-traveller, finds herself in 1933 after almost dying in 1944. She plays the same role as she did in the original manuscript, but her back story has changed dramatically. She is still a scientist. She's fierce, single-minded and intelligent, a true strong, female protagonist. A woman of action with a reputation as a troublemaker, something strong women battle with every day.

She pursues her goals with single-minded determination, but when the Germans over-run Paris, she doesn't hesitate to offer her services to the Resistance.

Wouldn't we all like to think that we would have done the same?

Fact check – Many scientists did offer their services to the Resistance. There were makeshift labs dotted across Paris and Northern France making improvised explosive devices (IEDs). The war dragged on, and as attacks and arrests took their toll on the ranks of the resistance, women scientists were recruited.

The working title was "Hotel Regrette Rien" but it was a pronunciation nightmare. Hotel Déjà Vu came to me during meditation. Rachel is perhaps a confection of who I might have been had I stayed in Paris all those years ago instead of coming home and falling in love. I have no regrets but it's intriguing to wonder what life would have been like in that sliding doors moment.

The meeting of Alex and Rachel at Versailles is based on my own meet-cute in the gardens many years ago, but that is a whole other story…(and that story is called Remembering Paris, my memoir which may or may not ever see the light of day.)

The house on Rue de Bièvre with the blue door is real. Just a few hundred metres from the Seine, the house is the main character, not just a backdrop to the story. I have stayed in this beautiful house and used to recommend it to everyone but sadly it is no longer operating as a B&B.

Arriving in Paris, exhausted after 24 hours travel, I thought I had found paradise just like Antoinette. A simple Google search of "Historic Paris

B&B" had yielded incredible results! A basement pool and a rooftop terrace! Many details I have included are accurate, but I really don't think I did justice to the incredible home. The huge carriage entry painted a deep blue is there, facing the ancient cobblestone laneway. The terrace is smaller than the one on which the ladies gather to enjoy tea and cognac, but the view of the towers of Notre Dame is real. The farmhouse kitchen, the enormous table, the lift, the stone stairs, the amazing showers…

Even the swimming pool in the basement is real but the time portal is, of course, a figment of my imagination. In the corner of the basement, behind the pool, there was a little wooden door which by my calculations would have opened to a space beneath the narrow street in front of the house. Of course, it was probably just access to the plumbing or something boring like that, but the idea for a time portal beneath an historic home in Paris was born. The home doesn't have a rear entrance as far as I know.

In the corner of the basement, behind the pool, there was a little wooden door which by my calculations would have opened to a space beneath the narrow street in front of the house, which was once a river. Of course, it was probably just access to the plumbing or something boring like that, but hey, the idea for a time portal beneath an historic home in Paris was born. The home does not have a rear entrance as far as I know.

I was inspired to start writing fiction again right there in that swimming pool.

Set in 2016, I have made no mention of the fire which tore through the Cathedral of Notre Dame de Paris in 2018. It was heartbreaking for so many lovers of Paris all over the world but heartening to see the phenomenal donations for the rebuilding process.

Monsieur Levy's violin shop on the corner near the house really exists. Other than its location, everything else is a figment of my imagination.

Karen…When I was originally working on this story, the Artist's name was Annie. Even though I desperately wanted her to be Annie, it had to change. I had Antoinette, Alex, and Agnes; Annie had to go!

Karen feels…everything. She is an accomplished portrait artist, but she is also a hot mess. She is desperate to be seen but like so many artists, terrified of not measuring up. At first, she forfeits her aspirations out of fear but a talent like hers can't be hidden for long. She is exposed. A second chance is exactly what she needs.

Each sightseeing opportunity and monument described is real and a Hotel Déjà Vu walking tour is a real possibility should anyone like to try. Kilo Shop is a must-see for lovers of vintage gear. Bertillon the place for ice-creamy treats. Ladurée and Angelina vie for lovers of hot chocolate. Each restaurant our ladies visit in the story was open in 2016. 2020 may have changed a few things in Paris but Paris will always be…Paris.

Having said all that, the characters and events in this story are fictitious and any resemblance to real persons, living or dead, is coincidental.